Resounding praise for
KAREN TRAVISS'
WESS'HAR WARS

"Traviss is a valuable addition to the world
of science fiction."
James Alan Gardner, author of *Expendable*

"Satisfyingly complex. . . . [Traviss], at times, evokes
the earlier moral fables of Le Guin . . . at other
times the revisionist critique of expanding human
empires . . . and at times the union of romance with
SF that we see in the work of Catherine Asaro or
Lois McMaster Bujold. . . . The fact that Traviss
manages to keep these sometimes conflicting modes
in balance, mostly through her strong sense of
character, suggests that she's a writer worth watching."
Locus

"Stellar."
Jack McDevitt, author of *Deepsix*

"Science fiction with teeth. . . . In Shan Frankland,
Karen Traviss has created a tough, interesting, believ-
able character."
Gregory Frost, author of *Fitcher's Brides*

"Traviss takes what could have been a rote colleetion
of characters (marines, cops, religious extremists) and
slowly adds depth, complexity, and color."
BookPage

Books of *The Wess'har Wars* by
Karen Traviss

CITY OF PEARL
CROSSING THE LINE
THE WORLD BEFORE
MATRIARCH
ALLY
JUDGE

JUDGE

KAREN TRAVISS

An Imprint of HarperCollinsPublishers

This is a work of fiction. The characters, incidents, and dialogue are drawn from the author's imagination and are not to be construed as real. Any resemblance to actual events or persons, living or dead, is entirely coincidental.

EOS
An Imprint of HarperCollins*Publishers*
10 East 53rd Street
New York, New York 10022-5299

Copyright © 2008 by Karen Traviss
Cover art by Chris McGrath
ISBN: 978-0-06-088240-2
www.eosbooks.com

First Eos paperback printing: April 2008

HarperCollins® and Eos® are registered trademarks of HarperCollins Publishers.

Printed in the U.S.A.

10 9 8 7 6 5 4 3 2 1

For my father

Acknowledgments

My grateful thanks go to Bryan Boult and Jim Gilmer for critical reading: to Suzanne Byrne, for saving me from being an ignorant Whingeing Pom; and to my editor, Diana Gill, and my agent, Russ Galen, for keeping me in line.

Prologue

"Shitty death, PM," said the driver. "Look at the *size* of that bloody thing."

Den Bari, Prime Minister of Australia, and Kimbell McKinnon craned their necks as far as they could to take a look at the spacecraft from inside the vehicle. In the end, they had to get out and stand in the morning sun, a shocking, breath-stopping 52 degrees of blast-furnace heat after the comfortable chill of the car.

And the ship was huge. It hung high in the sky over a desert of abandoned buildings, a smooth cigar shape, and when Bari took a look through the scope, it resolved into gently gleaming bronze metal with what seemed to be lights or sunlight flashing off it. Even without any real sense of scale or distance, he could see that it was bigger than anything Earth had ever constructed. But that wasn't what was most shocking. It was the fact that it seemed to be changing shape as he watched it.

And it was *alien*. It was from another solar system, the very first to visit Earth—unless all those nutters claiming they had probes up their backsides hadn't been hallucinating after all.

"Is that heat haze?" said Bari. "The thing looks like it's warping."

Kimbell shielded his brow with his hand. "No, sir, it's changing shape, all right. Look."

The cigar was thinning out at one point like a sausage of modeling clay rolled between a kid's palms. Where the metal was deforming—*was* it metal, did these creatures even *use* metal?—it was changing color, too, turning from bronze to the powdery blue bloom of a grape. Then the smaller section broke away and flew off, a perfect little rugby ball of a ship, silent and speed-blurred. It was just as if the damn thing had given birth.

"I suppose that's why they call it the mothership," Kimbell said. It was funny how he often drew the same parallels that Bari did. "You have to see it to believe it, I suppose. That's some tech."

The two of them watched the alien ship for as long as they could stand the heat. It wasn't alone. The rugby ball had vanished but more dark shapes, the same bronze color, appeared in the sky but with pebbled hulls as if they'd gathered barnacles on the journey.

It was a fleet.

Bari had known it was coming for the best part of thirty years. His teen years had been spent worrying about the aliens who were coming to punish Earth for nuking an alien world and to sort out its dirty, wasteful ways—hoping that Australia's cooperation would save his country. The Eqbas Vorhi fleet—the consequences of hubris, the judgment of godlike aliens—always seemed to be around an unspecified corner but never arriving, like the paperless office or peace on Earth. But it was here and happening. It was *now*.

And he was now the prime minister of the country playing host to them, while the rest of Earth held its breath.

How did we ever think we could pull this off? What the hell did we think we were doing?

It was the end of everything he knew and had taken for granted. Somehow, the images that he'd been studying for years hadn't prepared him for this moment.

Kimbell batted away a solitary fly. It was too hot even for them, most of the time.

"If they're a million years ahead of us or whatever, how can they even begin to understand us?" he asked.

"You think they even *have* to?"

"Well, at least we'll understand our other guests."

"They might as well be aliens themselves." Bari couldn't take his eyes off the ship. He was ready to believe that it was just an expensive advertising stunt "The colonists have never seen Earth either."

They were going to have a bloody hard time finding other Christians like themselves in this area, too, but if they'd volunteered to come back to a world that was baking to death, then maybe they knew something he didn't. Faith was a wonderful thing.

"At least they're used to living underground," Bari said. "They say they built an underground city with a church, everything carved out of rock. I saw it on that BBChan documentary. Michallat."

A lot of Australian cities had also moved underground when the temperatures got too high. All that was left on the surface now was a flat wilderness of a land once filled with ranches and wheat. The seas had reclaimed large parts of the south. There would be humans on that ship who wouldn't recognize the coastlines they'd left.

"Just as well they're used to roughing it, then." Kimbell opened the car door and stood in the draft of cold air that rushed out, arms held away from his sides. "And Michallat's a know-all ponce, PM. Can't stand him. I bet the Eqbas won't be anything like they are on the telly."

But Bari couldn't take his eyes off the Eqbas ship. It moved slowly east as if it was tracking them, and then it *fragmented.*

There was no other word for it. Chunks flew off, more mini rugby balls of molten-to-solid bronze, not in a random explosion but in a controlled burst like a fireworks display, spreading fragments in a uniform radial pattern. The parts dispersed, streaking across the sky in different directions, and the largest part lifted higher into the sky.

"Fireworks." Bari wondered how the Eqbas did that. "I always forget my cam when there's something amazing to see."

"Fireworks all right, sir," Kimbell said. They got into the vehicle; the cool relief of the aircon was one of the purest animal pleasures left in life. "The fireworks display to mark the end of the bloody world."

1

I have made it work consistently, Gai Chail. I am confident that I can remove c'naatat *from any human host, because I can remove it from Dr. Rayat after multiple reinfections. I plan to continue to work on removing it from wess'har, of course.*

DA SHAPAKTI,
biologist-physician of Surang,
in a message to Esganikan Gai,
pending her revival in Earth orbit

Shan Frankland rolled over, stomach heaving in disoriented protest, and found herself staring at the curved surface of a marbled planet from space.

She'd been here before, without a suit.

Shit, shit, shit, I've been spaced again, I'm spaced again . . .

Thin watery vomit came to a spattering halt in front of her face as it hit something solid, and she knew she wasn't treading vacuum this time—not drifting in the void, freeze-dried, yet alive and conscious—but on an Eqbas ship with its deck in transparent display mode. It wasn't the most reassuring thing to see when you were struggling to surface from cryosuspension.

"Shit," she said again. "Shit, you said I'd *sleep* through this."

Her voice came out as a rasping whisper as she inhaled the distinctive scent of an agitated Eqbas. The ship was alive with the noise, and smells of three species—Eqbas crew, ussissi aides, human payload. Then she fell the rest of the way out of the cryo pod, wondering why she wasn't lying in a pool of vomit. The deck was smooth and clean again, and also mercilessly transparent. When she managed to turn her head, she could see Eqbas crew gazing down at the planet below like tourists.

"Shan Chail—"

Shan was more focused now. "It's Earth. It's *Earth,* isn't it?"

"Have you been conscious for the whole journey?"

"Enough of it." Shan was on her hands and knees, trying to tell her instincts that she wasn't falling, her body returning rapidly to its normal temperature. *C'naatat* could do that. "Why didn't you check on me, for Chrissakes? Couldn't you see I wasn't unconscious?"

"We *did* check." The Eqbas crewman wasn't like a Wess'ej wess'har at all except for his scent. His flat brown face wasn't as striking as the elegant seahorse head and citrine eyes of his cousins, but he had the same citrus smell when agitated. "You triggered no alarms, *chail.* Perhaps *c'naatat* caused this. Perhaps we misjudged the bio-indicators for humans."

How long had it been? Five months? *Five months.* Five relative months to span twenty-five light-years. If the cryo hadn't put her out completely, then Ade Bennett might also have been trapped in that cold paralyzed limbo, drifting in and out of consciousness and unable to do anything about it, breathing and heartbeat so slow that it felt like death, and maybe Aras had as well. *Poor sods.* She had to find them and make sure they were okay.

It was just like that, being spaced. Only worse.

C'naatat had altered all three of them enough to make all kinds of unpleasant experiences possible. The parasite had kept her alive in vacuum when she'd stepped out of an airlock to keep it from human exploitation: she couldn't die. She hadn't even begun to scratch the surface of what the damn thing could do when it came to preserving and modifying its host organism, and that still worried the shit out of her. It had already showed her enough of its tricks to convince her it should never fall into the hands of those who would have the most use for it.

And here she was *bringing it back to Earth,* after she'd tried to kill herself to prevent exactly that.

You're fucking insane. Why didn't you stay on Wess'ej?

Because you've got a job to finish. Because you wanted to bring the gene bank home. Because you think the bloody Eqbas are going to wipe out humans like they culled the isenj on Umeh. Because Ade and Aras are right, and you really are an interfering bitch who thinks she can run the world better.

She couldn't recall ever worrying about humans before, and Earth could have done with a lot less of them. *Filthy, shitty things. We are, we really are.* Whatever had made her change her mind and come back eluded her now. Maybe this was part of thawing out, and in a while she'd have her old clarity back again. She tried to recall what it had been like to be revived from the mummification of three months in space, and remembered bizarre out-of-body moments when she didn't even know *what* she was, which one of *c'naatat*'s previous hosts, let alone *who*.

"I need to see Ade." It was Ade she thought of first, a microsecond before she worried about Aras, and she felt a little guilty about that as if she had betrayed him: but if you had two partners, one had to be first in the queue. She got up and steadied herself against a bulkhead. The structure of the Eqbas vessel was disorientingly translucent in some places but solid and impregnable in others, and it was hard enough to negotiate its shifting layout at the best of times. "Is he conscious yet? What about Aras?"

The Eqbas's two-toned voice had a placatory note, but she was probably imagining that. "Both of them have been revived and made no mention of being conscious during suspension. They've gone to locate the other marines."

Shan stared at the deck but still couldn't see where the vomit had gone. There was nothing. The hull material—liquid to solid, solid to liquid, whatever was required of matter to make a ship that could become a fleet and a squadron of fighters at a moment's notice—appeared to have disposed of it.

"So where's Eddie?"

Eddie Michallat, as permanent a fixture as her *c'naatat* parasite, was going to be a busy man. He could forget reporting. He had a proper job to do. He could handle all the bloody media wanting to know every cough, spit, and fart about the Eqbas, who had come on a far-from-unanimous invitation to put Earth's environment back together. Eddie would argue all that shit about his neutrality as usual, but he'd play the spokesman in the end. Esganikan Gai, the Eqbas commander, seemed to know how to press his buttons to get him to do what she wanted.

"Eddie Michallat is not on board," said the Eqbas officer.

Typical: he'd wangled an early disembarkation. "What do you mean, *not on board*?"

There were a lot more Eqbas milling around now, the females with that plume of hair down the center of their skulls like angry cockatoos. They glanced at her as if she was behaving oddly. Maybe she was.

The Eqbas officer—Cirvanali, Cirvenuli, she couldn't recall his name right then—smelled even more acidic, as if he was waiting for her to lose her temper. They were a totally undiplomatic people, so his hesitation was telling.

"Eddie Michallat chose to stay on Wess'ej, *Shan Chail*."

It took Shan a few moments to process the enormity of that statement. Eddie—the embedded BBChan journo she'd never wanted on the original mission, the cause of many of her woes, but also the solution to many of her problems— was twenty-five years in the past, 150 trillion miles away. He was as good as dead.

The last she'd seen of him . . . he was saying he'd be on board, and that he'd be in demand when he got back. He was planning on claiming his back pay from BBChan, 103 years of it.

"How could the bastard just *stay behind*?" It wasn't a question. She felt more bereaved than betrayed. "What did he say? Jesus, didn't he even give a reason? I need to talk to him. Get me an ITX link."

"I know nothing of his reasons," said the Eqbas, ignoring her demand. "But if you're arguing, then you must be well, and Esganikan has more urgent matters for you to attend to. There is nothing you can do to retrieve Eddie Michallat now."

The brutal simplicity of the statement stung. Shan still found it hard to accept that there really were things that she simply couldn't do. *C'naatat* had done little to disabuse her of the idea.

"Do Ade and Aras know?" But her gut felt hollow, and not just because she'd just emptied what little there was in it over the deck. *Eddie wasn't here.* "I'll find an ITX node. You go and do whatever you have to. When are we landing?"

"When Esganikan has completed her initial discussions with the *gethes*. And yes, your males do know that Eddie stayed behind. They seem equally displeased."

Gethes: carrion eaters. Sometimes it was descriptive, sometimes pejorative. But it always meant humans, because the wess'har species didn't eat other animals. They didn't touch them, exploit them, or get in their way. Eqbas just brought down civilizations that crossed their line of ecological morality, playing the galactic policeman. Shan wondered whether the humans on Earth had yet grasped the full implications of highly militarized vegans.

No, they probably hadn't.

"Okay," Shan said. "It's not like I'm going anywhere, is it?"

She made her way through the ship, fretting about Eddie. Jesus, he was just a journalist. The Eqbas could invade Earth without him. But she was damned if she was going to do his job and act as their liaison. *Stupid bastard.* What was he playing at?

No, it'll be twenty-old years before I see him again, and that means—

She'd already lost everyone she ever knew on Earth, jerked seventy-five years out of time by the mission that took her to Bezer'ej nearly three years ago. Now she was facing it again. *No Eddie.* No, worse than that: an Eddie in his nineties by the time she got back. And Nevyan, her friend, the wess'har who saved her life, who never gave up looking for her body when she was adrift in space—she'd be decades older too. But wess'har lived longer than normal humans. A *lot* longer.

Nevyan was staying on her homeworld. It was her duty, just as Shan felt hers was returning to Earth with the Eqbas fleet. She had to be here.

To do what, exactly? You think one poxy human, even

*you, can make a difference to a fleet that pretty well leveled
Umeh?*

The shifting bulkheads always made her feel like she was
negotiating a hall of mirrors. She almost tripped over the
communications officer as an apparently solid sheet of material thinned and parted in front of her, disorienting her
enough to make her think she was falling again.

"Shan Chail." The Eqbas put his thin spider of a hand out
to stop her but he didn't actually touch her. They were all
scared of catching her parasite, unlikely though that was.
"Shan Chail, you must adjust more slowly. You'll injure
yourself."

That was the very least of her worries. Almost any injury
or illness she could think of was simply temporary pain;
c'naatat could repair anything except fragmentation. She
wondered if all the Eqbas understood what the parasite
could do quite as well as Esganikan did.

"I'm fine," she said. "Where's Ade?"

The Eqbas pointed the way with an awkward human gesture. Shan followed the line of his finger to in the accommodation decks, neat rows of body-sized chambers stacked
at a slight angle like tilted honeycombs. There were still
dark shapes in some, but the two individuals who mattered
most to her—a Royal Marine sergeant and a five-hundred-
year-old alien war criminal—weren't among them. She
couldn't pick up their respective scents in the melee of
smells flooding the ship, and she had to stop a passing ussissi to ask for directions. The meerkatlike creature, chest-
tall and—to use Eddie's description—like a foul-tempered
Rikki-Tikki-Tavi, indicated aft with a jerk of his head.

She found Ade and Aras leaning against a patch of transparent bulkhead and gazing down at the planet beneath them
just as she had, like a couple of kids who were desperate to
go out and play in some exciting new place. They struck her
as oddly alike despite the fact that Ade still looked like a
regular man and Aras—however much human DNA his
c'naatat had scavenged—would never pass for a human.
C'naatat liked tinkering and rearranging its host's genome,
sometimes visibly, sometimes not.

"So we made it back." Ade managed a smile, looking her up and down. "Jesus, Boss, you look rough."

"The sodding cryo didn't put me out for the count." Shan was too self-conscious to greet either of them with a kiss. Somehow being the Guv'nor and showing affection in public still didn't mix. "I've been awake on and off for most of the bloody journey. You?"

"Dead to the world. Out like a light."

Aras seemed more interested in the spectacle below. "I recall nothing of being in suspension."

"So when did you find out that Eddie had stayed behind?"

Aras turned to look at her, eyes neither wess'har nor human but charcoal-black and sad like a dog's. "When I went to look for him. I checked on everyone I knew in cryo."

"Didn't you think of thawing me out and telling me?"

"Why? What could you have done? There was no going back."

Wess'har were scrupulously pragmatic. In a human, that behavior would have been riddled with ulterior motive, the kind of thing that corroded trust; but in Aras it was exactly what he said, no more and no less. He had occasionally lied by simple delay, but for all the changes that *c'naatat* had made to him over five centuries, his core was still wess'har—literal, uninterested in deception, and nose-bleedingly honest to the point of offense.

He was right, of course. She'd just have been impotently angry. Ade snapped back into sergeant mode and distracted her.

"How long do you think we're going to be here, Boss?" He still called her that, as if she was his senior officer, and she found it touching now rather than embarrassing. "Just asking. Stuff I need to do."

It was a reminder that he had a life that she knew little about beyond the memories that *c'naatat* had transferred to her. She found it odd to be that intimate with another person—there was no relationship closer than one between *c'naatat* hosts—and relive his most traumatic moments as vividly as if she were him, and yet have no idea where he grew up or what he'd regretted leaving behind. She'd have to find out. It mattered.

"Months at the very least," she said. "What did you want to do, then?" She tried to keep an eye on Aras. He'd wandered away and opened another transparent section in the bulkhead, as if he wanted to contemplate Earth without interruption. "You might as well make the most of the trip, because we won't be coming back again."

Ade shrugged and looked away for a moment. "I want to go back to Ankara and pay my respects to Dave."

Dave was his best mate, shot dead next to him in the battle for Ankara. Shan had relived the warm spray of brain tissue on her face as *c'naatat* plucked the event right out of Ade's transferred memories. She understood the compulsion at a level of empathy denied to normal humans.

"Draw up a list," she said. "I'll make sure you get to do it all."

She had a list of her own, but there were no old friends on it. There was the gene bank to hand over, and a court martial finding to be set aside, and macaws to return to the wild. When she thought about it, it sounded like a list of excuses for coming back, tasks that someone else could have carried out or that were no longer relevant.

And there were ghosts to be laid, but they weren't important now. She could erase her past anywhere, any time. She didn't need to make pilgrimages.

Then why have you really come back?

Aras still stood frozen at the temporary window in the bulkhead. Wess'har had a great capacity for standing completely immobile, unnaturally so, and it usually meant they were startled or stressed.

"Aras, are you okay?"

"I remember it," he said. "I remember Earth as clearly as I remembered Umeh before I saw it for the first time. How odd to remember what you've never experienced."

"I think we're all going to find Earth's not like we remembered," Ade said. "Except the colonists. Let's see if it lives up to their expectations." He gave Shan a fond swipe on the backside as if he was determined to pretend none of them were upset by Eddie's decision. "I'm going to make sure the lads are okay. Don't land without me."

"I thought they'd sorted out a landing site before we left," Shan said irritably. "But maybe a lot changed in twenty-five years."

"Apparently, Australia's had seven changes of government while we were in transit."

"I see you're up to speed—"

"No offense, Boss. I just asked the Eqbas when I woke up. I don't like not knowing stuff. Oh, and the FEU, Sinostates, and Africa have gone to their second-highest defcon state."

"Only second? Shit, I thought we were scarier than that."

"Give it time," he said. "They're just warming up."

He strode off looking as if he belonged on the ship and she watched him go. It was natural—sensible—for a soldier to orientate himself before arriving in uncertain territory. Shan hesitated to use the word *enemy,* but the Eqbas mission wasn't any more universally welcome than it had been when fighting broke out over it when it was first announced. Maybe the Australians had gone through a few changes of mind about the invitation to land on their turf and sort out Earth, too. But they probably realized what every world the Eqbas visited realized sooner rather than later: once invited, once their attention was focused, Eqbas didn't turn around and go home.

"Shit." She wandered over to Aras and put her hand on his back. "I wish I'd stayed out of the cryo. Lots of catching up to do now."

Aras indicated an interior bulkhead. It formed into a viewing screen at a gesture from him, and suddenly she was looking at a vaguely familiar logo and a scene she almost recognized. It took her a few seconds to work out that it was the latest incarnation of BBChan; the setting was familiar.

"Jejeno," said Aras. "I've been catching up on Eddie's broadcasts over the last twenty-five years. He's been prolific. And Jejeno has . . . changed."

It was all coming back too fast. Shan found herself looking at the once-crowded isenj homeworld of Umeh, the city of Jejeno, where every meter of land had been covered with high-rise buildings, every living thing that wasn't isenj or a food crop obliterated, every natural system destroyed and replaced by an engineered climate—until the Eqbas had shown up, and millions of isenj had died. By now, it was probably billions.

Aras was right: it *had* changed.

In shot, Eddie—a much older Eddie—was walking around an open area in the city that looked as if it was grassed parkland. On Earth, that would have been totally unremarkable. On Umeh, it was a miracle.

Isenj, black and brown egg-shaped bodies on spider legs, mouths fringed with small teeth like a piranha's, tottered through the background. They were an orderly people who looked nothing like humans, but who had far more in common with them than with their neighbors in the Cavanagh system, the wess'har. Some of them paused to watch Eddie doing his piece to camera, just like humans. The audio was muted, but the normality of the scene was shocking.

"What happened?" Shan asked. But she knew: Jejeno wasn't the dystopian urban landscape she recalled because most of the isenj population had been removed the hard way. "God. So they really did it."

But it wasn't the outcome of the war she'd walked away from that really shattered her composure. It was seeing Eddie Michallat now pushing seventy years old. He'd been younger than her when she'd last seen him.

Time was a bastard. It took everyone in the end, and this was somehow harder than first leaving Earth on a moment's notice and knowing everyone she cared about would be dead or senile by the time she was revived again.

But that's what c'naatat*'s like, too. It'll keep you going, repair you indefinitely, while everyone you know—everyone without the parasite—ages and dies.*

She'd known from the start that was how the bloody thing worked. It was a simultaneous curse and blessing.

Now, for the first time, she really felt it.

Eqbas Vorhi, office of Varguti Sho, senior matriarch of Surang: 2401 in the calendar of the gethes.

"If you don't act *now*," said Mohan Rayat, "Esganikan Gai is going to play right into my government's hands and give humans *c'naatat*. She's infected. And she's *on Earth*."

Varguti Sho, the most senior matriarch of the city-state of Surang, was new to the job. That meant she might be persuaded more easily than her predecessors, who seemed to think that while it was *irregular* for a commander to dose herself with a biohazard and fail to tell her own government, it wasn't a cause for alarm. They had done nothing in the intervening years despite his warnings. He had to make them understand.

Wrong. It's everything you want to stamp out. It's everything I've come to fear. It's a potential disaster. Didn't all this trouble with humans start there?

"Curas Ti trusted Esganikan to treat the parasite as an experiment," said Varguti. "And what can anyone do thirty light-years away, even if there was a problem?"

"Did she ever actually *tell* Curas Ti what she'd done?"

"No."

"Exactly—*I* did. Da Shapakti did. Has she even told her crew? Do you believe me when I say she infected herself deliberately?"

"Yes. Da Shapakti confirmed it. But motive is irrelevant—"

"Actually, *Sho Chail,* that's just not true." Wess'har—both the Eqbas here and their Wess'ej cousins—cared only about outcomes, not motivation. Most of the time that made them seem brutally hard-line; but sometimes it showed their blind spot about predicting risks. Vastly superior power had only compounded the trait. "If Esganikan was keeping it from you, she had a reason. It's not how wess'har behave. You're totally open. You don't *hide* things."

Varguti was beginning to waver. Rayat could see it. She was cocking her head, the four lobes of her pupils opening and closing, and then she froze for a couple of seconds. Wess'har always did that when they were alarmed.

"When we send armies to other worlds, the commander has complete autonomy." Varguti sounded as if she was trying to convince herself. "The time scales are too long and the distances are too great for any government to understand the situation she might find herself in. We do *not* need to know every small detail of her strategy, and we do not, to use your phrase, *second-guess* her."

Rayat was jolted out of the debate for a moment by the injection of English after so many years of being immersed in eqbas'u. *Home. Earth. I'll never see it again.* "But what if she becomes a problem? What if she's not competent to do the job?"

"You must justify that claim."

"She's lied by omission, and she's taken an infection to Earth—the very same parasite that I tried to destroy on Ouzhari because I thought it was too dangerous to give to my own government. They sent me to get it, and I don't disobey my orders easily, I can assure you." Rayat could feel his voice straining in his desperation to be believed. "*I started this.* I understand it better than you do—look, ask Wess'ej. Ask your cousins. They'll tell you."

Varguti knelt back on her heels, apparently more interested in some information shimmering in her ice-sheet of a desk. The office was all low tables and serene filtered light like an upmarket Japanese restaurant, something Rayat hadn't seen in a very long time and would probably never see again.

"I refuse to believe Esganikan would infect humans deliberately," said Varguti.

"*Sho Chail*, it doesn't have to be deliberate. The fact that a *c'naatat* host has reached Earth is the problem. Anything might happen. We've had an accidental infection before."

"Now I *know* you panic for no reason, because there are three more *c'naatat* hosts on that mission, and you have no fears about them despite the fact that two of them are human, and the wess'har Aras has already deliberately infected a human once. Where is your logic now?"

Rayat was helpless for a moment. He should have seen that coming. The reason he had dismissed it was because he *knew* Shan, and he *knew* that she would kill herself rather than let the parasite fall into anyone else's hands—because she'd done it before. Aras and Ade . . . well, he also knew that Shan wouldn't allow another misjudgment on their part. They'd already spread it once too often, both of them.

I know trouble when I see it. It used to be my job to cause it, more often than not.

"I *panic*," said Rayat, "because normal wess'har keep *c'naatat* at arm's length, and Aras is proof of what happens when the parasite takes hold. He spread *c'naatat* through his troops because it looked like a good idea. It wasn't. When he gave it to Shan, he did it to save her life—because he was too influenced by whatever *c'naatat* brought with it to just let her die like she should have."

"Like *you* should have, too . . ."

"I'm glad you're getting my point."

"You're not getting mine."

"You have to stop Esganikan. Recall her. Appoint another commander on the ground. Just get her out of there before anything goes wrong."

"She has done *nothing* to make me think she's a risk." Varguti seemed a lot more emphatic now. Rayat had lost her again, just when he thought he'd swayed her. The subtle tricks he'd been so adept at using when he was an intelligence officer dealing with weak, suggestible humans were no use on wess'har. "The risk is that *gethes* seize a host, but they don't have the capacity to breach Eqbas security. In the highly unlikely event that they do, then Da Shapakti now has the countermeasures."

Rayat felt his throat closing and his pulse pounding. *C'naatat* didn't do much to stop that. It seemed to think a little physical stress was good for him. "But you don't have a mass delivery system for that—"

"We *will* have one."

"—and do you really want to commit yet another task force to Earth simply to clean up the mess? Have you any idea of the social and environmental chaos that a zero death rate would cause even in a few decades on Earth?"

Varguti stared at him for a moment. She didn't have the

bright gold irises of the Wess'ej wess'har, and somehow it made all Eqbas look less ferociously intelligent; but that was a serious underestimation. *They just don't think like we do.* Rayat waited. There was no point angering her.

"Yes," she said. "We can predict *exactly* what it will do, far more accurately than *gethes* can. Yours isn't the only world we've adjusted in our history. And so far, I have no reason to think that Esganikan Gai is any more of a risk than Shan Frankland."

Rayat felt deflated. But he'd come through plenty, through a one-way ticket to Bezer'ej and becoming an aquatic creature and even living with the torment of nearly wiping out a sentient species. He'd been switched between mortal and immortal so many times that having his *c'naatat* back again seemed unremarkable. So a few spats with a dangerously optimistic Eqbas matriarch was just a minor setback. He'd try another tack.

"The reason to worry," he said, "is that her *c'naatat* has my genetic material, my memories, and I was an unscrupulous *bastard* ready to do whatever it took to get *c'naatat* for my masters, or keep it from their enemies."

Varguti had him on the back foot. "And yet you're not quite that *bastard* now, are you?"

"If you have evidence that Esganikan isn't behaving responsibly, *then* will you act?"

Varguti wasn't even mildly annoyed with him, just impatient. He could smell it. "Yes, within obvious limits."

Obvious limits. Esganikan was 150 trillion miles away, five years ahead of the second fleet sent to support her, with a loyal army of fanatical Skavu, a young and deferential Eqbas crew, and enough firepower and bioweapons capability to scour Earth as clean as Umeh. If she decided to do anything that the matriarchs here didn't sanction, there wasn't a lot they could do about it other than tell her to pack it in.

And would she obey?

If her *c'naatat* had changed her outlook as subtly as Rayat suspected, as it had all its hosts, then he wasn't placing bets.

"Thank you for your time, *Sho Chail*," he said.

Rayat left her office—unguarded, unremarkable, and open to any Surang citizen—and made his way down curving stairs onto the next walkway level. There was nowhere on Eqbas Vorhi he couldn't go, which was a strange situation for a prisoner; he'd stopped thinking of himself as one except for the times he felt an urge to contact Earth, which he was banned from doing because Shan had once told Shapakti that he was a slimy bastard who should never be trusted with a link, especially now that he had detailed knowledge of *c'naatat*. Shapakti, scared shitless of her and always mindful of an *isan*'s advice, made sure that Rayat didn't. Eqbas technology was nothing if not thorough. Wherever he went on the planet, the communications systems identified him and prevented his sending messages.

He had not yet given up.

Rayat waited on the walkway, looking out onto a city of impossible and breathtaking beauty. If anyone had pointed out Surang to him when he first arrived and told him that the structure was a vast ivory bracket fungus or coral, he might have believed them. But it was a city every bit as constructed as Moscow or Brussels. He took out his *virin* and checked the news feeds.

FEU ON HIGH ALERT AS ALIEN FLEET REACHES EARTH

Ah, Eddie. A dream headline for you, except you've already done them all now.

Rayat could access all the incoming information that he wanted, all the Earth channels still being picked up by the local ITX node, but eventually he'd stopped wanting to know what was happening back home. He almost had to force himself to check the daily digests. But now that the fleet had arrived, and Earth was in turmoil, he wanted to know what was happening very badly indeed.

I started this. I was tasked to investigate c'naatat *long before Frankland ever stuck her bloody nose in. I was the one who opted for the cobalt bombs. I'll finish the job.*

Nobody took any notice of Rayat as he leaned on a curved retaining wall and studied the selection on his *virin*. He'd been here so long that most Eqbas knew all about him, the exiled *gethes* who committed genocide and—somehow—

had been spared the usual wess'har justice. He flicked through the news feeds, gazing at the image that filled his palm like a face frozen under ice.

An evangelist was in full cry. "Judgment day is coming!" he roared. "Look at the signs—who'll be saved? Only the few—"

"You're not wrong there, friend," Rayat muttered. "Stand by for downsizing."

It wasn't as if Eddie's incessant torrent of documentaries hadn't given Earth the handbook for an Eqbas occupation. Humans just didn't take any notice.

Rayat worked through his options while watching the *paskeghur* boarding point. He liked to think of it as the metro. The transport route snaked through and under the city like a digestive tract, largely unseen, while the passengers within had the impression of being in a shallow boat skimming the tops of the vines that covered the heart of the city, with no sense of being in a subterranean tunnel. It must have been a similar technology to their transparent ships' hulls and solid sheets of microscope; but even after twenty years here, he still didn't quite understand how it worked.

And I don't understand how they think, either. Just when I feel that I do . . . I really don't.

Rayat glanced back to the headline feed on his *virin*. The FEU, Sinostates, African Assembly and the South Americas had now put their armed forces on the highest state of alert. Warships blockaded key waterways; fighters patrolled borders. Rayat thought it was a forlorn hope to try to stop the Eqbas that way, but then realized it was mostly to deter refugees who had already started fleeing.

There was nowhere to go, but they didn't seem to realize that.

He switched off and waited. It was easier than watching the wheels come off when he could do nothing. Eventually Da Shapakti stepped out of the *paskeghur* looking happy with life—Rayat could read Eqbas wess'har very easily now—and stared straight up at Rayat. He could probably smell him. The Eqbas biologist made his way through the crush, moving between the exchanges, the halls and chambers where Eqbas came to deposit surplus things and collect whatever took their fancy. It was busy today. Rayat gestured to Shapakti to stay where he was and ran down the steps to meet him.

They were friends and colleagues rather than researcher and captive specimen. Rayat felt a pang of guilt about the lab rats that Aras had rescued from him with a warning about his carrion-eater's habits, and wondered if it was his own shame or Shan's censorious voice deep in his mind. Even now, Rayat worked hard at separating his own thoughts from the ones *c'naatat* had created within him. Now that he was infected again, they seemed more insistent, but even during the periods that the parasite was removed from his body, they still nagged at him.

"Did Varguti listen?" Shapakti asked, stepping close to the exchange walls to avoid the pedestrians. "You should have let me talk to her as well."

"If I'd done that," said Rayat, "then she might have given you an order not to do something, and you'd have obeyed, wouldn't you?"

Shapakti tilted his head slowly. He knew what was coming, more or less. "You *know* I would obey the matriarch in matters of state. Besides, it's unlikely anyone would want to disobey the consensus."

"I have to call Shan."

"You're banned, and she never responded to you last time anyway."

I tried. Stupid cow. I've been waiting twenty years to get hold of her again. No, twenty-five, if I count the journey here. "Then *you* call her."

"No—"

"Or you let me call Eddie and ask *him* to call her."

"I'm not happy with this."

Rayat caught Shapakti's arm and steered him into the nearest exchange, a chamber that would have said *stock exchange* to any human. The trilling and warbling was at fever pitch as wess'har debated and chatted. Yet this wasn't about money—they had no equivalent economy—but *ideas*. It was a shop for exchanging ideas.

"Help me warn Shan," Rayat said, in English now. "If I can get her to listen."

"When you speak English, you're being deceitful," Shapakti hissed. "You put me in an impossible position."

"And what can Varguti do to you? Are you breaking a law? No. Help me do this. Just to warn Shan, or at least find out if Esganikan's crew know she's infected."

"And if they don't . . . what can *Shan Chail* do?"

Rayat had thought about that, long and hard. He'd had plenty of time to do it, too. And now he knew more about wess'har than Shan herself. She'd known them a few years; he'd lived with them for a generation.

"Long screwdriver." Rayat waited for Shapakti's comprehension. "It's what we call the ability to control frontline events on the battlefield straight from the top."

"Bypassing the field commanders . . . a foolish thing, because you can never see the situation as clearly as they can."

"But sometimes it has to be done."

There was plenty Shan Frankland could do thirty light-years away. He knew how the *jask* pheromone worked in establishing dominance among wess'har females, and *c'naatat* had given Shan the full chemistry set. If anyone could bring Esganikan into line, it was Shan, chock full of the dominant wess'har matriarchal pheromone and her own arrogant sense of messianic, world-saving, uninvited righteousness.

He had his long screwdriver. He had Shan Frankland.

If she'd listen to him, she would be his instrument on Earth.

Kamberra, Australia, Office of the Prime Minister.

This was the worst day of Den Bari's life, and he knew it had been coming for a long time.

"I don't want to talk to your foreign minister," he said, standing with his back to his desk. "I want your president. And no, I'm not prepared to wait."

He turned around to look at the conference screen, hands

in pockets, hoping he didn't appear as agitated as he was. *Agitated.* Nothing more than that. He wasn't afraid, and he'd do what he had to. Out of range of the desk cam, his own defense minister and foreign secretary—Andreaou and Nairn—stood listening like a couple of bookends, identically posed but mirrored, with one arm across the chest cupping the other elbow, knuckles of one hand resting against their lips. Whatever responses they were going to give him today, they'd be the bloody same.

I could have predicted this to the day. It's not like the Eqbas didn't give us plenty of notice. I just had no idea how exact they were.

"I'll get right back to you," said the FEU liaison.

Bari killed the link and looked to his ministers. "What does Europe think they're going to get out of this?"

Jan Nairn turned and studied the wraparound plot of the Australian Antarctic waters, now studded with real-time projections of naval and air activity. Mawson, the largest settlement in their Antarctic territory, was facing a FEU carrier group sitting just a few hundred provocative meters outside territorial waters.

"I don't think they fully understand the Eqbas capability," Nairn said. "Maybe this is just an excuse to expand east across the AAD border."

"I'd agree with that," said Andreaou. "It's pretty transparent—if they wanted to lean on us to do anything, they'd go for a mainland city. I thought they'd given up on the AAD claim, though."

"We'll see." Bari was trying to keep all the status screens in sight at once, and it was hard. The Eqbas ship had returned to a high orbit after checking out the Westside, the western landmass of an Australia looking ever more likely to split into two landmasses, and now it was just waiting, silent, while more ships appeared on the satellite image as if they were falling out of nowhere. "How the hell do they *do* that? How come we didn't detect them until the last minute, Annie?"

Andreaou folded her arms. "Because they're bloody aliens, Den, *advanced* aliens . . . they do that, you know. This isn't the time to piss off the defense staff."

"Okay, let me try to get some sense out of Zammett, and then we shift to the EM center for the duration." Bari turned to the doorway and called to his PA. "Sal? Sal, warn the FEU ambassador we'll want to see him today, will you? And tell the Uni to bugger off if they're still bleating about access to the Eqbas, because this isn't some academic thesis for their benefit. None of that international scientific cooperation crapola. We process this like any migration and resettlement issue."

They're our damn aliens. We invited them here. They're going to help us. Get your own.

There was still no response from the FEU. Bari was running out of patience. Andreaou switched to her earpiece.

"Chief of Staff," she mouthed at him. "She says there's more FEU navy heading our way . . ."

Bari ran out of patience and tapped the desk to call up the FEU link again, waiting for the image of the European portal to appear. "I really think it's time I spoke to your president, please."

He counted to eight before the screen turned into Michael Zammett's office in Brussels. Bari didn't have the same long history with Zammett as his predecessor, although that hadn't been a happy relationship anyway; so maybe a clean sheet augured better. But it was hard to see how it could be more cordial with a carrier off the ADD coast.

"Prime Minister," said Zammett, unsmiling. "I think we've all been caught out by the arrival of the Eqbas. Are you prepared to update us on that?"

Bari aimed for studied indifference and picked up his coffee. "I was rather hoping you'd want to discuss the carrier you've got rather close to our waters, Michael. Your GPS had better be *very* accurate."

"As we were saying . . . Eqbas?"

"They're here. We noticed. It shouldn't be a surprise, seeing as they gave us a pretty accurate estimate of their arrival years ago."

"And you still plan to allow them to use your territory as a base."

"That's what we've been saying for the last twenty-odd

years, yes . . ." *And I can't uninvite them. We found that out too late.* "Do you still have a problem with that?"

"It's massively destabilizing for the region."

"The Antarctic? Because we're all just fine about it down here."

"Our carrier group is simply observing."

"Look, the Eqbas are going to land. We've got accommodation for them, and no pressure is going to prevent them landing here. You think that they'll just drive around the block and then go home because they can't find a parking space? Just accept it and back off."

"There has never been any international agreement on this invitation."

Diplomacy had long since given up on the FEU relationship. "There wasn't any agreement when the FEU invited the isenj here way back when, either. If you cherry-pick international law, Michael, you just encourage the small fry like us to misbehave too."

"You could always come to an agreement with us."

"Over what? ADD land? I think not."

"No, that you don't allow them to carry out climate modification that'll disadvantage other states."

Bari looked at Nairn and just got raised eyebrows. Allow? He hadn't even spoken to the Eqbas yet, but Canh Pho had in 2376, and it was clear even then that the Eqbas didn't negotiate. They had their own agenda in which the conditions laid down by Earth governments didn't play a part. The sane response was to cooperate and hope to be the survivors.

It is, isn't it? To accept that there's no other way to win?

"I don't know exactly what they have in mind now," Bari said. "But I do know they want to try some of your people for war crimes."

Zammett wasn't fazed. He had a habit of simply ignoring any point he didn't like with an ease that made Bari wonder if he'd actually heard him at all. "We expect our returning military personnel to be handed over immediately."

"As soon as they've passed quarantine."

Andreaou caught Bari's eye with a raised finger and pointed to the status display of the Antarctic waters.

"On the move," she mouthed.

If Zammett thought the Australian Defense Force or any of its Pacific Rim allies were too stretched to deal with an FEU incursion, he'd get a rude awakening.

"Michael," said Bari. "I'm asking you to keep out of our waters, because we *will* respond. You know that. There's nothing to lever out of us now. It's just a good way of getting the wrong sort of attention from the Eqbas."

Again, Zammett just didn't react. "We'd like to be kept informed of the situation with the Eqbas. Good day, Prime Minister."

Bari knew dismissal when he heard it. Nairn yawned, feeling the long hours as keenly as the rest of them, and they stood in silence waiting for someone to state the obvious.

What do they really want from us?

"They're just skimming the territorial line," Andreaou said, jerking her thumb at the status chart. "It's pointless. Maybe they think we can dictate to the Eqbas what environmental measures they're going to implement."

Bari wasn't even going to try. He'd seen what happened to a planet called Umeh. It was a sad day when the best intelligence he had was a long-running series of documentaries from the Cavanagh system that most of the public had ceased to care about, because there were much bigger disasters at home.

We lost interest in life on other worlds. What does that say about us?

"They made their mind up a long time ago," Bari said. "And if it doesn't suit the FEU, that's too bad. I'm authorizing use of force under emergency powers. If the FEU crosses that line—turn them back."

Normally, a superpower's warship on the doorstep would have been the most pressing item on a ministerial agenda. But the Eqbas had much bigger guns, they weren't going to go away, and they were still the best chance this country had of surviving in a deteriorating global environment.

The Eqbas were Bari's priority.

2

*For it's Tommy this, an' Tommy that, an' "Chuck him out,
   the brute!"
But it's "Saviour of 'is country," when the guns begin to
   shoot;
An' it's Tommy this, an' Tommy that, an' anything you
   please;
But Tommy ain't a bloomin' fool—you bet that Tommy
   sees!*

"Tommy," RUDYARD KIPLING,
1865–1936

Eqbas flagship: Earth orbit.

Marine Ismat Qureshi stared at the ESF670 rifle in her
hands as if she knew it was as obsolete as a Lee-Enfield.
"She did it, then."

"Who did?" asked Barencoin. Beyond the transparent
bulkhead was an intense rust red desert. Ade had once
thought that all deserts looked the same, but they didn't. It
was red in a way that Mars wasn't. "Who did what?"

"Shan got us all home," Qureshi said. "She said she'd get
us back, and here we are. Back on the rock in one piece.
Well, *nearly* back."

Qureshi touched the bulkhead and the image zoomed
back with a speed that made Ade's stomach lurch at the illusion of instant takeoff. All she'd done was change the magnification; they were back in orbit again, looking down on
the blue-white globe they'd expected to see. The Arctic ice-
cap was a small patch even in January, and although the
very worst climate predictions didn't appear to have happened yet, it still wasn't the world they'd left.

Qureshi zoomed in with the bulkhead again, this time on
the Pacific to the east of the Sinostates.

"Shit, the coastlines have changed a bit."

Barencoin moved the focus. "Look, mum, no islands."

"God, look at Australia. The sea's really carved into the south."

"There's only so much you can do with sea defenses, I suppose."

"Whose bright idea was it to come back?"

"Izzy, you're the one who wanted a shag and a real beer. You could have been happy with sobriety and contemplative self-abuse, but no . . ."

Qureshi whacked Barencoin sharply on the backside. This had been Ade's sole objective—getting his people home alive. There was nothing he could do about the state that home was in.

Six out, six back.

They'd embarked in EFS *Thetis* for the Cavanagh's Star system in 2299, and all that mattered was that they were back in one piece. The scientists who'd gone with them hadn't been so lucky, but that was their own stupid fault for pissing about with the wess'har; but the rolling clusterfuck that the mission turned into wasn't the marines' fault, even if Ade still felt it might have been his. Now they were nearly home—*no, not home, not for me*—and somehow the injustice and shame of being court-martialed didn't seem to matter. They'd step off the ship, and people would just look at them as a five-minute wonder, people from the past. The world wasn't going to go on as normal. The Eqbas were going to turn it upside down.

Barencoin blew out a long breath. "Well, hurrah for the Boss, but we might have got home sooner without her." He was a good bloke, but he wouldn't say a cheery word even if his nuts were clamped in a vice. "We're still fucked."

"Okay, Mouth Almighty, that's down to me," said Ade. "I *could* have sorted a deal for you before we embarked, but there was the small matter of not being able to hand over Rayat, remember? Anyway, I'll bet they wouldn't have honored the deal. It'll be easier now we're back."

"What if we've changed our minds?" said Jon Becken.

"What do you mean, *changed your minds*?"

"Maybe we want to be civvies now. Jesus, it's going to be hard going back to the FEU now that it's almost at bloody war with Australia. You think we want to be fighting on different sides?"

"Who said Ade was going to be fighting?" said Chahal.

"Esganikan's got her army." Ade didn't want to think about allegiances. His was clear: he didn't belong on Earth, and he was here solely to keep an eye on Shan. "She doesn't need me when she's got that psycho bastard Kiir, does she?"

The rest of the detachment—Qureshi, Chahal, Becken, and Sue Webster—dropped the subject and occupied themselves tidying the remnant of their uniforms. It was that awful limbo period when the fighting was over and the euphoria of going home was tarnished by frustration at delays in disembarkation. But this time there was no familiarity to rush back to—no partner waiting at home, no pubs to stroll back into and regale the regulars with tales from the front, no relief at the return to normality, because *normal* was gone for all of them, forever.

It was the first time Ade had really *felt* that. It wasn't just him; he wasn't the only one permanently displaced. Even without his vastly altered genome, the other marines were now almost as alien as he was.

We were fucked as soon as we left Earth. We knew that. But it takes awhile for the reality to bite.

"Well, at least we've all got unique extrasolar experience of alien relations," said Chahal. "Five distinct species, and lived to tell the tale. Good ad-quals, eh?"

"Christ, you'll have a career ahead of you in civvy management," Barencoin muttered. He'd read international law at university and seemed completely unwilling to use it beyond being the proverbial barrack-room lawyer. "But you and Sue are all right. You're engineers. Engineers are never out of work, even if you have to build lavatories."

Webster played with the focus again. The Eqbas ship was almost like a fairground attraction at times, and they were bored. "Mind your manners," she said. "I build *brilliant* latrines."

"You can live off the fees for media interviews," said Qureshi. "You built a crapper on another planet. That's got to be good for five minutes prime-time."

They were way behind on Earth technology—as if that mattered now—but they had a story to tell if nothing else. Ade suspected the story would first have to be told to the intelligence corps. They'd want *details*. Maybe that was the way to open the batting and get them reinstated. *They want to be Royals again.* And so did he, he really did, and he knew it now he was back on Earth: it was over for him, but it would only break his heart if he let it.

"It's all right for the bloody navy," said Becken. He meant the remaining crew of the unlucky *Actaeon,* the FEU warship blown apart in reprisal for the bombing on Bezer'ej. "They're all squeaky-clean frigging heroes. They get welcomed back into the fold and debriefed, but we'll be told to fuck off."

"Cheer up, you miserable sod," said Qureshi. "You don't know that. I bet they're as short of recruits as ever. We haven't even made contact yet."

One of the Eqbas crewmen walked up behind them and trilled. "You look at Anarchic," he said, struggling with English. His overtone voice made him sound like an audio circuit glitch, two streams of sound trying to form the words. "Look at the warships."

"Ooh, Navy Days?" said Becken. "I used to love Navy Days as a kid. Made me want to sign up. So they still have navies, then."

"You still have *war,*" said the Eqbas, and jabbed at the image with a multijointed spidery finger. Not all of them spoke immaculate English like their boss. "But no to worry. As much trouble as isenj, they. Better view when we get remotes out."

"*Antarctic,*" Chahal said. "He means the Antarctic. But I think I like Anarchic better."

Barencoin and Qureshi vied for control of the bulkhead image, moving the focus along the Australian sector of the continent. There was a fringe of land exposed, dotted with small towns that had only been survey stations when they'd

first left Earth. And the Eqbas was right: there were warships off the coast.

Barencoin lost the battle for the zoom to Qureshi. "Is it
one of ours, Marine?" he said in a posh mock-officer accent,
but then the impression stopped dead. "Oh shit, it is . . ."

Ade watched as an aerial image of a carrier with FEU
deck markings and pennant code filled the bulkhead. The
shape of carriers had changed a little in the missing century,
but it was still a carrier, and still way out of FEU waters.
Nobody really needed carriers now. But nothing sat there
and loomed menacingly quite as well as a warship. It gave
you something to worry about for a long time.

"If I was an optimist," Ade said, "I'd believe that was the
South Atlantic guard ship."

"And what about those frigates?" Barencoin tapped the
bulkhead, but it made no sound. "Maybe they're hiring out
hulls as cruise liners to earn revenue. Peace dividend and all
that."

Ade caught a reassuring cedar-and-fruit scent of Shan and
turned to see her walking briskly down the passageway, not
exactly an elegant stride but always enough to make him feel
that things were under control and sorted even if they weren't.

"Maybe," she said, passing them without pausing, "you
need to find a news channel and watch the FEU getting
stroppy with the Aussies about our arrival. 'Cos they're waving
their todgers at each other in some macho display of bravado."

"That's all right," Becken called to her retreating back.
"We'll hide behind you, Boss. You show 'em."

Boss. They all called her that now, partly because Ade
did, but it still made him flinch. *That's my missus. Don't get
too familiar.*

"What's Australia got that the FEU wants?" Webster
asked. "Apart from a lot of dust, and some Antarctic land
when the ice melts completely?"

"Our undead oppo here," said Barencoin, giving Ade a
slap on the back. "Eh, Sarge?"

"They don't know about me," said Ade. "Rayat never got
chance for a call home after he found out."

"But I bet they know about Shan." Barencoin put a playful armlock on him, but Ade noted he was careful to avoid skin contact. "That's why they wanted her in the first place, isn't it? And I bet Esganikan told that Marchant bint that Shan was coming with us, and then Marchant told her buddies, and then it wasn't a secret any more."

It was bound to come out sooner or later. But there was nothing they could do about it. They'd have to get to her first.

Like me and Mart did. We took her down with just a couple of rifles, didn't we?

"Bollocks," said Ade, shaking Barencoin off.

"It'll be fun explaining your reluctance to rejoin the Corps after you made such a song and dance about reinstatement."

"You won't have to." Barencoin was too hard on the heels of his thoughts sometimes. "That's my job. You keep your trap shut and pick up where you left off, okay?"

"But if we go back to FEU jurisdiction, they *debrief* us. They'll want to know every cough, shit, and fart we've taken for the last few years. That's a bloody big story to keep straight between five of us. 'Oh yeah, don't worry, sir, Sergeant Bennett is the creature from the Black Lagoon on his day off. Now let's talk about this fascinating water reclamation scheme on Wess'ej.' They'll be happy with that, will they?"

"Well, maybe you should have started rehearsing it earlier." So what? Ade knew the FEU couldn't lay a finger on him whether it knew he had *c'naatat* or not. "It doesn't matter what you tell them. There's sod all they can do about it now."

Between them, Qureshi and Barencoin voiced all the fears and anxieties he still harbored, and asked all the troubling questions. It was a hard homecoming for too many reasons. His last conversation with the top brass on Earth had promised the detachment would be reinstated, more or less, *especially* if they could tell the FEU what had happened to Rayat. But that had been years ago, and anyone whose career depended on that promise being honored was long retired—or dead—now, and Rayat was thirty light-years away on Eqbas Vorhi. It was all academic.

Fuck 'em.

Barencoin shrugged. For once, he looked clean-shaven, which was no small feat. The cryo seemed to have slowed his beard growth.

"Yeah, the FEU's going to make a big thing about missing civvies. Just for something to do, if nothing else. How many payload came back out of seven? Hugel and Mesevy. Two. Out of *seven.*"

"Not counting Rayat and Lindsay," Ade said. "Champciaux wanted to stay."

"We only lost two, really, and one of those was a blue-on-blue."

"And Eddie," said Qureshi.

Barencoin shrugged. "Yeah, that gutted me. I never thought he'd stay behind."

"Why shouldn't he?" said Ade. *Shit, Eddie's my mate. I'm the one who's entitled to feel abandoned, not you.* It was still a massive shock, more like Eddie was dead than just separated from them by a generation. "He hasn't got any ties here either."

"I really thought he'd come. We need him to do the smarmy talk with the puny Earthlings, don't we? Shan can't do smarmy. Esganikan the Hun definitely can't. That leaves Deborah Garrod. She knows less about Earth than the aliens do."

There was also the small matter of her being the leader of a devout Christian colony; Australia's population was 45 percent Muslim. Last time Ade had checked, twenty-five years ago, the Christians were getting uppity again thanks to the apparently miraculous return of the lost colony complete with its precious gene bank. He marveled at the ability of people to grasp such flimsy things and build their lives and actions around them. But maybe that was what he'd done all his adult life, by hanging on to an affiliation that was another set of ideas held together by a little metal symbol: a globe and laurel instead of a cross.

The Corps was real, though, solid and visible in his comrades. Maybe Deborah Garrod saw what she trusted and believed reflected in her friends and family, too. He decided not to judge.

Becken sucked his teeth noisily. "What do you suppose Rayat's doing now?"

"I don't care," said Barencoin, "as long as the Eqbas are still shoving a fucking probe up his spook arse on an hourly basis."

He didn't mention Lindsay Neville. But she'd been a squid-woman for twenty-five years now, so maybe it was a subject he didn't want to discuss, because nobody wanted to imagine how much she'd changed with a dose of *c'naatat* and only a bunch of genocidal Nazi cephalopods for company. Ade was compiling a long list of things and people he had to check on as soon as he got time on the ITX link, from Eddie and Giyadas—Jesus, the kid would be an adult now— and the state of Jejeno, and even Lindsay and Rayat. What mattered most right then, now that he was sure Shan was fine and Aras was okay, was to look after his detachment, whose status was still an issue.

"It's always the bloody same, and it doesn't change, no matter what." Barencoin kept moving the focus around, changing the image in the bulkhead. Suddenly, he was getting images from 45-degree angles, as if a new cam had moved in. The Eqbas must have put their atmospheric remotes in place already. "All this frigging around to disembark. Not that there'll be anyone waiting on the jetty for us, eh?"

"Speak for yourself," said Becken. "I'm a bloody space marine. I'll be beating women off with a shitty stick."

"Not if we end up in the Muslim sector." Barencoin nudged Ade in the ribs.

"Can't you go and ask what the holdup is?"

"Are we there yet?" Ade lisped, mocking. *Shut up, Mart. Time enough to find out just how crappy things are down there now.* "Are we there yet, Dad?"

"I just want out of here."

"If you feel like hassling Esganikan, go ahead, mate. I'll stand back and enjoy the show."

"Seriously, what are *you* going to do? Are you really going to go ashore with that thing inside you?"

"It's only some kind of bacteria. Not a zombie tapeworm."

"You going to ring a bell or something to clear a path, then?"

Ade had already shown Barencoin the Eqbas smartgel barrier that turned from liquid to a thin film when you touched it. Eqbas tech was all about materials that reshaped and reformed into something else entirely. He shrugged, fumbled in his belt pouch, and pulled out the small ball of gel in its sac. "They're bloody clever, the Eqbas. This is a pretty good barrier."

"You're going to dress up in a giant condom. Classy, yet understated . . ."

Ade wondered how much to tell him, but distracting Barencoin was sometimes like keeping a kid quiet. Ade had developed the knack of getting the gel to flow over his skin like a liquid by prodding it just the right way. And it was all a matter of what you prodded it with, of course, but that was more than Barencoin needed to know right then. "It works okay."

Ade cupped the gel ball in his palm and pressed his index finger into the surface. It deformed and crept over his hand like a rising glossy tide, matting down to a more even satiny texture as it went. Barencoin stared. Becken craned his head to watch.

Ade withdrew his finger with a flick and the gel's progress stopped at his wrist to form a barely visible glove. Barencoin tilted his head, fascinated. Then he reached out and touched the back of Ade's hand.

"Feels clammy."

"That's to stop perves like you trying to hold my hand, Mart."

Becken tried an experimental prod too. "It's *still* a giant condom."

And that, of course, was how Ade had come across the technology. He'd had never been good at controlling his blushing; he blushed now. It wasn't a very marine-like thing to do, but Shan always said she found it *endearing*. It made him feel like a total pillock. Becken, ever alert to the little telltale signs of discomfort among his mates, sniggered.

"Don't tell me that's what Eqbas use," he said. "What

about this genetic transfer thing they do when they're shagging? They can't do that with a franger on, can they?"

It was a very old word for very old technology. Barencoin was always a more creative thinker than Becken, though, and he frowned. "Ade, you said you'd been done. Why did you need a condom?" The joke evaporated. Barencoin couldn't have known how painful a topic it was, and that meant he didn't know when to stop. "And she's past it—"

The wound was still more raw than Ade had thought. "You know the worst thing about *c'naatat*?" he snapped. "It fixes all that stuff. Yeah, we need 'em. Because it all went wrong, and we had to get rid of the baby. So shut the fuck up about it, okay?"

Barencoin's face was suddenly all regret and shock, which was rare for him. He didn't have any smart-arse comebacks for once. "Look, I wouldn't have taken the piss if I'd known. I'm sorry, mate. I had no idea."

Ade felt worse about it now than he had when the pain of the abortion was fresh, and had to walk away. He wasn't stepping back to avoid hitting Barencoin, but because it was so intensely private a tragedy—something Shan would never have wanted others to know—he was instantly ashamed of his outburst. It was one more thing in the growing list that he couldn't share with the people he'd trusted with his life up to now, and it left him with a bigger sense of loss than if he'd been physically separated from them.

"Hey, come on." Barencoin tried to go after him but Ade could hear him struggling to get past the tide of ussissi walking the other way. It was a busy ship right now. "Come on, Ade, I'm sorry."

Ade was halfway to the aft section of the ship when he realized he still had the gel coating on his hand. He slipped into a comms alcove for a moment. *Come on, you were handling this okay. People deal with it all the time, and do it for a lot less reason. You couldn't bring a* c'naatat *kid into the world.* He wondered how much of his reaction was realizing that the stupid fantasy of creating an average domestic life of the kind he'd never had was just that—fantasy. He would have to be content with having a woman he loved and who he knew he could trust. And it didn't matter that he had to share her with Aras. *Normal* had changed for good in the Cavanagh system. It was just a matter of accepting that there would be days when he slipped back into the basic human mold.

The ship moved.

Ade had to check that it wasn't just the visible horizon that had shifted. The views from the bulkheads weren't always exactly line of sight; they were projections of some kind. But he was sure the ship was moving. The crew going about their business around him reacted too. Then he saw why. Esganikan Gai strode through the ship, her copper red plume of hair bobbing as she moved like a juggernaut. Shan trailed after her. Ade somehow read the body language as Shan playing bagman to Esganikan, and he wasn't comfortable with that. The Boss *had* to be the alpha female. She could tear Esganikan up for arse-paper, he was sure of that.

"You can disembark shortly," Esganikan said. "We're landing."

"Where?" Ade asked.

"For the time being, the location called St George. There's accommodation provided for us elsewhere, but I want to inspect it first."

More saints, then: it boded ill. They hadn't had much luck with the islands of Constantine, Chad and Christopher back on Bezer'ej. Esganikan swept on but Shan paused and gave Ade a shrug. "Well, you wouldn't expect her to wait for the monkey boys to tell her where she can land, would you?"

"So who's doing the diplomacy and liaison?"

"Don't look at me. It's not my forte."

Ade had complete faith in Shan. She could do anything. She could even act as if she actually gave a toss what humans on Earth thought about her, for a while at least.

"You'll do a good job, Boss. You always do."

"I might," she said. "If the first job wasn't pursuing the FEU to hand over the tossers who authorized Rayat's use of cobalt bombs. I think that's going to get a bit hairy."

The Eqbas didn't believe in any statute of limitations. The order had been given at least twenty-five years ago, more than fifty if you counted the fact that *Actaeon* deployed with neutron bombs—BNOs, biohaz neutralization ordnance, banned for use on Earth—in the first place. Whoever gave Rayat his orders was old or dead, but the Eqbas didn't give a shit. If the guilty were alive, they wanted them; and their concept of guilt was just as inflexible as their Wess'ej cousins'. Only outcomes mattered, not motives, but giving an immoral order was as bad as obeying it. Ade was still struggling to reconcile the two. He wasn't sure that he ever would.

"It's been years since I arrested anyone." Shan felt down the back of her belt and withdrew her 9mm handgun, ancient and still in excellent, lethal working order. "Think I can still feel collars? Nick a few bastards?"

"Damn sure of it," he said.

He could have sworn she was looking forward to that. She was a copper, a hard street copper, back on the familiar beat of Earth. And she'd remembered what she did best.

He watched her go. There was nowhere obvious to secure himself for landing, and he wasn't up to facing Barencoin for a while, so he kept out of the way in the comms alcove and touched the bulkhead to see if he could make it transparent. It became an instant window on an Earth that was now an ice plain, not desert.

As the ship dropped—or the focus shifted, he was never sure which—he strained to work out scale and position, and failed. But it was white beneath, and there wasn't much snow left on Earth now. Where were they?

Jesus, she's coming in over the South Pole . . .

Esganikan probably just wanted to see for herself, like the big kid she sometimes seemed to be. She didn't have to worry about triple-A or even being detected. Ade wondered what would happen if the Eqbas ever came up against a civilization as advanced as them but as dishonest as humans. Maybe they already had.

Becken appeared and crammed into the alcove with him. "Shit, Ade, look at that."

"It's Antarctica, Jon. Big white flat place. Didn't you do exercises down here?"

"Not at this speed—"

A piercing rapid blipping sound almost deafened him. Something mid-gray and matte streaked backwards past them at eye level, then another. "*Shit.*"

"Fighters."

"Ours?"

"Not now . . ."

"*Shit.*" Ade hadn't even heard engine noise. It was like watching a vid minus audio. "She's coming in from the west, through FEU airspace."

Both marines looked at each other for a split second in disbelief before a searing white light blinded them and left green spots in Ade's field of vision. The jets had passed; now the Eqbas ship was clear of the ice and over tundra, a moss-green and gray blur, and then there were the tops of low buildings. The ship seemed to slow instantly with no feeling of inertia—Esganikan had given up sensors in favor of sight-seeing, Ade suspected—and came to a dead stop over a small town.

"Did we shoot something down?" Becken whispered. "Where are we now?"

"Christ knows." Ade gathered his wits long enough to touch the magnification. He was looking down onto a narrow street at the upturned faces of people as frozen as any startled wess'har. *Here's your first real UFO, folks. Be amazed.* "I can't see any flags. Jesus, if she's shot down an FEU vessel—"

The ship moved off again and passed the coastline at a more sedate patrol speed. Ade saw something he recognized: the angled boxy shape of a frigate churning a white wake behind her. The next thing he saw was a billowing mass of yellow flame and white smoke, and he was looking straight down the line of a missile.

Becken ducked instinctively despite the Eqbas shielding. Ade did too. Two or three seconds: no explosion. They straightened up and there was nothing out there but choppy sea smearing into a pale gray blur as the Eqbas ship headed north.

"Welcome home," Becken muttered. "Who shot at who?"

It wasn't a great start. It was Umeh all over again, except this was Earth, and that hurt.

F'nar, Wess'ej: Nevyan's home, upper terraces.

F'nar had been Eddie Michallat's home for twenty-seven years, but he never took the view for granted.

It beat the Leeds skyline for grandeur by a long chalk. At this time of the morning, Ceret—Cavanagh's Star to humans—had risen high enough to cast a peach light over the unbroken layer of nacre that covered the whole city, and gave it the name the colonists sometimes used: City of Pearl.

The gleaming layer was insect shit, deposited by millions of *tem* flies swarming on every smooth and sun-warmed surface. But it had the luster of extinct Tahitian pearl, and, as shit went, it was breathtakingly lovely.

Eddie stood at the irregularly shaped window and stared out across the caldera. He knew every house excavated in the walls of the caldera itself, every clan of wess'har who lived there, every territorial call of the matriarchs who ran the place. It was as much home as any place he'd ever known. He liked it here.

"Eddie, you know they've arrived, don't you?"

"Okay, sweetie."

"You've been waiting a long time for this."

"Okay."

He didn't turn around right away. The ITX screen was active—he could see the reflection on the glass bowl by the spigot facing him—and he knew he was going to have to psych himself up to see old friends who were now much younger than he was. For *c'naatat* hosts, age was irrelevant. But time had passed; time, and people, and events. In all those years, he'd been broadcasting into what felt like a silence, waiting for the reply that would come one day from his closest confidants. ITX no longer felt instant.

I miss you. All of you.

"Eddie, you knew this would happen one day."

"I did," he said, and turned around. "God knows we've

talked about this enough. Maybe I've worked myself up too much."

Erica was one of the civilian contractors who'd stayed behind on Wess'ej when *Actaeon*'s crew left, and had this been Earth, they'd have been celebrating their silver wedding. It was the longest relationship Eddie had ever had, lived out wholly in an alien city, quietly comfortable in the way of couples needing to stick together, and it had produced a son. Barry had seemed like a blessing until Eddie began to worry about what kind of life he had forced on a kid who would have to return to Earth simply to find a girlfriend.

Other than that, he had no complaints.

"You think Shan's going to go ballistic at you for staying here, don't you?" Erica said. "Look, she's half a bloody galaxy away. What's she going to do about it?"

"You never met her, did you? And it's not that far."

"I saw her a couple of times. But she's still a long way away."

"That's the problem. I let her down."

"Eddie, do you *really* want to be back there? With half the world waiting to start a war with the other? Oh, wait—that's just what you miss, isn't it? The good old days of watching someone else get their head blown off."

"Okay." Eddie waved vaguely, not sure if he was waving her away or waving her off. "Okay."

Erica turned up the audio. The sound of studio chatter filled the room. "Promise me you won't rant about what an inane bunch of wankers young reporters are today. Just accept you feel left out."

"No, I'll rant . . . it's a reflex when I see morons."

The insets at the side of the screen were far more interesting than the main image. There was a studio discussion between political commentators, a feed from a green rally, and another aerial mapsat shot of the FEU carrier group patrolling along the edge of Australian waters. Eddie focused on the rally and opted for the image, making it fill the screen; it had that excited sense of people waiting to see a movie premiere, not cowering masses on the brink of apocalypse. He wondered if they had any idea that even the massive environmental efforts they'd made in recent years might not buy them time with the Eqbas. And if the Eqbas didn't start a shooting match, the FEU looked like it would.

Nothing like an excuse to start up old feuds. The Eqbas are coming to cull the herd, and all we can do is squabble over who gets to be first in the queue.

Eddie had played the game of working out just what level of human population the Eqbas would think was viable to give other species a place at the table. Two billion? One? It sure as shit wasn't going to be the current seven billion.

"I still think Shan was mad to go back," he said. "I guarantee they won't be able to resist having a crack at grabbing her."

"Which *they*?"

"All of them. FEU, Sinostates, even the Aussies." Eddie had said too much at the wrong time about *c'naatat,* but he hadn't been believed by his news editor in the end. The FEU wasn't quite so quick to dismiss it; they wouldn't have sent Rayat to check it out in the first place. "They just need a sample. Nothing more. But that's Shan for you—she can't delegate."

As he concentrated on the green rally, he watched a reporter doing a vox pop in the crowd. Whatever a reporter was these days, he had no idea: some wannabe twat gagging to do the job for free or even pay for the privilege, just to get some reassurance that they existed by seeing themselves permanently recorded in some news archive, so they'd be somebody. Next week, they'd be back to serving donuts. When did reporting get to be about the reporter? In his day, it had still been about the story, outward-looking, inquiring; now it was a karaoke night. Maybe he was better off out here after all.

At times like this, Eddie missed Shan. She understood the therapeutic value of a good effing and blinding session. "Too many citizen journalists," he said. "Bloody amateurs. Shame the development of the human brain didn't keep pace with the expansion of self-publishing technology."

"You're right, it *is* a reflex, isn't it?" Erica leaned over his chair and kissed him on the top of the head. "I'm going to be back by lunchtime. Olivier found a cave system and wants me to put an optic line down there to chart it."

"But you're not going in, right?"

"No, that's what an optic line's for, poppet. Remember? White man's magic? The cam?" She paused at the door. "Why not go down to the exchange and see if Giyadas wants to watch this too?"

"Yeah. Maybe I will."

"And don't forget you've got to pack for Jejeno. You've a lot to do."

The door closed behind her as easily as she seemed to leave Earth's woes behind. This was a house full of memories today, because this had been Aras's home, the setting for so many painful, shocking and even wonderful times that Eddie had partly forgotten until now. The distance of years now lent a vivid relief to it all. Maybe the reality had been different, but he had—he absolutely *had*—seen Shan brought back like a mummified corpse from space, from the dead depths of absolute cold and airlessness, and he'd seen her breathe again. He hadn't imagined that. He knew exactly what *c'naatat* could do.

I bet Shan would be amazed at Umeh now. Another dead thing come back to life, at a price.

At sixty-eight, Eddie had a lifetime of headline memories to catalogue. The last years had been tame by comparison. But they had been spent living among aliens, and once again he was in a blasé period about that. Wonder waxed and waned.

What's it going to be like talking to you again, you old tart? You saw me a few months ago. I've missed you for a generation. The reunion's going to be very one-sided, doll.

How long had she been thawed out from cryo now? Maybe she'd call him soon, keen to share the experience with him. He envied her being in the thick of things, and if only he'd gone too, if only he'd been there right now—

"We're going to have to leave that report now and bring you breaking news—reports are coming in of an incident involving the Eqbas flagship and FEU fighters over European Antarctica," said the anchorwoman. She seemed to have no footage to run, and it was frustrating her visibly. Her fancy hairstyle quivered as she fidgeted. They were all used to simply jumping from feed to feed now, rarely interpreting, offering nothing to guide the viewer. No wonder news ratings had fallen off in the last few years. "We don't have pictures yet . . . I'm being told that the alien fleet is simply too fast for our unmanned newscraft to follow. We'll bring you mapsat or cockpit images as soon as we can."

"What incident, you silly cow?" said Eddie. "World war? Argument over a parking bay? Jesus H. Christ, this is the worst time to go with half a story . . ."

But his stomach was churning, and he knew how this would end, because he'd seen it all before. The last thing running through his mind right then were his fears for his buddies. He had complete faith—blind, even—in Eqbas might, but part of him, the largest part, felt a gut-churning dread for his world even if he'd never see it again. It was his son's future—and most of his own memories, which was all anyone was left with in the final days of life.

I'm only sixty-eight. This is insane. Stop the mawkishness.

Eddie grabbed a cup of tea, made from the bushes that Aras had planted for Shan, and settled in to be a very reluctant spectator for the rest of the day.

I should have been there, though. What a fucking story.

He thought of calling Shan on the ITX, but that was probably the last thing she needed right then. *Boy, I've got slack in my old age.* There was a time when he'd have called her on her deathbed and not felt a scrap of guilt, because the story came first, cold and pure. He waited a full hour before the first images began to show up, and as a blurred oval streak shot through a sky-colored frame—totally meaningless, minus scale, but the best they could do thus far—the ITX link chimed.

Eddie half stood, hand braced on the arm of the sofa, looking over his shoulder at the console to check the source. He didn't want a conversation right now, but it might have been Nevyan or Giyadas, and they didn't call for idle gossip.

But the light showed the link was coming in from Earth. From *home*.

At last, BBChan News Desk had remembered they actually had someone out here, someone who'd been under fire in an Eqbas ship, someone who'd had a front-row seat for the destruction of Umeh, their man in the Cavanagh system.

He'd try to be gracious. But they'd taken their fucking time. He got up and squeezed the *virin* in his palm, opening the link at his end.

"Michallat," he said, trying to sound busy yet distracted. There was nothing worse than making 'Desk feel that you waited on their calls like some love-struck teenage girl. He patched the link through to the main screen, but the icon was blank, just faintly crackling dead air. "Who's that?"

"Mr. Michallat," said the voice. "This is the office of President Michael Zammett. Can you talk? We'd like some independent input . . ."

For some reason, Eddie was disappointed that it wasn't News Desk.

Australia, Earth: St George landing site.

"That was just insane," said Shan, but she seemed to be concentrating on the screen of her swiss and cursing to herself as she walked along the main passageway of the ship. Ade Bennett followed her with that fixed lack of expression that indicated he was agitated. "Jesus, why provoke them? You could have waited a few days before starting a shooting match. So maybe we could unload the bloody *Actaeon* crew without this becoming an international brawl."

Esganikan had the feeling of being in a post-cryo haze from which she hadn't fully awakened; the present was there, but overlaid by an almost visible mesh of translucent images. When the hatch opened and the ship's ramp extruded from the bulkhead, she saw flash-frames of a city she didn't recognize, gray and square.

"I'm not bound by Earth's internal borders," she said.

Is this dreaming? I thought humans did this in their sleep.

Eqbas didn't dream as such, but these images, a whole random sequence of them, had begun intruding on her thoughts within a day or so of the *c'naatat* organism entering her bloodstream. They were memories of experiences she was certain she'd never had, and she was beginning to feel real fear about what *c'naatat* was doing to her.

"There's such a thing as not making more trouble than you need," Shan said, clearly angry even if her scent was suppressed. "It'll save you time in the long run."

Children. Human children. Whose? No, I can remember being one . . .

"You're too attached to Earth," Esganikan said flatly, making an effort to concentrate on the solid world in front of her. "I treat Earth no worse than Umeh, and you went along with that, did you not?" She turned to face Shan, and at that moment she couldn't tell if this was a woman with whom she had everything in common or potentially her worst enemy. "In fact, I showed much more caution. I merely flew over the European outpost and I fired no shots even when fired upon by that ship. If you recall, I destroyed a military base on Umeh for firing on us. That demonstrates my restraint."

"Well, the bloody warning flare ruined the pilot's fucking day, I can tell you *that*." Shan was furious, but totally devoid of scent. It always struck Esganikan as devious rather than diplomatic that Shan used her ability to suppress her signaling, even if she understood her unwillingness to emit *jask*. "The poor bastard had to eject. He's probably injured."

"He flew too close. He clipped the shield." Esganikan couldn't understand Shan's reaction. A vessel of war had behaved aggressively. Did she think humans would be treated any differently from isenj? "The FEU is not your ally, nor mine."

"This is about using an appropriate level of force. Why the hell did you want me along for the ride if you're not going to listen to advice from your tame monkey?"

Esganikan didn't fully understand the retort, either, and

had more pressing things on her mind. She couldn't seek advice from Shan about *c'naatat*: Shan didn't know that Esganikan carried it, and neither did the crew—yet.

It was an alien thing, this need to conceal facts. Wess'har didn't lie. But something in Esganikan said that she had to.

Shan will turn on you.

Your crew will not, but the Skavu will despise you for it, for being an abomination, and then you won't be able to command them.

Esganikan heard those thoughts almost like a stranger's voice whispering to her. This wasn't how she would have reacted in the past. She considered *c'naatat*, of the way it resurrected the attitudes and memories of previous hosts, and remembered thinking she would be better able to handle human deceit through the genetic memory of Mohan Rayat, an accomplished spy and liar.

I took on those traits. I have to be careful how I handle them. I have memories and characteristics from every host c'naatat *has passed through.*

It made sense to keep it from Shan, though. The woman was so adamant that the parasite shouldn't spread that she trusted nobody else with it.

This is how corruption begins. One small concession at a time. One thing you feel you have to do for a good reason.

Esganikan wondered what else *c'naatat* was going to change in her attitudes. Would she even know it was happening? That was what she feared. She'd been prepared for her body to alter out of all recognition, like Aras's, but not her mind. That was much more disturbing.

She walked down the ramp and onto the desert itself, through the defense shield that also maintained a habitable environment. Searing dry heat hit her in the face like something solid; she heard Shan puff out a breath. Ade Bennett fanned his hand in front of his face and said something about *redders,* which was incomprehensible, and the three of them stood looking at an undulating layer of air that warped the horizon into a hazy mass floating above the horizon.

"Home, Boss," said Ade. He turned to Shan and gave her a quick display of his teeth, eyes darting over her, but he smelled agitated and distinctly wess'har. They were all chimeras now, all a ragbag of species. "Hey, it still feels like . . . well, we did it."

"Don't get too used to it," Shan said.

Esganikan was satisfied with the location. It was as lifeless as she expected: no other creature would be inconvenienced by their arrival, and her Skavu forces could set up camp here away from everyone else, out of temptation's way. She didn't trust them close to humans. They would react, she suspected, as they reacted to the isenj, and she needed a more managed approach to restoring Earth. But Deborah Garrod's colonists would need to be removed to a more hospitable environment. This place was not for them.

"Well, you've got the prime minister trekking all the way out here to welcome you," Shan said. Aras walked past her with Aitassi, Esganikan's ussissi aide, followed by two of the environmental engineers who stopped to begin sinking probes into the ground to locate the deep aquifers. "Look. I bet they want to congratulate us for following their landing instructions so fucking inadequately."

Black shapeless blobs wobbled in the heat haze, as formless as Eqbas hulls in their transition phase. The shapes resolved into a convoy of vehicles kicking up plumes of dust, and which came to a halt a hundred meters from where Esganikan stood. Shan's skin and hair betrayed the slight gloss of the barrier gel, just like Ade's. They were taking no chances.

I could tell Shan. But I have enough to contend with now without starting a battle with her. I'll have to pick my time.

Esganikan could now see humans walking towards her, four of them, all obscured by what looked like environment suits. They came to a halt at fifty meters. She started walking towards them, and that seemed to start a panic.

"Quarantine," Shan said, keeping up with her. "Remember?"

"We're not at risk from them."

"It's not *us* they're worried about."

"We understand the human genome well enough now to guarantee—"

"That's not a good start," said Shan, and held her arm out in front of Esganikan in that gesture that said *stop*. "Let me handle it."

Esganikan stopped. Shan took a few more slow steps forward and made a gesture holding up both hands that Esganikan didn't understand.

"It's okay," Shan called. "We've done this before. We're not going to infect anyone. Eqbas are very efficient at handling biohazards."

Esganikan wondered if that was human sarcasm. It seemed to get no reaction from the welcoming party to indicate they understood it as that, and the figure in the center took a few more steps forward before pulling off the mask covering his head. It was Prime Minister Bari. She recognized him.

"Commander Gai? Superintendent Frankland?" The voice was a little shaky. "We had a more comfortable landing spot picked out for you, but since you're here . . . welcome to the Australian Republic."

Bari ignored a restraining hand on his arm from one of the men beside him and walked to close the gap.

"He's crapping himself," Shan said quietly. "He's scared, and he thinks he's taking a huge risk removing his mask, but it's so he can look you in the eye and gain your trust. So play nice. Okay?"

Esganikan saw no need to placate someone who had absolutely no choice, but she heeded Shan's advice about avoiding conflict, to save time. Earth wasn't something that could be wiped clean like Umeh was; the ecology was complex. Humans were needed—some of them, anyway.

Get him on side. He'll do your work for you.

It was that alien voice again: Mohan Rayat's. Esganikan was sure of that now. She took Bari's extended hand in hers, noting how he stared at the glove, and shook it as instructed.

"Are you sure this is going to be a suitable place to set up camp, Commander?" he asked. "Even temporarily? There's nothing out here."

"We leave no trace of our presence." Esganikan retrieved her hand. "And once we locate an aquifer, we can be self-sustaining indefinitely. We've worked in much less hospitable climates than this. But we have human colonists and military personnel who need other accommodation."

Bari's two suited escorts stood to either side of him as if they could protect him, while one—possibly a female— stood a few paces behind. *Gethes* were still a mass of fidgeting, twitching distractions; none of them seemed able to stand still by wess'har standards.

"We need to begin quarantine procedures for the human crew, at least," Bari said. "The FEU will insist on their personnel being screened before they enter their borders."

"They won't know what they're looking for, nor if they find it."

Shan intervened. "They'll know if they see mutated human viruses and bacteria, though."

"Very well," said Esganikan. An opportunity presented itself, and she took it without thinking, but it wasn't her own impulse. "Provide human pathogen data, and we can screen all the humans for you."

"The FEU will still want to quarantine them."

"That's their concern. But the colonists will remain here, so we can screen them for you and deal with any risks. Provide us with information on your genotypes and pathogen profiles, and we can predict if any contaminant carried by the humans on board will be a hazard to you—or if your diseases will harm them." Esganikan was more worried for the colonists she'd brought back to Earth than for the native population. They were the kind of responsible humans she thought fit to survive and, as Deborah Garrod put it, *inherit* the Earth. "Your diseases are most unlikely to affect us, the ussissi or the Skavu."

Bari hesitated.

Perhaps he needed to ask others in his government. Humans were bureaucratic creatures, always needing permission or seeking control, unable to act on their own initiative.

"We'll do that," he said at last. He was sweating visibly in the heat, but there was still no mention of the incident with the FEU fighter. "Commander, might I suggest we find somewhere more comfortable to continue discussions? The heat's a problem for us. I imagine it's unpleasant for you, too."

"Our next meeting will be at your offices, then," she said. "But in the meantime, I must speak to the FEU about those responsible for ordering the bombing of Ouzhari."

"I thought you'd dealt with all that a few years ago."

Bari meant the assassinations of FEU intelligence staff carried out by Helen Marchant's associates. But the response was out of Esganikan's mouth before she knew it.

"There were others," she said. Were there? *Yes, you know there were, don't you? You remember . . .* "And I must know if they're still alive. If they are, then they will be punished."

Bari took a noisy swallow. It was very distracting. "Might I ask you to warn us about your intentions towards Europe? We're in a very tense situation at the moment, and the incident with the FEU fighter is causing us problems."

Unlike the isenj, Bari didn't seem to be asking for help to defeat his enemies. Esganikan thought she might offer it anyway, by way of removing an irritant and reassuring an ally.

"If the warships cause you concern, we can remove them immediately."

Bari's expression was unreadable, but Esganikan knew what a stressed human smelled like. Shan made a noise in her throat, right on the limit of Esganikan's hearing.

"Thank you for the offer," Bari said carefully. Esganikan could see his jaw muscles working even when he stopped talking. "It would help me a lot if you *didn't,* though. Perhaps that's something else we can discuss."

The conversation was over for the time being as far as Esganikan was concerned. "I'll contact you when we're ready."

"We have climate scientists available to begin work with your team," said Bari. "In the meantime, this area is sealed off by our military, and we'll keep the media at bay."

"If they intrude, we can deal with them."

"We don't shoot journalists, Commander. They're useful."

Esganikan thought of Eddie. It was a pity not to have him on hand, but Shan could manage some of his liaison tasks. "Then we'll simply ignore them for the time being, and you can deal with them as you wish. Now I want the Federal European Union to honor its pledge to hand over the remaining members of its security services who authorized the use of cobalt devices on Ouzhari. Then I want to move the colonists into some permanent settlement, and then we will begin discussing the changes you need to make to restore this planet to a state of ecological balance for all its species."

Shan sighed quietly to herself. "What's the magic word?"

"Perhaps Superintendent Frankland could . . . lay some foundations for our discussion." Bari glanced at Shan as if he was keen to talk to a human and find out what the aliens were really up to. That was progress. "Despite all the discussion that's taken place over the years, I'm relatively new, and I still have some catching up to do."

"Yes," Esganikan said flatly. "If that makes you more comfortable. We'll contact you."

Bari stood waiting for a moment and then appeared to realize the discussion was over for the time being. The humans walked off and their vehicles edged forward to meet them halfway. Shan made a little puffing noise through her nose.

"You can *talk* to them," said Esganikan. Shan had been reluctant to come, and her annoyance showed even if it wasn't detectable in her scent. "Conversation commits you to nothing."

Shan glanced at a thin band on her left wrist, clasped her hands behind her back, and shook her head. "I have to hand it to you, Esganikan. We put our boots on Earth soil less than fifteen minutes ago, and you've already offered to kick off a world war and pissed over all the diplomatic channels. Not bad. Give us another hour, and we can start Armageddon."

"If you believe you can improve matters, now you have the opportunity." Esganikan could see Ade in her peripheral vision, hands clasped behind his back in much the same square pose as his *isan*. She felt she'd been exceptionally *consultative,* as Shan called it. She'd *given* the humans information; she'd *asked* them to provide information in return. She could have taken it. "We'll still do what we have to do. If you think you can make that easier by liaising with Bari in a way that I appear unable to, then I suggest you do it."

"Christ, when I'm the diplomat on a mission, then I know we're in trouble. And there's no point leaning on Bari to get the FEU to do anything." Shan frowned slightly. "And what do you mean, *there were others*? What others?"

It was what Ade called her *copper's voice*. Esganikan recognized it every time now. She was interrogating her.

I know there were others involved in bombing Ouzhari. I know, because I have Mohan Rayat's memories. I know who gave him his orders.

And now Esganikan had to practice that other gift from Rayat's mind: the art of lying.

It was getting easier.

"There are *always* others," she said. "It would have been a major decision for humans, and in your society, you rarely take those decisions without *committees*."

Shan gave her a long stare so devoid of emotion that it said everything. She didn't trust Esganikan. Shan always said she trusted nobody, but that wasn't entirely accurate; she certainly put great faith in her two males.

"I thought you drew the line somewhere in your guilt league," said Shan. "Are you going to go after the bloody committee clerks now?"

"I must balance this crime." A police officer like Shan would understand the need for justice, Esganikan thought. "There will be others, and if I have their names, and if they are alive, then I can make that decision."

"I'll ask around," Shan said sourly.

She stalked off, Ade close on her heels. Aras wandered after them at a distance, shooting Esganikan a glance that said he didn't approve of using his *isan* like that.

Esganikan could *feel* the name somehow. That memory was in there too. She might recall it before Shan discovered it; after so many years, finding it was a tall order even for an accomplished detective like her.

*This was our prime reason for coming to Earth, to bal-
ance the crime against Ouzhari. It must be dealt with . . . if
only to demonstrate that we mean what we say.*

And that was Rayat speaking for her, she knew.

An understanding of the thoughts of the spy—Rayat—
and the police officer—Shan—would help her deal with
humans. As she let the mirage of a distant ruined town lull
her into a meditative state, she could detect both of them in
her mind somehow, and they felt . . . *similar.* Both obsessive; both so committed to their mission that anything was
permissible in completing it.

And yet they hate each other.

Her hands itched inside her gloves. She peeled back the
cuffs, wondering if some insect had found a point of entry,
and thought she saw a flash of violet light. It took her a few
moments to realize the light was really there, winking and
rippling bioluminescence.

Shan had those lights.

It's gathering pace.

Ade Bennett had the bioluminescence too, but not Aras.
Somehow, genes from the bezeri had latched on to Shan's
genome through *c'naatat,* and now they were within Esganikan, a visible sign of her actions that would betray her
to Shan, and Shan would react badly.

*Am I going to end up looking like Aras? Nothing like my
own species?*

Esganikan fought down brief panic and smoothed the
gloves back into place. As she turned, she saw Shan, paused
in mid-step and watching. She was downwind; she had
smelled the scent of anxiety. Then the woman looked away
and resumed her walk back to the ship.

*I need her cooperation. She's a matriarch like me, not a
gethes. She could probably oust me at any time.*

C'naatat had bought Esganikan time, both to resolve
Earth's problems, and to give her the chance of going home
and having a life for herself before she grew too old and
lonely in the service of Eqbas Vorhi. Shan would never have
made that same choice—not for herself, anyway. But the
welfare of her males was a different matter, and that small

expedience made her no different and no more moral than Esganikan.

I know your weakness. You would rather die yourself than face the deaths of those you love, Shan Frankland, because love is rare and new to you.

Esganikan looked around for Aitassi. The ussissi aide was standing with her snout pointing into the wind, checking what might be out there. "Do we have access to any current Earth data links?"

The aide trotted back to her, kicking up dry red dust. "We had a link to the climatology database in Kamberra before we embarked. If other public databases use the same basic technology, then we can find a way to access those too."

"Good," said Esganikan. "We can't wait for the *gethes* to play their information games. Get the data so we can update the computer modeling."

Was that deception, or was it a unilateral decision? Guilt was a human emotion, and now Esganikan felt it for what it was. She was troubled by how unsettled Shan made her feel, and returned to the shelter of the ship.

Around her, the red plain was already dotted with shiplets that had broken away from the main vessel to form a camp of small bubble-like cabins.

The Skavu had landed too.

She could see their ships in the distance, still in one piece, waiting for her orders. The command center stood separate from the accommodation modules, and as she walked through the camp she could hear the sound of Earth's news channels drifting from the hatches. There was panic and speculation, the sound of demands for answers and reassurances.

When she'd dealt with Umeh, she was remote and insulated. Now she felt part of Earth, *among* it, and not simply because she was standing here. When she walked into the command center module, she inhaled carefully, trying to sense if Shan had emitted *jask,* but detected no trace of the matriarchal dominance pheromone that would make her submit to another *isan*'s will.

I never used to be wary of her, not like this.

But Shan had used *jask* for her own ends before, and

Esganikan couldn't rely on her instincts now. She no longer had any idea whose instincts they were. What she had in her altered brain was a library, a range of behaviors for any given situation, and she had to choose which was the most effective at the time.

Gethes rules applied here. Rayat's solutions might prove to be the best options.

Esganikan Gai settled down in her cabin, and concentrated on the part of her mind that was Rayat's, seeking not only guidance, but names.

3

I don't think we know the difference between a diplomatic visit and an invasion. If I were you, I would start thinking in terms of Earth being under Eqbas occupation. We certainly have, and we'll take whatever steps we can to protect ourselves, military or otherwise.

FEU President Zammett,
to Sinostates Foreign Secretary Evgeny Barsukov

F'nar, Wess'ej.

"You might have noticed," Eddie said kindly, "that I'm a few trillion miles out of town right now. I'm not sure how I can help you, Mr. Zammett."

If he thought he was getting a Mr. *President* out of Eddie, he was mistaken. Eddie was celebrating a late mid-life crisis with a little satisfying grumpiness, no longer needing to give a hand-job to political egos to get what he wanted. Zammett was familiar territory. Only the faces changed.

"We'd like to understand the wess'har—the Eqbas—better, Mr. Michallat, and you're about the only neutral person I can reach who knows them well."

There's Shan, and Ade, and the Royal Marines. But maybe you don't know where they are now, and you're trawling.

"I suppose I do," said Eddie. The five-second delay on the relay was a blessing sometimes, a little shakedown time. "What do you want to know that I didn't cover in nearly six hundred hours of features and doccos over the last twenty-seven years? I wouldn't have thought there was anything left *not* to know about. Even their sex lives and recipes."

Zammett had an extraordinary ability to sit completely still while waiting to speak. He was bred for live video. "We got off to a bad start with them, alas. They violated our Antarctic airspace, one of our air force observers got too close, and there were shots fired. The pilot ejected safely, though. We could still talk calmly with them at the moment."

Eddie shrugged. "If the Eqbas *had* opened fire, the pilot wouldn't have been able to bang out, except as vapor. If he saw a big flash, that's part of their mechanism for fending off collisions."

There was a longer silence than Eddie expected. "Unfortunately, one of our warships launched a missile."

"Well, is your office still in one piece? That means they weren't too upset, because I've seen them wipe out a whole city for that. And they don't have a concept of airspace and national boundaries."

"The missile certainly seemed to make no impression on their ship . . ."

"Mr. Zammett, have you actually *seen* any of my programs? The civil war on Umeh?"

"Not all of them."

"Well, get your secretary to dig up the BBChan archives and just watch the lot. That'll tell you all you need to know about their military capacity. *Capacity,* as in *you don't stand a chance.* They were spacefaring when we were living in caves. You know what they say—resistance is futile. Clichés are clichés for a good reason."

"It's hard," said Zammett, "to know that, and yet still be unwilling to be *downsized* like Umeh was without at least putting up a fight."

He'd absorbed that much, then. So what was he after? There was information, and there was special pleading. He didn't need military intelligence. The words *hundreds of thousands of years ahead of us* should have told him everything.

"What do you want from me?" Eddie decided to play for time. "My wife isn't keen on me getting involved with Earth matters these days, so I'd have to square it with her, but just tell me straight what you want."

"Just advice from time to time on who we should be talking to. Cultural advice. That kind of thing."

Right. If he'd seen the programs, then he would have known that he could just ask a wess'har anything at all and get a completely open answer. They didn't need diplomacy and good contacts.

"Okay," said Eddie, seizing a bargaining chip for the future. "For whatever good it'll do."

"You're a European citizen, Mr. Michallat. I don't think you want to see the English regions destroyed, however welcome the wess'har have made you."

Zammett was right, but the Eqbas would do whatever made sense environmentally, and singing "Jerusalem" to them wouldn't bring a tear to their eye and make them spare England. It wasn't even a green and pleasant land any longer. It was a cluster of storm-whipped islands, and far smaller than they'd been when he left Earth. "Anything else?"

"Long shot, but . . . do you know what happened to Mohan Rayat?"

Transparent as a glass of piss. What an amateur. "Not really." Well, that *was* true. He hadn't heard from him since the Eqbas left. "Why?"

"You must be aware that the Eqbas want to know who gave him clearance to use nuclear devices on Bezer'ej. I just wondered if he might still be alive and willing to say. Clear it up without the need for nastiness."

"I haven't seen him since . . . oh, 2376? He's not here, that's for sure. He'd be in his late seventies now if he's still alive."

"Thank you anyway. Please, get back in touch when you're ready to go ahead."

"I will."

Eddie closed the link with a sense of completely inappropriate elation. *Why the hell has that given me a buzz?* It was just the old juices flowing, being pivotal, knowing he was being set up and pulling a flanker on a smart-arse. All the old buttons were being pushed. Erica really *would* go nuts and lecture him about not being able to let go either of Earth or his old status, but that wasn't why he asked for time.

So Zammett wants Rayat—still. He wants Shan—still. Nothing's changed. Now, if you think your population is go-

ing to be wiped out like the isenj, what would you *want more than anything?*

C'naatat.

Eddie would have been surprised if Zammett hadn't worked out what he'd do next, but he had to do it anyway. He needed to warn Shan. The ITX wasn't encrypted; neither wess'har nor isenj cared much about secrets.

Giyadas would be delighted to help him contact Aras and cover his tracks. The little seahorse princess who'd wanted to be a reporter just like Eddie had grown up into a fearsome matriarch in her own right, wise to the ways of *gethes*.

Eddie grabbed his bee cam and headed for the pearl terraces to find her. He didn't need a poxy president to make him feel important. His best buddy was a wess'har warrior queen.

Earth, Australian Republic: Eqbas temporary camp.

The most alien trees Aras had ever seen weren't the cycadlike *dalf* of Umeh, or the *efte* of Bezer'ej, but the synthetic ones he was now looking at in the middle of a red desert so arid, so baked, so inhospitable that no real tree could ever have survived there.

In the relative cool of dusk, the trees looked unnaturally white, their rectangular upper paddles and rigidly straight lines at odds with the natural curves of the landscape.

They weren't decorative—humans used artificial plants for enjoyment, he knew that—but devices for carbon dioxide capture, trapping CO_2 and pumping it as liquid sodium carbonate for separation and routing to vast underwater gas injectors to bury the gas forever in the sea bed.

Forever was a very flexible word. *Forever* was, in this technology, millions of years. That wasn't *forever* at all. Aras could envisage forever, and now it was troubling him. He thought of Umeh, of visiting the city of Jejeno that he'd never seen but that he recalled from the memories of his isenj captors more than five hundred years before.

What was I before c'naatat? *What mattered to me? What gave me joy?*

It was as if the intervening centuries hadn't happened; long lonely years of self-imposed exile on Bezer'ej, where every day was the same except for the changes of garrison personnel, followed by fewer than three years of the most bittersweet joy, agony, war, and deaths that completely changed his life and the future of both Earth and two other star systems.

I can count my time with Shan in single years, and my time with her as my isan *in months. I executed my best friend. I mourned Shan's death and then she came back to me. I have a house-brother again, at last. And still . . . I dwell on what I was, because I can hardly recall it, but I need to. I need to know who I really am.*

Aras preferred to do his thinking in the open air. The huge scattered camp of shiplets was quiet, and flickering status lights in bands of red and blue chevrons marked out each fragment of vessel. The defense shield now enclosed a more humid environment, and insects had appeared from nowhere to dance around the blue-white displays. The red lights didn't seem to appeal to them.

"How do they *do* that?" asked a woman's voice.

Aras should have smelled Deborah Garrod's approach, but he was too engrossed in his thoughts. She startled him.

"Do what?"

"The moths. How do little things like that get past the shield when missiles can't?"

"The shield recognizes them as harmless," said Aras, realizing she was trying to keep him company rather than seeking a lesson. "Like the barrier around the Temporary City on Bezer'ej recognized wess'har DNA, or the biobarrier around Constantine separated the terrestrial environment from the native one. It's the same technology."

"I thought you'd be with Ade and Shan."

"I wanted to think."

"You sure of that?"

"Yes. Besides, Ade needs more of Shan's time than I do. Human males are quite insecure, even sensible ones like Ade."

"He's a nice man. I'm glad you're all happy. I think all of you had such lonely lives before."

Aras wondered if it was wise to discuss loneliness with Deborah after making her a widow. Josh Garrod had been his closest friend, and yet Aras hadn't hesitated to kill him for helping Rayat—and Lindsay Neville—detonate bombs on Ouzhari. Deborah had convinced herself that she bore him no ill will because her god had planned for it all to happen. Aras still wasn't sure if he envied her ability to mold reality to what she needed to cope, or pitied her, or if—such was the certainty in her face—she was actually right.

But if she's right, and her god is a real entity, then I have more questions about his failings and methods than his indefinable love that I can't actually see working anywhere.

"I think I resent loneliness," said Aras. "It accounts for ninety-nine-point-nine-five percent of my life."

"You calculated that?"

"By years, yes."

"Ah." Deborah sat down on the outcrop next to him. "I forget that."

Aras had seen no evidence of any god's love in all those years. He saw detached abandonment, the balanced cycle of life and death, ebb and flow, and the inability of just one species to accept the ephemeral nature of all worlds. God was a good coping mechanism for humans.

"Do you feel content at completing your mission?" he asked.

"I'll tell you when I do it," she said.

"You saved the gene bank and brought it back."

"I have to see what happens to it yet."

"Where will you be settling now?"

"I've been talking to the government resettlement people on the link. There's a refugee camp to the northeast, in the Islamic sector. A community of vegetarian Muslims has offered us land nearby."

"They're not the same faith as you."

"Neither are you, but we were happy to share your goals."

"No faith at all is easier to reconcile than a different one."

"I know, but we do many impossible things each day, don't we?"

Aras took abstinence from all involvement with other

animals as a given, but for humans it was still a distinct life-style, and one the Muslim township clearly found some kin-ship with. Shan said Esganikan needed to understand that you couldn't put religions like those together and expect them to *play nicely.* She cited wars and mutual persecution. Deborah seemed to see the same thing that Esganikan did, so perhaps Shan was wrong for once.

"You realize that many of the gene bank's species have no habitat to be placed in now," he said, wary of mentioning religious war.

Deborah nodded. "I worked that out when I wondered what would happen to the macaws." She'd been stunned by the two blue-and-gold macaws that Shapakti had resurrected from the gene bank as an experiment. She'd grown up in a small and very limited copy of Earth's environment on Bezer'ej, where there were just food crops and pollinating bees. The wild planet beyond the biobarrier on Constantine island was utterly alien, and had Aras not intervened and created the environment, the first settlers and all their dreams of returning the gene bank to Earth would have died. "Sometimes it's hard to look beyond the next hurdle, isn't it?"

I could have saved the gene banks myself and let the humans die. I know that now. Would it have been kinder, more in keeping with the balance of life?

Aras had inherited the human tendency to fret about things in the past that couldn't be changed, but not their delusional certainty about the future that they called *faith.*

"I know," said Deborah. "I feel that way sometimes. I wanted to know where the macaws would go and if they could be set free. Then I found the rain forests were gone."

"There are still some surviving areas, and there'll be more forest in the future."

"But not in time for *them,* though. Where are they?"

"The survey team is caring for them. They plan to release them in a sanctuary in Canada."

"Not a real forest, then."

"No. I think they have little idea how to survive in the wild even if there were habitats for them. At least they'll be with other captive macaws."

"Ah," said Deborah. "I know how they must feel."

It summed up all of them—him, the colonists, everyone who'd returned. Place was tied to time, and the places were still here, but the *time* was not.

"Aras, did we make a mistake bringing back the gene bank?"

He'd never heard her express doubt before. "I don't believe so."

"You never lie, and you've restored planets yourself. Convince me."

"Think of it as a staged process. Everything in it can be resurrected when the conditions are right." Aras risked putting his gloved hand on her shoulder, suddenly conscious of her neck and seeing Josh's seconds before he swung his wess'har harvesting knife at it. "The alternative was losing all life that might have survived, had humans not driven it to extinction. I would say you did the only thing you could."

"You know, I can't help thinking we've brought it back for Judgment Day."

This was where rational, pragmatic, calm Deborah Garrod became someone who alarmed Shan. Deborah switched from demonstrable reality to unfathomable belief, seamless and certain. Shan would try not to look embarrassed, biting her lip and talking patiently to Deborah as if she was a child—a human child, not a wess'har one. Wess'har children needed no fairy tales. Humans—of all ages—seemed unable to live without them, and Aras could still see no difference between morality tales and the word of their god.

"Why would your god destroy what he created, unless he felt he'd made a mistake?" Aras asked. He didn't do it out of cruelty, but out of a frustrated need to understand. This faith was a massively powerful motivator for good and bad in humans, and he had never fully grasped it. "Is he culling, like we did to the isenj?"

"In a way. He'll save the righteous and give them eternal life."

"And the sinners are cast into Hell, yes?" Aras remembered that bit. He wondered about it from time to time, and

if he would be considered a sinner. It struck him as unfair.
"So he doesn't forgive."

"Oh, God forgives."

"Then who goes to Hell? I asked your ancestor Ben about
this many times, and I never understood where God drew
the line between those he forgave and those he didn't."

"I don't have an answer."

"Do you think you'll be saved? Because you did what you
thought God wanted and preserved the gene bank?"

"I *hope* I'm saved, because I want to see God.
And . . . Josh."

Aras knew he would have made the same decision today,
right now, and killed Josh for helping destroy Ouzhari. He
still missed him. He still pitied Deborah. He still didn't feel
guilty. It had to be done, or there was only chaos to follow.

It was *judgment*. He understood that.

Aras wanted to find Shan and Ade, and shelter in the
comfort of his family, but the conversation had transfixed
him and he felt on the brink of genuine discovery after so
many years of confusion. He was acutely aware of the language used in the conversation, because he'd struggled with
the concepts for many years. *Forgiveness* had taken him
years to unpick, but he had a better idea of what *guilt* was.
There was also *redemption*, which he still thought of as selfish and irrelevant, and then there was judgment, which he
understood when he saw it as *balance*.

"Billions of humans will die when this planet is restored,"
he said. "Is that Judgment Day? Does it have to be God who
kills them to count as that? Or is this what you call *working
through man*?"

"Do you realize how profound your theology can be,
Aras?"

"No. I understand too little."

"I think that's what makes it profound."

"Well, is it? Will that be Judgment Day? Is it the end of
Earth, or the end of humans? Because this won't be the end
of humans, not unless Esganikan—"

"You're scaring me now."

Deborah had never said that before, not even as a joke.

And she *was* scared: her pupils were dilated and she smelled of anxiety. How could she fear death if her god was going to reward her for doing the right things in life, and reunite her with Josh?

"I'm sorry, Deborah. Why?"

"Because if this is God's judgment coming, then I have to rethink my whole life."

Aras thought of something Shan had said to him a long time ago when he made a grave and headstone for Lindsay Neville's premature baby, and asked Shan about the afterlife.

Every miracle's got a mundane explanation. Your City of Pearl is actually insect shit. Eternal life is a parasite. The bubbles in champagne are the farts of yeast colonies. That's just the way the universe is. And you can choose—you can look at the wondrous surface, or you can look at the crud beneath.

He had a moment of revelation, of epiphany—ah, all those god words again, the god words the colony always used—that made perfect sense of it all. He knew now, or at least he had a theory. It would comfort Deborah.

"But that means you were right," he said. "That your faith has been proven."

"—I like to think so. We all struggle with faith, Aras, because if we didn't we'd be wasting the minds that God gave us."

"Your Bible is looking increasingly factual."

The expression on her face was suddenly unreadable. But there was still fear on her scent, and not of him. "You surprise me by saying that."

"It's a matter of perspective. The future of the planet is being determined by the Eqbas, which is judgment. Only a relatively small number of humans will survive, which is the righteous. You've seen the City of Pearl in F'nar, and eternal life in *c'naatat*. And whatever environment is left here may well be the world to come. Doesn't that vindicate your views?"

As soon as he finished the sentence, he knew he'd said the wrong thing. Deborah didn't turn on him, but there was the

faintest slackening of the muscles around her mouth and
eyes, a little human tell that he knew could mean anything
from dismay to well-hidden shock or grief. He thought she
wanted to know the truth, to be proven right after all, but
he'd got it wrong again.

*They're within you. You have their memories, you have a
human* isan *and house-brother, and yet you still don't know
humans at all, not even now.*

"In a way," Deborah said, "I hope the Bible is wrong in
that respect."

"I'm sorry."

"Don't be. Humans—believers—have always tried to tie
the scriptures to real events and to second-guess God. I think
that's why we shunned literalism in the colony, all of us, whatever branch of Christianity we came from. Our intellects
aren't enough to comprehend God on that mundane level."

It was as kind a way of being told to shut up as Aras had
ever heard. He felt he'd wounded her.

"I didn't mean to undermine your faith."

"We all question belief, Aras. It's not wrong."

"I never really understood it."

"Faith keeps you going when there's no logical reason to.
In its way, it keeps life going. It keeps *people* going, having
kids even though the future looks bad, because they believe
it'll get better. I hear that even Mohan Rayat found comfort
in his faith. Commander Neville did too."

"But after they *sinned.* After they destroyed Ouzhari. Do
we have to sin to find faith? Do we—"

Aras was desperate to continue the debate. He wanted to
understand so badly. But he stopped short of the logical pro-
gression, of pointing out that as far as he knew, other animals went on reproducing without a formal belief in God,
and that eventually the Earth and the whole solar system
would die when the Sun reached the end of its life. But that
was something she literally didn't need to hear.

There was always the chance he was wrong. He hoped
so, for her sake, and wondered where he might stand if he
were. God must have found a way of dealing with an ever-

increasing population of people who were eternally alive. He must have learned a way to deal with a kind of *c'naatat* that lay beyond the scope of ecologies. Perhaps the humans' god would *forgive* an alien who had faced similar choices to his own.

Deborah stood up and looked at Aras, tears in her eyes. He could see the glistening liquid welling in the dying light.

"You'll visit us many times before you return to Wess'ej, won't you? Promise me."

"I will. I'll visit as often as I can."

"Good." Then she hugged him. It was rare for any human other than Shan to touch him, and Shan had transformed his life when she took his arm for the first time. A hug was an exceptional thing. "You're part of the miracle, Aras. I wish you peace, and an answer to your life in the fullness of time, because even *c'naatat* can't outlive God. Thank you. I'll miss you."

She walked back to the camp of shiplets, kicking a little dust behind her, and was swallowed up in the cool darkness of the evening. The desert was empty except for him and the silent camp. Aras felt an *end*. One job was over forever. The next—

He didn't know what came next.

He *needed* to know what happened next. He needed to know what he'd done so many years ago, saving the Bezer'ej mission from disaster, had not simply created more problems for the many species of Earth. He wanted all of it saved, the whole gene bank, and he wanted the various worlds he knew to go back to the way they were: when Bezer'ej was clean and unpolluted by colonizing isenj, when Earth was peopled with the species that filled the gene bank, when Wess'ej hadn't yet been drawn into a terrible war.

Humans said you could never turn back the clock. But wess'har—Eqbas especially—could.

Aras walked back to the shiplet for the night, wondering how far Shan and Ade would turn back their own clock if they could.

Eqbas ship 886–001–005–6: command center module.

Esganikan studied Da Shapakti's message again with a
mix of relief and apprehension. He'd done it; he'd managed
to remove the *c'naatat* organism from Mohan Rayat, not once
but a number of times.

The parasite's capacity to adapt and resist removal had its
limits. Shapakti had found a way to beat it—in humans, at
least, there was.

Esganikan found herself looking past his recording on the
screen set in the bulkhead of her cabin, straining to see
something of her home city, Surang. She missed it: the longing was sharp, sharper than she had ever known on previous
missions, a craving for a normal life and a clan of her own.
She knew his words well enough by now. She didn't need to
listen, just to see.

She'd talk to Shapakti tomorrow. Her life depended on it:
c'naatat would have to be removed one day, or she would
have to be removed from it by fragmentation. She had no intention of ending up like Aras, alone for unthinkable periods.

And then there was Rayat.

Could she allow him to return home now? She'd once told
him he could come back to Earth. What harm could he do
once *c'naatat* was removed? Without the parasite in his pos-
session, nothing he knew could help humans to find it and
exploit it. And they would never reach Bezer'ej again, she'd
see to that.

Is that Rayat's voice persuading me?

Shan would fight to stop him returning; she'd try to kill
him again, Esganikan was sure of that. Shan thought knowledge was dangerous and needed to be controlled, one of her
few blatantly human failings.

Esganikan searched as best she could in the jumbled
memory that wasn't wholly hers, trying to test Mohan
Rayat's motives. She felt the passing touch of an isolated
child who wanted to please his grandfather. The memories
of the humans through which *c'naatat* had passed emerged
with a fragmented but surprising clarity. The wider picture
eluded her, but she saw *snapshots,* as Shan called them, fro-

zen moments of great detail. She felt his intense devotion: family, nation, but no wife, no child, and a conscious, aching gap where they should have been.

How similar all creatures are, deep down.

Esganikan could feel Shan's desperate dread of *c'naatat,* a fear that had drowned out her own needs—a nightmare of supersoldiers, uncontrolled population growth, wars over the privilege of owning the biotech, a battleground between the haves and the have-nots, the destruction of the fabric of the ecology, the economy and society. There would also be something called *stupid, wasteful bloody beauty treatments* derived from it without a thought of the long-term consequences, although Esganikan was still working out what that meant.

All life was meant to end. Humans were far too obsessed with stagnant permanence—in mortal or spiritual form—in a universe already predestined to end and begin anew.

Esganikan distracted herself by catching up on the latest climate modeling that the ecosystem analysts had produced in the last few hours. It would probably upset the *gethes* that she'd taken information from their systems rather than waiting to be given it, but this was not their timetable to dictate. They were squabbling among themselves just like the isenj had done, except that their wars would damage other species, and so they had to be *managed.*

If Shapakti failed to find a way to remove *c'naatat* from Esganikan, she would face the same choice as the wess'har once had—at what point to give up her unnatural life.

Stop this. You've been on Earth less than twenty-four hours. Deal with that when you have to. You knew the risks.

The climate changes on Earth weren't as extreme as the first Eqbas model had predicted: humans had tried to mend their ways again, but it was never enough and they always stopped short of the necessary measures. She gazed at the three-dimensional animated models of expanding and contracting ice, isotherms, storm systems and sea levels. The warming had slowed; so had the deliberate destruction of many habitats, but humans had no technology for putting things back the way they were. The reports emerging on her screen showed a debate growing between her ecology analysts about how much of that slowdown could be attributed to declining human numbers, remedial action, or the planet's natural cycles. The *gethes* were dying in greater numbers from famine, floods and disease. There still seemed to be an ample and renewable supply of them, though.

"Aitassi," Esganikan called. "Aitassi?"

The ussissi normally hung around the cabin, but sometimes she disappeared to be with her clan, complete with infants, subordinate females and the complex hierarchy of males. Ussissi traveled in packs, and Esganikan understood why. Only a handful of her crew had families back home, waiting for their return in synchronized suspension. When a ship landed, and the crew was revived, their kin back home were as well, so that they could have the illusion of a shared life with no time dilation. Most of the crews were therefore young, unmated, and relatively inexperienced. Those with families endured a peculiar thing that Shan referred to as *hell*.

The sound of skittering claws announced Aitassi's arrival, and she appeared in the hatchway with a small infant clutched under one arm like a piece of baggage. That was how ussissi transported their offspring; it looked so casual to a wess'har that Esganikan was always worried for their safety, but the little ones seemed perfectly secure. At that age, their finely ribbed skin—Shan called it *corduroy*—made them look appealingly wrinkled.

It was impossible to get away from reminders of family and offspring. Aitassi made no introduction of the new baby.

"What do you want, Commander?"

"The climate projections. Have you looked at them?"

"I have, but I don't fully understand them."

Esganikan, kneeling in the most comfortable resting position for a wess'har, looked at the projections and interpretations again. She was a soldier, a planner and strategist, not a scientist: she wanted to be absolutely certain she understood what she thought she was seeing in the data. The information had been prepared by the senior analyst in the biodiversity team, Balagiu Je.

"Get Balagiu for me," she said. "I think we have a hard decision to take."

"What would that be?" asked Aitassi. "Which humans to cull?"

"I don't think that will be difficult," said Esganikan. "The environmentally responsible ones are easy to identify, and *Shan Chail* will help with that. No, this is a matter of what kind of Earth we help them restore, because it may not be the same world the species in the gene bank were taken from. The issue is how far to reverse the damage already done. We're not here to recreate a museum."

Aitassi considered the dilemma and appeared to understand. The baby under her arm—her grandchild—began squealing, demanding food and attention. "I fear this will be the major point of contention between you and the host government. They clearly have their own expectations of what will be offered."

"Shan called it a *theme park mentality*, but I suspect she wants the entire gene bank revived."

"You should watch more of the gethes' factual programming output. That's what we've been doing today." Aitassi hoisted the baby into a more comfortable position. "It always seems to be an outpouring of their wishes and opinions. They should at least *ask* for what they want, so we're all clear."

"They're humans. They're oblique and manipulative." Esganikan still hadn't had a response from the FEU to her demand that they hand over the last of those responsible for the destruction of Ouzhari. Europe was running out of time and didn't appear to realize it. "I think I shall do what Shan calls *cutting to the chase*, whatever that actually means, and make their situation clear to them as soon as possible."

"We have the genome and disease data, anyway. It's simply a matter of completing the processing against the genetic templates."

Esganikan couldn't avoid mentioning the restless infant any longer. "Is this Hilissi's child?"

"Yes. Gorossi. I have to feed him now. Will you excuse me?"

"May I hold him?"

It was an unusual request for an Eqbas. Aitassi paused and then held out the tiny creature to her.

"He already has teeth," she said. "Mind out."

Esganikan took him in both hands. She had never handled the young of any other species. There was no such thing as a *pet* in wess'har society, because non-wess'har of any kind were *people* to be left alone to pursue their own lives. Gorossi, warm and utterly alien, looked up at Esganikan with an expression of indignation, revealing an angry, demanding mouth fringed with tiny needle-like teeth.

And yet he was perfect: a creature of pure wonder.

It was shocking moment for Esganikan. It stirred memories that were very definitely not hers, of lost children and unfulfilled lives—ah, Lindsay Neville's memories, no doubt—and a craving so profound that she was distressed by it. The fact that she *knew* this was an inherited memory didn't dilute the pain one bit.

"Here," she said, holding out the child for Aitassi to take him back. "He's very fine. I envy you the prospect of continuity."

It didn't come out as she'd planned. As Aitassi left, Esganikan regained her composure and tried to look at the memories more dispassionately. No, she really hadn't bargained for this when she insisted on an infusion of Rayat's contaminated blood. It was far more intrusive than she had ever imagined. How did Shan or any of the others cope with this chaos in their minds? It made her feel invaded rather than guided, and that was totally outside her experience.

She shut her eyes and groped for a wess'har memory, something that she could feel more at ease with. It was Aras's—Aras, realizing what *c'naatat* actually was, and what his isenj captors had accidentally given him along with the terrible wounds that healed over and over again almost instantly during torture.

Five hundred years ago. Yet it's so vivid.

A wave of regret and dread—Aras's—almost took her breath away; thinking *c'naatat* simply healed, then realizing it was far more than that, and knowing he had made outcasts

of his comrades and that none of them dare breed. Esganikan could see the sunlit courtyard wall he was staring at
when the full realization hit him, could smell the cut foliage
scent of the vegetable roots in his hands, and the near pain
in his chest. *I can never be a father now. What have I done?*

She had to physically shake her head to get the image out of
her mind and reassure herself that she was still Esganikan
Gai. Perhaps the memory felt so vivid because it was a preoc-
cupation of her own—the urge to have family. It was one of a
number of yearnings and regrets from so many other lives.
She recognized Lindsay Neville's grief for her dead baby son,
an image of a little grave with a stained glass headstone de-
picting flowers; then she was suddenly underwater and watching the bioluminescence flickering and fading in a small
bezeri body. And she could clearly identify another creature
mourning the loss of family, but not a child—parents and
siblings. That was more alien; isenj, she thought. When she
concentrated, it was tied to an image of white-hot flame and
explosions as the colony of Mjat on Asht—yes, Bezer'ej, when
the isenj overran it—was destroyed by wess'har air strikes.
By Aras.

She saw the whole world from many eyes, and it hurt
more than it educated. She wanted the longing for offspring
to go away. She also preferred not to see the world through
the eyes of isenj under wess'har attack, although she'd never
been squeamish about such things before.
Get a grip.

Esganikan thought it was Shan's fierce discipline surfacing in her, but it was that all-too similar voice, the spy Rayat;
they were both so tenacious, such survivors, so *driven.*

A sense of detached calm overwhelmed the other memories. She saw a small illuminated data screen with meaningless words on it, but a very clear recollection of the names
and faces associated with them.

For a moment, she was Rayat, receiving orders to salt
neutron bombs with cobalt, and ensure that the *c'naatat* organism dormant in the soil of Ouzhari island was totally
destroyed, put beyond the reach of any of the FEU's rival
states.

Michael Leard.
Jaime Callard.
Rav Mynor.
Katya Prachy.

So those were the names. She knew that three on that list had been killed by environmental activists before she'd left Bezer'ej, twenty-five years ago, when Marchant had contacted her and promised to deliver the guilty. One was a civil servant; the other was an intelligence officer, a *spook* like Rayat.

But the woman, Prachy . . .

The woman was guilty too, and now Esganikan had her name. That had been worth those moments drowning in alien memories.

If the woman was still alive—she could check that, with or without Shan Frankland's investigative skills.

Europe faced overwhelming restoration measures anyway, but Esganikan didn't want a *probable* death. She needed to carry out the death sentence on Prachy, and be certain of it.

It was about balance. It was about *judgment*.

4

We still have six Royal Marines and a naval officer listed as dismissed the service. Commander Neville's dead, but the marines are still on board that ship, and maybe now is the ideal time to bring them back for debriefing. Let's resurrect the Judge Advocate's recommendation to set aside the findings of the court martial. It was only a political gesture to appease the wess'har. Get them back with the rest of our people. Good intel, good bargaining chip.

Head of Military Intelligence, FEU

Australian PM's flight, en route for the Eqbas camp: next day.

Bari didn't care if he had to crawl over broken glass to see Esganikan Gai. His place or hers, it didn't matter; if she wanted to sit it out in the bloody desert for a few more days deciding if she liked the color of the wallpaper, that was fine.

Right now he needed to know what his visitors could do to warn off the FEU. Another carrier was heading south from the FEU's main Spanish base. The worst thing was that Bari had no idea what concession he was expected to make. The saber rattling made no sense.

"Shukry, just tell me the damn accommodation's ready," he said, not looking up from the surface of his makeshift desk. It filled the width of the small charter aircraft. A private jet was unacceptable even for the PM, except in a national emergency, and it had to be a *very* small aircraft to avoid accusations of environmental vandalism. The desk screen showed him the split feed from the emergency response center, the military navsat array and the UN, but the latter might as well have been a bloody freeze-frame for all the action they were taking. "And the quarantine's sorted, right?"

Shukry Aziz looked at Persis Jackson, Bari's PPS. "Well, Esganikan said we're safe, and she thinks *she's* safe, so . . ."

"Frankly, if we catch the Black Death, it'll be worth it just to go and cough over Zammett," Persis said. "Eh, PM?"

What the hell does Zammett want from us? He knows we can't kick the Eqbas out, and this isn't about the Antarctic territory. I'm fed up guessing.

Esganikan Gai could put her highly advanced boot up Zamett's backside. That might get him to put his cards on the table.

"I'm going to trust Eqbas tech," Bari said. "But I didn't think we'd managed to get all the data. Still waiting on the Nairobi Disease Center, I thought."

"She says she has it anyway," said Persis. "So I think we can forget passwords and encryption. Everything's hackable as far as they're concerned."

Shukry grunted in agreement. "No concept of secrecy. Like they don't understand borders."

It was the little things that reminded Bari not to push the Eqbas too far. The plane flew over a surprisingly large crowd clustered at the perimeter fences the army had erected, and then dropped down on a scene that looked like an orderly snooker table. He could see the defense shield clearly now, a layer of shimmering air sitting over the whole camp like a flattened dome, and there were figures moving around, some almost human in size and shape, some like . . . large dogs. He had no other description. It was just as well he'd seen the news footage from Wess'ej over the years or the culture shock might have killed him. *Ussissi.* They were ussissi. He wasn't just dealing with one alien species; counting the Skavu, who he hadn't yet seen, there were three.

"You think they could generate a shield like that for the whole country?" Shukry asked. "It was bloody amazing how that jet bounced off it."

"Yes, Zammett's backed down on the claim that the Eqbas opened fire. Common sense says he finally worked out that the FEU can't go on pissing off wess'har and not be turned into charcoal."

"Bit late for that," said Persis. "It's still top of her agenda. Esganikan wants Zammett to hand over an ex-spookmaster called Prachy for the bombing."

"Oh, she's got a name now?" Somehow Bari had expected Esganikan to tell him first. "They do hold a grudge, don't they?"

"The FEU did a lot of damage."

"Says a lot for their patience that they don't just fry Europe from orbit, actually."

Shukry looked back over his seat. "They don't think like us. It sounds obvious, but everyone forgets because they speak English so fluently. They're not patient. They're *precise*."

"This is the wisdom of Michallat again, is it?"

"He's the only definitive source on the wess'har, PM. And he says to beware trying to mix wess'har and human concepts of guilt."

"My, the useful things you can learn from televids. Now, is that refugee center ready for them or not? It'll make all our lives easier if we can get them to move."

"The army says it is, but they think the outer perimeter needs to be extended to take in the town. Or the residents will be driven nuts by media, apocalyptic dingbats and assorted sightseers. There are only a couple of hundred people, and it beats having the center full of asylum seekers trying to escape before they're deported. Townsfolk seem to prefer real aliens."

"Okay, do it."

The aircraft landed a cautious distance from the edge of the camp, and they made their way across open ground that was already searingly hot. Bari took a deep breath. *Yes, you're strolling into an alien army camp. It's no big deal.* He hesitated at the visible edge of the shield and wondered if he was going to get a massive shock from it until he noticed ussissi trotting back and forth as if it wasn't there. When he plucked up courage to walk through, the hairs on his arms stood up and he felt a mild tingling; but the most shocking aspect of it was the cool, moist air that enveloped him.

"Whatever it costs, I'll buy it," Shukry said, basking in the blissful sensation. "Oh, this is great . . ."

"It's a damn shame we didn't get to meet them when we weren't on trial."

Bari had a fleeting thought that this single piece of technology alone could transform an economy. He couldn't even begin to imagine the power source. And then there was the gene bank. And ITX. What else?

No, don't even think about profit. Concentrate on not ending up like most of Umeh. Concentrate on the environment.

Esganikan Gai ambled towards them with a slight swagger that might have been indicative of trouble brewing, had she been human. It was the first lesson about assumptions in what was likely to be a very long list. Behind her, Shan Frankland's body language was much easier to read. She looked like she was used to having people scatter in panic before her; she was six feet tall, and although her uniform had seen better days, physically intimidating. That wasn't the kind of woman Bari was used to. He wondered which of the two he'd really be dealing with.

That was disorienting, but it was nothing compared to the interior of the bubble-shaped ship that formed Esganikan's quarters. The first thing Bari did was almost slam into a translucent bulkhead that seemed to move.

Oh my God. I'm in a spaceship. A real spaceship.

"Yes, it's like a hall of mirrors in here," Frankland said, oddly chummy, although her expression wasn't sociable at all. Bari sat down on what he hoped was a seat. "And the scenery moves, so mind how you go."

Bari turned to Esganikan. "What do you want to discuss first, Commander? We've got accommodation ready for you to inspect, and a complete team of environment scientists waiting to start work when you're ready. You tell me."

"I must have custody of the woman called Katya Prachy," she said bluntly. It was very matter of fact, and yes, she really did have a double-voice like one of those Tibetan singers. It was riveting, especially as she seemed to have a faint English accent that was nothing like Frankland's, and he could *hear* who taught her the language—Michallat. "This is what you call a war crime."

"I've called in the FEU ambassador to tell him we're starting extradition proceedings."

"No. Inform him that he has to hand her to us as soon as he locates her, and if he fails to deliver her, then we *will* act."

"I'm not sure what you mean by that." Bari avoided Shukry's eye. He didn't want to hear more of the world according to Eddie Michallat. "But relations between us and the FEU aren't very good at the moment."

"Then it makes even more sense to do things our way."

Frankland looked weary. "It's probably a good idea to stand back and be *uninvolved,* Prime Minister," she said. "The FEU won't like the task force being based here while it carries out its operations, but from what I've seen they're putting the frighteners on you anyway."

"We still have concerns about their naval activity, yes."

"We've seen the news this morning."

"It might result in firing warning shots. I'll be frank with you—I don't know what their real intention is, because you're not about to leave, are you?"

Esganikan's plume bobbed like the crest of a Roman helmet. "Perhaps they think we might back down over Prachy if pressure is put on our hosts."

Frankland didn't look convinced. "Have you asked them?"

"Yes."

"Maybe we need to call the ambassador in and ask again."

Esganikan didn't even look up. "Prime Minister, I used to have discussions with Jim Matsoukis and Canh Pho. They were aware of how we *remediate* planetary environments, and that your neighbors beyond the Pacific Rim States may be greatly upset by this. Are you prepared to experience what the isenj Northern Assembly did when Umeh was prepared for restoration?"

"What's the alternative?"

"We'll restore the planet with you or without you."

He believed her. It was impossible to doubt now, even if Brussels seemed to think it was a bluff. Did they learn *nothing*? "We invited your intervention, so we stand by our decision. We even held a referendum on it, and the majority of the population still support it."

"This will be beyond war. What follows will be nothing like peace. It's fundamental and permanent change, the curbing of your species, but your nation will escape the worst of it. Do you understand what I'm saying?"

Esganikan said it very quietly and it was all the more terrifying for that. Bari knew; he'd always known. But feeling it in the pit of his stomach was new and sapped his confidence.

The FEU started this, remember. They brought the trouble to the door. So make the best of a bad job.

It didn't feel like betrayal at all. It felt like survival, and Zammett would have nuked Australia for less.

All empires had their day, though, and all fell, so the FEU would have to make its own choices.

"Okay, let's give their personnel the choice of remaining here, and ship the rest home if they want to go, given the likelihood of conflict. Shukry, you can arrange that." *At least I don't send those poor bastards home just to be fried.* Bari stopped short of asking her what she meant by *the worst of it.* "I know I should be talking about consultation with the UN, but the FEU doesn't listen to them."

"The UN has no power to deliver results," Esganikan said. "So I'll deal with those in power."

"Why don't you let me talk to the FEU ambassador?" Frankland asked. "Tell him he's running out of time."

Frankland kept looking at her watch, as if she had some other planet to invade with her alien chums. How did a copper like her ever get in that kind of position? The gloves bothered him for some reason. Nobody wore gloves in this heat, no human anyway. Esganikan wore them too. Perhaps it was some Eqbas etiquette thing.

"What do you think you can achieve?" Esganikan asked her, as if they hadn't planned any of it and were just mulling things over.

"I like to do things by the book," Frankland said. "Whatever the state of my warrant card, I'm still a copper, and I have rules."

The two women stared at each other for a few moments and Bari felt forgotten, not a feeling he was used to as prime minister. Then Esganikan nodded as if she was just giving Frankland permission to take a day off.

"We'd like to talk to you about the gene bank, too," Frankland said. "That's my part of ship, so to speak. Would your government be prepared to produce seed from the non-patented food staples and distribute them at cost?"

There hadn't been unpatented seed available for at least two centuries. Bari had to think twice about it. He was too firmly stuck on the impending showdown with the FEU to concentrate on agriculture. "That's going to upset the European and Asian agricorp multinats."

"I'd hate to do that, Prime Minister." It was the nearest Frankland had come to a smile. "Yes, it's going to destroy their business. But that's not my problem, and I don't have shares."

Esganikan Gai looked at her with an expression that could have been anything from disapproval to curiosity. "But this might interfere with natural population decline. If you distribute food crops that have resistance to drought and heat, then the natural reduction by famine is lost."

Frankland didn't even blink. "But it drives out genetically engineered crops, so it contributes to the overall remediation."

Jesus, they're debating whether letting more people starve to death is a bad thing. Aliens . . . okay, but a human saying that?

Bari knew he was still avoiding the most painful issue. It wasn't just about replanting the forests, or reducing temperatures, or finding a home for those macaws they were so worried about. It was about reducing the number of humans on the planet by *billions*.

Slow or fast? He wasn't sure whether he was cooperating with genocide or staving off inevitable disaster with hard pragmatism, but either way it was going to happen, and his duty was to make sure it didn't happen to Australia. Technically, he had a duty to his Pacific Rim allies too, but he found his focus had narrowed fast.

And there was still an FEU carrier group in the neighborhood.

He'd focus on that. Maybe he'd be a hero in the end, but he also ran the risk of being a monster. It was hard to judge. All he had was the here and now, and he couldn't stop the Eqbas on his own even if he wanted to.

"I'll call in the FEU ambassador this afternoon," he said. "Meanwhile, we'll send in our resettlement and immigration teams to get the colonists moved. Let's leave the *Actaeon* crew until we hear what the FEU has to say for itself."

As meetings went, it was the most surreal imaginable. He couldn't think of anything to say as they flew back to Kamberra. Persis and Shukry sat scribbling on their handhelds, heads down.

"You think I've sold my soul to the devil," Bari said at last. "And not even discussed with the full cabinet."

"No, PM."

"Not at all, PM . . ."

"Come on." Damn, he was going to have to tell the cabinet that it wasn't for discussion. Nairn and Andreaou realized that, but the others would want to complicate matters. If he could hand them a quick win, something spectacular that made life a lot better for a lot of people, *their* people, then they'd face facts. "Look, there's been no shooting yet but we're at war, and not with the FEU. I'm collaborating. I don't happen to think the Eqbas are a hundred percent wrong, either. I'll go to the country on it if I have to."

"Like you said, PM, the Eqbas aren't leaving any time soon," said Shukry. "I'm not sure that going down in a blaze of glory defending all mankind is any more moral than saving your own tribe if you can. It just makes better movies."

Persis, ever the pragmatist, nodded. "And the FEU or Sinostates wouldn't think twice about paving us over for a vehicle park."

That made it all right, then. Bari leaned his forehead against the window, imagining the endless arid bush irrigated and alive again, and realized what a bloody hard job it was to be judge and jury.

Surang, Eqbas Vorhi: Da Shapakti's clan home.

Rayat rushed to check the headlines as soon as Shapakti's son Mejiku opened the door. The family were used to him by now. He was Dad's loony *gethes* pal, not an alien lab specimen, and it was comforting to have at least one place in the galaxy where he wasn't automatically mistrusted.

"The *gethes* are very afraid," said Mejiku, following him into the huge central living room that doubled as a kitchen and general meeting place. "I've watched the transmissions. They have all their armies ready to fight."

"We're so lovable, aren't we?" Rayat gazed at the news feed, unsurprised. "You could call it the indomitable human spirit, but given the inevitable outcome, I'd call it stupidity."

Eqbas families were as strictly matriarchal as the Wess'ej wess'har, but males were the majority by only two to one; the huge clans of four or even five husbands per *isan* that he'd seen on Wess'ej were very rare here. Rayat still found it hard to think of the Wess'ej wess'har as the redneck cousins. He stood watching the BBChan coverage of the standoff between Australia and the FEU. He had to do it now. Shan would have too much on her plate to spare him any time once the fighting started.

You could have taken the call twenty-five years ago, Shan. I was trying to do the right thing.

"Come on, Shapakti," he said. "Make the call."

Shapakti seemed to be checking that his *isan,* Fenelian, wasn't home. "I think you're right," he said, darting into a corridor and disappearing for a few moments. Mejiku smelled anxious and took the opportunity to slip out. Avoidance wasn't a wess'har trait. He might have been simply giving his father space because he was so agitated. "This has to be done."

"What made you change your mind?"

"Because you talk like *Shan Chail* sometimes, and I know

her level of commitment. She killed her own child. That takes a certain rigidity of principle."

Rayat didn't think anything could take his mind off the matter at hand, but that bombshell did. He wondered if he didn't understand eqbas'u as well as he thought. "What do you mean, killed?"

"She conceived a child, without intending to," Shapakti said, completely unabashed. "Her internal organs regenerated. She removed it herself, and was very distressed by the action, but she wouldn't bring a *c'naatat* child into the world, she said."

Rayat found he'd lost a little righteous steam.

"Dear God," he said. "I had no idea. When was this?"

"Not long before we left."

Rayat couldn't quite take it in. It was whole new side of the woman that he could never have imagined in a million years. Given her callous intolerance of Lindsay Neville's unplanned pregnancy, he had trouble imagining how Shan had handled her own.

"Why have you never told me this?"

"Because you never asked. It didn't seem relevant. So she's the person who would make a decision about Esganikan with most objectivity."

If Rayat ever got to speak to Shan, he'd find it hard not to let the revelation color his attitude. He'd always thought of her as a thuggish, humorless, moralizing bully without a scrap of human emotion, whatever the nature of her relationship with Ade and Aras. Then he found himself wondering how the hell she defeated *c'naatat*'s defenses to terminate the pregnancy, and having a vivid picture of exactly how she might have done it—how he might have done it in her position. He felt uncharacteristically sorry for her.

He'd expected he would gloat if he ever heard her bad news. Life wasn't like that any longer, though, and neither was he. Maybe it was having a little of all of that bizarre little family in his head.

"Let's do it," he said.

Shapakti opened the ITX link on his *virin* and called Shan's device. Rayat hovered. Shan would take notice of

Shapakti. He'd get her listening and convince her. Rayat couldn't expect him to do more than that, because no wess'har would interfere with a commander in the field.

"*Shan Chail*," Shapakti said. Rayat could hear both sides of the conversation. "Do you remember me? Shapakti?"

Shan's voice was remarkably clear. "Of course I do. How are you?"

"I'm well. We watch the news from Earth. It won't be an easy task."

"Did you want to speak to Esganikan?"

"No, to you."

"Any luck with *c'naatat*?"

"Yes. I sent a message to Esganikan. I can remove the parasite from humans now."

Shan paused. The link was instant, routed via the ship's node, so there was no delay on the relay and the pause was significant. "She didn't mention it. Is that what you called to tell me?"

"No." Shapakti froze for a moment and Rayat thought he was about to lose his nerve. "Mohan Rayat has a message for you. He tried to call you twice all those years ago before he left."

There was another long pause. "We're done here, Shapakti. Sorry, but I'm not in the mood for his games. He wants to talk to me? He's got my code."

"He's here, but the *virin* system is set to prevent him contacting Earth. I'm relaying this message."

"This is one of his stunts, and he's got you to play along with it—"

"It's very serious."

"I'll call you back," she said. "I've got a couple of crises running at the moment that are higher on the list. He's waited twenty-five years, so he can wait a bit longer. Oh, and don't contact the FEU for him, you hear? You might *think* you know him by now, but you don't."

The link went dead.

"Shit," said Rayat, defaulting to English. "Shit." If Shan was anything, she was pragmatic and detached in an emergency. She didn't hang up in a fit of pique. "I know what it is.

All she heard was 'remove *c'naatat*' and now her world's in disarray again. You know what she's doing now? She's getting into gear to kick Esganikan's arse for not telling her. Forget everything else. It's about trust and her sex life, in that order."

"I think," said Shapakti, "that she fears you're trying to manipulate her, and she doesn't want to hear anything that might make her doubt herself. She's not a self-centered person."

"Hoist by my own petard again, eh?"

"Deception destroys the fabric of interaction."

"You're full of them today, my friend."

"She may well know that Esganikan carries *c'naatat*, and chooses not to admit that to us."

Rayat was already on to the next strategy. He couldn't wait around for Shan to come to her senses, or rely on her working it out for herself. Who else was there? Who else took the risk of *c'naatat* as seriously as Shan?

Kiir. Kiir, Fourth to Die, the commander of the Skavu troops.

The Skavu made Shan look like an amateur when it came to green zealotry. He'd heard the ussissi talking about their dread of *c'naatat*. And Kiir was all for exterminating Shan, Ade and Aras. Abominations, he called them.

"You have to trust Shan," Shapakti said. "She will *know*."

"Trust her to turn a blind eye to stopping the thing spreading if it's in someone she likes or needs?"

"She spaced herself to stop *you* having it."

"And she's still around, so she obviously changed her mind about self destruction."

"If you doubt her, then why rely on her? Why is this so crucial, anyway? No wess'har would infect another species, especially *gethes*."

"You've got a short memory for a wess'har. Aras infected Shan. *C'naatat* makes you do all kinds of things you never would otherwise. I swear it influences its hosts."

Shapakti did that little annoyed head-jiggle, side to side, to show his irritation. "Like making *you* decide that it was your duty to *stop* your masters getting hold of it, counter to your patriotic mission—"

"It's called new data in the equation. It's more dangerous than I first thought."

"I think, Mohan, that you still want to win. To be right."

It was Rayat's job to protect national security. It was his remit to take decisions on his own, do anything he felt was necessary. For a moment, he wondered if he'd simply been out of contact for too long and too altered by *c'naatat* to have unclouded judgment. If Shan deposed Esganikan, there was still no guarantee that *c'naatat* would never get out into the human population. It was there. It was on Earth, and it shouldn't have been.

"I need to find out how I can get in touch with the Skavu command," he said. "I need to talk to Kiir."

5

You suggest that if they're so anxious to acquire Katya Prachy, then we want a prisoner exchange. We have grounds for Frankland's extradition that are still on the public record, so if we can't get Rayat back, then she'll be a fair substitute—maybe better. BBChan might not have believed Eddie Michallat's report about her surviving spacing, but we do.

FIONA BARTOLEMEO,
FEU Foreign Secretary to Intelligence

Yarralumla, Kamberra: early evening.

Kamberra still existed, unlike Perth, but it was a ghost town of apparently abandoned suburbs glittering with solar collectors in the setting sun.

It was only when the Eqbas shuttle passed over the center of the city that Shan could see that not all life had gone underground. The capital, neat roads in concentric circles, had lost what little grass she remembered from the ITX images and acquired a number of giant canopies. Kamberra made a defiant statement that Australia was still open for business, even if it tended to wait for the cooler hours before emerging.

Food production had changed out of all recognition. Space-station technology generally hadn't traveled far from Earth, but it now came in handy at home to grow crops in a very hostile environment. Shan thought of the isenj, living in their sterile world and growing their food indoors, and tried not to see omens all around her.

"Nanites could clear all that now," Esganikan said, apparently offended by the miles of deserted houses.

"They might want the option of coming back topside," said Shan. She bent over with her hands braced on her

knees as she looked down through the deck, out of habit
more than necessity. If she needed to see better, she could
magnify the image; but that stopped her from looking at
Esganikan. If she did that, she doubted she could resist the
urge to demand why the commander was still keeping
things from her. "That's what they're looking for from us,
remember. Climate management. Which the FEU *doesn't*
want, because we have a history here of ballsing up that
kind of project. There's your flashpoint."

"The FEU could behave sensibly and benefit as well."

When are you going to come clean with me? "You're new
here . . ."

"I realize Europe will *not*."

Shan tried not to meet Ade's eyes, but it was impossible.
He gave her that wounded and wary look that said *don't
start it, not here*. They'd been here before, anyway; it
wasn't the first time they'd realized they didn't have to be
c'naatat hosts any longer, that they could return to normal,
and the dilemma and self-recrimination started all over
again.

*What about Aras? Can Shapakti remove it from wess'har
too?*

*And if I think it's that dangerous, why am I still walking
around?*

It was one thing to make the noble sacrifice yourself, and
quite another to kill someone you loved for a principle.

Esganikan was still musing over Australia's potential,
oblivious of the suspicion festering in Shan.

"They still appear to make insufficient use of desalination," she said. "We could resolve that for them very easily."

Shan acted out cold normality. "It was always expensive
tech."

"What could be more expensive than destroying your environment?"

"Don't try common sense arguments with humans. Just
scare the shit out of them and give them orders, or we'll be
here forever." Shan straightened up and nudged Ade with
her boot. He was sitting cross-legged on the deck, elbows
on knees, gazing down. "That's like putting your arse on an

image scanner, Royal. What an inspiring view of the invading army."

"I've got my pants on, Boss." Ade got to his feet in one fluid movement, using his arms to develop momentum. He looked into her face, frowning. "Besides, I think it looks opaque from the outside. Doesn't it, Esganikan?"

Ade squeezed Shan's shoulder one-handed and went back to studying the terrain through the deck. He seemed to have become used to it. Aras wasn't concerned by it at all; wess'har didn't have that falling reflex. Some of the crew had found it hilarious to watch Eddie or the marines edging onto a section of deck when it became transparent, as if they might fall through. Shan still checked the deck instinctively when she moved around, just a glance down, but Ade seemed totally immune.

"Lots of sightseers," he said. "Magnify." The deck resolved into a view from a hundred meters. "Yeah, plenty of people out gawping today. Hey, that UV canopy must have cost an arm and leg. Look at the spread of it."

Shan risked a glance at Esganikan, willing herself not to bawl her out. The Eqbas seemed to be more interested in Ade. She was watching him, head cocked, then turned slowly to look at Joluti, and for a moment Shan got that irrational feeling of wanting to warn her off looking at her old man.

Don't be stupid. She's Eqbas. Ade's not her type.

"So we've got the full house." Ade consulted his *virin*. He was more at ease with the transparent device than Shan. It required a guitarist's wrist to manipulate the controls. "Can I punch out the FEU ambassador?"

"Ladies first," said Shan.

"Can I smack him after you're done with him, then?"

"I'll see what I can leave in one piece."

Even though she was invulnerable, and a lifetime of police work had accustomed her to every encounter being a hostile one, the prospect of another awkward confrontation didn't thrill Shan. Her jokes were whistling in the dark. As the shuttle reached the airspace over the grounds of Old Government House, the media pack and their swarms of bee cams—

smaller and faster than Eddie's obsolete model—made her wonder how this was being viewed in other parts of the world, and she could guess. She could even see the shot in her mind's eye.

"That's a distressing image to give the hacks," she said. "That'll be on every bulletin. Guaranteed."

Ade stepped back from the transparent section. "What will?"

"Try imagining what this looks like from the ground, with your bee cam tilting up . . ."

Aras rocked his head as if in irritation. "Iconic."

"Don't blow the roof off, will you, Esganikan?" Ade gave in to laughter now. "It'll look like cheap theatrics."

"Will they see it as a joke or an omen?" Aras asked, obviously understanding the unspoken idea that still eluded Esganikan. There was learning the language, and then there was knowing cultural reference, like movies, and Esganikan didn't.

"I'm putting my money on the latter," Shan said.

The shuttle settled on the ground and Esganikan stood facing the bulkhead waiting for the hatch to form. She rolled her head like an athlete easing kinks out her neck muscles, and Shan wondered if she was nervous too, or if trampling over another planet was like any routine day for her.

It's never routine. Kicking down doors never got routine for me.

From the transparent section of the hull, Shan could see the crowd beyond the police cordon, curbed by a simple red cable and demonstrating what good rule-followers humans could be when they put their minds to it. All that compliant *Homo sapiens* needed was a good dominant example to norm with, she thought, but that had been tried before with varying degrees of abject failure. She settled for being satisfied that anybody still respected a police cordon. It was still way too close to the building for her tastes. The white mansion sat isolated on an ocean of neat gravel fringed by desert plants, a fitting icon for a world drowning in its real seas.

"Lay on, Macduff." She stepped close up behind Esgani-kan to chivvy her along. "Make a good entrance, at least."

"Beachhead landing," Ade muttered. Aras seemed preoc-cupied with other thoughts—Jesus, hadn't she told him enough times that she wouldn't leave him, *c'naatat* cure or not?—and walked down the shallow ramp that extruded from the ship's casing, followed by Joluti and the senior en-vironmental analyst, Mekuliet Nal. It was all a matter of not looking around, of concentrating on that long gravel path up to the doors.

Ade nudged Shan in the back.

"Look," he said.

She did, and turned away immediately. A knot of people pressed close to the cordon, two of them holding a banner with letters that flashed and sparkled, scrolling slogans. The words took a little effort to read, but one phrase was clear enough: GAIA'S GUARD. Another read SAVED.

"They probably mean the gene bank," said Aras.

Ade raised his eyebrows. "Well, they sure as shit don't mean humanity."

There was another banner-waving group to the left of them, though, proclaiming WELCOME GOD'S BOUNTY HOME and another in Arabic that Shan couldn't read, but at least the two groups appeared engaged in friendly conversation. They looked ecstatically happy. She wondered if they had the slightest idea what had happened to Umeh.

Ade nodded in the direction of an ornamental pond with a fountain in the grounds. "You might want to walk on that, Boss. Give 'em a thrill."

"Bollocks." It was a waste of scarce water, but it was probably switched on solely for VIPs' visits these days, and an alien warlord coming to scour your planet clean was as V as an IP got. "I can put up with Bible-bashers like Deborah, but I'm not getting sucked in by that lot to further their agenda."

"You including the Muslims in that, Boss? Izzy can help you out there."

A cheer went up and someone shouted, "Frankland! Hey, you did it!" That section of the crowd dissolved into shouts and clapping, and the bee cams tracked rapidly to the spot like missiles.

"Fucking pathetic," Shan muttered. "This is exactly what I wanted to avoid. How the hell do they know who I am?"

"Eddie's transmissions."

"Helen Marchant, more like. I bet I was her green recruiting poster in my absence." Shan slipped past Esganikan and headed for the refuge of the colonnaded doorway. "Just as well I haven't come back to do undercover duties."

By the time they climbed the few steps to the entrance, a group of people stood waiting in the hall by the open doors, tidying their suits and looking nervous. Shan glanced back over her shoulder at the group with the Gaia's Guard banner and wondered if she should now use her influence to mobilize the greens. But what could they do? Now that the Eqbas were here, she had no need to seek out the militant element willing to use direct action against governments and corporations, the eco-terrorists she'd used for her own unofficial enforcement purposes a lifetime ago in EnHaz. There was a whole Eqbas task force waiting to do give the un-green a good kicking; they could kick a lot harder, too. It was now all about identifying people who'd work with the Eqbas and put their plans into effect, the kind of cooperative partnership stuff she'd never been very good at. Nobody called in a cop like her to set up joint working parties.

There were bound to be plenty of humans who wouldn't cooperate, of course. Shan was waiting for the emergence of the anti-alien movements, the folks who'd watched too many vids and thought that Earth could be defended from vastly superior forces by good old human grit and unfeasibly simple countermeasures like computer viruses and water. It was the kind of mythology that developed only in countries that had no experience of being invaded by a bigger neighbor.

Why the hell did I ever come back?

Shan suspected the silent influence of her *c'naatat* these days, and interrogated it fiercely. Were these really *her* thoughts, *her* aims? She tested them all against logic, and faced up to the fact that she was as likely to be here now through excessive faith in her own power as through the subliminal urging of her parasite to carry it further afield to propagate.

Neither was a particularly edifying thought.

"Is that a real weapon, ma'am?" asked the police officer on the door, glancing down Shan's back. She still carried her 9mm pistol, ancient but perfectly reliable. "Because we have gun control here."

Shan wondered if the officer had noticed that Ade was carrying a big fuck-off ESF670 rifle over his shoulder. Maybe he thought it was simpler to ask a woman to surrender her arms first.

"I can control it just fine," she said, trying to keep in mind that the bloke was only doing the same job that she had for so long, and it wasn't his fault that she was a stupid cow who'd been conned yet again by her own gung ho sense of duty. "And I've still got a firearms permit with *Superintendent* Frankland written on it."

They stood with gazes locked for a couple of seconds until the officer got the idea and gave her a brief nod. She wasn't a cop any longer, not technically, not *really,* because she had to be past compulsory retirement age by a few decades—on paper; and she remembered leaving her warrant card in the cairn of rocks that Ade had built as a memorial to her while she was still dead—on paper.

Sometimes it was all about how you carried it off. She still felt like a copper and thought like one, and she probably always would. She hadn't even wanted to be one; she'd been drafted. Now she had no idea how to be anything else.

"It's hard to quit," Ade whispered. "Isn't it?"

They had a lot in common, her and Ade; everything, in fact. The queue of civil servants lining up to pay their respects were unashamedly mesmerized by meeting real live aliens from another planet. Their faces had a uniform childlike quality, wide-eyed and chins slightly lowered, that erased all gender and ethnic variations between them. Bari looked relieved. But he also looked astonished.

Shit, I did that once. When I first met Aras. A real live alien. A miracle.

She wasn't about to take Aras for granted again, and made sure she caught his wrist and steered him close to her. Esganikan ambled down the polished hallway looking from side to side with her hands clasped as if she was considering putting in an offer for the place. Shan played her automatic game of picking out which suspects in the lineup looked as if they were breaking sweat, just to see if her old copper's radar was still working. As they walked into the elegant period room at the end of the hall, she spotted one.

Him.

He was a little too young and plump to fit her stereotype of a career diplomat—thirty, maybe, with a face as polished as the floor and a shock of black hair—but he looked the most nervous of the bunch.

Let's see.

Shan held out her hand, protected by gloves. The gel barrier was just too clammy to touch, not that she gave a shit if the FEU's ambassador thought she had a limp handshake. She squeezed his fingers hard enough to see the reaction on his face.

"Superintendent Frankland," he said. "John Pettinato, Federal European Union Ambassador to the Republic of Australia. I apologize again for the naval incident. Our ship thought the Eqbas had opened fire on our aircraft. We understand now that it was a *collision*."

But his carrier group was still on station south of here. "No hard feelings," said Shan. "You've got a chance now to make it right."

Bari leapt in, clearly adept at heading off trouble in inappropriate places, and ushered them into what felt like a ballroom. "We nearly sold this place for luxury apartments last century. Costs a fortune in maintenance, but we do love our continuity."

Shan laid claim to a chair next to Esganikan while Aras sat on the other side of her. Ade, still in his DPM rig, ended up at the far end of the long white table with his rifle propped against his leg. Incongruous didn't even begin to cover it.

Esganikan fixed her gaze on the young diplomat and didn't wait for introductions. "You're John Pettinato."

"Correct, ma'am." He went into a commendably calm and polished routine. "I'm the FEU ambassador here. I'm delighted to meet you at last."

"I have instructions for your government," Esganikan said.

That, for her, was diplomatic. It was fascinating to watch two cultures racing head-on down the same stretch of road towards each other. Shan had grown so used to wess'har in-your-face frankness that she had to remind herself that it would seem brusque and aggressive to a regular human. She watched the body language around the table, and inhaled the generic scent of agitated *Homo sapiens*. Nobody spoke.

"Where is Katya Prachy?" Esganikan clearly felt she had waited long enough. Maybe if Pettinato tried saying *sorry,* a word she seemed to interpret as a slow preamble to doing as she ordered, it might have got off to a better start. "I gave your government many years' notice that we would come to exact balance for the crimes committed on Ouzhari, and that shielding the guilty would be a crime in itself. Why have you not complied? I've even given you her name."

Pettinato was holding his own. "Ma'am, we have to look into the allegation and locate Prachy, then consider where she should be tried. This is a slower process than you might wish."

"You record all your citizens' births and deaths, and all their affiliations and movements. You must know where she is. She still lives. *I* know that."

Pettinato didn't flinch. He turned his head to Shan as if to invite her into the conversation, not a trace of concern on his face, and then turned back to Esganikan.

"Yes, we know where she is," he said at last. "But she's an elderly woman now."

"And you have no need of a trial. Hand her over to us."

This was the point at which all human rules went out the window. Age and the judicial process meant nothing to Esganikan. Shan wasn't sure that age had ever meant anything to her, either; surviving didn't erase any crimes or bring anyone back to life. But now she was back on Earth, Shan felt uneasy about words like *no need of a trial.*

Fucking ironic. I used to manage without them quite often, didn't I?

"You *must* hand her over to us," said Esganikan.

"Commander Gai, we really do regret what happened on Ouzhari, but let me put this in context." Pettinato had a remarkably calming voice, and it seemed a shame to waste it on an alien who wouldn't respond to it. "A government servant acting lawfully has immunity from prosecution, so not only can we not agree to try this woman for any crime—yet—but we also can't hand her over to any foreign power, either. We'd have to hold an inquiry into whether she acted within her powers first, of course, but as some of the people involved in managing those events have since died, and recollections are inevitably faded by time, I think we would find it hard to place any confidence in the findings of such an inquiry."

Shan braced. Esganikan paused, head cocked. "That's a very long way of saying *no*."

"It's not so much a *no* as not knowing where we might start to establish culpability, and where she might be tried if it was decided there was a case to answer."

"If you're not already aware, Dr. Mohan Rayat was in contact with four individuals who instructed him to go ahead with the use of cobalt weapons on Ouzhari, which are still illegal here, yes?"

"They are. But—"

"Three were executed on our behalf by what you term eco-terrorists. I wasn't aware of a fourth until very recently. There are may have been more people involved in the chain of command, and if there were, I want to know who they are and if they're still alive. In the meantime, I'll take Prachy and the direct matter of the bombing will be closed, unless the FEU knows of others who are responsible, and then shields them, in which case there will be more people held accountable. Do you understand me?"

Pettinato didn't seem thrown at all. Maybe this was the kind of tirade that he faced most days, but if it was, he probably didn't realize that wess'har were absolutely literal.

That was where it had all started. Shan tried not to catch

Ade's eye. Aras watched with his usual detached fascination; this was the same conversation she'd had with him, more or less, after Surendra Parekh had killed the bezeri child, all misunderstandings and—eventually—shocked revelation.

"You might understand why we want Superintendent Frankland to stand trial in Europe, then," Pettinato said, lobbing in his verbal grenade. "Or at least submit herself for a preliminary investigation regarding the killing of Dr. Parekh."

"Oh, I do understand," said Esganikan. "You want to swap Prachy for her. But she won't place herself in your custody, and I won't give her to you. These matters are not connected."

Shan cringed. It was like being a kid again, with the grown-ups talking above her head about what a naughty girl she'd been. *Shit, I wish I had pulled the bloody trigger on Parekh.* If she admitted now that she hadn't, then she'd look like she was afraid of facing the consequences. But that didn't matter a damn now. She had a much bigger problem, and she knew now exactly what game the FEU was playing with Australia: make it uncomfortable enough, and they might think that it was easier to hand Shan over to Europe than to be harried by the FEU forces for months on end.

"I'm not turning myself in," Shan said. "I know why you want me, and it's nothing to do with Parekh—who was a child killer, by the way. She broke the local laws. She ignored my orders, too. There's no leverage you can apply to this country, either, because you're dealing direct with Eqbas Vorhi—no offense, Prime Minister. Shall we move on?"

Pettinato didn't miss a beat. "That brings us to Dr. Rayat, then, who's still missing, our naval personnel, the civilian contractors, and the Royal Marines detachment," said Pettinato. "We would like them released."

"The personnel from *Actaeon* can leave at any time they wish," said Esganikan. "Dr. Rayat is currently on Eqbas Vorhi, and we have no plans to return him. The detachment were dismissed from your armed forces in their absence, and they are no longer your personnel—unless you agree to reinstate them, *and* they want to be reinstated."

Shan could see the slightest flicker in Pettinato's eyes as he tried to work out the moves and counter moves that just weren't there. If she interrupted now to help him out and explain that Esganikan was listing facts, not negotiating, he probably wouldn't believe her.

"I'm sorry about this, Prime Minister." Shan gave Bari a polite half-smile. If she hadn't felt so sorry for herself right then, she'd have felt sorry for him. "As soon as we get this out of the way, we'll move onto the real business."

"We do have an extradition treaty with Australia," Pettinato pointed out. "And we intend to invoke it."

"But that obviously doesn't extend to diplomatic personnel." So Bari wasn't playing. "Superintendent Frankland is a resident of Wess'ej and part of the Eqbas mission. We'll happily provide transport for your military personnel, though. And please bear in mind *you* were also summoned *here* to receive my strongest possible objection to your navy's continued aggressive presence on the edge of our territorial waters."

"What about the marines?" Shan decided now was as good a time as any, and it was probably her last chance to screw anything out of the FEU for them. "We need an answer." She aimed the question at Pettinato, but Nairn cut in.

"We'll process them with the returning colonists and grant them Australian citizenship," he said, "seeing as they're civilians."

"They're FEU citizens," said Pettinato.

"They're free to stay," said Nairn. He and Bari were both looking right at Pettinato now, and Shan got the feeling this was less to do with backing up Esganikan's buddies than taking a chance to piss over the FEU. "You've never claimed there was any criminal matter outstanding against them. I checked. The only sentence was *dismissed the service.* Because you didn't expect them to come back once you'd flung them to the wess'har to get the matriarchs off your back."

"Ah, and there was I thinking the language of diplomacy

was still French," said Shan. "I'm glad we're back to plain English."

It was Esganikan's turn to watch now.

"It was a bad decision taken a long time ago by a different administration," Pettinato said. He couldn't have thought Shan would do a deal, but he might have known she spaced herself, and that would have made him think she was prone to grand gestures of self-sacrifice. "We'll agree to let them rejoin the FEU Defense Force, of course. But we'd need to know they weren't complicit in the deaths of Parekh . . . and Dr. Galvin."

Oh, that was a punch Shan hadn't seen coming. She had to hand it to the bastard: he'd done his homework. Rayat must have filed his reports diligently, and, by Christ, they'd gone through every word in the intervening years, looking for some lever. Yes, Galvin had died with an FEU round in her—probably fired by Ade.

"If you've read Rayat's reports," Shan said carefully, "you'd know Galvin was caught in crossfire with the isenj after she breached a curfew. I was there."

"We know. We also know you took a serious head wound and survived . . . somehow."

Ah. They just couldn't leave it alone. It really was all about *c'naatat.* They were staring into the abyss, with an Eqbas task force sighting up, but they still wanted the parasite. Shan had to admire their persistence.

"Look, can we cut the crap?" She really shouldn't have come. She really shouldn't have changed her mind. She should have stayed on Wess'ej. "The coffee's getting cold and this is the first decent cup we've had in three years. You want me? You come and get me, son. Personally. No deal."

Shit, if I hadn't come . . . they might have swapped the detachment's reinstatement for Prachy.

I blew it.

Do they even call it reinstatement?

Pettinato still seemed to think he was negotiating. "Then it doesn't give me anything to take back to my government to persuade them to hand over Katya Prachy."

Esganikan looked bored, red plume bobbing. "Very well, hand her over, or we'll come and take her ourselves."

"End of the week," said Shan, trying to be helpful. Esganikan wasn't very good at specifying deadlines. Everything was *now*. That, at least, was very wess'har: chilled or punching. *Threat is now*. It was one of their defining phrases. "Because we'll find her anyway. It's what I do."

The ambassador paused for a moment, looking as if he was going to ask her to explain, and then thought better of it. "I believe our business is concluded, then, Commander Gai." He stood up and smiled perfectly pleasantly, as if it was just a mild disappointment, like finding they couldn't fit in lunch after all, and nodded politely at Bari. "Prime Minister. Our door remains open."

Shan had plenty of practice at toughing out hostile situations. Nobody liked a copper, at least not the kind of copper she'd been; she hadn't been in the business of giving school talks on road safety or directing tourists to the monorail for a long, long time. But she felt guilty. Impossible as the deal was, she'd become the sticking point.

Bari waited for the doors to close and resumed the meeting.

"I'm sorry this has turned ugly," he said. "But you're aware of the conflicting interests here, and at least we know what the FEU's really after."

"We are," said Shan, cutting off any discussion of why she was such a point of contention. "Let's discuss the marines."

"The immigration department will process them, no delays. After that, they're eligible to enlist in our defense forces. I'm sure we'd welcome uniquely experienced special forces troops." Nairn looked at Ade, not realizing yet that the deal didn't include him. "We'd like to put that straight as far as we can, because we committed ourselves as a nation to accepting your help. We're not proud of Earth's involvement in destabilizing your system, even if we had no hand in it."

Esganikan turned to Bari. "Will you still feel that positive when we have to deal with the FEU's intransigence, and you're seen as acting as our military base?"

"I'm a pragmatist," Bari said. "We're already seen as that, and we need your goodwill infinitely more than we need theirs. The problem with superpowers is that they eventually alienate so many other countries that they find themselves in a world of enemies, and they collapse. Every empire dies in the end. You won't find the rest of the world piling in to condemn us or helping the FEU."

"Is that an indication that I can remove the warships?"

Bari kept looking at Shan. But this part wasn't her business, and she didn't join in. "I assume you could."

"If an attack is likely, it's simpler to remove the source than to maintain a defense shield across an entire country." Esganikan seemed to be sliding into a defense pact again. "Which can be done, but it may take many weeks to create the infrastructure here."

"Source . . ." said Bari. "Do you mean the fleet, or the FEU?"

"Which would you prefer?"

The Eqbas could destroy both, of course. It wasn't remotely funny.

"It would be helpful if the carrier group could be persuaded to go away. Loss of life is always the last resort."

Shan caught Ade's eye accidentally, and wasn't surprised to see his face locked in that blank I'm-not-going-to-react expression. They were talking about blowing his comrades out of the water. He didn't know them, and they were a century apart in real terms, but the FEU navy was still his tribe.

We're all way too close to this. But didn't I realize that it was all heading this way?

"Let's give them a warning demonstration, then," Shan said, trying to be helpful. "Now that Pettinato's telling them Mr. Bari's not in the driving seat, and they know they're dealing direct with the Eqbas or not at all, they might react differently."

"Warnings are only relevant if you want to educate," said Esganikan.

"Humor me."

"There will still be many deaths in the coming years."

"Maybe, but launching missiles at ships upsets me. Eddie would suggest you target the politicians instead."

"Assassination, or attacking their capital?"

Bari's face lost all color. Shan was used to wess'har being utterly literal, but now that she was back in a more familiar human context, the idea of killing politicians and erasing problems that contained living people made her uneasy again. She'd done enough serious shit herself over the years, but that didn't make it right.

Dead's dead. You always say that. Does it matter if it's a bullet or if they die of starvation or disease when the Eqbas start culling?

But Earth made everything look different, more complicated. It had been a bad idea to return.

"Look, why don't I leave you to do the international stuff, and I'll make a start on locating Prachy." Shan got up and gave Esganikan no chance to keep her there. "I'll be in the shuttle. Call me when you need me."

"Don't you want to discuss the gene bank?" Bari asked.

"My role in that is finished," she said. "I got it back here. That's all I was tasked to do. The rest is up to you, although I'd be pretty upset if any of it got wasted. Maybe we should aim to reset Earth to the climate conditions prevailing when the bank was assembled."

She didn't mention the duplicate gene bank back on Wess'ej; that was asking for trouble. Ade and Aras got up to follow her and she found herself trying to remember the way back to the main doors. A member of staff directed her outside and she gulped in hot air as the air-conditioned environment of the building was left behind. She was torn between standing there and going back to the shuttle, and looked up to check for bee cams, but the modern type were much harder to spot than Eddie's. The crowd was still there on the cordon.

"You knew it was going to degenerate into this very fast," said Aras. "It's wise to let Esganikan handle it, because she won't listen to you unless it suits her."

"Don't I know it."

"So what are you going to do about Prachy?" asked Ade.

"Find her."

"And?"

"And what?"

"They won't hand her over, Boss. It'll be another shooting match, and Esganikan isn't going to write her off as a bad job."

"Okay, maybe *I* need to go and get her, then. I think I can manage to arrest a granny."

"With Eqbas assistance, perhaps." The ramp emerged from the shuttle again and Aras stood back to let her enter. It was good footage for somebody, that small glimpse of wess'har technology. "However proficient you are, *isan,* you're not experienced at infiltrating what is effectively enemy territory, locating a target, and assassinating her."

"You've not seen Reading, have you?"

"Be serious. This is best left to the Eqbas, or the Skavu."

"And who said I'd assassinate anyone? *Arrest.* And fuck the Skavu. I don't want them on my op, thanks."

"*Isan*, they are *on your op* anyway. You can no more dispense with them than you can Esganikan."

Ade gave her a weary look as if he was being asked to volunteer. For some reason, the FEU hadn't worked out that he carried *c'naatat* too—which meant Rayat hadn't been able to make contact again after he was seized from Umeh Station—and there were no signs that they might make a grab for Aras. That explained their focus on her.

"Assassination's easier," Ade said quietly. "Then all you have to worry about is your own exfil. No struggling body to haul with you."

"If it's that or the Eqbas frying half of Belgium, maybe I don't have a choice."

"You have a very long life ahead of you," said Aras. "All of us do. After a few years, your view of what you can cause and influence will alter, believe me."

Aras lived so much in the moment that it shook her to be reminded of his age, and that, after five hundred years, he saw events in a different context. It was a kind way of reminding her she didn't run the universe, and she wasn't responsible for it. For some people that would have been tantamount to being told they didn't matter, but she grasped at it as an escape from feeling she was to blame for the way events were unfolding.

Shan sat back against a bulkhead and took out her swiss to see which networks she could still access; there was nothing except the ITX, and that was useless for communications on the planet itself. The Eqbas pilot glanced at her, but he was more interested in watching the BBChan feeds displayed in the bulkhead, a spread of five channels that he seemed to be able to watch simultaneously. It was the only window Shan had on how the rest of the planet was reacting.

At the UN, Canada was pledging to support the Pacific Rim States. Closer to the action, the Sinostates had closed its borders and ports to the FEU refugees.

"Where do they think they're going to go?" Ade asked. "There's nowhere to run from the Eqbas."

"Haven't a clue. People just run."

"No joy with the swiss?"

"'Course not. Here I am, interstellar fucking traveler, and I can't get a poxy signal. I'll have to buy a bloody handheld. Or scrounge one."

"That means going outside the cordon," Aras said. "And I think that's a bad idea."

Cordon. There was an easier option, or at least a more immediate one.

"Don't follow me," she said, wagging finger at both of them, and left the shuttle to crunch across the gravel that they said had once been a splendid lawn. The crowd still waited in that baking heat; even the police were taking turns to slip back into their vehicles to cool off, and it was nearly dusk. Noon must have been intolerable. As Shan got closer to the cordon, some of the media reacted and the police turned around with that oh-shit expression Shan knew she'd worn so many times herself.

"It's okay," she said to the inspector who intercepted her. A cloud of tiny bee cams caught her eye, and one of the officers started yelling at the media to get the things back on their side of the line. "I'm not going out there to meet and greet. I need to speak to the Gaia bunch. Grab me one of their reps, will you, mate? And ask them if they can lend me a handheld."

Surang, Eqbas Vorhi.

Rayat found a surprising lack of interest among the Eqbas about events on Earth. Maybe they'd seen it all before; after a million years, many of them spent imposing the Eqbas environmental will on unenlightened worlds, it was probably a minor news story for them.

One thing he'd learned over the years here was that the majority of the population never left the planet. They respected their galactic policing program, and were happy to contribute to it, but—like so many similar tasks on Earth, he thought—it was something that they neither saw nor took part in, and so it was invisible. The citizen militia philosophy of the Wess'ej wess'har didn't exist here. They had a professional army, one most of them rarely saw.

He left Shapakti to go back to his laboratory and walked the curved pathways of the city, pausing to watch debates in the ideas exchanges and to ponder the problem of getting a call through to Kiir, the Skavu commander. He'd never even spoken to a Skavu, although he knew a little about them and the small, savage war against them in Eqbas colonial history. It helped him to think of the Eqbas in terms of a colonial power; even if they usually left when their adjustments were complete and planets were restored to what they thought of as their proper state, they had all the other trappings of empire.

But they didn't have embassies. Rayat couldn't call on his old spook skills and find an unsuspecting diplomat to work on.

I could try Eddie, though.

He hadn't spoken to the journalist in a long time. He could have told Eddie years ago, but he hadn't, because things told had a habit of becoming things shared, and that was the last thing he needed, for the FEU—anyone other than Shan, really—to know that there were more *c'naatat* carriers. It was bad enough with Shan and her menagerie being there. If Eddie could be persuaded to tell Shan, would she believe them? Why would she *not* believe him? What motive could he have for driving a wedge between her and Esganikan?

Maybe Aras wouldn't think it was such a good idea, either. But both he and Ade had passed on *c'naatat* to others for their own reasons, ones that had seemed perfectly noble to them at the time, but now left more messes to be cleared up.

It needed to be a hardliner who heard the news. And that meant Shan, because she could oust Esganikan from command with that *jask* thing, or Kiir, who at least commanded the shock troops and so had some influence on the situation.

He'd ask Eddie. Somehow, he'd get past this comms blackout and talk to him. If he couldn't beat the technology, he'd try social engineering.

As he passed another ideas exchange, an Eqbas he recognized beckoned him inside. The Eqbas seemed to spend an extraordinary amount of leisure time in them when they weren't eating or tending their plants, almost as if they were bars or social clubs.

"Come," said the Eqbas. Rayat always thought of him as Roger, although his name was Rujalian. "We're talking about cultural change. We have theories about changing human nature."

"That's nice," said Rayat, edging his way into the packed chamber to avoid physical contact. He was infected again. It really was like a crowded pub, but without the beer. "I suppose you want input from a human, then. I used to be one."

Wess'har didn't laugh, but some things did elicit a trill that Rayat always interpreted as amusement. The trill went round the room. "How do we select humans who will live like wess'har?" asked Rujalian. "Or can they be converted, like Skavu?"

Rayat took up a seat in the corner, a little upholstered alcove. Eqbas seemed to like their creature comforts a lot more than their ascetic wess'har cousins, with their rock-hard sleeping ledges and kneeling stools. And as he was *c'naatat*, he could drink their beverages and eat their snacks with impunity. It was one way to spend an afternoon.

"You'll find humans can be rabid converts," he said. "There are also plenty of humans who live low-impact lives. You'd get on fine with some religious sects like Jains, and all kinds of humans. But not most."

"What makes them different?" asked another Eqbas. "Not genes. If it were, it would be simple to cull the ones who didn't have the correct genetic profile."

It was all very matter of fact. They were talking about his species, about exterminating troublesome creatures like him, and yet saw nothing offensive in that. But that wasn't half so hard as reconciling that fly-swatting attitude with their reverence for all life. It seemed that once you broke the rules and did the exploiting and pillaging, then all bets were off. Where the line lay between collective and individual guilt, Rayat was never sure.

In twenty years, Rayat had merely come to accept wess'har morality.

"Tell me about the Skavu, then," he said. "Have any of you met one?"

"Not face-to-face," said Rujalian. "But I have a neighbor who creates the ship updates for them."

Ah, that was interesting. It was no direct use to Rayat, because the Skavu were light-years away, but it would help him understand their mindset better, perhaps. He grabbed any intelligence he came across and stored it for possible future use. Knowledge was never wasted. Information really *was* power.

"They use Eqbas ships?"

"We gave them our old vessels, yes. So they require updating from us."

Rayat was thinking shipyards for a moment, vapor hissing from robotic presses and the smell of hull composite being formed. But that wasn't how Eqbas built ships. They used nanotech, creating ships that could be grown from templates and whose form and function could be changed dynamically by altering the materials at a molecular level.

"So how do they get updated?" he asked, imagining them

limping back to port for a refit of some kind. "And why don't you just break down the old ones with nanites? You can do that. I know you can. I've seen it."

"Why deconstruct them while they still have use for others?" Rujalian looked as if he was groping for simpler language, probably doubting Rayat's ability to understand eqbas'u. "We transmit new instructions. The component materials have to be told how to change the way they react and behave. There are limits with the older nanites, of course, but that's no bad thing with allies like the Skavu, is it?"

There was more trilling and a cacophony of discussion, in their two-toned voices that sounded as chaotic as a birdhouse. "Hang on," said Rayat, "is that like sending them an updated program? An upgrade made up of instructions?"

"Yes, it is. Are you *sure* you were a scientist?"

Rayat didn't know who or how, but something in his head said *message vector,* and that was something he needed very badly right now. "How often do you do this?"

"Whenever they request it."

"Do you . . . ever send updates without their asking?"

"Occasionally."

"Do you run diagnostic checks?"

Rujalian looked at him with his head cocked so far on one side that it was comical. "We can, but why?"

"Just curious."

Rayat *was* curious, that was true. But he was far more interested in working out how he might get a message to the Skavu, in terms they understood, that their mission commander was an abomination, a *c'naatat* carrier.

He knew he could rely on them to do the right thing. All he had to do was work out how to send an intelligible message.

"*Roger*, my friend, tell me more about your neighbor," he said.

Rujalian seemed to find it very funny to be called *Roger,* and trilled happily. Wess'har were very open if you asked them questions. That was common to both sides of the family. Humans were pretty helpful too, most of the time, but not as unfailingly detailed. Rayat left the ideas exchange armed with the knowledge that once every few weeks—he kept the Gregorian calendar running alongside the Eqbas one even now—a maintenance status check was downloaded to Skavu vessels via the ITX. He also knew who sent it, how they sent it, and what he had to do to add code to it, for want of a better word.

He also knew the Eqbas responsible for it didn't speak or read English—very few did—and wouldn't notice if the words YOUR COMMANDER HAS *C'NAATAT* were embedded in the code, and so the message would end up shunted to the diagnostic display that showed parts of the program that wouldn't run for some reason. Eqbas, being the efficient bastards that they were, didn't have many duff lines of code. The Skavu would notice that, he hoped—and they *did* process English through their translation collars.

"Once again, the *lingua franca par excellence* comes into its own," he said aloud as he walked back into Shapakti's office.

"Latin *and* French," said Shapakti. "And you seem smug."

"I think I have a solution to getting a warning to Earth."

Shapakti wafted agitated citrus again. "Eddie Michallat may have the best chance. You could have passed him a message by now."

"Old habits die hard, Shap. I've found a way of getting a warning direct to the Skavu fleet."

Shapakti filled the room with his anxiety scent now, as pungent as grapefruit peel. "I think that's a bad idea. Telling *Shan Chail* is, as you call it, the long screwdriver. She can be relied upon. Telling the Skavu is pulling a pin from a grenade. That's the phrase, isn't it? They are *volatile*."

Rayat paused to consider what the worst thing that might happen. The Skavu understood *c'naatat* enough to know that it needed to be destroyed by fragmenting the host. All he wanted was for *c'naatat* to be taken out of the Eqbas armory before it got out of control.

"I'm going to have to do it, Shap. You *know* that. Things are going to be bad enough on Earth without adding a plague like that. Have I ever showed you *zombie* movies? Funny how they never addressed the whole population problem aspect of the not-quite-dead. But *zombies* don't go on breeding, of course."

Shapakti had frozen in that classic wess'har shock pose, and he didn't ask what zombies were. "I would seek to dissuade you. You may cause a problem where none existed before. There are three other *c'naatat* hosts on Earth, remember. All four may yet come home without incident."

"How strongly do you feel about that?"

Shapakti was very still; not quite frozen, but motionless enough for Rayat to gauge his mood.

"I would stop you if I could," he said. "So don't ask me to help you."

"Okay." Rayat nodded. He liked Shapakti. It wasn't fair on him to push this further. Rayat preferred to do his intelligence work alone anyway.

It was just like old times.

Rayat spent the rest of the day reading up on ship construction and nanite command codes via the communal library link, an easy task because Eqbas were every bit as open with information as their wess'har cousins. Shan might have been unwise to return to Earth with her parasite, but she wasn't as big a risk as a wess'har with a hidden agenda. Esganikan wasn't at all like Nevyan or the wess'har Rayat had known in the past; he couldn't trust her, and he didn't know what she'd do next. She might have wanted to explore extended life for all kinds of practical reasons, but now she had plenty of Rayat in her, and Rayat knew how his own mind worked.

She had to be exposed, and stopped. He couldn't trust her not to be Mohan Rayat. And he couldn't count on her being Shan Frankland.

St George, Eastside Australia: Eqbas temporary camp.

Aras stood in the blazing heat with the *virin* cupped in his palms, and stared at the image that had formed within it.

"Is she angry with me?" Eddie's voice hadn't changed but

his hair was thinner and grayer; his face was deeply lined. Wess'ej, clean and unspoiled, still took its toll on humans with its higher gravity and austere life. "Look, I'll face it like a man, Aras. Just let me talk to her."

"She's . . . regretful. I would not say *angry*."

"Does she understand why I had to stay?"

"Ask her yourself. She's busy talking to the government here, but she'll always have time for you." The *virin* had a limited field of view but it was clear there was someone else with Eddie. Behind him, Aras could see the shimmering city of F'nar reflecting light like a covering of snow, and a shadow moving. "You've been meticulous in cataloguing the progress on Umeh. A little remiss in keeping us updated on your own circumstances, though."

Eddie shrugged in a way that usually indicated benign embarrassment, as if he felt uncomfortable with praise. When he reached out of the field of view and pulled someone into the frame, Aras understood why.

"I have a family now," he said. "This is my son, Barry."

Barry was around fifteen with sharp features and light brown hair. Aras assumed he was the likeness of his mother, a woman Aras hadn't yet seen.

"Hi, Aras," said Barry Michallat. *Eddie has a son.* Even Eddie, solitary and obsessed Eddie, had a child, but Aras didn't. He should have been happy for Eddie, but all he could feel was shocked betrayal that made absolutely no sense. "I've heard all about you. How's Earth?"

"It might be dying," said Aras. "Or it might be going through a normal cycle in its life. Either way, life is changing here."

"But the Eqbas can fix it, right?" Eddie cut in. "Have you seen Umeh? Seriously, have you seen it?"

"I've seen your programs, yes."

"Has anyone on Earth taken any notice?"

"Time will tell."

"Aras, it's been just about scoured clean and the population is below one billion. In *twenty-five years*."

Ferociously efficient nanites were a standard wess'har method of remediating polluted land and stripping down the detritus of construction. Nanites had reclaimed Ouzhari and

the surrounding area after the isenj had been driven from
Bezer'ej: nanites had left Constantine pristine again, as if no
human colony had ever settled there, and no mission had set
up base. But Eqbas nanite technology, ten thousand years
removed from that of Wess'ej, seemed to have done much
more in the time available.

"Show me the latest images," said Aras. He hadn't yet
checked all the ITX links from home and what might be
available now. It was hard to know where to begin to pick up
the threads of his interrupted life after five hundred years of
relative stability. "The last I saw were years old."

"It'll knock your socks off." Eddie grinned, but uncon-
vincingly. He fumbled with something in his hand. "Here's
the view south of Jejeno today. Live."

Aras pressed the *virin* to accept output from the Wess'ej
ITX node. The image stirred no recollection in him, neither
from his conscious recollection of the all-encompassing city
nor from the more fleeting genetic memory of isenj who had
hosted his *c'naatat* before him. Where there had been tight-
packed towers and spires covering every meter of land as far
as the horizon, there was now a more open vista with patches
of light green vegetation and light yellow cycad-like trees.
The sky was clearer; the whole impression was one of a city
that had been thinned out. From this altitude and angle—the
observation point must have been relatively low in the sky,
perhaps a monitoring remote left by the Eqbas—he could
see no living rivers of isenj packing the streets and moving
in carefully managed traffic streams.

But this was Jejeno, the capital of the Northern Assembly
on the Ebj landmass—just one of Umeh's nations. There
were three more island continents. This was *not* the complete picture.

"Now show me the Maritime Fringe," he said. "Show me
Pareg, Tivskur and Sil."

It took a few moments for Eddie to patch through the images: Aras didn't need to see them all, because Tivskur's
coast summed it up. What had been a packed coastline cren-
ellated with ports and inlets, with towering structures right
up to the pinkish gray polluted sea—the dying sea—was

now completely flattened. It reminded him of Ouzhari after the cobalt-salted neutron devices had incinerated it. It had a velvety uniformity; not a wasteland, but a blank sheet. The buildings were gone, utterly gone without even ruins to show where they'd stood.

Aras had used nanites for clearance on Bezer'ej post-war, and years later when the colony of Constantine was evacuated, so he knew what he was looking at without any prompting from Eddie. The built environment and everything in it—including corpses—had been broken down into their components by nanites. It was bare soil, barren, but clean. Like a new volcanic island erupting from the sea and cooling, it would in time become colonized by . . . what? The isenj had destroyed everything living that wasn't of direct use to them, and were eventually forced to manage their climate with brilliant but doomed engineering on a planetary scale. They would import native flora and fauna from the isenj moon of Tasir Var.

There were no isenj in Tivskur, of course. They were all dead.

"So the genome-targeted bioweapons were used," Aras said at last. Somehow he thought the phrase *knock your socks off* implied a positive surprise, but this wasn't. Part of him—and not his inherited isenj memories—took no pleasure in seeing the demise of a people even if they had once tortured him as a prisoner of war, and reviled him as a war criminal; in fact, he regretted the loss of talented engineers who might have had elegant solutions for some of Earth's problems. "Was it Minister Rit who decided to use them, or Nevyan?"

"Rit," said Eddie. "Deployed by wess'har craft."

"Just as they agreed to do."

"I didn't say I *approved* of it, Aras. Just that . . . well, desperate situations sometimes require extreme solutions."

Aras wasn't shocked by the mass slaughter. He was wess'har, and no life-form was more valued or sacred than another; but those with choice and control had more responsibility for exercising it responsibly, and if they didn't then balancing had to take place.

He'd done that balancing. He'd led the assault on the isenj colony on Bezer'ej centuries before, when he was just a normal wess'har male, because they'd polluted the seas and caused the deaths of bezeri. He would do it again without a second thought. This was the ethos of his species.

But to see that isenj could kill isenj in those numbers . . . as Rit had said, change could only come if whole lines of genetic memory were wiped out, not just culling for the sake of numbers. *Thinking* had to change. Isenj were physically hidebound by their genetic memory.

"Tell me," he said, dragging his gaze away from the *virin*, "do we now have a population made up almost wholly of the Northern Assembly isenj?"

"I reckon so," said Eddie. "Ethnic cleansing, by genome."

Barry was still in shot, looking awkward and bored. He'd grown up in a world where this was normal—but it would not be normal on Earth. Humans were appalled by racism and yet hardwired to seek out and favor their own kind, their closest genetic match.

And wess'har didn't care. Numbers were what mattered: they just reduced the number of isenj to the level that the global ecology could support. How and who didn't matter, no more than humans discriminated when they culled numerous animal populations.

"I think humans will find that very hard to understand," said Aras.

For a moment, he and Eddie looked at each other in silence. It struck him that twenty-five years was too much time to lose in a friendship.

"Get Shan to give me a call, will you, mate? And Ade." Eddie put his arm around Barry and gave him a rough paternal hug. "Tell her it's important. The FEU have been sniffing around, asking me for what they loosely term *advice*. I think they're going all out for grabbing *c'naatat* because that's one good way of surviving an Eqbas clean-up, isn't it?"

Aras thought of Mjat, the isenj colony on Bezer'ej that became Constantine, and how he'd destroyed it, *c'naatat*-infected or not. "It doesn't always help, and that's why I was known as the Beast of Mjat . . ."

"Sorry, mate. Look, warn her, will you? You've all got to be bloody careful."

"It's not as dangerous as you think," Aras said. "Shapakti has perfected a technique for removing *c'naatat* from humans."

Eddie's expression was blank for a moment, as if he was waiting on the five-second delay of the relay, but this was point-to-point transmission, and he was simply surprised by the news.

"So now you tell me," he said.

"Make sure that Nevyan has been told. We can't rely on Esganikan to keep us informed. Shan is very angry about her silence on the matter."

"I'll bet . . ." said Eddie. "But we've been here before, right? It won't affect you three. So don't fret about it."

Aras thought it was interesting that Eddie focused on the impact it might have on his relationship with Shan and Ade. The whole issue of wider human contamination and its countermeasures fell by the wayside. That wasn't a journalist's reaction; it was a friend's.

"I regret missing so much time with you," Aras said gently. "I'll return as soon as I possibly can, and then . . . then we can catch up."

Eddie compressed his lips for a moment in that expression that often preceded tears. "I'll try not to die, then," he said, and forced that laugh again. "Get Shazza to give me a bell, okay? I've really missed a good swearing session with the old ratbag."

After he closed the link, Aras stood in silence contemplating the emptiness of the desert. The sun was low in the sky, casting long shadows from the rocks and hard-baked stumps of trees, every bit as dead and sterile as Tivskur. Life had moved underground. It was like the Constantine colony.

And Eddie has a son.

Aras knew how isolated Eddie had felt and saw the paternal affection he had for Nevyan's child, Giyadas. Now he had a family. It was good to see your friends' lives come right in the end.

He has a son.

For that, Aras envied him; no, it was much more than envy. It was jealousy, that ugly human thing, but he was unable to dismiss it.

Eddie had a child, and Aras didn't.

Giyadas Chail, *forgive me for contacting you, but I need your advice. The matriarchs of Surang see no need to intervene in the Earth mission, but Mohan Rayat is pursuing an alarming path. There is something you need to know, and that you need to tell Shan Chail. She refuses to listen to Rayat. She will listen to you.*

DA SHAPAKTI to Giyadas,
breaching the agreement not to contact
Wess'ej unless invited

Nazel Island, Bezer'ej.

"Are you sure you want to do this?" Giyadas asked.

Eddie knew he didn't, but there was wanting to and having to. He hadn't seen Lindsay since she was a regular human, a woman with a lot on her conscience and no way out. The least he could do now was give her one bit of good news.

She could go home.

"I am, doll."

"You'll be shocked."

"I've done shock." But he'd never seen a friend turned into another species. Not even Shan, or Ade—they looked like their old selves, except for a little bioluminescence. "I can handle this."

The biohaz suit felt too gauzy and insubstantial to be proof against the pathogen that now protected the planet from incursions by humans. There was one to stop isenj getting a foothold again too, but the one that mattered to him was the human-specific one, created and put in place here by the wess'har to stop humans returning, not the Eqbas. The biological box of lethal tricks had a long and ancient pedi-

gree and predated human bioweapons by thousands of years.
It did him good to remember that sometimes, when he thought
humans were unique in their destructive ingenuity.

Eddie trudged up the shore of a rocky island south of
Constantine that he'd never seen before, feeling like a bee-
keeper in a shroud. Biohaz suits were supposed to look
macho and spacesuit-like; this was practically a frock.
Giyadas walked beside him, needing no suit, with one hand
ready to steady him in case he tripped over the loose folds.
The suit was built for wess'har, and tall ones at that.

"Did you ever see normal bezeri?" Giyadas asked.

"I saw the lights in the sea," Eddie said, straining to see
some sign of terrestrial squid, as fantastic an idea as any
he'd come across in the Cavanagh system. "And I saw the
pictures of dead ones. But I never went in the water, no."

"You'll find this interesting, then."

As they moved beyond the beach and into the knee-high
heathland foliage, the clearing was visible, and with it the
sight of a settlement that looked like a collection of giant
wattle-and-daub warbler nests. There were other structures
too: some like drystone walling, others built from timber
giving the overall impression of an eclectic Bronze or Iron
Age village.

A large ITX screen—a sheet of the typical wess'har blue
metal—stood in the center of the village.

"Christ," Eddie said, "are they getting ready to watch
football or something? Squid soccer hoolies pissed up on
lager. Now that's *got* to be worth a feature."

Giyadas didn't laugh, but pointed past the screen. It was
then that he noticed the huge shapes like glass sculptures
lounging in the trees or protruding from the doorways. They
were alive with lights.

"Wow." For the first time he could remember, he didn't
rush to grab a few shots with his bee cam. This wasn't for
any bulletin, because *c'naatat* bezeri on Bezer'ej had to remain a secret. He waved, helpless. Could they hear him,
being glass squid? Of course they could. They lived in air.
"Hi, guys!"

"Eddeeeee . . . the hack!" said one with a rumbling voice

like a tuba. They could speak—and they knew who he was. Giyadas visited regularly to check they hadn't bred out of control, and she must have mentioned him. He wondered how she'd describe him if they'd learned the word *hack*. "How do you like our modest home?"

What could he say? For once, he had to think hard.

The central building of the village, a semi-submerged roundhouse with a plaster dome, reminded him of other places in the Ceret-Cavanagh-Nir system; the ussissi village, with its painted eggshell roofs, and the domed skylights of the subterranean colony of Constantine.

"It's pretty damn good," he said. *My God, I'm having a chat with an intelligent immortal land-squid. This is the fucking ultimate journalist moment, but no bloody viewers to stun with it.* "You're way ahead of us apes. It took us quite a few million years to start building things once we got out of water."

Eddie thought that if he kept talking then he might recognize Lindsay while he scanned the shapes, and slide tactfully into a conversation. He dreaded showing any reaction. There was a polite English core of him that still thought it was bloody rude to stare, even at the extraordinary sight of walking, talking, house-building squid.

He looked around, helpless.

"Eddie!" said a voice. He recognized it. It was completely human except for a slight vibrato in the lower registers. "I never thought I'd see you again."

Lindsay had no trouble recognizing him even after all these years, but he struggled to match the voice to the shape, and prayed that his shock didn't show. When she got close enough to peer through the transparent visor, he didn't recognize her. He'd looked past her just as he looked past one of the bezeri ambling around the village like a glass ghost. She wasn't even humanoid in shape, just an upright column of bipedal gel studded with shadows like variations in density. But there was a definite bulbous formation at the top of the column—a head. Eddie struggled to find eyes to focus on.

"Eddie," she said. "It's me. Here."

Had she still been in human form, she'd have been over fifty, and probably looking much older thanks to a hard life of largely manual labor spent outdoors, but he'd have *known* her from the little unchangeable things that survived the erosion of time.

"Lin?" he said. *Oh God. She's not human anymore.*

"It's okay. You can say it."

Eddie was a man with a heart who finally let it get the better of him, something he once thought a journalist should never do. He tried to spare her feelings. A knowing grin—professionally manufactured, but probably not enough to fool her completely—spread across his face, and he was damned if it was going to slip.

"There's something different about you," he said. "New hairstyle?"

"How are you, Eddie?"

"I'm good."

Yes, her voice was almost the same, another of *c'naatat*'s odd touches. He could see a hole in her throat—more or less—opening and closing. "Long time."

"I know. I should have visited years ago."

"But . . . seeing the rest of them back on Earth got to you, yes?"

He nodded. "It seemed a good point to . . . I dunno, catch up." He glanced over his shoulder. "Giyadas and I have some encouraging news. We need to talk about it."

"Oh, you're here to soften me up for something."

"Not exactly. I really wanted to see you anyway, but . . . remember Shapakti?" Eddie took a breath. Blurting seemed to be the best policy these days. "He's found a way of getting rid of *c'naatat*."

Giyadas intervened. "Let us be precise, Eddie," she said. "He can remove it consistently from *humans*. He doesn't know if it can be done with other species."

Humans. Lindsay, a translucent biped who was more like a cartoon pillow than a humanoid, reacted to that word with a brief glitter of colored lights. Eddie wondered what she might be left with if all that *c'naatat* had made her suddenly vanish. Would *he* have accepted the bloody thing? If he had—could he have given it up? It was a terrible choice either way, and one he was thankful never to have had to make.

"This is all about the tests on Rayat, isn't it?" Lindsay looked around as if to check who might be within earshot. She seemed to default to human habits forgotten for decades. It told Eddie a lot. "So did he survive? What was left? What did it do to him?"

"He was perfectly healthy each time," said Giyadas. "I've been in touch with Shapakti, and he says Rayat returns to the state he was in when the organism infected him. Shapakti repeated the infection cycle and it worked consistently every time. He's managed to defeat its defense mechanisms."

"It's taken so *long*." Lindsay sounded wounded. "Or has he been sitting on the news?"

"I don't know. But he succeeded, and that means you have choices beyond fragmentation."

Eddie had to judge Lindsay's reaction by tone. There was no face to show emotions that he could recognize, and the lights told him nothing. *So she can go back to being blond, petite Lindsay Neville. She was quite pretty back then. Does she even remember her own face in the mirror?*

"Does Shan know?" Lindsay asked.

"Yes," said Eddie.

"Is she going to have it removed? Is Ade?"

"I haven't asked her, but remember they don't know yet if it'll work on wess'har."

But Lindsay doesn't care. She can go home now.

It was the simplest, most animal of thoughts, and it ambushed him again. Lindsay had lived with *c'naatat* for a very long time, much longer than Shan in real everyday terms; even Rayat had carried it for longer. For some reason, Eddie thought of mentioning it as some kind of reassurance but then wondered if she might be offended by mention of such a petty thing as if it were evidence of not being wholly in Shan's overwhelming shadow.

"You've come to send me back, then," she said. "But I can't leave David here. If I go, he has to come with me. I can't leave him here, all alone. I have to exhume him."

It seemed suddenly to become her dominant thought. Eddie had a distressing image of her sifting through soil to find a fabric shroud and heartbreakingly tiny bones. He hadn't thought about it before; but that was why she'd scavenged parts of the stained glass headstone from David's grave and taken them to the bezeri settlement underwater. She still needed a physical focus for her grief.

Faced with the crushing reality of a grave 150 trillion miles from home and no hope of returning to visit it, Lindsay was probably doing what many parents would. But restored to normality, wholly human and around thirty years old, would she have another baby in due course, and would she find that a solace or a reminder? It was an awful choice. Once again, it was one Eddie was grateful never to have to make.

But who'll understand her back on Earth, after all she's been, and been through?

"Well, not *send* you back, exactly." Eddie's tone was set on *soothing*. "Not if you don't want to go, but we need to find out now if Shapakti can do the same with bezeri and return them to normal too. Then they can rebuild their society in the normal way. I mean, it's what they want, isn't it? To be able to breed and spread out, and not worry that *c'naatat*'s going to turn them into a plague like the isenj."

Is that it?

"What do you want me to do, then?"

"We want a bezeri volunteer," said Giyadas. "Perhaps you might persuade one of them."

"But what if they don't want to be normal again?" asked Lindsay.

"Do *you* want to?" asked Giyadas. "Do you want to give up the bezeri and wess'har components in you? Did *you* prefer that first life you had?"

"Is this part of a bargain?" Lindsay asked. "I give you a bezeri to play with, and you let me become a human again?"

"There *is* no bargain," said Giyadas. "Just a question."

Wess'har didn't go in for those kinds of games. There were never strings attached, but the downside was that there was no bribing or persuading them with an exchange of favors, either. Every action was a separate process carried out for its own purpose. Their reason for offering Lindsay a way home would not be linked in any way to getting the bezeri to cooperate.

It was one of many reasons why humans thought they understood wess'har but didn't. Even their Eqbas relatives seemed not to mesh with them completely. Even after decades living here, Eddie sometimes couldn't fathom them.

"I'll *ask* them," said Lindsay. Eddie noted that she said *them,* not *the others,* as if she'd started withdrawing into human territory right away. "But I honestly have no idea how they'll react."

Maybe she remembered them as they were when she infected them all those years ago: the last remnant of their kind, almost all elderly and infirm, waiting to die and too old to repopulate their world. What if that was the state they were restored to? Why would they ever want to do that, if *c'naatat* had made them fit and young again? It was a rotten kind of normality to crave after years of vigor.

Eddie thought of Shan aborting her own child, and had a glimpse of the impossible dilemma of anyone with *c'naatat.* It was an all or nothing kind of thing. Having any *c'naatat* around changed the whole nature of life, and whether you couched it in Deborah Garrod's religious terms of a satanic temptation, or just looked at the basic maths and social implications, it wasn't a boon for anyone or anything. It was a terrible burden.

"I'll ask them," she said again. "Come back in a week or so."

Lindsay could go home. Eddie could hear it in her voice, real human relief coupled with desperation in case her hopes were dashed. He felt a strange empty guilt that she'd been here for so long among a tight-knit community, and yet the prospect of being human again and going back to Earth made her react as if she was being rescued.

It was a glimpse of hell: unending existence in a situation you didn't want to be in. Eddie got back into the shuttle and wasn't sure what to say to Giyadas.

"Upsetting, isn't it?" she said.

"I feel like I abandoned her."

"It was a choice she made, Eddie. She went to a lot of trouble to get infected. She also caused the catastrophe for which she sought to atone." Giyadas was a wonderful, supportive friend and exceptionally restrained for a wess'har, but wess'har she was, and so her thinking was that once you made your bed then you bloody well had to lie on it. She wasn't being callous. She was simply linking cause and effect, wess'har style, to make Eddie realize that this situation wasn't his fault. "But now she has a solution. She could quite easily have been executed like Josh Garrod and Jonathan Burgh, and then none of this soul-searching would have been necessary."

She made a good point. Wess'har always did.

"Seeing as I'm wearing my hazmat rig," he said, "can I see Ouzhari?"

He'd never been there, although he'd seen the apocalyptic images after the bombs had detonated. *C'naatat* was native to the island and nowhere else. Now he wondered how, and why, and if it might have come from another place. It was a question he knew he shouldn't pursue, ever.

"The radiation levels are back to normal." Giyadas fired up the shuttle's drives. "But the biohazards are still there, yes."

"Let's go, then," he said. "Please?"

Ouzhari was the smallest and southernmost island in the chain that started with Constantine nearest the coast, and it had first been named Christopher, although they all had bezeri names; Eddie couldn't remember which island went with which saint, but they all began with C. Aras had described the landscape as glossy black grass and pure white sand. But even from half a kilometer offshore, Eddie could see that while the sand was white again, the grass that had grown nowhere else had vanished for good. Nothing had regenerated. The vegetation now colonizing the island was the same as on the islands north of it, a mix of bronze and blue-gray spiky stuff like aggressive heather. Eddie, with his eye for a good shot, could imagine the visual drama of the way it had once been.

He suited up again when they landed. He walked along the shore with Giyadas, savoring the tranquillity and the rhythmic wash of the waves.

"All for nothing," said Eddie. *C'naatat* survived the cobalt bombs intended to destroy it, but not much else had: not the species that lived on Ouzhari, not the relative safety and peace of Earth, not the comfortable wess'har isolation far from Eqbas Vorhi, and not friendships. He thought of Aras and Josh, and pitied Aras having to live with the memory of executing a friend. "What a fucking mess."

Eddie turned around to look at the footprints he'd left in the icing sugar sand, and very nearly crouched down to grab a handful of it like any beachcomber. But there would always be the risk of dormant *c'naatat* lurking in it. The idyll ended right there.

"I'm done, doll," he said. "Time to go."

He almost asked to visit Constantine and relive the brief months of wonder and terror, when alien planets were exciting stories, and he had been a much younger, blinder man. But he wasn't in the mood now. He'd come back one day, maybe with Aras, just as the big guy had promised.

Eddie missed him. He had a long wait until he saw him again.

Aliens' accommodation, Immigrant Reception Center, twenty kilometers south of Kamberra.

Barencoin dropped his bergen on the lobby's dusty inlaid floor and looked around the entrance to the hotel.

"I suppose it's too much to hope they kept the bar open," he said. "But my first stop after I have a pee is to search the stores."

"That's the spirit, Barkers." Jon Becken consulted his handheld. Eqbas crew and ussissi milled around them with the occasional Skavu officer, looking even more bewildered than Ade felt. "Seeing as there's no porter to carry our luggage, allow me to show you all to the presidential suite."

Some of the Skavu had already moved into the center—officers, Ade guessed, because there were too many troops even for this huge complex to swallow—and they gave Ade a long wary look that said they knew who he was, what he was, and that they'd all heard about his robust disagreement with their Fourth To Die, their commander, Kiir. *Stupid titles. But if he comes the acid with me again, I'll make the fucker live up to it.* Ade and Shan were *abominations* to the Skavu, who played their environmental credentials like a fundamentalist religion. It had exploded into violence twice, and Ade was fairly sure it would do so again. He was counting on it. He'd promised Kiir that he'd kill him. Ade didn't like to disappoint.

"What do you suppose their planet's like?" Chahal asked, staring back at the Skavu. "You're right, Izzy. They do look like fucking iguanas."

"I bet it's all frigging cycle routes," Barencoin muttered, and joined in the staring. One of the Skavu barked a sound at the others, and they walked away with some reluctance. "But they can come and have a go if they think they're hard enough."

Ade listened carefully for a hint of unhappiness in the voices of his RM detachment, but they were tired, disoriented, and just grateful to be in a place that said *Earth* to them. He didn't know how long that would last. The bioscreen in Becken's palm, a computer grown into living flesh, had lit up again but wasn't showing any data; they all had one, except Ade. It was a redundant system that still functioned but had nothing to connect to, just like them. *C'naatat* had expelled Ade's early on in its makeover of his genome, but he checked his palm again anyway. He had its own lights, thanks, and his *c'naatat* knew where it wanted to put them.

Ade was still living down the piss-taking about the bioluminescence that had gravitated to his tattoos. It was fine with the ones on his arm, but sometimes he regretted getting so rat-arsed with Dave Pharoah that he'd had his dick tattooed for a bet. It kept Shan amused, anyway. That was worth any number of neon knob jokes from Barencoin.

I'm going to visit the Ankara war graves. I said I would one day, Dave. They can't stop me.

"I'm a lost soul," said Chahal. "I hope we find something to keep us busy."

"Fed up, fucked up, and—well, not that far from home, eh?" Barencoin jerked his thumb over his shoulder at nothing in particular as they climbed the stairs. "Christ, Chaz, I'll give you a list. Smartening up this place, for a start. Filling out your ADF forms. Getting your bank account released. We've got plenty to crack on with."

The lift to the upper floors wasn't half as interesting as the huge stairwell, which had obviously begun life as the central feature of a place that had once wowed tourists. Then it had been turned into a place to store visitors who weren't so welcome before shipping them out again, which struck Ade as an ironic thing for a country founded on transported criminals. The water feature was disconnected now, and a white chalky deposit was all that was left to show an artificial waterfall had been there; but it was still bloody big and impressive. Barencoin sprinted up the stairs with his bergen on his back, which was relatively effortless given the lower gravity and higher oxygen levels of Earth. They still had their Wess'ej muscles and lung capacity from a few years' acclimatization in a tougher world. For a while, they'd find the place a stroll, boiling hot or not.

"Poser," Qureshi called after him. "There's no women here to impress now."

"We've got to keep fit for upcoming shagging duties, though," Becken said, pausing to look over the staircase into the abyss. Ade could see empty beer containers down there. "Even Ade still runs every day, and he's a real superhero who doesn't have to."

Ade smiled. "Piss off, Jon."

"*C'naatat*—I mean, it does amazing stuff. Does it improve sex too?"

"Yeah . . ."

"Really?"

"I'm not telling you. I told you before. Don't ask."

"Well, if Shan hasn't kicked you out, and Aras has two dicks, then you must be getting good at it."

"Leave him alone," said Qureshi. "It's romantic. Don't spoil it, you crude bugger."

There was the usual chorus of *oo-ooo-oo!* and she gestured eloquently with a finger.

Ade shrugged. "I'm going to get married, *properly* this time."

He almost wished he hadn't said it, and braced for barracking. Barencoin leaned over the banister above him. "Who's the lucky woman, and have you told Shan yet?"

"There's your alternative career, Mart, comedy . . ."

"Seriously. Do we get an invite? And who's going to do it? Don't you have to have a passport or residency or something?"

"If the Aussies can process you lot in a few days, they can turn a blind eye to *any* paperwork."

No, he hadn't asked Shan. They were as married as they could ever be, even down to his mum's ring because there was nothing else he owned that he could give her at the time, but it wasn't enough now that they were on Earth and he could do it properly. Anything less smacked of . . . of lack of commitment. *Until death us do part* really meant something when you had *c'naatat.*

"Won't it be bigamy?" asked Becken.

"I was never married before," said Ade.

"I mean Shan. There's Aras. It's not strictly legal, polyandry, is it? Not here."

"Can you even spell it? Sod what's legal here."

"Okay, Aras is an alien. I think she can argue that one of you doesn't count towards her recommended daily allowance. I'll be best man."

It was a joke that started Ade fretting. His mates ribbed him about sharing her, but it was a mix of the usual good-natured banter and general human curiosity about the *logistics* of it all, approached with a kid's need to know the scary stuff. They never asked him the really important things, like if he was worried she had a favorite, or if he thought that

Aras was better at it than he was, or if she would leave him for Aras in the end. It was that messy emotional side of life that still worried him, even if he picked up their memories from the genetic transfer during sex. He *knew* what Shan felt about him from right inside her mind. No regular man could have that certainty.

But he wasn't absorbing the memories now. The gel barrier condom stopped *oursan*. That meant he didn't pick up Aras's memories via Shan either, although she must have been getting them. It made him feel suddenly out of the loop.

Ade stopped at the top to gaze down the full depth of the stairwell, hoping to see Aras somewhere. He'd been very quiet since they landed. Ade hoped it was just the usual stunned silence at seeing a new planet—shit, how many humans could even say that and mean it?—and not some sense of dissatisfaction. There was no sign of him.

Yeah, I've been all over Shan, hogging her attention. I'm like a kid. I'm home, sort of. I know there are things to do and see. I'm excited. Does he feel left out? I just don't know. And I can't know now, not if he won't tell me.

"Ade, come and look!" It was Qureshi's voice. "This is the life!"

He followed the sound. The rooms allocated to the marines were on the coast side of the block. Qureshi and the others clustered on the balcony of one of them, looking out to sea. There was plenty of it.

"Wow," said Chahal. "What a view . . ."

They'd seen alien worlds of astonishing variety—pearl cities, underground cities, cities that covered a whole planet and reached into the sky—but here they were *oohing* and *aahing* about a glittering sea that filled the horizon, standing on a balcony in a disused hotel that needed more than a lick of paint.

Humans were bloody weird. But Ade found it an amazing sight too, probably because he never thought he'd see it again.

"Okay, settle in, and we'll meet back here in ten minutes," Barencoin said. "Then we plan an op to locate and liberate some fucking *beer*."

The banter started again. "Shit, he's taken command, Ade . . ."

"Can we shoot him for mutiny?"

"Not until he's got the beer."

"If I'm promoted over you in the ADF, Jon, I'm going to work on being *unreasonable*."

Ade was relieved they were back on form. They seemed to like the idea of joining the Australian forces; there was no longer a Corps of Royal Marines to feel excluded from, and somehow they'd latched on to that as a source of sanity. There was also the small matter of the FEU being the proverbial sack of cunts not deserving of their loyalty, and probably about to get a serious good hiding from the Eqbas, which added up to a valid pair of reasons for not begging Brussels to be let back in. Ade hadn't been able to bring himself to look at the news coverage of the regimental amalgamations. It would be in some archive somewhere, some badly researched load of shit that got all the dates and military terms wrong—Eddie would have got it right, he knew—and went on about the end of a proud and unique history spanning centuries, and outliving even the monarchy that gave it its name.

But I can keep my badges. It's history now.

He tried to remember where he'd put his medals. Shan had fished them out of the memorial cairn he'd built for her when he thought she was dead, and shoved them back in his pocket. He had another grave now where they'd find a home; Dave Pharoah's.

"Stop moping, Sarge," Chahal said. "What's up with you now?"

"Thinking. That's all." Ade leaned over the balcony. There was a breeze, but it was still too hot. Arriving in January in the southern hemisphere was bad news. "Are you pissed off with Shan?"

"Why?" asked Qureshi.

"Because she wouldn't do a prisoner swap."

"Well, she can't, can she?" Qureshi dropped her voice. "Not with *c'naatat*. It's bad enough knowing Rayat and Lindsay are still out there somewhere without handing the thing over to the government."

Becken joined in. "Seriously, mate, if she'd done that just to get us back in some bloody regiment *pretending* to be

Royals, I'd have had to shoot her, even if she *is* the undead, just to show my displeasure."

Shan respected the detachment. They knew that, even Barencoin. But she was also fond of them, and they probably *didn't* know that, because she was good at being unreadable even when she didn't need to be.

"She thinks the world of you lot," Ade said at last. "She was still trying to lean on the FEU to get a result. I think it mattered to her more than it did to me in the end."

"Not a problem," Barencoin said, checking his watch. "The Corps is gone, the government shat on us and would shit on us again if we stood still long enough, and we're welcome *here*. Job done. Bring the old cow up here for a beer when we've accomplished our mission." He leaned a little further out over the balcony. "See? Buildings. Town. Beer. We'll be back in an hour, even if we leave the transport here and yomp it."

Qureshi held her transfer chip in her hand, the first time she'd had to think about a bank transaction for years. At least they'd been able to keep their accounts open. "Yeah, it's a bit much going into town with a spaceship . . ."

"Do these chips still work?"

"They promised that they would. The FEU can't legally block them, not that they give a toss about the law. Why would they want to, anyway?"

"Because they're shit-houses," said Barencoin. "And they think we don't notice. Of the two, I hate them more for the latter."

"Well, that'll teach 'em to bin us before they worked out if they might need to debrief us . . ."

They remained unspecified, but it didn't matter. Ade would reassure Shan that she hadn't made the detachment make an impossible choice. You could never go back, they said, and it was one of those insultingly stupid reassuring noises people made—like *we can still be friends* and *time's a great healer*—but it was one that also happened to be painfully true.

Everyone needed a fresh start. He had his; now they would have theirs.

While they were calculating the optimum amount of beer in self-chilling bottles that six Royals could fit in bergens and carry in temperatures of more than 40 degrees, Ade caught a whiff of sandalwoodlike scent and turned to see Aras wheeling in a trolley.

"I know you too well," he said, grim as ever, and took off the cover.

The trolley was laden with packs of beer, wine, and some cartons that looked like snacks of some kind. It didn't actually matter if it was shit: it was *Earth* shit, things they hadn't seen for years and sometimes thought they'd never taste again. It was ambrosia by default.

There was a moment of breath-holding silence that really was genuine shock. Then they started laughing.

"Aras, old mate, you're a fucking *king* among baron stranglers," Becken said, a real note of adulation in his voice. "You sure you haven't got any Royal Marine in you?"

"That's more than we really want to know," said Barencoin, and for once he had the grace to stop there. "Thanks, Aras."

The sense of relief in the room seemed to lower the temperature by several degrees. As the impromptu party got under way, Ade felt a door close on him, and settled for grasping the solid, settled feeling in his gut that said he'd done what he had to, and got his mates back in one piece with their self-respect restored. They could take a short leave and enjoy a brief time being civvies for a change before the ADF processed them. The Aussies would want extensive intel debriefs too, but nobody had any illusions, and so far the ADF hadn't crapped on them. Ade's job was done.

"One more task before we put on the old bush hat and corks," Barencoin said, tipping his bottle in the direction of the ocean as if he was toasting it. "Prachy. Extraction and retrieval."

"Come on, Mart . . ."

"I mean it. Just to clear the books. If we hadn't helped Commander Bloody Useless Neville land the beano bombs in the first place, then Ouzhari would still be a nice beach resort."

"Don't I know it." *I should have said no. I should have*

refused Lindsay's order. It's not like I didn't know she might use the bloody things. "It's *my* job."

"It's *our* job, Ade. Come on. For old time's sake. A bit of blowing shit up and causing mayhem. Haven't done that in a bloody long time." Barencoin spread his arms to canvass opinion from the others. "Who's in? Snatch squad. Grab a granny."

"That's your sex life in a nutshell," said Becken.

"Come on, grow a pair. Once Shan gets a location from her paramilitary bunny-huggers, we could be in and out like a greased weasel."

Qureshi, ever the big sister, took a ladylike sip of her beer and wiped her lips on the back of her hand. Her pronouncements carried weight. "I'm in. Can't turn back the clock, but at least we can avoid the crazy parrot-woman nuking Brussels to find her."

They made it sound like a lark. They were bored; the last couple of years had been boring by Royal Marines' standards, by *any* military standards. But this was their way of saying they still felt guilty about Ouzhari and that they had to claw back a little self-respect and decency.

"We're all in, then," said Chahal. "Right, Sue?"

Webster nodded, bottle to her mouth, and swallowed. "Beats building lavatories, mate."

Ade had no choice. He would have done it anyway. Shan might have been a terrific cop and as hard as they came, but she still wasn't a commando, and he was. It was nice to be the best at something.

All he had to do now was talk Shan into persuading Esganikan to let them do the job.

Kidnapping old ladies wasn't how he thought he'd finish his special forces career, and it probably wouldn't make much difference to Earth in the long run.

But some things were *right,* and had to be done.

Reception Center, fifth floor.

Shan stopped in her tracks. "Oh, for fuck's sake," she said. "Tell me you're just reading that for research."

Esganikan was kneeling in her comfort position—which still made Shan's eyes water at the thought of the pressure on her knees—and reading a battered Bible. She looked up with a jerk that made her crest of red hair bob alarmingly.

"I want to know what Deborah Garrod believes is taking place," she said. "I found this book in the cupboard by the bed. This is Revelations."

"Oh." *Thanks, Gideons. Whatever crazy ideas she gets now will all be your fault.* "There was never a sequel, was there? Just a happy ending."

Esganikan did her angry parrot impression, crest of hair quivering as she tilted her head. It was actually curiosity, moving her head to get a sharper focus with those cloverleaf pupils, but it didn't send that message to humans. "Why is this bad? Your disapproval is obvious."

"I didn't say it was *bad.*" Shan helped herself to the jug of water on the table and poured a glass. *Human room: human stuff.* It might have been an abandoned hotel, but it did feel good and familiar. There was a lot to be said for decent upholstery and plumbing. "I just have a recoil reaction to people who base policy on noncontemporaneous reports written long after the incident and translated through a number of languages. It's a cop thing. Personally, I'd wait to take a statement from God if I were you. Get him to sign it, too, in case he retracts."

Esganikan either didn't understand the references and wasn't going to stop to ask for explanation, or she didn't think it was an incisive analysis. "But much of this work says that you have to treat your fellow beings with consideration, as you would want them to treat you. I can find nothing to object to."

"It never caught on," Shan said. "They usually skip that bit and concentrate on the smiting, destruction, and vengeance."

"But not Deborah's people."

Shan gulped down the water and teetered on the brink of challenging her. "Chances are," she said, "that half the faithful out there think this is the Second Coming. Not just the Christians, either. Lots of religions say their deity will come back one day and mete our judgment to the sinners, and then make things all better again for the good guys. I'm sure you can join up the dots on that one."

"They ought to welcome necessary but harsh measures on this planet, then."

"We've always had lunatics who wanted wars to happen so the apocalypse could take place. Funny way to love Jesus." The nearest wess'har had to a religion was the doctrine of Targassat, an economist with a noninterventionist, eco-friendly outlook. It was also the philosophical rift that made some wess'har leave Eqbas Vorhi and settle on Wess'ej for a simpler lifestyle that didn't involve policing the galaxy. Shan thought it was a good example. "Look, you might agree to differ and move to a new planet rather than fight over Targassat, but humans have slaughtered each other over their imaginary friend. Get it?"

"Should I explain things to humans in those terms? Would that make things run more smoothly?"

Shan nearly choked on her water in her rush to kill that idea stone dead. "Whatever you do, don't drag religion into this. It'll happen anyway. You won't like it."

"Very well. But I understand human reactions better now."

"Not all humans believe in god."

"Religion has its roots in the human way of thinking, though." Esganikan closed the Bible like a kid being told to turn off the light and go to sleep, as if she couldn't put it down. Shan decided she preferred the cliché where aliens got the wrong idea about human culture from watching TV instead. "If there is no deity, then they imagine it. That must come from something fundamental in their minds. If not, then the deity exists."

"Eddie is better at analyzing this than I am. Aras, even. Look, I haven't come to discuss theology. There's some stuff we need to get straight."

"Very well."

"Why didn't you tell me that Shapakti had worked out how to remove *c'naatat* from humans?"

Esganikan seemed unmoved, as Shan expected. "Does it matter to you? You don't want yours removed."

"No, but it's rather *relevant* when you think that the FEU is frigging well herniating itself to get a slice of me, isn't it? And when it means you could have a countermeasure for the bloody thing."

"You're angry."

"I like to be kept in the loop. Especially where my personal parasites are concerned. If you don't keep me in the loop, I get worried and think you're hiding things from me, and then I'm a real pain in the arse, I promise you. It's a cop thing."

"And an Eddie thing."

"Level with me in future, okay?" Shan's gut said that Esganikan wouldn't, but wess'har really did have different ideas of relevance from humans. Nevyan had failed to tell Shan things, too, and Nev was as straight as a die. Maybe she was being too hard on Esganikan. "The other thing is that I'm now talking to greens in Europe, indirectly, and pinning down Prachy's location. I'm going to extract her, probably with the marines, and bring her back here for trial."

Esganikan didn't bat an eyelid. "You must shoot her."

"Well, this is Earth, and I'm still a copper one way or another, and this time we'll do it my way. Quietly. No flattening cities. Okay?"

"You're foolish."

"You're welcome." Shan hadn't expected approval. Her gut told her, as it had told Ade, that they really ought to do it by the book, or as far by the book as an obstructive FEU would make possible. "And you're going to give me the speech that she'll be dead in the end, and so will half or more of Europe, so why do I bother with the pantomime. Well, I'll save you the speech, and tell you that I stuck to wess'har law on Bezer'ej with Parekh, and now I'm sticking with human law on Earth."

Esganikan picked up the Bible again and flipped through the pages to near the end. "I shall kill Prachy anyway. The laws of Eqbas Vorhi are in operation."

Shan's moral compass rarely let her down. It was a stupid gesture, maybe, but the alternative was to stand back and do nothing, or take part in something that rankled with her.

"I've stepped way outside the law," Shan said. "Beating up prisoners. Making bastards disappear for good when the courts couldn't or wouldn't. Using terrorists to do my dirty work, even. I'm not saying I'm right, but I know what I can sleep with and what I can't. Okay? Illogical, but true."

Esganikan stared at her for a while. "If you fail, I shall have to do it."

"I better not fail, then."

"You think Prachy is in your former homeland, don't you? You fear for England."

"I'm not doing any special pleading for home. I know the score. But I won't enjoy thinking of the Skavu being there."

Esganikan didn't answer.

"Okay, Commander, I'm going to be putting pressure on the FEU via Eddie Michallat, on the off chance that they'll give in to our demands, and then I'll let you know when we're going in. Okay?"

"Agreed," said Esganikan, and went back to reading.

Shan left before she began venting useless anger and walked down the stairs, listening to the echoing cacophony of Eqbas voices and ussissi, and wondering what the Skavu found to live on in the desert. Most were still camped out at St George, thank God. The thought of thousands of them swarming around here made her shudder. At least she could delay their deployment in Europe until the FEU got the picture.

You seriously think Earth can be adjusted *without it ending up like Umeh, a global war? Bioweapons?*

But as Eddie was fond of saying, every little helped. And adding a pebble to the avalanche was still adding a pebble that wouldn't otherwise have been there.

Shan found Ade waiting in the lobby, stretched out in a chair with his eyes shut. He was wearing new clothes, a major development in itself. It was just plain blue pants and a white casual shirt, the current style with a turned-up collar, but he might as well have been wearing a tuxedo. She'd only ever seen him in some variation on his uniform, and—very rarely—light brown wess'har working clothes. He owned nothing else. It made him look very different.

"Hey, where'd you get the new rig?"

Ade looked up. "I bought it."

"Jesus, have you been off camp?"

"I asked Bari's bagman Shukry to convert some of my account and pick up some stuff for us." He held up a new charge chip. "I thought the lads might be able to walk around town without being recognized if they tried. The uniform really sticks out a mile here."

"Good thinking." She looked down at her own clothing: a mix of black police uniform, sports vest, and brown riggers' boots, the boots Ade had gone to great lengths to acquire for her from the crew in Umeh Station. She treasured them for that reason, but they were inherently scruffy, and she'd have to smarten up soon. "I'm not exactly in best blues. Where's Aras?"

"He wants to stay here."

"Are we going somewhere, then?"

"Yes."

"Oh." She really didn't feel able to concentrate on leisure right then, but Ade had that appealing expression that said it mattered a lot to him. "Where?"

"There's a bar down on the waterfront. I'd really like that beer we talked about."

"We can't go out and leave Aras here on his own."

"He won't come. I tried. He says people need to get used to aliens first or we'll end up with a crowd staring at him all night."

It was another thing that hadn't really hit home before now. She'd become so focused on the job and so immune to differences between the species she dealt with that she'd forgotten what a public order problem Aras would create simply by going outside among humans, even within the security zone. She was mortified. She thought of him sitting in their scruffy room, alone and miserable, and felt she was losing him somehow, that a gulf had opened between them. She couldn't let that happen.

"You have to start taking him out, Ade. Take him to a wildlife sanctuary or something."

"It's okay," Ade reached up and gave her hand a brief

squeeze. "Barencoin's taken him under his wing. The lads are working their way through the beer he found for them and keeping him entertained."

"Okay."

"I promise I'll drag him out soon. Shukry's given me a list of places he can take us so Aras can see animals." Ade lowered his eyes for a second. "I thought I might take him with me when I visit Ankara, too. Dave's grave. Is that okay?"

Shan still felt as if she was abandoning Aras, and now guilty that she found herself ready to just walk out of this bizarre situation—a disused refugee hotel full of alien invaders, which included her—and sit down with a drink where nobody knew anything about her.

"Of course you can, sweetheart," she said. "You don't have to ask me."

"Did you know they've got a memorial to *Actaeon* in Leeds now? If I could trust the FEU not to play silly sods and try to detain us, I'd want to go."

Shan wasn't sure if she was ready for that yet. The FEU warship *Actaeon* had been blown apart by wess'har missiles in retaliation for its role in events that led to the destruction of Ouzhari, and to her apparent death. Deserved fate or not, the news made her uncomfortable when she finally heard it. She felt worse about it as time wore on.

I wasn't dead. Okay, that wasn't the plan, and I really meant to die, but I *wasn't dead. And a bit of me thinks that Nevyan destroyed* Actaeon *more out of vengeance for my death than for that bloody island.*

But wess'har didn't think like that. Did they? So *Actaeon*'s fate wasn't her fault.

Shan ran her fingers through her hair to tidy it as best she could and gestured to the doors. "Okay, let's go, then. Let's fantasize about being normal and drink beer that can't possibly get us drunk."

"You have no idea how long I've waited for this."

"You're a cheap date."

"And better hide the sidearm. If locals see it, I think they'll get overexcited."

"Good point." She slid the 9mm from the back of her

belt into her jacket. "But I think they'll still know who we are."

It was funny how she could embark on an extrasolar journey at a moment's notice, convinced by a subconscious briefing that it was a noble mission, but walking half a kilometer down a coastal road to a bar felt like a leap into a terrifying void.

You've trod vacuum, girl. You've drifted in space. Try, just try, to see things in that context.

The cordon around the hotel was manned, and at the perimeter there were ADF troops patrolling who didn't seem to be expecting anyone to be entering and leaving on foot. Uniforms hadn't changed that much, but they had no visible body armor. Shan resisted the urge to ask the corporal who stepped cautiously into their path if she could see what he wore for ballistic protection. This was no time to covet new kit. It wasn't as if she and Ade would be staying, or even needing it.

"We're just going for a walk," she said.

The corporal looked around him. "How far, ma'am?"

"The town, or whatever those buildings are over there."

"Okay, that's within the outer cordon. You shouldn't get any unwelcome attention there."

"It's not derelict, is it?"

"No, ma'am. It was easier to leave the locals in situ, so they're inside the cordon too. It's a tiny place. Couple of hundred people."

"No passing trade, then," Ade said cheerfully. "We'd better do our bit to keep the local economy going."

There were tables outside on the paving; a couple of people looked at them when Ade went to the bar to get a couple of bottles, but nothing was said. Shan tried to shut out the intervening years, the century and more between leaving for Mars Orbital and the moment she felt the sunbaked seat burning the backs of her legs through her pants.

Mundane routine was liberating, if she could keep it up.

"Cheers," Ade said, placing the bottle in front of her. It was already running with condensation. The sensation of ice-cold liquid in her mouth and the near-frozen glass in her hand was almost as good as orgasm. "I think we ought to get married. Legally."

She wasn't expecting that, but it was Ade all over. "Only legally on Earth. Wess'har rules are different."

"That's a *no,* then."

"It's a *yes.* I love you. You didn't really expect me to refuse, did you?"

"Not really. But I don't pick up your memories any longer, so I'm not sure if you've changed your mind about me."

"Shit, no. Why would I? You're what a bloke would be if I'd designed Mr. Perfect to order."

It was hard to tell if he was blushing in this heat, but it was the point at which he usually did. "Thanks. It means a lot to me."

"You get to choose the venue and all that guff, then."

Ade took a long pull at the bottle and they gazed out to sea and let the sounds and scents wash over them. And she worked out what the quay was: it was actually part of massive flood defenses that looked as if they extended along the entire coastline. The small detail of climate change brought things home to her even more than the unfamiliar coastline.

The unfamiliar environment made Shan hyperalert, and it was never going to be a regular night out. It was a brief interlude that she might look back on in a hundred, two hundred, even a thousand years and recall with mixed feelings. That upended her more than anything. She couldn't tell if she was happy or sad about it, just that she felt it *intensely* to the point of feeling her eyes sting with suppressed tears.

"If the memory thing bothers you, Ade, we can ditch the gel," she said. "You know. Old-fashioned unprotected sex."

"I'm not putting you through *that* again."

That was never spelled out. "I check myself daily with the ultrasound on the swiss, you know that. Nothing's grown back. No uterus. I can't conceive again."

"I don't know . . ."

"Just a matter of checking, that's all. It won't sneak up on me again."

"I just didn't realize how much I'd come to need to know what goes on in your head. And Aras's, come to that."

Sharing memories came from a strange fusion of two different genetic systems, the wess'har transfer of DNA between male and female—*oursan*—and the genetic memory of the isenj. Maybe there were no other creatures alive who had evolved a system like that: *c'naatat* was the element that made it possible. Shan felt Aras had the measure of *c'naatat* now, and whether it had conscious purpose or not, it behaved like *Toxoplasma gondii*, influencing the behavior of its host for its own ends. She was still grappling with it.

C'naatat, like God, moved in mysterious ways, and Shan wasn't submitting to either's whim.

So where did Esganikan get Prachy's name? Better ask Eddie to ask Rayat . . . the bastard.

She drained her bottle. "I need you to know what I think, too, Ade," she said. "Let's forget the gel for a night and see what happens. Okay? You know I'll run the checks first."

"As long as you *tell* me if something goes wrong this time, Boss. Don't ever go through that alone again, will you?"

Ade was the most decent human being she'd ever met. She wanted to take every pain from him and put his life right—breathe for him, even. She felt that about Aras, too, but sometimes Aras was harder to reach. It was comforting simply to take Ade's hand and mesh her fingers with his.

"If Esganikan looks you over one more time, I might even punch her," Shan said.

"I'm irresistible, Boss. Maybe she heard about my novelty lightshow."

It was worth seeing if Ade had any suspicions. "Does she strike you as acting strangely?"

"She's a *long* way from backup without the resources she expected to get, she's got trigger-happy Skavu, she's pulling back-to-back tours of duty, and she has to work out a whole new plan in theater because the situation on the ground keeps changing. Been there, Boss. It makes you sweat at night."

That was true; the planning for this mission was still sketchy. A million years' head start on humans and a much more sensible outlook didn't solve every problem.

When do I decide it's time to pull out and go home? When I see some environmental progress? When I'm sure the Skavu aren't going to lose it and trash the place?

The more she looked, the more she found elements that she could—*should*—deal with.

If Aras was right about *c'naatat* and *Toxaplasma,* then the bloody thing had made her anxious enough to come on this stupid mission in some hope—whatever that meant in terms of microorganisms—that she might give it a lift to new hosts. She couldn't get that thought out of her head.

Bad call, Germ Boys. You didn't realize whose arse you crawled up, did you? I'm wise to you. I'm here because I need to be.

Ade stretched luxuriously, distracting her for a moment. It was turning into a balmy evening; a refreshing breeze had picked up, laden with interesting scents of seaweed, hot metal and frying food. *Chips.*

"Another beer, Mrs. Bennett?"

"I'll force one down if you insist, Mr. Bennett. Shall we see if there's anything safe on the menu?"

"I'd really fancied a fried egg," said Ade. "Until the memory popped up of what Aras thinks of them and where they come from."

Wess'har were vegan anyway, but the prospect of eating items that emerged from an animal's backside seemed to horrify them on a whole new level. She recalled an embarrassing mealtime explaining human eating habits to a wess'har. "I do smell chips, though. Let me inquire."

Damn, she hadn't been this person in years, and not just chill-sleep years. This was the relatively carefree days of her time as a detective sergeant, and a few laughs in the police social club bar after the shift finished.

Just a few hours' break. The Gaia contacts are seeing what they can dig up. You've got time for this, at least.

Chips. She inhaled and followed the aroma.

Yes, it was definitely turning into a nice evening. She pushed Esganikan to the back of her mind, and got a strange look from the barman. It was obvious that she and Ade weren't local.

"You security?" asked the barman.

Nobody got into the area without authorization. Shan indicated the pistol-shaped bulge in her jacket pocket. "Do I look like an alien?"

"Nah," he said. "I can spot a cop at ten klicks. Tell all your mates we could do with the extra custom."

It was strangely comforting. She could never shed that Detective Superintendent persona "I'll do that," she said, a carried a big plate of fat, oil-glazed steak fries back to the table. It was the most wonderful meal she could imagine.

Ade closed his eyes and placed a chip in his mouth with perfect accuracy. He chewed, a slight frown creasing his nose.

"No offense, Boss," he said at last, "but this is as good as sex. I swear."

"Yeah." Shan was transfixed by the perfection; crisp skin, meltingly fluffy interior, and the optimum sprinkling of salt. Back home—yes, home was still F'nar—chips never turned out quite this good. It was the oil, or the way the soil influenced the taste of the spuds or something, but F'nar chips would never be Earth chips. "I'm with you on that, Ade."

"Shukry said he could get us legal clearance for a civil wedding ceremony," he said. Rare delicacy or not, the chips hadn't distracted him from tidying up his life. "You can wear a dress."

"I'd look like a gorilla in drag."

"You'd look lovely."

"You really want me to?"

"Only if you're comfortable in it."

Shan wouldn't be, but it was only for a matter of hours at most, and she found she'd do pretty well anything to make Ade happy. Like Aras, he hadn't had enough harmless joy in his life. She was considering the possibility of a smart dress, nothing frothy or girly, the Prachy issue still in her forebrain but dulled by the bliss of a plate of chips, when her swiss chirped.

"I never get junk messages now," she said, flipping open the screen and inserting an earpiece. She didn't want the few drinkers at the far table to hear her.

F'nar ITX.

It was Nevyan. *Shit.* She hadn't called her. It was still just days ago in Shan's mind, not twenty-five years. "Nev, I'm sorry, I haven't called Eddie either—"

"It's Giyadas." The voice was tinged with overtone, but it was Eddie's accent, perfect English. Little Giyadas had grown up. Shan wasn't quite ready for that. "I remember you, Shan. You must speak to my mother later, but first I have bad news for you."

"Eddie?" It was her first thought. "Is he okay?"

"Eddie's fine, and you have to speak to him too. But first, listen—Esganikan Gai is carrying *c'naatat.* She infected herself with Rayat's blood, but I don't imagine she told you, or else you and I would be having a very different conversation right now."

"Oh shit . . ."

Shan's evening was suddenly heading downhill fast. Ade paused in mid-chew, listening intently to Shan's side of the exchange.

"You're a citizen of F'nar, Shan," said Giyadas. "A matriarch—an *isan.*"

"I know." Shan struggled to work out a plan on the fly, and stood by for a bollocking from Giyadas for not spotting Esganikan's ruse already. "Give me a few minutes and I'll work out how we tackle this."

"No need," said Giyadas. "The matriarchs of F'nar have asked that you kill her. In fact, we *order* it."

7

*The Holy Prophet Muhammad was asked by his compan-
ions if kindness to animals was rewarded in the life hereaf-
ter. He replied: "Yes, there is a meritorious reward for
kindness to every living creature."*

BUKHARI

Immigrant Reception Center, south of Kamberra: next morning.

Aras could see uniformed police on the road leading to
the center's outer perimeter fence, building another barrier
with posts set in cement and a brightly colored gate that
folded neatly into the upright sections on both sides. They'd
begun work just as it was getting light and the air was still
relatively cool.

He found that staring out of the window helped. They'd
been discussing Esganikan for hours now. Shan had paused
to argue about the time scale with Giyadas, who seemed to
have grown into an even more formidable matriarch than
Nevyan.

"Yeah, and I'm saying that we *have* to get another credi-
ble commander in place before I do it," Shan whispered. It
was a ferocious hiss, as loud as she dared speak in case she
was overheard beyond this room. The ancient device had its
limitations. "Or the whole thing goes to rat shit, and I'm not
taking over this fucking mission, okay? I'm not competent
to run an army and an environmental remediation team. I'm
a bloody copper."

Ade watched Shan getting more agitated and considered
taking the swiss, telling Giyadas to mind her own business,
and destroying the ITX link for good. He'd also considered

taking a device and removing Esganikan himself, but that
had been pure anger, and it would only have made Shan's
situation worse. He could hear Giyadas's voice very faintly.
She seemed in a hurry.

Shan waited, listening, but she was blinking rapidly, jaw
muscles twitching. "Okay, so Rayat might find a way to tip
off Kiir . . . so? Well, I'll take that risk. I'm the one on the
ground here . . . no, I can't do that. You have to trust me on
this. I have to have her second-in-command in place first.
Laktiriu Avo. She needs to get up to speed."

The argument slowed to a weary series of grunts, then
Shan shut the link and sat down at the small table again.

"I'm doing this to my time scale," she said, as if they
needed convincing.

"Okay, Boss." Ade put his hand on her arm. "I still think
you should leave Prachy to me and the lads."

"No, because if I pull out of that, Esganikan will wonder
why." Shan shook her head. "We go ahead with that. Here's
the op order, then. I get Eddie to do a BBChan piece outing
Prachy, and if that doesn't get the FEU to give way by the
deadline, we go after her. Then I concentrate on Laktiriu as
Esganikan's successor. Then, when I think she's up to it, I do
the job."

"Then," Ade said quietly, "we get married, and then you,
me, and Aras go home. Yes? Because if you stay after that—if
any of us stay—then I don't think we'll *ever* be able to go."

Shan stared at Ade for a few seconds before she did that
little adoring frown at him, as if she'd hurt him and regretted it. Aras seldom seemed to evoke that in her these days. It
didn't trouble him, but he did take note of it; Ade was in-
dulged like a child, and Aras was expected to be an adult.
That seemed fair, given that he was the senior house-
brother.

"Why do you agree to assassinate one woman and yet go
to great lengths to stop the killing of another—who'll be
killed anyway?" Aras asked.

Shan looked fixed and grim. It was her *don't start with me*
look. "Because one is a serious biohazard, and the other
isn't."

"That wasn't the answer you gave Esganikan about Prachy."

"Okay, Aras, maybe I'm getting wess'har about things. The two are not related. One target fits in one ethical framework, and the other fits in a different one."

"Human rules for humans, wess'har for wess'har."

"I hadn't thought of it that way, but it's one possible explanation, yes. All I know is that they look like different situations to me."

"Motive doesn't matter."

"And they'll both end up dead. But yes, motive still matters to me most of the time."

Shan was very pale now, pumped with adrenaline. She wasn't a woman who took the easiest path through life; she agonized over what was right, and frequently did what was least convenient for herself, an unusual thing in a human. The only surrender she had made to expedience was to let him and Ade live. They were bio-hazards too, just like Lindsay and Rayat—and Esganikan.

Ade kept squeezing her arm, almost as if he was reassuring himself she was still there. "How do we work out if she's infected any of her crew?"

"That worries me, too."

"Wess'har are poor at feigning reactions," Aras said. "If the Eqbas crew show caution about physical contact with me, it's a fair assumption that they aren't carriers."

"But do they *know*?"

"I'd say not."

Shan raked her hair with her fingers. She needed to get some sleep, *c'naatat* or not. They'd been debating this all night. "Okay, one piece at a time. Prachy first. Let me call Eddie. Lovely, isn't it? The first thing I say to him in twenty-five years is, 'Hi, mate, do me a favor, will you?'"

She got up and went into the bathroom, probably for privacy; that was Shan's habit at home. At least the hotel complex now had a good water supply, thanks to the desalination pipeline the Eqbas technicians had set up. Government engineers had already arrived to cluster around it and marvel at its efficiency.

"It's outcomes," said Ade, scratching his hair. "Shan's all about outcomes. You know that. Very clear about consequences. Esganikan's a risk."

"*We're* risks. *We've* both infected a human deliberately. Esganikan hasn't. We live, she dies. Does that not trouble you?"

"Are you *defending* the crafty bitch? Or saying we should be fragged too?"

"No, I'm simply saying that it's inconsistent, and that it causes me distress as a result. I have no answers or better suggestions, other than to walk away from it."

"Then why are you riding Shan about it? Life's full of dilemmas we never solve."

"Because I always feared that she would be used, Ade. She's very loyal. She's been used by the matriarchs before. I don't want to see her killed carrying out the orders of matriarchs who summoned the Eqbas in the first place."

"Hey, we were bloody glad they did at the time, remember? When we thought Shan was dead? We wanted the shit kicked out of the FEU. The only thing that changed is that Shan came back. Everyone and everything else is still *dead*."

It was true, of course. Aras wondered how they might be looking at events on Earth now if they had all spent the last twenty-five years living out their lives on Wess'ej. Perhaps the whole situation would have seemed more like an ancient wound, a scar, the incident recalled but the pain forgotten. It certainly wouldn't have felt this urgent. Cryo-suspension had done nothing to stop the momentum of events that thrust them forward back then. Aras sat in silence with Ade, not wanting to talk further, until Shan came out of the bathroom toweling her hair.

She took a comb and tugged at tangles. "I wonder if the FEU appreciates the irony that the only reason Esganikan hasn't just dumped a metric fuckload of human-specific pathogens into their atmosphere and finished them off is because she doesn't want to harm other life as a side-effect—like power stations going critical and a few continents of decaying human flesh polluting the place."

Aras tried to draw the line between venting his own distress and being helpful in a situation that seemed to be escalating out of control. "I think Esganikan badly underestimated the time this restoration would take."

"No shit, Sherlock." Shan looked crestfallen for a moment. "Look, I came because I felt I had to keep an eye on her, as if I could do a damn thing to stop the Skavu and the slaughter and the whole shebang, as if there was a *nice* way of removing humans to make way for other species. I know bloody well that there isn't, and I know I've presented the FEU with temptation just by being here. But I'm bloody glad I *did* come now, because if I hadn't, who would have dealt with Esganikan? But I swear we *will* go home, as soon as this is over, and that removes all temptation for anyone else to make a grab for *c'naatat*. No us, no Esganikan. It'll be over."

"So, as ever, you make the best of a bad job, and find a retrospective justification for it."

"I said we'll leave *as soon as I'm done here*."

"You miss this kind of life."

"What?"

"This is what you do best. I can see it on your face. You like *sorting* situations. You have no idea how to do anything else."

Shan paused for a second as if Aras's accusation had hit a nerve.

"I think the novelty wore off a long time ago."

"Accept, then, that the FEU may not hand over Prachy, that you might not be able to find her, and the outcome in fifty years will be exactly the same, except for the state of your conscience."

"Come on, knock it off, you two," Ade said. He hated arguments, and Aras regretted reminding him of the way violence always started in his childhood home. But some things had to be *said*. "I agree with the Boss. Sorry, mate."

"And Prachy can't *vanish*," Shan said. "Europe's the most heavily cammed, scanned, and recorded society in the world. She can't leave her house without public security surveillance picking her up, or even buy groceries without the transaction being scanned, recorded on her medical records, and charged to her account. She can't move anywhere without passing through a monitoring system." Shan held out a small device, flipped it open from a small penlike tube to a flat sheet, and laid it on the table. "She never had to assume an identity, you see. Just a civil servant who never thought anyone would come after her, not a spook out in the field like Rayat. Detective work is mostly sifting the obvious. Look." Shan pulled a file of documents and screen grabs on the display into a fan so they could see some of each one: directories, publications, and lists. "PRACHY. Patchy audit trail, starting with the Civil Service Staff Association's list of retired members. Cross-referencing with awards, I find the field she claimed to work in—treasury forecasting—and then I find her writing papers at some university, because smart people don't usually want to pack it all in when they have to retire. Combine that with a few totally unconnected comments she's made in public fora about the state of her local waste management service, and I pin her down to one of three cities. Get one of the Gaia crowd's friend of a friend of a friend to check the mass transit passes database—because Europe really got a taste for tracking people's movements in the twenty-first century, and never stopped—and I have her home address. It took me four hours, start to finish. No rocket science necessary."

Aras and Ade looked at each other. It seemed like an impressive feat, but then Shan was a police officer, and an expert at taking one or two pieces of a puzzle and working out who might give her the others. Eddie would have been proud of her. They worked the same way.

"I take it she's not at home," said Ade.

"No, the word from greens on the ground is that she hasn't been seen for a couple of days, and the transit guy lost her at the port authority data portal. So my guess is that the FEU moved her to the mainland to lose her. It wouldn't be so hard to find her in a few small islands with thirty million people, as I've shown, not if she kept her real name until the last few days."

As far as Aras was concerned, Prachy was missing, and

the deadline would not be met, and Esganikan would launch an attack on those she held responsible for harboring her, the FEU government. The whole stalking exercise was a massive waste of effort. It might also put Shan in danger. He was getting more frustrated and angry by the minute.

"Aren't you going to ask me what I do next?" she asked. She held up the flattened communications device. "Transit guy's database includes full ID. Hologram image, biometric security markers, the works, so, ironically, the security services can track naughty people when they need to. All those can go out via BBChan when Eddie does his piece. Now, tell me—would *you* want to shelter her once you saw what was coming down the pike? Someone will see her, sell her a coffee, let her ride the monorail. Someone will grass on her. Humans are lovely creatures like that."

"It's a shame you can't ask Esganikan if she remembers any more of what Rayat remembers," said Aras, deadly serious. Shan seemed to take it as sarcasm.

"It's obsolete data anyway. Unless she wants to have a trial and call witnesses." She snapped the sheet back into a tube and took out her swiss. "Time to loose the hunting hacks, gentlemen."

Cabinet Meeting Room, Government House, Kamberra: four days after landing.

"Frankland has to be in intelligence." Niall Storley, the attorney general, had such a quiet voice that he could stop a meeting dead simply by forcing people to strain to hear him. Bari rather admired that strategy. "Records say she was Special Branch and an antiterrorist officer, and then she got busted over some eco-terrorist op and she resurfaced in En-Haz, as it used to be. All the same line of work, strong gene-tech component, and then she ends up in the Cavanagh system at the same time as an FEU spook called Rayat. That's looking like she's got some data they want back. I doubt that the FEU would go to the brink over a simple criminal extradition. They want Frankland for something else."

"Biotech fits," said Andreaou. Everyone had been scouring the archives. "That was the rumor at the time."

"Well, we can't swap her for Prachy, even if we were minded to," said Bari. "One, the Eqbas don't want it. Two, if it's biotech she has access to, we want it. Or at least we want to deny it to the FEU."

"So why are we even discussing it?"

"Because, Niall, I would love to be able tell the UN to shove it, stop trying to broker some *understanding,* and concentrate on reminding the FEU that piling up military assets around a nation's maritime borders is bad form."

Bari had expected a very rough ride in Cabinet for making a string of decisions on the hoof without discussion. Instead, ministers took it all quietly and seemed almost grateful that he was going it alone. Perhaps they wanted someone to blame afterwards, if they thought there would be any *afterwards* when the shit finally hit the fan.

"It must be bloody significant biotech if they're going to all this trouble," said Nairn. "And nothing concrete's coming out of intelligence?"

Storley shook his head. "Nothing. I can't help being curious, even though I know it's not really the biggest issue on the table."

Bari kept an eye on the various status screens in the cabinet room showing the positions of ships, news feeds, and diplomatic contact activity. "It's academic, and I'm damned if I'm going to upset the Eqbas by asking Frankland what makes her so special, but let's keep an eye on that."

"Here's my worry," said Andreaou. "The FEU got away with opening fire on the Eqbas once. They might think they can get away with a lot more without serious consequences."

"Could they?" Storley asked. "I know the Eqbas trashed Umeh, but would they do the same on Earth?"

"We're no more special than the isenj to them, but we have a hell of a lot more wildlife that would be collateral damage."

"I'm not worried for the welfare of the Eqbas, PM, I'm worried about *us*—because if they launch an attack using us as a base, especially bioweapons, then we're automatically an international pariah and we'll come under attack."

Nairn held up a finger. "Our ambassador in Beijing has had private assurances that the Sinostates won't intervene if Europe takes a pounding. Noises, condemnation at the UN, but no action."

"Clears the world stage for them, doesn't it? How about the African Assembly?"

"Waiting and watching. More concerned about stopping refugees coming across its borders."

"Everyone's expecting a shooting match centered on Europe."

Bari sat back and scrolled through the screens to see where the FEU had moved its warships. It was just a gesture. If they were going to attack, they'd use air assets, but it still didn't reassure him.

"I'm going to see if I can get some undertaking from the Eqbas that they'll defend us if we take stick for their activity. I think that's the most I can do." Bari turned to the communications director. "Mel, our ratings?"

"Eighty-seven percent still in favor of going with the Eqbas plan," she said. "But a tangible benefit would help a lot right now."

"I'll get the desalination stepped up and ease water rationing in the major cities. Any other grim business?"

"Prachy, PM," Storley said. "I hear there's a motion going to the UN from the Canadians, asking for Prachy to be handed over to the UN International Crimes Directorate to be tried in neutral territory. The ambassador here says they think it'll take the confrontational heat out of it."

"Niall, I know they've stayed on side since Canh Pho's day, but I wish they'd keep their lovely polite expansionist noses out of it." Bari tried to imagine how an Eqbas would take that move: peacemaking gesture, or trying to obstruct their justice? "Keep me posted, especially if they manage to find any *neutral territory* on this planet. I'm seeing the Eqbas next."

Bari grabbed his folio and walked up the back stairs to his office to wait for Esganikan and her environment scientist,

Mekuliet. He needed a show of Eqbas largesse, something that would not only reassure the Australian electorate that there was some benefit to having aliens in the backyard, but also to show the rest of the world that this was rescue, not invasion. He'd gloss over the population issues. It wasn't as if they were new, or if no human had ever suggested equally draconian measures. There were even humans who'd suggested self-extinction. They'd be recruiting for the Eqbas now.

Esganikan and Mekuliet were sitting in his office, not entirely at ease on chairs, watching the feed from the UN chamber for a few minutes in bemused silence.

"*Should* I have done this through the UN?" Esganikan asked.

"A lot of member states are concerned that you haven't started from that platform," said Bari. It was as good a time as any. "They could extradite and try Prachy for you."

"The UN has shown no ability to make nations unite, so it's of no tactical importance to us. It couldn't even protect the gene banks it set up in the past. The Christians had to step in."

She didn't seem bothered by the extradition idea. "Nevertheless, it's the only truly global organization we have."

"The world can hear me as well from here as it can from the UN headquarters. As I recall, Australia extended the invitation to us to restore global ecology, so *that* is where I start, with the society most likely to be willing to maintain the planet once restored."

"You have to deal with the whole planet eventually."

"Prime Minister, if every nation realized that their boundaries are no protection against a deteriorating environment, I wouldn't need to be here except to punish those responsible for the genocide on Bezer'ej."

Bari chewed the thought over. It was a long way to come just to smack a few humans. Wess'har seemed a remarkably motivated species. "Has your team finished their estimates?"

"Yes. The global population needs to be reduced to approximately one billion or fewer, zero growth to prevent further premature extinctions of other species, and to free up resources to reintroduce species whose habitats have been destroyed by human activity."

So, five or six billion had to go. It was the time and manner of their going that made the difference. But he'd definitely seen worse scenarios. A billion . . . that took Earth back to the population of the nineteenth century. Life wasn't too bad then. It wasn't Year Zero. This was *survivable.*

"We've had *worse* estimates from climate modeling," he said. "We've even got a movement, been going for a few hundred years, dedicated to voluntary human extinction, except it's still here, which always strikes me as being like an anarchists' group drawing up a rule book."

"You'll go extinct anyway," Esganikan said. "Either through the natural course of evolution, or by bringing a disaster on yourselves. The issue for us is how many other species you destroy by altering the environment beyond its normal fluctuations."

"Okay, we pay for the climate change we caused. We still can't agree on how much is down to us."

"You forget that climate change is only one aspect of this. There's killing other life, and irresponsible land use too, and direct poisoning from pollution. Tell me, Prime Minister, when you see images of Umeh, do you see that as your own future?"

"It's hard to get humans to see that. It's hard enough to get them to stop eating things that they know will end up killing them in a few years, let alone something that'll affect future generations. Which is why we're in the mess we're in now."

"But there are many who do heed warnings. They change their lives to reduce the harm to other life-forms, and refuse to use other species for their own benefit."

"I like to think we've got a lot of people like that here."

"Presumably you don't have the monopoly on them."

"No, but we have a long history here in the Pacific Rim states of environmental responsibility and protection."

"Then I'll be looking to you to demonstrate a more

sustainable and civilized lifestyle here, which would include ending all livestock farming and use of animal products."

Bari knew it wasn't going to be easy, and common sense told him this was coming. *Gethes.* Carrion eaters. Humans ate other animals, but didn't need to. He tried to see it through Eqbas eyes: people here objected to dog meat and it was banned, but other cultures couldn't see what the fuss was about. It was still going to be a bloody hard sell. On the other hand, drought had been the end of most cattle and sheep farming, and 90 percent of meat sold now was cell culture anyway.

It'll just be the rich bastards who can afford natural meat . . . and then there'll be a black market in it. . . .

He thought he'd check anyway.

"Does this extend to vat-grown meat and fish?"

Esganikan looked at Mekuliet. Bari thought it was an ethics issue, but the Eqbas seemed not to separate ethics from anything.

"We still find it repellent," Mekuliet said. "But for the time being, it can remain, because no live person suffers."

"Person?"

Esganikan looked puzzled for a moment, then the light went on. "All creatures are people. We have no concept of our own species as being unique."

"Got it," said Bari. If he'd thought negotiating was hard, then non-negotiating was even harder. Did he dare ask for some sweetener to balance that? He imagined the headlines when this went public—GO VEGAN OR ELSE. It was the kind of small dumb thing—and it *was* small, in the scheme of global catastrophe—that brought down governments while much bigger sins like sleaze, death squads, and dubious allies passed unremarked. "Time scale?"

"As soon as you can."

Bari wished he'd studied the interminable Michallat programs more thoroughly. One thing he recalled was that wess'har—and Eqbas were still wess'har—came out straight with whatever was on their mind. It had to be worth trying.

Esganikan certainly wouldn't understand the give and take that was expected and unspoken, and he had no cards to play anyway.

"Can I ask you two direct questions, Commander?"

"Yes."

"If the FEU attacks us, will you give us military support?"

"Australia is our *pilot project,* as you call it, just as the Northern Assembly was our basis for progress on Umeh. Yes, we would defend you."

Shit. That was so simple. "And is there any environmental improvement you could carry out in the short term to show our citizens what's possible? Hope is a great motivator for humans. Most of our grand climate change remedies haven't worked as well as we'd hoped."

Mekuliet, who'd been speaking when spoken to up to that point, suddenly perked up. "You have inadequate models. I saw your attempts at reflecting solar energy with devices in orbit. Your concepts are promising, but your calculations are flawed."

Puny Earthling. He really expected her to say it. "There's also the complication that countries don't like geo-engineering because it might benefit one nation's environment but screw theirs. Very contentious. Wars have been fought over it."

"We have to think in global terms," she said. "While we decide whether to accept *Shan Chail*'s wish that the planet be restored to a much earlier optimum state, such as the early twentieth century, what measure would *you* find most useful for your country right now?"

"Water," Bari said. He didn't even have to think about it. "We need more water. Always have."

He had no idea if Canh Pho had this conversation with Esganikan in the past. But even if he had, it was worth repeating. Bari wasn't sure if he was asking for rain-seeding or sophisticated recovery methods, although he'd seen the Eqbas tapping deep into the desert to find water that engineers here couldn't get at. Bari was ready to believe that a million years head start on humans bought you something akin to magic.

"Desalination," said Mekuliet. "You use it, but we can do it better. Your engineers have seen how we created a desalinated supply for the reception center."

She made it sound so simple. Bari knew he should have involved the scientists right from the start, but he hadn't, and now he was glad he'd played it that way. They would have dived straight into detail when what really needed doing was to look this relatively benign army of occupation in the eye and ask if they would take care of the place if the residents behaved.

It *was* that simple. Now the scientists could get on with the job. He had no doubt that the Eqbas would play it exactly as they saw fit, and roll over any interdepartmental rivalries.

"I'll get the Minister for the Environment to see you right away, *Chail*," he said, pleased with himself that he'd picked up at least one honorific.

The two Eqbas left, and Bari took a few minutes' breathing space to reflect on the fact that it was barely a week since they'd landed and he was getting results. The planet hadn't been plunged into war. Death rays hadn't reduced the place to rubble. The future was going to be horribly hard, but not for Australia or its neighbors, and weaning the country off meat was a small price to pay.

He sipped his coffee, kept hot since early that morning in the socket on his desk. So Shan Frankland had enough influence to make Esganikan think twice about the restore point for Earth; that was something he hadn't realized.

Nobody was ever going to hand her over to the FEU, then. And if the FEU were going to get shitty over that—well, now there was a new line of defense.

The Eqbas fleet and its Skavu army.

Surang, Eqbas Vorhi: Place of Maintenance and Innovation for Fleet Vessels.

Rayat still had time—days anyway; maybe months.

He sat among the transparent panels of the maintenance control room, feeling as if he was in a room full of shower curtains. The sheets of material were alive with colors and movement, looking very much like *virin've*—the transparent Eqbas communication devices—after a nasty accident in a rolling mill. When he reached out to touch them, they were soft and pliable. This was the live code that instructed the extraordinary liquid-solid nanite technology of the wess'har to create a home, or a robe, or a constantly changing warship. Wess'har could program matter.

"These each correspond with ships in the fleet," said Rajulian's obliging neighbor, Co Beyokti. "Each collection of materials—each ship—recognizes its parts, and only those, and communicates instructions from this *banivrin* only to them. So we have no accidents where parts of other objects merge with each other, and the technology doesn't run wild and start deconstructing cities. Does that make sense to you?"

Rayat's eyes searched for patterns in the shifting colors, and the bioluminescence in his hands, the legacy of his time among the bezeri, flared into wild rainbow sequences. He could speak in light, even if he'd fought hard to keep his vocal abilities during his time underwater; but the lights were random, like someone mimicking an unknown foreign language to try to squeeze meaning from it. Rayat quelled the signals with an effort and looked up into Beyokti's face. His head was cocked completely to the right.

"They told me you could do that," he said. "But seeing it is quite another matter."

Rayat had him distracted. *Good.* He could handle the programming sheets any time and not draw attention, then. "It's my party trick. I used to be aquatic, for a while . . ."

"I think you must be very brave to face that."

"Drowning isn't so bad after the first few times. It's like going to the *dentist.* You can will yourself not to feel fear or discomfort."

Beyokti didn't know what a *dentist* was, seeing as he understood no English at all, but drowning had seized his attention anyway. Wess'har loved to hear everyone's stories, something the Eqbas and the Targassati exiles on Wess'ej still had in common. Learning eqbas'u and mastering the overtone—*c'naatat* could do wonders with a human larynx—had been one of Rayat's best decisions. It opened the planet to him, although not quite enough of it.

"You must tell me more," said Beyokti.

"I will." Rayat draped a program sheet over one arm. *And I don't even have to lie.* "I've lived here twenty years, and I still don't understand how you do all this. I know the principle, but that's all. It's quite astonishing. How do you input the code changes? With a stylus?"

Beyokti took out a glove that was made of the same transparent, color-shot material. Transparent materials, from the tough and beautiful glass all wess'har used to the slab of gel that formed those extraordinary Eqbas "tea tray" microscopes, were a wess'har obsession. Rayat slipped the glove onto his hand, noting how it reshaped itself from long multijointed spidery fingers to fit his shorter, thicker human hands.

"Here," said Beyokti. He guided Rayat's hand to a blank area of the sheet. "Trace your finger like so . . ."

A line of magenta light followed Rayat's fingertip. He touched the tips together, as if using a *virin,* just to see what would happen, and the color changed to a vivid green. For a few seconds he was lost in a childlike finger-painting moment.

"Now tell me what I just did," he said, smiling. Eqbas seemed fascinated that humans showed their teeth to indicate good humor. It came of living alongside ussissi, whose display of teeth meant anything but a good mood. "I bet I didn't write a coherent program change there, did I?"

"No." Beyokti trilled, amused. "The template will recognize that as useless data, and won't attempt to incorporate it into any instructions. But the engineers on board a ship currently in ten light-years from here will see a pretty scrawl appear on their redundant code screen. It simply spits out what it can't use, and shows it to the crew in case this is significant."

It was perfect. Rayat was careful not to sully his faith with the dirty necessities of his job, but there always seemed to be a solution at hand when he most needed one. His pragmatic self told him that he was the one who worked bloody hard to find solutions, not a higher being.

"Where are the programs for the Skavu fleet on Earth?" he asked.

Beyokti led him through the forest of gently swaying sheets. "Here. They don't look any different from the modern fleet, but the ships are much older, and the technology less flexible. But they still work—and we waste nothing."

"Very commendable," said Rayat, just managing to stop himself mentioning Targassat. It was hard to offend any wess'har, but it would be a robust debate that he didn't have time for at that moment. "Show me the flagship. If I can't do any harm, may I write something on this for the commander to see?" Then he slipped in the only actual lie he had told in the whole process. "Fourth To Die Kiir. I met him briefly."

He hadn't, of course. But Beyokti wouldn't check that, not for a long time anyway.

"Certainly."

"Can I schedule it to be sent?" asked Rayat.

"We update the Skavu fleet in about six days."

"Ah, that's soon enough." Rayat let himself smile, thinking that it probably looked like happy recall of meeting the Skavu officer. "Maybe he'll reply. Like a *message in a bottle*."

Rayat wrote carefully, and Beyokti watched him with as much comprehension as Rayat would have managed faced with a sheet full of kanji.

KIIR, ESGANIKAN HAS INFECTED HERSELF WITH *C'NAATAT*. YOU MUST ASSESS THE RISK. DOCTOR MOHAN RAYAT.

It looked very pretty, in vivid turquoise light that quivered slightly as the sheet flexed. And he hadn't even urged the Skavu to do anything; merely to assess the risk.

There was always the chance that Kiir would do just that, and shrug it off, but from what he'd heard from Shapakti about Skavu and their fanatical views, he doubted it.

"There," said Rayat. "And you're sure that won't cause a drive shutdown or anything unpleasant?"

"I'm sure. It'll get transferred to the diagnostic screen."

"It won't get lost?"

"If Skavu engineers follow our procedures, they'll pass it up their command chain. And it's such regular script—they can see it's not random. How I wish I could learn to read it."

"I'll teach you," Rayat said. "Now, let's have a pot of tisane at the Exchange of Ideas, and I'll tell you all about my time living with the bezeri. *All* of it."

8

We have two choices. One is to sit back and allow Australia—and its allies, who don't seem to be getting much from this deal—to benefit from the local climate changes the Eqbas can put in place at the expense of the rest of the planet. Remember the disasters that unilateral climate engineering caused in the past. The other is to give Australia a very good reason to bring the Eqbas to the UN table to talk to us all.

MICHAEL ZAMMETT, FEU President,
addressing the UN Security Council

Immigrant Reception Center,
Shan Frankland's quarters

"You know I wouldn't ask a favor of you unless I really needed it, Eddie."

Shan shut her eyes and waited. Eddie's voice hadn't aged at all: no cracking, no hoarseness, just a measured and confident tone that made you stop and listen. Eddie always sounded as if he knew what he was talking about and that it was the holy truth.

"I'm amazed you've kept the vultures away from you for this long, doll," he said. "Have you punched one out yet? Hope you wore your gloves . . ."

"Ade and Mart have been shooting bee cams for target practice. Y'know, calibrating for Earth gravity and air density. Cams are tiny things now. They even use dust tech."

"How very modern," he said. "It's obvious, I suppose."

Twenty-five years, lost in a heartbeat. I hate this. I hate time. I hate being outside *time.*

"I need a real journalist, Eddie," Shan said. "I won't dress it up. I want to leak something and put the FEU in a corner. It might stop Esganikan bombing the shit out them."

"No pressure, then."

"I can't rely on the camera kiddies out here."

"That's my girl. Never ask a wanker to do a man's job."

"There was another jobsworth involved with Rayat's orders, and the FEU won't hand her over to Esganikan or even the UN. You can guess the rest. The name's Katya Prachy."

"P, R, A, C, H, Y?"

"Correct. I need her flushed out—either to show the FEU it's a good idea to play ball, or, worst comes to worst, for a snatch team."

"So she'll end up dead, won't she? Like the others."

"Strange as it might seem, that wasn't my doing."

"I know that. Are you heeding my warning about the FEU making a grab for you?"

"Of course I am."

"The man himself contacted me to ask if I could give him advice on the wess'har from time to time. The fucking FEU president. I'm sure you can join up the dots."

"So are you up for it, Eddie, or has Zammett bedazzled you by making you the court anthropologist?"

"You're sure you got the right woman?"

"Esganikan's adamant. Must have come from Rayat. Do you ever have any contact with him?"

"Zero. All I've heard is what I got third-hand from Nevyan, that they've extracted *c'naatat* from him a few times and he survived. I'm amazed he talked after all this time."

So Eddie didn't know about Esganikan. *Probably.* "Well, can you put a piece together saying Prachy has been named as another bastard who ordered the bombing of Ouzhari, and that serious shit will happen if she's not handed over? I've got her ID holos for you, her biometrics, the lot."

Eddie paused. "She'd be what, sixty, seventy now?"

"Eighty-odd."

"Ooh. Extraditing little old ladies for war crimes is always iffy, PR-wise."

"They were ready to swap her for me."

"Well, you're getting on for a hundred and fifty . . ."

"Eddie. Please. I need pressure put on the FEU to give Esganikan what she wants before she starts taking Brussels apart. It's going to be bloody enough as it is without that. You've got the whole BBChan machine, no other hack gets near the story, and it goes without saying that I'll get Esganikan to front up and do the resistance-is-futile interview. And Rayat isn't aware of this yet. Cards close to the chest, mate, okay?"

"I recall warning *you* way back that he was going to be serious trouble," said Eddie. "Look, I'm not sure people even remember why the Eqbas decided to visit Earth in the first place. Twenty-six, twenty-seven years ago? I think I'll need to remind them."

"They think it's to teach them to hug more trees."

"But you realize they'll ask why we bombed the place to start with."

"Tell them."

"About *c'naatat?* Jesus—"

"Say it's valuable bacteria. Be vague. Make it sound like some lunatic government project. Like trying to train commandos to walk through walls."

"That'd be *lying.* That'd be propaganda, not reporting. I still know the difference."

Shan had never asked him to lie. Eddie's decency was also his biggest flaw, at least when you were trying to get him to do something irregular. "Look, if you say the government thought it was something that gave the user eternal life, it's *true,* and it's also so fucking crazy that the public will nod and file it under *Yet Another Waste of Our Taxes.*"

"I never said I wouldn't do the lying bit. Look, a question for *you,* doll. Not for the record. Does Esganikan really know what she's there for? She was sliding into mission drift even before you set off. Not a good sign in a war."

Did Eddie know? No, he'd have told her if he knew about

Esganikan's *c'naatat*. He would never sit on anything that
dangerous now. "At least she seems to have an exit strategy.
That's a big plus."

"Time will tell. Look, it'll still be dead squid as far as
humans are concerned, but Ade and Aras got some great
shots of the bodies strewn along the shoreline for me."

Shan realized she didn't find the short leap from *great
shots* to *bodies strewn* at all callous, and wondered why the
newscasts weren't running that again now. But it was all so
long ago, and humans couldn't even keep the causes of terrestrial wars straight in their heads a week afterwards. They
didn't even care much about dead humans who were different from them.

*I ought to come clean with him. But where do I start? Am
I telling him what he needs for his own good, or dumping
on him?*

Shan began to frame her confession to Eddie and then
swallowed it whole. "Time is of the essence, mate."

"Pedaling as fast as I can. Keep watching the skies . . ."

Shan flicked the key and shut down the link. *Isn't that
something? I can just call a man a hundred and fifty trillion miles away, right away, and for free.* The corporations
would be sniffing around again soon, war or not, trying to
find the Eqbas price for technology transfer: ITX, morph-
ing structures and ships, biodegradable metal, contamination remediation nanites . . . weapons, nice clean minimum
residue weapons to fight nice green wars.

*A ship that can split up into any number of vessels. Isn't
that something?*

She could step into one of those right now and go anywhere she wanted.

Yeah, that's something.

And she could call in a favor and have a retired intelligence officer exposed to the world's media, and get her
killed, but maybe head off a regional war.

Yes, that was something, too. But in the end, not one
damn bit of it mattered. It would all end the same way.

Billions would die, sooner or later, and Earth would be a
very changed place.

F'nar, Wessej.

Barry leaned over Eddie's shoulder and peered at the screen. "What are you doing, Dad?"

"Dusting off my adrenal glands." Had Barry ever seen this footage? Eddie couldn't remember. "I haven't had a really urgent story in a bloody long time. I'd forgotten how good a deadline felt."

"What is it?"

"Bodies." Eddie leaned back to let Barry see the rushes that had been sitting in his archive file for years. It was much more graphic than he remembered, but maybe he was getting soft in his old age. "What effect does that have on you?"

"I can't tell what they are."

"Dead bezeri. After the bomb on Ouzhari."

Barry watched the sequence intently. "Oh God. That one's moving. Oh . . . its lights are still flickering. Horrible."

"Thanks." Eddie hit the edit point and marked the section for later. It was tough to get apes to empathize with squid, so he had to use a heavy hand. "Just testing. I just want to be sure that it says *genocide, tragedy, dead aliens.*"

Barry tried to show interest in his father's trade, but he'd grown up in a world without mass media. "Tell me why it's urgent."

"I'm interfering again. I'm exposing a spook. Don't you just *love* that word? I like it a lot better than *spy*. Anyway, when this breaks, there'll be a big row."

"Right." Barry didn't ask any more questions and just watched. Earth was as relevant to him as Mars, somewhere he knew a fair bit about but that wasn't home or even the Promised Land, and didn't hold any memories. "Why are you doing it? Keeping your hand in?"

Eddie was secretly disappointed that Barry didn't find current affairs the most hypnotically addictive subject in the world, but the kid didn't have that hunting instinct. *I fathered a normal human. I was so sure he'd be a hack.* Barry didn't grasp the enormity of Earth's predicament because he'd been a regular visitor to Umeh since he was a baby, and that was local for him.

"It's to help Shan out," said Eddie. Sod it, Barry was old enough to wrestle with the realities of the job. "The Eqbas went to Earth to sort out the people who authorized the bombing. It's a war crimes thing. And if I name this woman and stir up some trouble, then the FEU might hand her over and avoid having the Eqbas cream Europe a city at a time to find her. Or the loony greens might assassinate her. That would avoid any international nastiness, actually. Maybe they'll oblige."

Barry frowned. "Is that what a reporter should be doing? Setting people up to get killed?"

That stung, but a fair bit of the job could be seen that way. You didn't spike an uncomfortable story because there might be unhappy consequences for those scrutinized in it. Deliberately aiming to do that was only a few salami slices away from being impartial.

Yes, you did *spike stories. You did it all the time. You* definitely *did the first time you saw what breaking the* c'naatat *story unleashed.*

"It depends. The outcome could be slightly better than if I didn't do it. So wess'har would say I should, and humans would say I shouldn't, because I've set out to make something happen, not report the facts as objectively as I can."

The look on Barry's face said it all. *It's wrong.* Well, at least his boy had a strong moral anchor, and that was no bad thing.

"Don't you get scared, Dad? Being responsible?"

"Yeah," said Eddie. "I do."

Eddie wondered from time to time what his life might have been like had he gone back to Earth with the Eqbas, but since the landing, he'd been thinking about it all day, every day, and admitted to himself that he regretted it. Not enough to sour the rest of his life, but a little niggle of pain when he thought what might be happening right now in Kamberra, and what he could be doing, and . . . shit, he'd be in his forties, not staring at seventy.

But going back when your news editor accused you of fabricating the *c'naatat* stories . . . no, that had been the turning point. That was the moment he rethought his whole existence, even if he didn't realize it at the time.

*I'm not like Shan. She let people think she'd fucked up,
and didn't give a shit what anyone thought of her, because
she thought that the thing she was protecting was more important than her reputation. Me . . . I did the martyr act.
But I cared what they thought of me, all right. I still do.*

"I'm going out for a bit," Barry said, obviously feeling
he'd feigned the required period of interest in the item. He
held his *virin* out so Eddie could see he was taking comms
with him as a routine safety precaution. "I won't go any further than the mesa. Okay?"

"Be home in time for dinner, or your mum *will* go nuts
this time."

What was he worrying about? The worst that could happen to Barry was an accident. There were no drugs, gangs,
perverts, murderers or drunk drivers out there. And you really didn't need to lock your doors, unless the wess'har habit
of walking in without knocking really bothered you. Privacy was alien to them, but wess'har made great neighbors;
they'd trash your planet if you broke the rules, but other than
that, the worst he could say about them was that they were
tactless and nosy.

*That's worth staying for. I love 'em. Now I remember why
I'm really still here.*

Eddie had all the elements of the story now; the archive of
the attack on Ouzhari—nice iconic mushroom cloud shot
from a ussissi pilot, he'd forgotten that—and confirmation
of Katya Prachy's identity with a bit of life history. Added to
a brief but *au point* piece from Esganikan saying that she
wanted Prachy or else, and a *no comment* from the FEU
supplied by the BBChan bureau on the ground, it said guilty,
guilty, guilty.

*Why bother, Shan? It's not going to make any differ-
ence.*

*And why did Rayat wait until now to name Prachy?
Maybe he didn't. Maybe he grassed her up before the fleet
left—which was probably recent as far as the task force is
concerned. I keep forgetting Esganikan's been on a different time scale to us.*

Eddie got back to editing the death sentence on Katya

Prachy. It didn't feel like he was doing that at all; it felt like any other story, one that he weighed and polished.

Eighty, is she? She looks like she's had a stress-free life.

It didn't feel like pulling the trigger until his finger hovered over the Send tab for a few seconds longer than normal.

He hit it anyway.

Former hotel restaurant, Immigrant Reception Center: three days to deadline.

"Here's how you do it," said Ade, happy to be useful again. He upended the tumbler and covered the saltshaker. "Spider and glass. It's how the Eqbas took the Northern Assembly government building. Simple."

The detachment and Aras watched the demonstration. Shan tapped her thumbnail against her teeth, lost in thought, and kept taking out her swiss and the borrowed handheld to stare at the screens for a few moments before putting them back in her jacket pocket.

"Not exactly covert," said Barencoin.

"Doesn't need to be, mate. Eqbas tech. We've seen that shielding bounce missiles, remember."

"It's okay with a salt cellar, because they're pretty easy to subdue." Barencoin reached across the table and lifted the glass to slide a pebble beneath it. "But put this bloke inside with his piece, and you're still confined with him. They'll have close protection for Prachy. All we can do is seal off a building from the air."

"But it's still a whole lot simpler than inserting covertly into God knows where in Europe and getting the old girl and us out in one piece again."

"Does the FEU know the Eqbas have those kinds of isolating shields?"

"Thanks to Eddie, yes. Remember all the footage he pumped out from Umeh?"

"Oh well, knowing it's there doesn't mean they can do anything about it."

"Except surround Prachy with a load of big blokes with big guns." Barencoin turned to Qureshi with a smile. "Or a load of teensy little women with big guns, of course."

Qureshi shrugged. "Well, then it's a case of who's got the better body armor."

Shan looked as if she was suddenly paying attention. "Maybe this isn't such a good idea. Might be simpler if I walked in and just slotted her like Esganikan wants."

There'd been a time when a full-on nuke couldn't have shifted Shan once she'd made up her mind. Now she was wavering. The one thing she couldn't do that a good officer had to was to put her people in harm's way. It was different for coppers; they usually expected to come home each night in one piece. And the detachment was her volunteer militia, civvies, not protected by international law. Shan cared about stuff like that.

"You couldn't do it now," Ade said kindly. "You have to *insert*. It means flying in, and any journey originating here is going to get FEU attention. Plus you're a known face to the FEU, Boss. We're doing it, period, and then it's up to the Eqbas to process her."

"It'll all hinge on where they stash her, anyway," said Becken. They had a small audience of ussissi now, all watching the discussion as if it was a chess game in a park. "One thing we know is that whatever building they use, we can isolate it without touching the ground, and then clear out whatever's inside. No overground exfil."

"I lose, then," said Shan. "And shouldn't we have a pilot here for the planning?"

Aras raised his hand. It was a peculiarly human gesture and he almost looked as if he was taking the piss.

"I am," he said. "I can do this."

Shan didn't look convinced. "You've never flown an Eqbas ship."

"I was a pilot. All wess'har ships have much in common. Besides, you want to return to Wess'ej before the Eqbas fleet withdraws, don't you? How do you imagine you'll do that?"

"Good point," she said, without emotion. She turned to Ade. "Look, when this kicks off, you won't be able to stroll into Ankara afterwards, so if you're going to visit the war graves, you'd better get on with it while you can. It's going to be tense enough getting into Turkish airspace as it is."

She walked out into the main lobby. Barencoin gave Ade a sympathetic pat on the shoulder. "I reckon so. It's not going to be like the Fourteen-Eighteen War, playing football with the Hun in the tea break between shelling. Get going."

Chahal and Webster spent the next couple of hours working through the live map databases of Europe, speculating on where Prachy might end up, which seemed to entertain the remaining ussissi. The money was on the main FEU complex in Brussels, because that was the kind of up-yours gesture that Zammett would make; he'd defy the Eqbas to trash the center of government because they hadn't zapped any of his ships, Barencoin reckoned. Ade couldn't work out why they didn't just hand the woman over. She was expendable. Everyone was in the end. And they had to know by now that they weren't getting Shan, whatever pressure was brought to bear.

"Fucking mess," Ade muttered to himself, and made a conscious effort to stop his mind wandering back through the timeline to the point where it had all started to come unraveled. He knew it was that day on board *Actaeon,* back in orbit above Umeh, when Commander Lindsay Neville tasked him to find a way of infiltrating Bezer'ej to capture Shan Frankland.

Jesus, don't I ever learn? I'm doing it again, aren't I?

No, it wasn't then. He could have clawed it back after that. It was the moment in the armory when Rayat asked him if the BNO bombs could be transported to the planet, and he said he . . . he said they *could* be, but shouldn't be. Ade had lost count of the times he'd imagined himself telling Rayat and Lindsay to fuck off, because there was nothing they could have done to force him, and he was bloody certain that the rest of the detachment would have dug their heels in too, regardless of disciplinary action.

My fault. I tipped events.

He didn't dare talk about it to Shan any more. She always got exasperated and went through a long list of all the other ways that the nukes could have been deployed on Bezer'ej, and maybe with even greater loss of life all round, but it never quite made the guilt go away completely.

Fuck it. It was done now, and the least he could do was clean up the last turd. He took out his *virin* and began planning the trip to Ankara.

"I'll pilot a shuttle," Aras said, looking over his shoulder. Ade hadn't realized he was watching so closely, but Aras had that wess'har mood radar. "It will be excellent training for the mission."

Aras was a good bloke. There was no doubt about it.

An hour later, Shan walked back into the restaurant. Her expression was that odd mix of chalky unblinking anger and something that might have turned into a smile, but a humorless one. Someone had just lived up to her worst expectations, or she'd been outflanked. Ade knew it. Aras tensed and stood up.

"God bless the Canucks," she said. "Now they've upped the ante. The UN backed their extradition idea."

"To where?" said Chahal. "Surang?"

"Canada." Shan pointed at Barencoin, cueing him. "Now, may I have an opinion from m'learned friend Judge Barencoin over here?"

Barencoin perked up. The mouthy, aggressive image hid the fact that he did international law at university, a regular intellectual, but he never liked revealing that side. "Do they have the death penalty? Come to that, do they do piddly nitpicking stuff like real trials, and risk acquitting people? Because if they won't lynch her, Esganikan won't consider the case closed. I won't bill you for the legal advice. It's common sense."

"I'm obliged, Your Honor. That's the question the Aussies are putting to them now." Shan looked at them all, asking for a response. "Well, do we still want to get involved?"

"It's legal," said Becken. "I'm up for overseeing a handover too. Even if it's not as much fun as extracting her."

Qureshi nodded. "Better, actually."

"Shame it wasn't that Sinostates place, right on the African Assembly border," said Ade. "Last time we looked, they were beheading everyone for anything, just to be on the safe side."

"It's Canada," said Shan, and Ade knew everyone was thinking the same thing; they'd still have to go in and haul out Prachy anyway. "And if Prachy had any sense of duty, she'd save everyone the trouble and top herself. Ade, if you're still going to Ankara, make it very soon."

Shan wandered off.

"If Prachy *does* stand trial," said Barencoin, savoring his bit of legal exercise, "it's going to be fascinating procedure."

9

*Okay, do you remember the first contact we had with the
isenj in the 2300s? One of their ministers told us that
wess'har made their soldiers "immortal" in the past and
could do it again, so we shouldn't underestimate small
numbers. The isenj aren't primitives. I think we should take
the threat as seriously as they did. Look at Umeh if you
don't see why.*

BENEDYKT JANIAK, FEU Foreign Office,
at ministerial briefing

Immigrant Reception Center's airstrip, late afternoon.

"Do you have time for this trip?" Esganikan demanded.
"Shouldn't you be planning the arrest of Prachy?"

Aras watched Shan for signs of a reaction but she remained glacially calm. Knowing her temper, he thought it
was a remarkable feat of self-control when she almost certainly wanted to round on Esganikan for her deceit more
than she wanted to remove her. Aras didn't think Shan *wanted*
to remove her at all. There was no rage or passion in this,
just that dull sense of having been deceived again, and he
remembered how much that rankled with Shan when she
discovered what the politician Perault had done to her.

As always, Shan chanelled the sense of betrayal into the
strict performance of her duty, by way of vengeance.

"This will only take seven hours, tops," Shan said quietly.
"Canada's discussing the handover and there's nothing useful I can add to that. Ade's never going to get the chance to
visit the graves again, and I intend him to have his wish. I
hope we're clear on that."

"I'll come too," Esganikan said. "As will Kiir and Aitassi.
We have never seen war graves, and Aras needs an experienced shuttle pilot with him."

"I don't think either Kiir or Ade would welcome that."
Shan's tone was completely neutral, not that Esganikan
would have been swayed by her emotional state anyway.
"This is a very emotional event for Ade. Kiir had better stay
behind."

Ade lowered his chin. "It's okay. He might as well see it. I
think he'll understand humans better if he does."

Esganikan paused for a moment, then motioned Kiir on
board. It was hard to tell if the Skavu had been ordered to
come or if he was genuinely curious. He said nothing and
stepped into the shuttle, saber slapping against his back with
each stride, and vanished into the gloom of the ship.

Shan nudged Aras discreetly. "I'll keep an eye on him,"
she whispered. "You concentrate on learning to fly that
bloody thing properly."

Esganikan was totally unperturbed by the tension. "We
shall need to extend this area to accommodate all the vessels," she said, changing topic completely and gazing around
the dilapidated field. Slabs of cracked concrete poked
through dead grass as if there had been other buildings here
once, or at least parking. She seemed to have made up her
mind. "An area of fifty square kilometers so we can bring
all the Skavu inside the perimeter. Then we can make this
a temporary city."

That was what wess'har called their garrisons; there was
never an intention to remain. Empires prized permanence,
but wess'har were simply passing through, putting things
right and enabling the native population to maintain what
they had re-created. That was how they saw it, anyway.

"Well, I think it's time we made a move," said Shan.
"Seeing as you're concerned about my time management."

Aitassi let Aras slip into the pilot's seat and watched
from the position beside him with wary matte black eyes.
None of the controls felt as familiar as Aras had hoped,
despite his training. Shan settled down on a seat that emerged
at her touch from the bulkhead, and Ade gave her a silent
thumbs-up. Aras wasn't sure why. It was just something he

did to bond with her. Perhaps it was approval for not punching Esganikan when she must have wanted to.

"I'll apologize in advance for this," Ade said. He kept his eyes on the deck, possibly to avoid meeting Kiir's gaze. The Skavu commander sat silent in the aft section of the shuttle, his sheathed saber flat across his knees. "I'm going to be upset when we get there. Don't be embarrassed."

"'It's okay," Shan said. She had an eye on Kiir, though. "You do whatever you need to."

The shuttle's deck became transparent. Ade knelt down to watch the eastern seaboard of Australia streaking beneath them, and as they passed over the coast they could see patrol vessels leaving brilliant white wakes as they moved south.

But it was beyond Australian airspace where the reality of the Eqbas visit became suddenly visible. Their days of peaceful isolation had been an illusion. Now Aras could see exactly how the world was reacting to the arrival of the Eqbas and the tension with the FEU, in the shape of a Sinostates carrier battle group on station to the north.

"Is that for us?" Shan asked.

"I doubt it," Ade said. There wasn't a lot a carrier could do against Eqbas air power, and everyone must have known that by now. "I think it's to block off more refugee movement when things start to go pear-shaped."

The bulkhead displays were showing clusters of yellow lights on the long-range chart, the point where the FEU, African Assembl, and Sinostates borders met; they'd have company in Ankara. Aras hoped the FEU had the sense simply to look, and not try to touch.

They reached Turkish airspace at 0925 local time. The first of the fighters picked up the shuttle fifty kilometers out from the coast, and stayed with it across a country that seemed to be either dense cities or arid wasteland.

"It's time I took over the helm," Aitassi said. "This is no time to practice your skills."

"Ussissi never fly combat roles," said Aras "Your neutrality is important to you."

"This," said Aitassi, showing a hint of teeth, "is not configured as a fighter, and ussissi can certainly defend themselves."

"I think that subtle point might be lost on our buddy up there." Shan pointed up through the deckhead, now set to transparency. A wedge-shaped craft trailing an occasional ring of vapor was keeping pace with them. "He's probably just observing. I bloody well hope so."

When Esganikan magnified the image, Aras could see the FEU roundel on its undercarriage. The tracking display showed twelve more were within a ten-kilometer radius of the shuttle.

"Not a Turkish squadron," Ade said. "Central European. Off their usual turf today."

"You worry about nothing," said Esganikan. "They can do you no harm, and observing an act of mourning is hardly going to provide intelligence for them. Aitassi, connect me to their traffic control. I warned them we were coming, and I want no interference."

Ade didn't seem comforted. He was often consumed by guilt; Aras knew he would feel it now, and would blame himself for everything that happened from this point. Some humans absolved everyone around them of responsibility, and Ade was one of them, still punishing himself for not saving his mother from his monstrous father. Aras didn't understand why a child felt he had to be more adult than his own parents.

"I don't want to start anything," Ade said. "Not today, and not here. Please."

"Do you want to turn back?" Esganikan asked.

"If this is going to cause a—"

Aras interrupted. "No. This is important for Ade. He has to do this."

Aras *understood*. Wess'har didn't bury their dead or create memorials, but he remembered how he had clutched helplessly at the soil on Ouzhari, on Bezer'ej—two hundred years ago, yes, just after the *gethes* sent their first unmanned mission—and mourned for his comrade Cimesiat. There was no body to leave for the scavengers, for the rockvelvets

or *srebils,* because Cimesiat carried *c'naatat:* so he had finally ended his own life by fragmentation.

*Everyone should be returned to the cycle of life. Every-
one needs somewhere to mourn.*

"You know who's flying those fighters, Aras?" Ade asked.
"Ordinary blokes like me. They're the ones who get hurt,
not the tossers in Brussels who start this shit. I know a lot of
them are going to die sooner or later—but not today, and not
because of me."

Esganikan waited with unusual patience for contact with
the Turkish air controllers. "I have no intention of firing on
them unless they attack on us."

"You don't have to return fire at all," Shan said. "You
don't need to. You've got shielding."

"If I don't, then how will they learn that we mean what we
say?" The shuttle was well inside FEU airspace now with its
fighter escort. "They must be able to see where we're heading. Perhaps they think a small vessel is also a vulnerable
one."

Ade glanced up through the deckhead a few times but
his attention was on the ground. Finding a specific location
on Earth was simple; Aitassi turned for the cemetery with
a burst of speed and left the FEU fighters struggling to
catch up.

It wasn't hard to spot from the air.

Aras was used to two kinds of artificial landscape; the
near unspoiled, like F'nar, making as little visual impact as
possible, or the wholly urbanized, like Umeh had been. What
he'd never seen before was manufactured emptiness. The
cemetery covered a vast area of land south of Ankara, nowhere near the city itself; hectares of arid, empty land covered with perfectly precisely spaced white objects that threw
shadows. Magnification showed him what they were: headstones. This wasn't a wess'har custom, but he knew what
headstones were because he'd made a stained glass one for
Lindsay Neville's dead baby. What was new and shocking to
him was the sheer number and the space they occupied.

*Why should this shock you? You were responsible for the
deaths of many more isenj than this.*

He tried to work out if the distress was from his own sorrow for lost comrades or the influence of Ade's memories. The shuttle hung motionless above the cemetery. There had to be thousands of headstones down there. It shook him to his core despite his rationalizations.

Shan had now switched her attention to the scene below, all scent suppressed, and she took Ade's hand without looking at him.

Aras turned to him. "You knew all those people?"

"No," said Ade. "I only knew my mates."

"How will you find the right grave?"

Ade tapped his pocket. "I got the coordinates from the public register. The rows have numbers and directions. It's like a city."

"Tell Aitassi where to go," Esganikan said. "She'll maintain a shield over the area so you can do what you need to without interruption."

Unlike Shan, Ade couldn't shut down his scent signals. Even normal humans gave off scents that a wess'har could detect and use to gauge their mood, but Ade had an extra dimension of wess'har genes and so communicated his feelings much more clearly. He was scared and angry. Aras watched him carefully while the shuttle took up position over the section where Dave Pharoah was buried, ready to offer some comfort if Shan's tight grip on Ade's hand wasn't enough.

Is he reliving the battle? Or is he reacting to the moment?

Turkish air-traffic control responded at last. Esganikan seemed more interested in the graves.

"Eqbas vessel, this is ATC Ankara. You've entered FEU airspace—"

Esganikan's tone was subdued. "I informed you we wished to visit."

"You have no *formal* permission to land. But the cemetery has now been closed to the public for the duration."

"Are you a soldier?"

"Eqbas warship, say again?"

"You. Are you a soldier?"

"This is a military traffic center, yes."

"I have one of your former comrades on board, a man who fought for the FEU many years ago. All he wants to do is to visit the grave of his friend, and then we'll withdraw. Do you understand his need? If it were your friend, would you not want to do the same?"

"Eqbas warship, I don't have authorization to respond to that."

Shan cut in quietly. "Esganikan, I don't think you understand what's being said. He's not actually stopping you. He's not giving you permission, because that might compromise his government, but he's not *stopping* you. Get it?"

Esganikan played along as best a wess'har could. "Very well, then tell those who do, and by the time they decide how to deal with me, we'll have left your territory. We won't fire on your vessels."

Esganikan closed the link. This wasn't the commander who laid down her rules of engagement and applied them without concession on Umeh. Aras caught Shan's eye.

Yes, you think that's unusual too, don't you?

"Are you going soft?" Shan asked, treading on thinner ice. Aras willed her not to confront Esganikan now.

"I see no point in engaging in conflict that won't achieve anything," Esganikan said. "My curiosity will be satisfied and Ade will have more positive memories of a day that has great significance for him."

"You've pulled, Ade," Shan muttered. "Get your coat."

Aras could work that one out from her expression. Esganikan certainly liked Ade just as the rest of the Eqbas crew seemed to, but wess'har weren't swayed by appearance anywhere near as much as humans, and Ade now emitted wess'har male scent. Wess'har females were never attracted to males already bonded to an *isan,* though. Sexual jealousy was a human trait. Aras hoped that Shan was indulging in a bitter joke to postpone that inevitable confrontation with Esganikan. It was hard to tell—even for her, sometimes.

"He has a very long life ahead of him," Esganikan said, with the slightest hint of annoyance. "Being burdened with a painful memory is that much worse for *c'naatat* hosts, is it not?"

Ade did his usual trick of defusing the situation. "Thanks, ma'am," he said. "I appreciate it."

The graves looked identical, but Ade knew where he needed to go. Aitassi waited in the shuttle overhead while the rest of them descended to the ground. Within the defense shield projected by the ship, the air was still; beyond its heat-haze boundaries, the breeze whipped dust from the finely chipped pink-tinged stone that covered the ground between the gravestones. Aras couldn't see a single living plant. This was either a wasteland, or meticulously maintained. Around them, all the headstones were carved with the same globe emblem that Ade had worn on his beret; these were all men and women from 37 Commando Royal Marines. It said so on the headstones, along with their name, rank, age and date of death.

Aras felt a sense of complete desolation. He had no ghosts here, no real memories, but the seemingly endless ranks of uniform white slabs left his stomach feeling scraped hollow.

"Give me a minute, will you?" said Ade. "I need a bit of time on my own."

He meant Shan too. He set off at a slow pace, pausing at each stone to read the inscription, and finally stopped at one in particular before squatting down on his heels, elbows braced on knees, hands clasped.

Shan seemed to be focused entirely on him, frowning slightly. Esganikan, distracted by the sound of two rotary-winged aircraft overhead, looked up into the sky.

Aras forgot Ade. All he could see in his field of vision were ranks of white stone that appeared to be moving slowly away from him, and the moment when he and his comrades, a tiny wess'har army faced by millions of isenj, had decided in desperation that whatever resistance he'd developed on Bezer'ej while in isenj captivity was worth trying for its healing properties.

We didn't know then what it really did.

But later . . . later I knew all too well. And I still infected Shan against her will because I couldn't bear to see her die.

Aras knew how easy it was to fall to *c'naatat*'s temptation. He also knew the consequences better than Esganikan
ever could. Looking at the stones, he tried hard to remember his brothers—not comrades, not *brothers in arms* as
Ade sometimes called them, but his first house-brothers.
He'd been the youngest, the smallest, and hadn't had time
or chance to father a child when the bezeri begged for help
to remove the isenj colonies from Bezer'ej. He was a brilliant soldier and pilot. His *isan* was proud of his precocious
talent.

A hard war to win. But I lost. I lost everything.

Self-pity was an ugly thing, and he rarely fell prey to it.
The seemingly endless ranks of graves had triggered the
thoughts.

Shan turned. She was seldom an emotional woman, but
her eyes were glazed with unshed tears.

"Sad, isn't it?" she said. "War graves always do this to me.
When you see them all together . . . you can see just how
many lives and families were ripped apart. I hope the bastards who sent them had a fucking good reason they didn't
share with the rest of us. Either that, or I hope there's a hell
for them to rot in."

Ade had never passed an opinion on that. He was still
squatting by the grave that mattered most to him. Shan
walked over to kneel down beside him and rub his back re-
assuringly with one hand, then reached out and placed a
pebble on the ledge at the foot of the headstone. Humans
seemed to do that as some kind of personal act of memorial.
Eventually they both stood up and walked slowly along the
rows, Ade pointing at some of the stones and stopping, shaking his head sadly.

It took some time. Kiir stood behind Esganikan like a
statue, hands clasped and resting on his rifle rather like a
human honor guard—and Aras wondered if, for all his very
vocal and violent dislike of *c'naatat,* he felt for Ade as a fellow soldier.

Ade and Shan walked back towards them, stopping to
touch Dave Pharoah's headstone again. Ade, who found it
much easier to express his emotions than Shan, wiped his

eyes with the back of his hand and let her put her arms around him.

No hurry, Ade. We all need time to say goodbye, and it'll be a long time before you see this again, if ever.

Eventually Ade seemed to have had enough. He walked briskly to the shuttle and almost ran up the ramp. Aras followed and settled down next to him, Shan on his other side.

"I always find goodbyes hard," he said. "I didn't get chance the first time."

Shan squeezed his shoulders. "I think he'd appreciate the gesture. A hundred and fifty trillion miles is a hell of a long way to come to say goodbye."

"Bit of a downer for you, Boss."

"No, I'm honored that you let me come along." Shan pressed her temple against his. "It's right. It's very right."

It was a moment of complete and exclusive intimacy, just a second or two where the rest of the world—including Aras—vanished for them. He never minded, but he wondered why he didn't experience the memories of Dave Pharoah's death as vividly Shan did. It was an oddly lonely feeling that passed as soon as it began.

The shuttle lifted, and Aras moved forward to the cockpit to sit next to Aitassi and learn more about the Eqbas navigation system.

"We have our escort again," she said. "Look."

Four fighters appeared on the bulkhead display, two above and two below. Aras didn't know the capabilities of FEU aircraft, but he was a pilot, and he knew that they were far too close.

Kiir said nothing but gestured to Aitassi to let him have the controls. She slipped off of the seat and let him move into it.

"So they know we're Eqbas," Shan said quietly, "but have they worked out who's on board?"

"FEU knows exactly who you are and can recognize you from aerial surveillance," Aras said. "So I think this will be an unpleasant episode."

"Sorry, Boss," said Ade. "My fault."

"No, it's the pilots' choice to harass us or not, Sergeant

Bennett," Esganikan said. She turned the hull to transparency. "As it's also their choice to withdraw. We've done no harm here."

The fighters stuck with them across country, keeping a constant distance but swapping positions from time to time. The coast came into view. Aras suspected that they didn't want an incident in Turkish airspace. It was a country that could easily slip from the FEU to the African Assembly if provoked, Barencoin had told him. An incident like that might tip it.

"I could simply outrun them," said Kiir. "But I anticipate they'll attempt to intercept."

Esganikan watched impassively. "As long as they don't try to force us down, continue."

Kiir accelerated south, climbing a few hundred meters. One of the fighters streaked ahead of him, dipping down and blocking his path. It was clear to Aras that they still didn't know what an Eqbas ship could do; they seemed to think they could force it to deviate by threatening a collision. Kiir carried on, building speed, and now there were two fighters ahead of them and two on their tail. The transparent bulkheads with their full visibility were an advantage in a combat situation. It was only when he glanced over his shoulder and saw Shan and Ade looking alarmed—quiet and calm, but definitely alarmed—that he realized how vulnerable an invisible hull made them feel.

One of the fighters dipped its wing and cut across the shuttle's nose. Kiir didn't seem bothered; he could have simply increased speed and left the fighter behind, but he seemed to be assessing it.

"He's telling you to follow him and land," Ade said.

"He's trying to capture us?"

"Stupid idea, but yes."

"Slow to learn," said Kiir. "Too slow."

The ITX link burst into life. It was probably the only band that the FEU was certain it could use to get the attention of Eqbas ships.

"Eqbas vessel, change course and follow us to—"

"FEU craft—withdraw before I fire on you."

The nearest land was Sinostates or African territory, neither of which appeared to be supporting the FEU at the moment. If the fighters were trying to force the Eqbas ship to ditch, then they probably knew that any *c'naatat* hosts would survive and so it didn't matter who was killed with them.

But forcing an Eqbas vessel to do anything when it was cocooned in countermeasures was next to impossible. Kiir, showing unusual restraint, waited until he saw the flare and trail of a missile before he fired one burst of light that split into three; the missile and both fighters ahead of them exploded in a ball of flame. It lit up the whole shuttle and Aras heard Shan's shocked grunt.

"Shit," said Ade. "Shit."

The two fighters on their tail broke off the pursuit and Kiir streaked away at top speed towards the Arabian Peninsula.

"From tomorrow," said Esganikan wearily, "we return to normal rules of engagement."

It wasn't an act of invasion by a long stretch of the imagination, but Aras knew it would be recorded as the first attack by an alien vessel on a human ship in its own airspace. As things went, a war had definitely begun, regardless of legal status. Aras simply felt sorry for Ade, having his day of such emotional significance marred by more deaths that needn't have happened.

But if the FEU had wanted to capture Shan, the missiles hadn't been fired to hit, merely to pass close and intimidate. It was another tactical mistake based on treating the Eqbas as humans.

The FEU never stood a chance of seizing Shan from a ship like this. Ade sat forward with his head resting on his hands, elbows braced on his knees.

"Sorry, Dave," he said.

Reception Center: Eqbas officers' quarters, meeting area, 5th floor.

"So you went out of curiosity?" Laktiriu Avo asked.

"I did," said Esganikan. "The graves are so *orderly*.

Humans seem to find more reverence for each other when they can no longer benefit than while they're alive. They always come to their senses too late."

She watched the BBChan transmissions, fascinated by the flurry of activity that the shooting down of the fighter had caused. The FEU was enraged. Michael Zammett, the leader who Bari seemed to dislike so intensely, appeared every ten minutes on one channel or another declaring that it was an act of war and that the Australian government was complicit if it harbored the Eqbas aggressors. There was a certain irony in that.

"You could have your say on that channel," Laktiriu pointed out. "Premier Bari's office tells me they've had hundreds of requests to *interview* you."

Esganikan knew all about interviews. Eddie Michallat had been an excellent teacher, and when she decided it was time to speak, she would address BBChan exactly as advised. It was a pity he hadn't come; but he was a human with a strange conscience, just like Shan and Ade, and so he'd be a hindrance as often as a help. The exposé of Prachy had made the top headlines for a full day.

"I'll wait," she said. "Let's see."

The reporters were pressing Zammett to say if he thought the *repeated incursions,* as they kept calling them, were connected to the Eqbas demands to hand over Katya Prachy. Zammett snarled defiance. He didn't mention Shan, though. It was yet another confirmation that they wanted her as a biological sample, and didn't want anyone else to focus on her. Bari's aide said a formal request for Shan's extradition was sitting on the Prime Minister's desk, and that he was using it as a coaster.

"I feel pity for Ade Bennett," said Esganikan. "Still mourning his friend after so many years. He even mourns the pilots we shot down yesterday. He's too sensitive for his line of work, I think."

Laktiriu didn't look up from her *virin.* "Yet he still does it well."

"And it pains him each time. *Shan Chail* feels her losses too, but she's so much better at ignoring them."

Esganikan spoke not only from observation but from the many perspectives her parasite gave her. She felt as Shan felt, occasionally, and as Ade Bennett did. They lived painful inner lives. So did Aras. Small wonder they clung together.

"She looks impervious to me," said Laktiriu. "I can't even detect her mood from her scent."

"She's *far* from impervious." Esganikan hadn't worked out significance of the large humanoid animal, the one who kept gesturing frantically in Shan's memories, or the sheet of flame that sometimes flashed into her mind, or even the flaking blue door, but Shan certainly wrestled with demons. "She collects painful events and seems not to know what to do with them."

"So you two talk more than I imagine. I thought she found you difficult to deal with."

It was as good a time as any, Laktiriu was pragmatic and would understand. Sooner or later, Esganikan would do something that would reveal her condition—an accidental wound that healed immediately, something she couldn't plan out of possibility—and that would demand explanations.

"I have her memories."

"I don't understand, Commander."

"I carry the *c'naatat* parasite."

Laktiriu stared at her, utterly still with shock. "She *contaminated* you? When? Is there nothing you can do to remove it?"

"I acquired it deliberately, from Rayat, and so I have his memories, too, and several others'. It would make sense to Laktiriu in the end, she knew it. "I was prepared to experiment, knowing that if Da Shapakti is never able to remove it, I have the option of a quick death. But if we can control it—as we now appear to be able to control it in humans—then it offers us huge advantages on long deployments like this."

Laktiriu's pupils were snapping open and shut. Esganikan had almost expected someone to notice how different she was becoming, but not even Shan seemed to have spotted it.

"I think you're foolish to sacrifice yourself for an experiment," Laktiriu said at last, "but it's very courageous."

"I haven't mentioned it to anyone else. I wouldn't want the Skavu to know. They reacted very badly to *Shan Chail* when they found out what *c'naatat* was, and I have to maintain control of them. So sensible discretion is called for, and I know how unnatural that is for us."

"Understood. But we face unnatural challenges."

"If any of you want to join me in the experiment, you're free to do so. The matriarchs of Surang are fully aware of what I've done." Esganikan hadn't spoken to them since leaving Bezer'ej. Hers was another ongoing restoration now, expected to carry on quietly unless there was a serious emergency she couldn't handle. *C'naatat* made that even less likely. "Shan is not aware of it. Like the Skavu, she reacts in an extreme way, and I don't want this mission disrupted. She even aborted her own child to stop the spread of the parasite, Shapakti says."

That silenced Laktiriu. Wess'har could consciously control their fertility, so the idea of an unplanned and unwanted child was beyond them. It simply sounded nightmarish; and it was. Esganikan felt a surge of the conflicting memories of both Shan and Lindsay Neville, and how very differently they'd felt about Lindsay's accidental pregnancy. She wondered if either of them had regretted their decisions in the weeks that followed, but she would never know now unless she asked them. She could hardly approach either of them for a top-up of their body fluids to experience what they'd felt since their *c'naatat* infected the next host. Esganikan had to make do with the snapshot the parasite gave her up to the point of infection. That was distressing enough.

"I shall be discreet," Laktiriu said. "Let's change the subject."

It was a prudent approach, and one Esganikan expected of her second-in-command. And somehow she felt very much better for having told at least one member of her crew.

If there was one thing she knew she had inherited from Shan rather than Rayat, it was an unforgiving conscience that muttered quietly in the corner, while the bold Rayat within her told her that risks were there to be taken for the greater good.

After Laktiriu left to get a meal, Esganikan summoned Kiir. She didn't like leaving things to chance now, and the more she saw of emotional human reactions to inevitable death, the more she wondered if Shan and the marines would have been capable of seizing Prachy, knowing she would be killed anyway.

They might have turned squeamish, though. Kiir never did. Skavu always made sure that the job got done.

Immigrant Reception Center.

"Kiir," Shan said, "I need your assistance. Come here."

The Skavu commander straightened up slowly and stared at her, turning his back on the chart laid out on the table. She'd already punched him out once for suggesting that an abomination like her should be killed. She didn't want to leave him with the impression that she wouldn't do it a few more times for fun, and indicated the doors with an imperious jerk of the thumb.

It wasn't fair, she knew, because in his own world he was probably just like Ade and others, ordinary people doing a rotten, thankless job, and she wondered if she shouldn't cut him some slack just for wearing a uniform. Slaughtering unarmed isenj—well, she couldn't get too pious about that. She slept with a wess'har who'd killed an awful lot more isenj civilians than Kiir could probably count. It was one of those ironies of life that Ade adored Aras but would kill Kiir if he got the chance.

"What do you require of me, Shan Chail?" His tone was level but there was almost a thought bubble sketched over his head with *abomination* penciled in it. Qureshi was right about the iguana thing. "I'm preparing to repel FEU threats to our hosts."

Shan was determined not to mention the shooting down of the FEU fighters. Ade's remorse had left her feeling even more raw about it. She knew she'd never get used to deaths in wars, because her police training was all about death being unacceptable, and not something to be chalked up to experience, however many autopsies she watched impassively with a sandwich in one hand. There was inuring yourself to personal pain to do the job, and there was kidding yourself that people had to kill each other, and she never wanted to find that she couldn't tell the difference any longer.

"It won't take long," she said. *Am I being disloyal to Ade? He hates this bastard.* "I need weapons."

Kiir didn't ask why. "What are you competent to use?"

"Most small ballistic firearms. Haven't got a clue how to use energy weapons, except a PEP laser for those pesky public order situations." He knew all about her 9mm and Ade's rifle. "But what I want is a fighting knife and a few grenades. You know. Small explosives. Ade trained me."

"Why do you need explosives?"

It was a fair question. "Because I'm an *abomination,* as you so kindly pointed out last time, and if I fell into enemy hands I'd like to fragment myself as efficiently as possible. I've tried spacing myself. Doesn't work."

"I meant what *task* you require it for, because that will determine what kind, and how much you need."

"Ah." Shan wondered how much was lost in the translation; Skavu could speak eqbas'u, as could she, but they wore thin metal collars that interpreted languages for them. "Large biped, like me. And I'll take a few more for my abominable men folk as well."

"You mock me," Kiir said flatly. "I'll get you the grenades. But you have a blade. Your sergeant confiscated one from me."

"Your sword, you mean." Skavu all carried a large flat saber sheathed on their backs, which seemed quaint and ceremonial like a naval officer's sword, except the Skavu really did use them. Ade would have had the scars to show for it if he hadn't been *c'naatat.* "I want a small blade." She held her forefingers apart to indicate length. "Fifteen to twenty centimeters, if you have one."

Shan was suddenly aware of Ade approaching from the right, casual and careful. He stood with his hands in his pockets, head cocked, but in Ade it signified disapproval rather than curiosity.

"You could borrow mine, Boss," he said quietly.

"No, you better keep it." She turned back to Kiir. He stared at Ade and then looked back at her, unfathomable. "Kiir, I'll be here for a while, so if you could get those for me, or have one of your men do it, I would be grateful."

"It's good to be prepared to fragment yourself, *Chail*," Kiir said. "The consequences of humans' acquiring the organism would be disastrous."

Kiir summoned a junior officer and sent him on the errand while he went back to his planning session. The breakfast table was covered with a chart of the Australian coastline; it was exactly like the device that Shapakti had used as a microscope when he was surveying the irradiated soil of Ouzhari, a thin sheet of transparent material that Shan thought of as a tea tray. Like the opaque-to-transparent hulls of the Eqbas vessels, it could zoom in and out to different magnifications. Kiir and his officers pored over a global chart of the southern hemisphere as seen from Antarctica and then the image changed instantly into a much more detailed chart of harbors and inlets.

Ade cast a discerning eye over it at a tactful distance, and then steered her away to the lobby with gentle pressure on her elbow.

"You okay?" she asked.

"Fine."

"I'm sorry, I really am."

"You forget what I did for a living, Boss. Just because we've had a few relatively quiet years doesn't mean I didn't see a lot of dead blokes in my career."

Shan didn't regard them as quiet years at all, but the marines certainly hadn't seen frequent action. It seemed all too frequent to her, though.

"Okay. I'm still sorry."

"Look, I paid my respects to Dave. I'm glad I got the chance. Now let's concentrate on the task in hand. Prachy."

"Where's Aras?" Shan asked. He was getting left out. She needed to drag him along with them whether he felt like it or not. "I don't want him brooding."

"He's helping set up hydroponics. Boss, I'm a grown-up now. Treat me like one. Why ask Twat-Features for kit when you could ask me?"

Yes, Ade really was an adult. Shan wasn't blind to her own double standards in keeping things from him for his own good, and then yelling at him for doing the same to her.

"You don't have any more grenades," she said.

"I could get some, and at least I know what I'm doing. What happened to the last one you kept? You had it before we left." He was doing his instructor–sergeant routine now. It was actually quite intimidating, even by her standards. "Cops know how many rounds they've got and how many they've expended. I'm like that with frigging ordnance."

She opened her jacket. "I didn't leave it on the bus . . ."

"And the knife?"

"I've not got one."

"I've got a *lovely* knife. Old pattern Fairbairn-Sykes. And you could have—"

"And *you* need it."

Ade wasn't giving up. When he was locked on to a target, no chaff could distract him. "I know some oranges can put up a fight, Boss, but why else do *you* need a knife now?"

Shan could have used the blade in her swiss, or maybe found a sharp enough knife in the reception center's restaurant, but her first thought had been something separate and disposable so she didn't risk contaminating herself with even the faintest trace of Mohan Rayat. That was one mind she didn't want sharing space with hers. There was one easy test she'd used on herself to check for *c'naatat,* and that was slicing a chunk out of someone: you could watch the wound heal instantly.

It wasn't that she didn't trust Shapakti's judgment, but before she took anybody's word—Rayat's word, especially— that Esganikan Gai had given herself a dose of the parasite, she wanted proof. If they were wrong, the consequences might turn out to be even worse than leaving things alone.

"I'm still waiting, Boss." Ade looked disappointed and—yes, *hurt*. Did he know how hard that hit her? "I think I can guess."

He didn't even need her memories. He just knew her.

"Okay," she said. "It's as good a test as any, isn't it? I need to be sure Esganikan's what we think she is."

Ade beckoned her outside where they could talk in the remains of a pebbled forecourt that might once have been a Zen garden. In the containment of the defense barrier, it was a pleasantly warm day. Overhead, in the reality of a searing January morning, a police drone craft was making lazy circles in a bee-cam-free sky while it emitted regular pulses of light from its nose.

It must have been disabling media surveillance dust. Journos had no bloody ethical standards these days. Eddie would have had something to say about it. From time to time, a fighter streaked across the sky at a much higher altitude. The FEU carrier was still nudging at the territorial waters and everyone was still jumpy.

"I liked your method best," she said, watching the flickering ship. Her hands pulsed violet light for a moment and then gave up.

Ade ambled along the pebble border. "Can't shoot dust, unfortunately. "So who's going to drop this turd in their lap, then? And what about her bosses back in Surang? Can't they see this is enough to warrant relieving her of command?"

"Shapakti told Nev that they won't interfere because they don't second-guess commanders in the field."

"D'you know, that's the first time in my life that I've thought that might be a bad idea."

"What would you do, then?"

"Just tell the crew. They can't all be stupid. One of the females might even do the *jask* thing and take over if Laktiriu doesn't. But whatever happens, don't let it be *you*."

They sat down on an ornamental bench. Shan wondered if Ade knew her better than she knew herself, and could see her becoming convinced of her own responsibility to be in charge. No, she hadn't the slightest idea how to run this mission properly; she was just an intelligent, competent copper, nothing more. All her opinions of how she'd run the world, her instant knee-jerk wisdom, were hopelessly inadequate when she tried to apply them to a big, complex system like Earth. Shoot all the bloody wasters, shoot all the fucks who harmed kids and animals, shoot . . . well, she'd shot a few on a very personal basis, but now that she was looking at a more dispassionate, rational, and industrial scale approach to culling humans, she'd lost her nerve.

And you thought you were so hard, didn't you?

What if she made the whole mission unravel by compromising Esganikan? The Eqbas rescued planets for a living. Shan might have been an EnHaz veteran, but she was just a tourist compared to an Eqbas commander.

But what if this is how c'naatat escapes into the human population, and I could have stopped it? What if that happens, and removing it isn't as easy as it was with one human in a lab? Didn't I try to die to stop this very thing happening?

Yes, she had. But that didn't mean she was right this time. She listened for some quiet word on the breeze from her commonsense guts.

It told her not to hope for the best. This was Earth, after all.

"Deadline's getting closer," she said. "Come on, let's root for gentlemanly behavior and the rule of law."

Shan wondered how she would feel if she looked into Katya Prachy's eyes and saw not a callous bureaucrat who dispensed careless genocide at 150 trillion miles' remove, but an old woman.

She was a copper, though, and she was long past feeling pity for criminals.

10

The FEU has until midnight to hand over ex-EFI5 agent Katya Prachy to the Canadian authorities for involvement in alleged war crimes in the Cavanagh's Star system. The Eqbas Vorhi task force is also seeking custody of Prachy, but is said to be in talks with Canada about dropping the claim pending a UN war crimes tribunal held under Canadian law.

BBChan 445 international bulletin

F'nar, Wess'ej.

"Are you coming to bed, Eddie?"

Erica leaned against the doorframe and pulled an exasperated, weary expression that was exactly like Serrimissani's disapproving scowl. Eddie didn't risk telling her that she looked like a stroppy ussissi.

"I have to watch this, doll. Sorry." He gestured at the ITX link showing BBChan live. "You've got no idea how frustrating this is."

"You want to see Brussels wiped off the map, is that it?" She walked across the room in front of the screen and started boiling water and rattling glass cups. "Armageddon, live and uninterrupted. Lovely. But we've got hours yet. Time to get some beer and snacks in, and make a night of it."

"If I'd *gone,*" he said sourly, "I might have been some use."

"If you'd *gone,* poppet, you might have made it *worse.* And you're still sticking your oar in, aren't you? I saw that piece on Prachy. I can't believe you did that."

"It needed saying."

"Shan needed you to say it, more like."

Erica made the tea and held the cup out to him, a beautiful piece of wess'har domestic art, all violet and gold swirls; they made the most wonderful glass. Transparency was their obsession. The drains running from terrace to terrace around the caldera were a kind of glass too, like all their utensils, and on Constantine, before Aras had let the nanites loose to erase all signs of human settlement, even the church bells had been royal blue glass like antique Bristol ware. One of the things Eddie had grown to love about wess'har was that what you saw was exactly, painfully, and unremittingly what you got. They hid nothing.

If they said midnight was the deadline, they didn't mean 2359 or 0001. And the consequences would be swift.

"If anything," Eddie said, responding aloud to his own thoughts, "Esganikan's gone soft. I'm piecing together what I'm getting from the news with the little I hear from Shan, and I'm amazed no shit's hit the fan yet. The Eqbas expect the death penalty. They can't even imagine that a trial would acquit, either. Big cultural mismatch there. Lull before the storm, maybe."

"If memory serves, the Eqbas were hanging around here for ages before they started on Umeh."

"Did it scare you, knowing they'd turned up?"

"Bloody right it did. You?"

Eddie tried to remember. He'd logged and recorded a museum's worth of experiences since he'd first come here, but recalling his emotional state accurately at any one point was hard. "I think I knew it was scary, but I was more wrapped up in the ethics of how I reported it all. My footage kicked off riots. It's like realizing you've pulled the trigger without looking where you were aiming."

"What, like with Prachy?"

"The alternative is never to report anything in case it upsets someone, and almost all stories do. That's news for you."

Erica seemed to take some time thinking that over. She sat down beside him on the sofa, the one Shan had made with her own hands, which looked white unless you were wess'har. They saw the fabric as peacock blue. It had needed a few repairs over the years, but Shan had done a solid job of building it.

"I'm fed up seeing you sit in judgment on yourself every night." Erica slid her arm through his, slopping his tea. "You're not the only person in the universe with free choice. You don't run it. It's as much the viewers' bloody responsibility to react sensibly to what they see as it is for you to report it properly, so for goodness' sake stop *doing* this to yourself."

"Yes, Mum."

"Come on, you and Shan—you've got the same self-focus. Everything you do is of global importance. Only you can save or condemn the world. That kind of arrogant bullshit."

"You know what they say about great power."

"Is that in the Bible?"

"I think it was in a comic, actually."

Eddie leaned back and watched the images in silence for a long time, Erica's resting against him, and wondered if they'd woken Barry. Brussels mattered. The whole planet did. Barry, and the Champciaux kid, Jérôme, would be the last humans left here one day, a lonely fate however good the wess'har were as neighbors, and that meant that sooner or later—sooner, probably—they'd have to go to Earth to have any hope of normal life. Eddie now fully understood why Shan aborted her kid. It wasn't just curbing the spread of *c'naatat;* it was saving a child from the fate of being utterly alone for a very long time. Having *c'naatat* parents there for you until Kingdom Come didn't make up for not being able to have a lover and all that went with it.

"Esganikan had better get this right," Erica muttered.

So she was thinking the same thing.

"If she can't, who can?"

"If you're going to wait up for the deadline, I can heat some soup."

"I'm not hungry. So you're going to keep me company to watch the fall of Rome."

"Is that on the hit-list too? Can't be much of the place left anyway."

"Figure of speech, dear, just so you know I'm not a totally uneducated oaf."

Eddie had once been used to waiting for deadlines to

expire and wars to start. They were never *called* wars, of course, always something short of that to satisfy legal niceties, but he'd never seen one on his home turf. Umeh didn't count. If he ever saw one of the British regions scorched and crushed like the Maritime Fringe, he wasn't sure how he'd take it. Zammett had hit a nerve there.

The room filled with the smell of leek and potato soup, grown in the Wess'ej soil still protected by a biobarrier to maintain a little bit of Earth a long way from home. Was it too hot or dry to grow good spuds in England now?

"How long to go?" Erica asked, settling down again beside him to eat.

"Four hours."

"Ah. You'd think they'd run some old movies, like the countdown to New Year."

Just hand Prachy over. She's expendable. Ouzhari was.

Would it make any difference in the end? Sooner or later, the Eqbas would use force.

They were lovely neighbors, wess'har, until you crossed that line.

PM's office, Kamberra: two hours to deadline.

"Okay, this is the agreement, or at least what's in place so far," said Storley. "We have a location for any handover that's yet to be agreed. The FEU Mitterand Air Base."

Bari lined up the coffee in anticipation of a long night. Shukry looked in need of it too. "Why there?"

"Access for Eqbas ships as well as the Canadians."

"Talk me through the timeline."

"First critical thing is the response from Canada," said Storley. "Because the Eqbas want Canada to agree to a death sentence, and they're still kicking that around. Expectations will *not* match. The Eqbas assume that a trial will convict, because they don't factor in motive. We have to prove specific *intent* in genocide cases, or else it's just a list of murder charges, which won't get the death penalty in Canada anyway. Either the Eqbas are blind to that, or they're nodding and smiling with the intention of lynching her anyway."

"I'm not sure what Canada is playing at." Bari got up for a walk around the office to keep his circulation going. The whole ADF was on standby now, because Bari could see this going off like a chain of firecrackers. "Once they have Prachy, and the Eqbas work out she won't die, they've got a ticking bomb in their lap."

"They're mindful of the risk. They're looking at bringing a general war crimes charge based on the cobalt bombs, and seeing if a death penalty option can be attached to that. Cobalt is only there to wipe out life indiscriminately, no other use. Let's not even get into the legal status of the assault. No war declared, obviously. It's a mire."

Eqbas didn't like mires. They wouldn't wait through a year of legal pretrial argument. Bari had no intention of saying it explicitly, but he knew Storley and Andreaou thought it too: the cleanest option would be for the Eqbas to kill Prachy there and then, leaving the FEU to decide if it was up for a shooting match with a massively advanced alien navy. It was going to be ugly, but not quite as ugly as the same scene happening on the soil of an ally.

"Who do we have at the location now?"

"Just a diplomatic service observer. No visible involvement to drag us in—the Eqbas are sending the private military contractors and a few Skavu to ride security."

"By contractors, you mean the former marines."

"And Frankland. No, she won't be on the ground. No risk or hint that we might hand her over, accidentally or otherwise."

"Okay, so this is only a question of the size of the turd entering the turbine, not *if* the turd will hit it."

"I'm afraid so. But we're within the law, and *observing*."

"Niall, your precision is laudable, but the Eqbas are the law from now on. And if they do have a legal system, I'm too scared to look at it."

"The air force is on alert five, anyway," said Andreaou. "But I would still like to see the trial, and let the Eqbas loose later."

Bari drained his cup and refilled. "Damn, you said it . . ."

It was just a matter of waiting. Bari waited another ten minutes before the desk system chirped and Persis's voice said: "They've agreed. It's on."

He wasn't sure whether to be relieved or not.

FEU Mitterand Air Base: 2330 hours CET,
30 minutes to deadline.

It was a big airfield, and Ade felt edgy and exposed in the middle of a lake of fierce light.

To the marines' left, the Canadian handover party waited; a diplomat, and what looked like cops in anonymous black coveralls with no signs of armor or weapons. To the right, an FEU military police vehicle was idling next to a group of men and women in suits; diplomats or lawyers, by the look of them. Above, an Eqbas command ship hung motionless at five thousand meters, projecting a defense shield that took in the whole airfield and tower right to the perimeter.

And just in front of them, four Skavu waited in a line, completely silent and stock-still in the mild night air.

Chahal nudged Ade. "Tempting," he said.

"I hope they took their calm pills." Ade could hear chatter from the command ship in his earpiece. Shan was talking to Esganikan, reminding her that the Canadians were worth being nice to. "Shame, I really fancied a proper raid, one last time."

"Careful, or the FEU's going to ask for our rifles back," said Qureshi. "For the museum."

They were a remnant of a proper commando outfit, reduced to standing around in battered kit, minus any badge or rank to wear. They looked like a weekend skirmish hobby team, but with real and serious ESF670 assault rifles. The rifles might have been obsolete weapons now, but they could still do the business. Ade assumed everyone realized that.

"Boss, what's happening?" Ade checked his watch. "Fifteen minutes to go."

Shan's voice popped in his earpiece. "They're bringing her onto the tarmac now. Watch for the police vehicle."

"Here she comes," said Barencoin.

The police car came to a stop at the line of FEU lawyers and someone jumped out to open the door. The woman they helped out wasn't the frail old lady that the description suggested, but one in reasonably good shape and walking well.

"Bang goes her sympathy vote," Barencoin muttered. "She needs to get that helpless granny look down a bit better before she goes on trial."

Prachy, accompanied by a lawyer, walked across in front of the Skavu and stared at them for a second or two before the Canadian diplomat stepped forward and some words were exchanged. The two men nodded at each other, taking those little gradual steps backwards that preceded turning and walking away. Prachy looked as if she wasn't sure what she was supposed to do next.

Once she was in the Canadian vehicle, it wasn't Ade's problem any longer. The men turned away from each other as if on cue and Prachy was left standing between them, exposed for a moment.

Something zipped past Ade's head like an insect. A loud crack split the night air.

Prachy stumbled forward, arms held away from her sides like a diver for a moment before she crumpled onto the concrete. The marines dropped instinctively into a contact formation; there was no cover unless they ran for the cars. For a second, everyone froze, including the Skavu.

"Sniper!" Ade yelled. If anyone had gone to Prachy's aid, he couldn't see. The round had *passed him*. "Ground level, over there—"

Another shot rang out; it sounded as if it came from behind them this time. And that was the one that plunged the handover into disaster. Ade knew it as soon as he heard the wet thwack of a round hitting flesh. Turning, he saw a Canadian officer on the ground and his buddies aiming their short automatics as if they thought the shot had come from the Skavu. Then the Skavu turned towards the Canadians, rifles raised. It was as if a switch had been thrown: the shooting started.

Ade's brain slipped into a different time frame. Everything ran slowly, agonizingly, and Prachy was forgotten. In the crossfire, Ade heard another *thwack* and Becken slumped forward. Shan's voice filled Ade's earpiece saying, "Get them out—" but the sound cut off.

"Cease fire!" Ade yelled. "For fuck's sake, it's *snipers,* you twats—"

The firing stopped. He could hear everyone panting. He looked around frantically, checking where his people were. He couldn't see Qureshi.

"Jon?" Chahal scrambled towards Becken. "Jon? *Jon!*"

"Izzy? Where the fuck's Izzy?"

Barencoin must have caught something in his scope; he opened up at a position right of the tower that was well inside the perimeter. Ade ran at a crouch to Becken and tripped over Qureshi.

"*Oh shit.* Oh shit, shit, shit . . ."

It was all over in thirty or forty chaotic seconds.

The airfield was silent for a moment before the sirens started. Ade, still running on adrenaline, checked who was alive and who wasn't; one Skavu was down and so were three of the Canadians, two of them with visible burns from Skavu energy weapons. The civvies were squatting or lying flat on the tarmac, too scared to move, and Prachy's head rested in a pool of tarry blood.

So did Jon Becken's.

Chahal was checking Becken's pulse, fingers on the man's neck. It was a waste of bloody time. Becken was an ordinary bloke, not *c'naatat* like Ade, with miraculous powers of recovery; a chunk of his head was gone, and he wasn't going to regain consciousness a few days later and carry on as normal like Shan did back on Bezer'ej. Ade shut down at that point. If he let himself feel anything right then, he'd slot the next bastard who moved. He ignored the sudden noise around him—ambulances, shouting, recriminations, the noise of vehicles screaming into position—and concentrated on Qureshi.

Barencoin leaned over him.

"Fucking idiots." Barencoin spat out the words. Ade felt

the spray on his face. "Fucking amateurs." He started yelling, but his voice seemed to be coming from a long way away. "*Medic!* Get a fucking medic over here!"

Qureshi lay on her side with her legs bent awkwardly behind her, blood spilling from her mouth and spattered over her jacket, but still alive. She was making a gurgling sound. Ade's emergency first aid kicked in. He checked the wound; a ballistic round had penetrated her neck below the larynx and she was choking in her own blood. *Airway, get the airway clear first—*

"Mart, help me keep her neck stable. Izzy? Can you hear me? Don't you dare bloody well die on me." The blood was frothy. Her eyelids fluttered. Barencoin pulled off his jacket as used it as a pad to cover the wound while he held her head steady. "You're going to be okay, Izzy, hold on."

It was a lie; Ade knew it.

He tried to clear her mouth of blood with his fingers. Then a hand grabbed his shoulder and he batted it away before he realized it was the ambulance crew taking over.

"About fucking time," said Barencoin. "What's the matter, you got stuck in traffic or something?"

Ade watched numbly as the paramedics clustered around Qureshi and tried to stabilize her. But she stopped making that awful rattling sound and went limp. They worked on her for what seemed like a long time; it was probably minutes, no more, but Ade had lost all sense of time. Barencoin tried to haul him away.

"Come on, mate, nothing we can do now—"

"Is she dead?" He pulled away from Barencoin and caught one of the paramedics by the arm. "I said, *is she dead?*"

"I'm afraid so, sir," said the paramedic.

Ade knew the words had sunk in, just as he knew Becken was dead too; but it was all still unreal and distant, as if events were so fresh that he could change what had happened if he tried hard enough. It had all gone to shit in moments. That was how big the gulf was between life and death: not hours of battle, but a fucking stupid stray shot after some bastard got spooked and started firing.

The ambulance crew started to move Qureshi's body. That was the final straw for Ade. They weren't going to take her, or Becken. Ade was suddenly aware of Webster holding him back and telling the paramedics that they'd deal with the bodies. He hadn't even seen where Webster was during the shooting.

"Who started it?" he said. Like it mattered: it hadn't been a Skavu weapon that had killed either Qureshi or Becken, but his money was on those fanatical bastards. "How did two fucking snipers get inside the cordon?" He turned, not sure if he was going to take it out on the Canadians or the Skavu first, and found himself in Barencoin's arm lock. He railed at the Canadian cops anyway. "Jesus Christ, don't any of you bastards have proper *procedures?*"

"Easy Sarge." Barencoin was close to breaking his arm. "Time for that later. I promise you. Now's not the time."

Ade didn't give a shit about looking controlled and professional. Two of his mates had been killed in a simple hand-over. People got away with friendly fire incidents all the time, but not on his watch.

A section of Eqbas ship had already plummeted to the ground in shuttle format. By the time it crossed Ade's mind that he could have sliced a chunk out of his hand and got some *c'naatat* blood into Qureshi or Becken, and let Shapakti sort out the infection when they were well again, Shan ran down the ramp of the shuttle with a couple of Eqbas and grabbed him.

"Get the bodies inboard," she said. One of the Skavu made a move as if to help. "Not *you,* you arsehole."

In that stupid way of firefights, Ade now panicked about *not taking biohaz precautions,* stupid bastard, stupid *stupid* bastard, and started gulping in air, transfixed by the sight of two bodies being wrapped in something like a translucent body-bag. The Skavu tried to board the shuttle. That was the point at which Shan snapped.

"Get fucking out!" she yelled. She had her 9mm in her hand and she smashed it across the face of the first Skavu who put a boot on the deck. "Not in here. Just fuck off."

She wouldn't let them board. The shuttle lifted and Ade

found himself in what felt like a bubble filled with the smell of blood. Shan was the only one talking, saying something to Webster that the FEU had slotted Prachy to stop her giving embarrassing evidence, and shot one of the Canadians too, just to spread confusion. It had done that, all right. Once the Canadian cops went down, nobody stopped to work out who was firing.

"Bastards," said Barencoin in his ear. Who? Canadians, Skavu, FEU? All of them. Ade couldn't take his eyes off Qureshi's face, all that was Izzy gone for good leaving just this blood-smeared frozen mask looking at nothing. He couldn't see Becken's face from this position. "Fucking idiots. Why didn't we armor up?"

I should have got them all armored up, helmets, the works. But it was just a handover inside the defense shield, and so they hadn't. Ade wanted to go on the rampage, and then he realized why Shan had forced the Skavu out of the shuttle, because she knew him so well.

"Jesus, I should have known the FEU would do this," said Shan. "We got back all this way, all alive, and I get them killed in this poxy fucking waste of a place."

Ade was certain right then that had he not reverted to training, he would have said sod the consequences and saved them both, like Aras saved Shan. Later, when his adrenaline started to ebb on the way back to base, he thought that he wouldn't have. He swung between if-only and I-couldn't-have for a couple of hours in complete silence. He just didn't think of it first.

Esganikan had her "balance," though. Prachy had been executed, and the matter was closed.

If she ever said that to him, though, he'd kill her.

11

Let's revise the old adage for our times. All that it requires for evil to succeed is that enough lazy, stupid bastards believe everything they're told.

EDDIE MICHALLAT

Reception Center's landing area: six hours later.

Shan wasn't sure how she was going to last another hour on this shithole of a world without killing Esganikan where she stood.

She found herself almost hammering the shuttle's bulkhead with the heel of her hand to get the bloody thing to extrude a ramp. Aras set the vessel down. There was a second or two of numb silence, and then Barencoin got up and stood beside her. She couldn't even look at him.

All she could feel, over and over again like a vid loop, was the splash of something warm against her face. It was a flashback she had far too often: Ade's memory of Dave Pharoah's brain tissue spraying him at Ankara. But the guilt that went with it was fresh and all her own.

"Aras," she said. The voice wasn't hers; it was Superintendent Frankland taking over and handling the incident, pure reflex. "Aras, leave the—leave the bodies for me to deal with, and get the detachment to their rooms and *keep* them there." She didn't want to yell at them at a time like this, but she knew what they'd do: they'd go after any Skavu they could identify, or even one that just looked at them the wrong way, and someone else would end up dead. She knew that urge all too well herself. She didn't care what happened to the Skavu, but she was damned if she was going to lose one more marine. She didn't care if the whole planet was destroyed; she would *not* lose one more

Bootie. She'd got them home after all that shit, all that insane *shit* trillions of miles from home, and now two of them were dead because she'd fucked up and not seen trouble coming.

Of course the FEU would kill Prachy before she could stand trial and embarrass them with her revelations. *Of course* they'd shoot one of the Canadians to muddy the waters. They probably didn't even realize it would tip a tense situation with the Skavu over the edge. And no inquiry would ever identify the gunmen as FEU agents.

That's how it works. Always has. And you should have seen it coming.

The two deaths weren't Esganikan's doing, even if the Skavu were the wrong troops for the job, and they weren't even the FEU's. It was down to Shan. If she'd stopped the marines going, the outcome at the air base would have been the same, but Qureshi and Becken would be alive.

"I don't want anyone going near the Skavu for the time being," she said. "I'll deal with Esganikan."

"Ma'am, we'll take care of Izzy and Jon." Barencoin's voice was quiet, a different man's entirely. "They're our own. No offense, but we want to do it. Not you."

"Okay." Shan managed a glance at him, burning with shame and grief. *I got your mates killed.* "I don't even know where to start saying sorry, so I'll do what I have to and see that bitch."

Ade caught her arm. For a moment Shan thought he was going to take her handgun from her, even though the bloody thing wouldn't have done any lasting damage to Esganikan now. "Don't do it, Boss. Wait a while. Let's all calm down and think."

For once, Shan didn't *want* to think. She wanted to kill Esganikan Gai *now,* buoyed up on pure clean hatred, because the fucking cow deserved it: she deserved it for lying about *c'naatat,* and sending Skavu in, and probably for a lot of other things Shan didn't even know about yet. But most of all she wanted to kill her because Qureshi's and Becken's lives were over before they'd even had a real chance of living them. If she felt this grief, she dreaded to think what was happening to Ade. His anger had now collapsed and left him quiet and spent.

"Look," she said, taking slow breaths to calm down. Her anger tended to build after an incident, not ebb. "I have to see her. So get out of way, and let me do what I have to."

"I'll go with you," said Aras.

"You will *not*. Look after Ade. I'll be right back."

"I don't need looking after," said Ade. "Please, Shan, if there's any scores to be settled, we do it cold, right? We do it *later*."

She didn't know what to say, so she left. The worst moment was stepping out of the shuttle and leaving the marines with their friends' bodies. It seemed the ultimate act of callous abandonment. It had been a long time since Shan had lost anyone close to her, and her mind was an explosion of assorted bereavement: her own memories of being told that Baz had wrapped the area car around a tree, Ade's numb horror more times than she realized, and Aras mourning his comrades. It was an eruption of grief and guilt. *Jesus, is this how they felt when they were told I was dead?* She had to get a grip. Ade was right. She had always yearned to stop her automatic shutdown of strong emotions and to be able to chase the pain or love to its ultimate expression, but now she knew how the floodgates could be opened again, it was the wrong time and place. If she didn't slam the door on that emotion now, it'd overwhelm her when she most needed to function.

As she walked up to the center, a big black official cruiser was parked right outside the doors; Bari was already here. So he had political flak to handle. Tough shit.

What was it now? Five days? Six? It wasn't even a week since they'd landed, and it was already falling apart. Maybe Esganikan had another definition of *according to plan* that she didn't know about. By the time she had sprinted up the stairs and reached the fifth floor where the Eqbas officers had set up camp, Bari was walking slowly downstairs, head lowered, with his bagman trailing him.

"I suppose you'll be wanting an explanation from me, Prime Minister," Shan said as she passed them. They stopped. "Because I doubt you got one from Commander Gai."

He looked into her face. He was dark, mid-forties, with a tight mouth that hinted at a bad temper kept in check. "What happened? The Canadians are going nuts. I'm getting stories about a sniper."

"The FEU slotted her and a Canadian, I'm bloody sure. The rest—someone drew, the Skavu reacted, and my people got caught trying to stop it. Tell the Canadian ambassador to shove his head up his arse."

"Commander Gai, believe it or not, is satisfied. She's *satisfied* because Prachy's dead. *Outcomes.*"

And that's why I've got to hang in there and have an orderly handover of power. That's why I've got to get Laktiriu ready to step in, and make sure she's up to the job.

"If it's any comfort," Shan said, "I'm going in there to slap the shit out of her because two good people got killed. *My* people. I'm doing everything I can to manage this, too."

"But you're human. This is *your world.* Can't you bring some pressure to bear?"

Shan considered telling him things would be changing before too long, but thought better of it. "That's what I'm doing. Maybe now you realize you're dealing with people who don't think like we do."

Bari and his assistant carried on down the wide stairway. Shan found Esganikan sitting at the desk in her room with the door wide open like it was a regular day at the office. The walls were covered with displays that seemed to be the same as those in the ship.

"I think the usual opening line is 'What the fuck are you playing at,'" said Shan. She had to check that she wasn't reeking *jask* everywhere. The effort of containing it was almost painful. "Two of my people are dead. Your Skavu didn't exactly help matters, either."

Esganikan never reacted. That was what made Shan really want to punch her face in; the complete lack of anything to come back at. "I told you to let us deal with it in our own way. But you wanted to follow some pointless ritual. Prachy is dead, but your marines needn't have been there, nor you.

In the future, you might be better employed sticking to the liaison role, which is your reason for being here."

Two people weren't supposed to matter more than a whole planet, but right then they did. Shan would never know how she did it; but she kept her *jask* under control, and yet totally lost her temper. She lunged forward and sent Esganikan flying backwards on the stool, crashing flat on her back, and jumped on her chest to pin her down with one arm across her throat. Her 9mm was in Esganikan's face before she even thought twice about it.

It won't kill her. She'll hurt like hell. But then she'll know that I know what she is.

"You keep your Skavu shit under control," Shan hissed. "You've got five years before the main fleet arrives. And the only reason you're still in command is because *I allow you.*" Esganikan's pupils were snapping open and shut at an incredible rate. She was taller than Shan, but she wasn't any stronger, and that realization gave Shan a massive burst of adrenaline. *I can take the bitch, I really can.* "You know I can depose you, don't you?" She leaned harder on Esganikan's neck. "*Don't you?* You want to smell it?"

Esganikan didn't struggle. Shan—animal Shan, not Superintendent Frankland—wanted to lose control and get it over with. She couldn't, though, not yet. She eased back an inch or two. Esganikan seemed to be playing along with the idea that the gun could kill her. She had to know that it couldn't. The act just made Shan angrier, because this wasn't like any wess'har she knew.

"If you depose me, the Skavu won't answer to *you*," said Esganikan. "And then you'll have to use the Eqbas personnel to put down any rebellion in the ranks, which I'm certain there'll be, and then the mission will be a disaster."

It was another good reason for getting Laktiriu in place first. Shan knew she'd have to find another outlet for her rage and grief, which was what all this scuffle was about. But she'd shown Esganikan that she could give her serious personal trouble, and that would have its uses.

"Maybe I don't give a shit about that," Shan said. "Maybe it's worth it to—"

"Commander!" Laktiriu stood in the doorway, head cocked on one side. Matriarchs didn't brawl on the floor. It stopped her dead. "Commander?"

Shan got to her feet and put the 9mm back in her belt.

"Your boss and I had a difference of management opinion," Shan said. She hadn't planned this moment, but it was there to be seized as an excuse for her next move. "You'll excuse me if I avoid her for a while. I'll deal with you instead, Lieutenant, or I might be tempted to blow her fucking head off."

Shan had no idea what rank Laktiriu went by, but now she had a good reason for spending time with her and steering her into a coup. Her own cold opportunism while Qureshi and Becken were lying out there in pieces suddenly disgusted her. As she ran down the stairs, pulse pounding in her throat, random thoughts hit her: What would Eqbas Vorhi do when they found out that Wess'ej had ordered her to execute of one of their people? How many more *c'naatat* were there now? Had Esganikan infected anyone else?

Laktiriu had to be Shan's focus. Right now, though, she had to support Ade and the others.

When she got back to the shuttle, Barencoin and Chahal were securing a body bag. Ade knelt over another, busy with a cloth and a bottle of water.

Webster wandered across to Shan, arms folded across her chest. They'd rarely chatted; Webster was one of those scrubbed, cheerful women who looked as if they belonged on a farm or at the church fete selling cakes, and Shan knew very little about her background.

"Ade was very fond of Izzy," she said. "He wanted to make her look as nice as possible."

"Is there anything remotely useful that I can do now, Sue? Other than shutting the fuck up or apologizing?"

"We've got it all under control. And the last thing we do is start throwing blame around. We all volunteered to do this."

That still didn't get Shan off the hook. "What do we do about burials?"

"Shit, they can't even have a military funeral," said Barencoin, straightening up. He kept taking deep sighs as if he was having trouble holding back tears. "We didn't get as far as enlisting with the ADF."

"There's somewhere they can both be buried," said Aras. "The Muslim town where Deborah's taken the colonists. That would satisfy both their final requests, I think."

"Yes. That's nice." Ade nodded. He pulled Qureshi's collar into a neat shape and stood up, a small chain dangling from his hand. "They'd have liked that."

Maybe Ade was getting too used to digging graves for people he cared about. He just seemed quiet. Shan put her arm around him and wished that he hadn't had to see yet another image that would haunt him.

"Okay, let's move them inside." It would have to be in the food store again, just like it had been on Bezer'ej when they needed to store cadavers from *Thetis*. "I'll give you a hand."

Shan had dealt with a lot of bodies in her police career and she could always switch off, in some cases more easily than others. This time, she didn't want to.

In a few days' time, Becken would have been best man at her wedding. Qureshi was going to do her hair.

And both of them—she could have saved them, just as Aras saved her. She could have saved Lindsay Neville's kid. But Ade, unlike Lindsay, would have the good grace never to remind her.

PM's briefing en route to the UN hub.

"You can't suspend parliamentary questions again, sir," said Persis.

The sky was filling with clouds as the cruiser emerged above ground level, a warning of the severe storm forecast for later that day. The display screen in front of Bari, set in the blast-proof partition between the driver's cab and the passenger seats, laid out too many news feeds and messages for him to take in. But as they all said the same thing, that he'd plunged the world into deep shit, he didn't have to worry that he was missing anything.

New Zealand seemed to be unhappier than the FEU.

Jesus, how much alien tech did they expect to get their hands on right away? They watched too many movies.

"I've had a busy week," Bari said. "Or didn't they notice the aliens land? UN first, then the local stuff." He checked the defnet satellite images: no sign of FEU vessels in AAD waters or anywhere else in the region. That was a start. "Have we got teams from all the Rim States on the desalination tech transfer project?"

"Just us at the moment."

"Well, ship in some Pacific Rim delegates fast. Get everyone feeling they're involved. Show that we're going to look after our neighbors."

The UN hub was an anachronism, but participating in a meeting via an implant in your head just didn't cut it like sitting down with other humans in that tribal way. It wasn't the full main session in Brussels—the FEU could kiss his arse now—but every region clustered in its own hub because long-haul travel was antisocial behavior, and budgets were tight. The trade-off was business done on the hoof in the corridors and coffee shops; that was where political relationships were built.

But right now Bari only had announcements to make. There was no horse trading left to do.

The hub conference room looked in need of a lick of paint. The New Zealand delegate, Jackie Rance, was deep in conversation with the Indonesian rep, Charlie Nyoo. And, apart from the small army of diplomats and advisers sitting in the viewing area, that was it.

"You'd have thought we could have turned out a few more bodies for the end of civilization as we know it, wouldn't you?" said Bari, reaching out to shake hands. "Better look like a crowd when the cam's on. Don't want to remind them how small we are down here."

"The storm's coming," said Rance. "Travel problems."

"Never mind."

"I see you got off to a cracking start, then . . . not a pretty sight."

"Mistakes were made," said Bari. "But I'm not in a position to stop them happening . . . yet."

Nyoo just looked at him, chin resting on his hand.

"What?" said Bari, checking the array of time zone clocks on the wall; five minutes to get his story straight. "Look, there'll be terrific benefits coming out of this for us all."

"Den, I just want to know if it's a case of *what* we get out of it, or *if* we get out of it."

"You want the truth? Both. Because the Eqbas strategy is to reduce the world population to a billion. We either win big or lose big."

He'd rehearsed that line in his head so many times that it came out like a mantra. If he said it often enough and fast enough, it might not only be believed, but it would happen. Rance and Nyoo both made a long *shhh* sound under their breaths. Bari could imagine how that figure was going to go down with the wider UN community.

"How long have we known about this?" Nyoo asked.

"If we'd paid attention, twenty-five years."

But Australia, and by default the Pacific Rim, *had* paid attention; and it got the seats in the lifeboat.

The screen that formed the entire wall went live, and Bari was looking at a packed chamber that was a composite of overlays from regional hubs around the world, creating a reasonable impression of being in a real session except for the delays on the links. Now that was something that ITX could fix, he thought; but there were more important applications for it.

"Here we go," said Rance.

There had always been rules about life on Earth up to now, and the main one was that if you annoyed the superpowers, you paid the price. Now it *didn't matter*. It struck Bari just as Michael Zammett—not a regular speaker at the UN—got up to call for sanctions against Australia.

It was an awfully quiet chamber.

"Mr. Zammett," said Bari, "I have to point out that, so far, no Australian vessel, aircraft or citizen has crossed your borders. All we seem to be guilty of is thinking ahead."

Zammett wanted his moment. "You're allowing aggressors to use your country as a safe haven."

"The Eqbas don't *need* a safe haven, Mr. Zammett.

They're safe from us anywhere they go. I truly regret the loss of life in the incident yesterday, but the FEU is responsible for security on its own air bases, and let's not forget the roots of the whole crisis—that the FEU committed an act of genocide on a planet for its own military ends, leaving the rest of this world to share the consequences. You had a quarter of a century to do as the Eqbas asked and punish those responsible. You didn't. You made it worse for us all. All Australia is doing now is saying to the Eqbas that we understand their anger, and that we also recognize things have to change here if humans are going to have any kind of future." Bari paused for effect. Hijacking a question was fair game, and while he had a world platform he was going to wring every advantage from it. Nyoo was making notes. "They're not going to go away. They're not going be driven off or defeated. There's no simple germ that's going to kill them off in the nick of time. The only choice we have is the speed at which we reduce our population and our consumption. Here's the clue—a planet called Umeh did it fast. Anyone who doesn't want to end up like that—sign up to an agreement to a more frugal way of life, and get some help from a race who can actually do something about cleaning up the planet. It's that simple."

There was a silence. Some of it was the delay on the relay, but then it was clear that it was just a bombshell coming to rest.

Zammett made one last stab. "That doesn't deal with the matter on the table. The FEU asks for sanctions against Australia for harboring terrorists, and it asks Australia to honor its extradition treaty and hand over those individuals we want to stand trial in an FEU court. I'd also call on all countries not to cave in to an invasion—because that's what it is—and to resist an occupying army."

It doesn't matter.

It really doesn't.

Bari stood his ground. "And in the unlikely event that the Eqbas leave, Mr. Zammett, then we don't have a future anyway, do we? We're out of ideas for slowing climate change.

Let's treat this as the opportunity it is for humankind and the planet."

The vote for sanctions was taken; the Sinostates were among the abstainers and Canada and Norway voted against. It was never going anywhere anyway. Bari was grateful for the chance to do his global savior speech, but slightly shaken by the awareness that he wasn't exaggerating one bit.

"Nice job, PM," said Persis.

Now all he had to do was get Esganikan Gai to start addressing the rest of the world, and not routing everything through him. And all she had to do was deliver on the promises of turning back the environmental clock.

En route for Rabi'ah community, Australia: seven days after landing.

"Can we make the bulkheads transparent?" Shan asked. "It's getting claustrophobic in here."

The shuttle pilot, Emrianu, obliged by clearing the nose section. Small patches of expensively irrigated crops, shielded against evaporation by canopies, stretched along both sides of a highway punctuated by clustered houses and silos partly buried in the ground. Some people refused to retreat below the surface.

Everywhere Shan looked now reminded her in some way of her first sight of the Constantine colony on Bezer'ej: the vivid colors, the sunken buildings, and the sharp delineation between the cocoon of cultivated land and the wilderness beyond. And Rabi'ah, as they called it, had one more parallel with Constantine. It was a religious community.

Shan could imagine how Deborah had reacted when she saw the place. She was probably measuring it up as another miracle inside five minutes.

"Is that enough?" Emrianu asked.

Shan savored the view, missing the open spaces of F'nar and what now seemed like a simpler life. "Thanks," she said. "That's plenty." She turned her swiss over in her pocket, trying to find the right time to call Eddie about Qureshi and Becken. He'd know now; he'd have seen it on BBchan, even if the two weren't named. He'd *know*.

I have to face him. Shit, it's hard enough to face Ade.

"We could give them biobarrier technology," said Esganikan. The ceasefire between the two matriarchs was just that—an awkward unspoken agreement not to rip into each other again. Shan resented every second spent with her. "That would be more efficient than these canopies they use everywhere."

Shan's suspicion reflex kicked in. "Is there any way it can be misused? I'd hate to think of you losing your edge."

"I want to make Rabi'ah an example of the template for *gethes* to follow. Let's see what we can do for them in the very short term."

The debacle with Prachy was evidently history for Esganikan now. Nobody could accuse her of spending her time in working parties and meetings. If she hadn't come straight from Umeh in operational terms, then maybe she'd have had the patience to spend a few more weeks settling in before she embarked on anything, but her sense of urgency was manic.

Shan had her own reasons for making Rabi'ah a priority visit. Aras had suggested that this was where Qureshi and Becken could be buried. She wanted the graves in good hands, and she could think of none better than Deborah Garrod.

It was a vegan community established by Muslims. Now it was host to the influx of Christians from Constantine and already working out how to move them out of the nearby temporary camp as soon as possible. Shan tried hard, but she couldn't think of a logical reason why a multifaith vegan community could be bad news, other than that it was too good to be true, and she never trusted faith not to turn into something more bizarre and sinister when her back was turned. They'd said yes to the graves without a moment's hesitation. Their generosity made Shan despise humans even more. If these people could behave decently, there was no excuse for the rest.

"Well, I can't think of a better model," she said. "You going to make it compulsory? Because a lot of Muslims won't play well with Christians and vice versa. And you've only just scratched the surface of religion. We've got a long list of faiths with feuds and schisms."

Aitassi, who'd been curled up against a bulkhead, edged into the conversation. She didn't seem happy; Esganikan had been making less use of her services, especially as translation wasn't needed now, and she'd come on board that morning with an air of not wanting to be left out.

"Religion seems to be the most powerful motivation for humans, even more than greed for wealth," she said. "Look at Constantine, a mission that no company or government would attempt because they felt it wasn't worth the resources. But the colonists gave everything they had because they thought this god of theirs wanted it done. How do we implant ideas that powerful?"

Shan could now jump a few stages ahead in that inexorable logic. "Religious people can also think their god wants them to kill anyone who disagrees with them, or commit mass suicide so they can join the mothership. It's a lottery as to what they think God wants. So if you're thinking of using religion to drive this, that's very dangerous ground that your million years of civilization can't prepare you for."

"Restoring Earth is a long process," said Aitassi. "It needs custodians with a long-term view. Religions seem to make a better job of that."

Well, don't expect me to hang around forever. Once I've sorted you out, I'm leaving. You've already cost me two good friends. "How did you do the triage of good guys on other planets?"

Esganikan tilted her head to one side very gradually, looking past Shan and through the not-there bulkhead at the panorama of a parched continent.

Shan noticed her distraction and tried to see the Earth mission through Eqbas eyes. They'd ended up with just a few months in total to plan the complete remediation of a planet, instead of the five years they'd counted on, and with data interrupted by time dilation in transit they were flying partly blind. It was like arriving in modern Rome with a copy of Tacitus's *Annales* as a handbook and then trying to catch up on the run.

It was also like responding to a disaster anywhere, and Shan had done that as a copper so many times that she should have known better. The basic plan of things that had to be done whatever the situation, from moving people out of danger to clearing up the aftermath, was planned for and tested on exercise. But the detail of the real emergency was always new, always different, always something you couldn't plan for until you got to the incident and took stock of what was unfolding around you.

And what you did on a moment's instant decision shaped everything that followed.

I closed off a highway and diverted traffic onto another route because the flood barriers had overtopped and the road was awash. I didn't know that the route I was sending it down was blocked by a collision, because someone's data stream failed, because I couldn't get an aerial view, because . . . , I made the wrong call in a situation that was all bad calls.

Now multiply that by a planet.

Esganikan was just the first responder on the scene, and her backup was years away. Shan tried to make an effort now to see the adjustment of Earth as an incident, with strategic, tactical and operational elements. It didn't change a damn thing in her plan for Esganikan, but at least she had a better idea of the problem.

And it scared the shit out of her. A million years' head start didn't make wess'har into gods. Yet that was what she'd expected in some subconscious way: omniscience, at least. It was the second time that God had failed to show for her.

I hate being right. Really, I do. I want the universe to be better than this, a commonsense place. I didn't want humans to be typical. I was so sure we were the idiot dregs.

"Shan, can you hear me?"

No, she hadn't. "Yes. Go on."

"I said that we identify the individuals in the most capable species who can maintain the world when we leave. It's normally the first step. And if there are none, we remove them and allow other species to develop."

"Not as scorched earth as I thought, then."

"Only Umeh was that clear-cut, to our knowledge."

"You must have done a lot of world makeovers in your time, then. If you're at the zero-growth stage, that must be a drain even on your resources." *Bang goes omnipotence. And I never thought infinite mercy was on the menu from the start. Bye-bye, God.* "But you've still got the main Eqbas fleet on its way. Just tell me they haven't started defense cuts back home."

Esganikan gestured to the pilot to land, holding her hand flat and lowering it like ordering a dog to sit. "No, there are still six ships in transit. I expect to leave a more sustainable situation here for them to take over."

"And how long is Eqbas Vorhi prepared to stay?"

"I won't speak to the matriarchs in Surang until I see how the next year goes. The outcome for Earth is as much in the hands of humans as it is in mine."

It was one of those platitudes that was true and probably not believed; humans always needed to think Mum and Dad would be there to run to and make things all better. When Shan realized she did too, only on a far bigger scale, she finally felt herself ripped from her moorings. She'd always known what to do, rock-solid, her core of right and wrong as fixed as a navigation beacon, and humans had been the playground bullies in a universe where the smaller kids were just victims and someone grown-up was ultimately out there to break it up and punish the wrong-doers. But animals did almost all the bad things that humans did—rape, war, child neglect—and the grown-up aliens did their bad stuff too, and couldn't always control the kids or get things right.

All animals really are equal, and I don't like it. Shapakti said I wanted humans to be the only bad guys around. I think I do. It gives me a bit of hope that there are galactic grown-ups out there.

"Okay," Shan said. She suddenly felt physically smaller. "Let's think of this as assertive enabling, then."

It was liberation, or disappointment on a scale that crushed souls, and she could choose which if only she knew.

The ship landed with barely a vibration as it settled onto the bare earth on the outskirts of the town. The port bulkhead opened and extruded a ramp, letting in the real world and a gust of hot air.

"I'm so glad you came," said Deborah Garrod, face illuminated with a certainty that Shan had just lost. "This is the leader of the town council, Mo Ammad. We're so sorry about Izzy and Jon. How's Ade coping?"

There was no lecture on morality or any mention of the circumstances. "You know Ade," she said. "He's solid."

Shan didn't ask if Mo was short for *Mohan*. It would have rattled her at a time when she'd had enough rattling. Ammad greeted Aitassi without turning a hair, squatting at the knee to meet her gaze at eye level rather than looming over her, and Shan took a shine to him right away.

He looked like any other fifty-something dark-haired bloke and not like a religious nutter at all, and he held out his hand. *That saves me worrying if I'm breaking some religious rule on shaking hands. Decent of him.* She'd worn gloves again. Nobody seemed to comment on that.

"What does it do to the liter?" Mo asked, looking back at the Eqbas shuttle.

"I don't even know where they stick the fuel," she said. "Weirdest thing you ever saw. You should try it."

"That'd be something to tell the kids. No security crawling all over you, I notice."

"There would be, if we told them where and when we were moving."

"You used to be a cop."

"I did. I think I still am."

"A ride in the squad car, eh? They'll love it."

"My treat."

It was a spontaneous offer and Shan didn't ask Esganikan. *Hearts and minds, remember?.* They headed towards the town in a dusty farm vehicle that brought back memories of her first contact with Constantine: *Sam.* Sam, that was his name, and he was probably here now, the man who collected her from the *Thetis* shuttle in her biohaz suit and took her to an underground city with a completely incongruous Norman-style church built at its heart. From humbled amazement to planning an assassination took her fewer than three years.

And you knew then that you'd never be able to come back home, in any real sense of the word.

"I admire your ability to keep uprooting yourself, Deborah," Shan said, trying hard to be sociable. "There's a lot to be said for carrying your sense of belonging around with you."

The Constantine colonists had coped with Bezer'ej—thinner air, higher gravity—and brief confinement on the Wess'ej island of Mar'an'cas, a cold wet rock. Earth, even during an Australian summer, seemed to be just another challenge they took in their stride.

Deborah nodded. "If you can do it once, you can do it as many times as you have to."

"Commander, we didn't know what food would be safe for Eqbas," Mo said, half turning his head from the driving seat. "Biochemistry and all that. But at least you know none of it will be animal products."

Esganikan was exceptionally still for a moment. Something made her nervous; it might have been Mo's driving, or it might have been the realization that she could eat anything now that she was *c'naatat*. "Wess'har have eaten some terrestrial crops without harm," she said, surprisingly gracious. "I'll regard it as an experiment."

The town looked like a cluster of enclosed shopping malls that had settled several meters after an earthquake. Inside, it was a lot cooler and the filtered light fell on an impressively green, leafy landscape where the buildings seemed to be drowning in vegetation. The Umeh Station biodome in Jejeno was probably built with similar technology; it was sobering to see how it had developed here in what was—Shan had to pause and count—an intervening fifty years or more.

A utilitarian-looking but rather short tower was the most striking landmark. It was a minaret.

"There's a lot more underground," Mo said. "But we need light, being the delicate flowers that we are. Deborah says the wess'har could pipe sunlight into Constantine. That must have been quite a sight."

I didn't even record any images. It's gone forever. Do I even have any pictures of Jon and Izzy? God, the first time I met him, I bollocked him for setting off the defense grid. Poor sod.

"It was," Shan said, wishing for temporary amnesia. "It really was."

She didn't ask where the Christians gathered. She had no idea if a church was a contentious issue here or not. There were plenty of places on the Earth she'd left where it would have been, and enough of others where a mosque would have been unwelcome too. Wars left very deep divisions that even the shift in global power didn't heal. But this place gave every impression of being a regular town where the inhabitants—watching carefully, inevitably curious about real live alien visitors—just had a few more headscarves than usual. It could have been any city in Europe.

"Do you need a police force here?" Shan asked, smiling as best she could and waving to some fascinated small boys leaning over a wall that was one big flowerbed. They reached out to pat Aitassi like a dog, and Shan braced for the screams, but the ussissi just accepted it. Everyone seemed to be in a tolerant mood today. "Even traffic cops?"

"Why, are you looking for work, Superintendent?"

She'd once asked Sam, her guide to Constantine, if there was crime in the colony. "Just curious. Always am."

"Oh, we have cops, all right. Nobody's perfect." Mo kept looking at Esganikan, who seemed very interested in the kids. Shan could almost see her evaluating their long-term potential as reliable curators. "But we don't have anyone holding secret barbecues, which is probably more of an indicator of our ability to live what we believe."

"Not even grilling soy links?"

"Nah, the bloody things fall through the grid."

Yes, Shan could do business with Mo Ammad.

In the town hall, a small group of men and women waited for them in a committee room that had a whiff of fresh paint and cinnamon. They'd laid out a good spread of what Ade called *small eats* that would have been serious currency for the marines on Wess'ej. Shan had to suppress a reflex to grab a bag of treats to take back for their entertainment. She'd already spotted something that Qureshi would like before reality crashed in and reminded her that Izzy was dead.

Esganikan examined slices of mango with an expression that said the scent was all too familiar, but tried it anyway. *Go on, you crafty cow. You know you could eat it even if it was strychnine.* Esganikan seemed to be surprised by the flavor.

"I intend your settlement to be a model for the rest of this planet," she said suddenly. "There have to be others like you."

Town councils everywhere were used to hearing that. It meant *pilot project* to them, though. That wasn't what Esganikan had in mind. There would be no fact-finding missions to persuade other authorities what might be done. This would be enforced, one way or another, sooner or later.

One of the women councillors took out a handheld. "Are you asking if there's a network of towns like this?" She tapped a control and then held out the screen so that Esganikan could see it. "Because there are, all over the world. Look. We stay in touch, share ideas, occasionally visit. Very different beliefs, some very diverse populations, not all vegan, but we've all aimed to build minimum-impact, zero-growth communities. Some have been around for a few hundred years."

"That," said Esganikan, "is slow progress."

"She doesn't do charm, folks." Shan abandoned any pretense of tact and took a sandwich. She was briefly distracted by a wonderful flavor and sensation she'd almost forgotten—avocado, buttery and green. When she'd left F'nar, the prized dwarf avocado tree hadn't fruited. That'd be something to look forward to when she got home. She craned her neck to look at the handheld Esganikan was scrutinizing, and saw a world map with locations picked out on it and a text list of names.

"What makes you different?" Esganikan asked, gazing into the councillor's face.

"In what way?"

"If your community sees the need to live this way, why don't all humans? You all have the same information about the state of the planet."

"I don't really know," said the woman. "We just want to . . . stop doing more harm, I suppose." She turned to Deborah as if in a plea for backup. "I can't imagine anything worse than that planet in the documentary. The one with nothing but buildings."

"Umeh," Shan said.

"Yes, Umeh. If you believe in a deity, you have to respect everything he made. But you don't have religion, do you, Commander?"

"No." Esganikan seemed enthralled by the discovery, judging by the tilt of her head and her dilated pupils. "But motive is irrelevant to us. We care only what happens, and your aims are the same as ours. That's all that matters."

"So what can we do that's useful, Commander?" Mo asked.

"Someone will have to take responsibility for the gene bank when we release it. I'll give you ownership in due course." Esganikan lobbed in the decision like a grenade. "I won't give it to a government until the nature of government changes, and is not influenced by commerce."

If Shan had ever kidded herself that she had some joint status with Esganikan, or even the basic courtesies due a sidekick, she'd been mistaken. One minute she was changing their entire policy simply by saying that she wanted an Earth where the whole gene bank could be restored, and the next she didn't even get told about the ownership of the bloody thing.

Or that the CO gave herself a shot of c'naatat.

Shan didn't want to crack the image of a united front, but whatever humans thought, wess'har didn't regard disagreement as a loss of face. It was just discussion, reaching the consensus. She tried to keep her challenge conversational. "Isn't that a lot to expect of lay people?"

"I'll appoint experts in their fields to advise on reintroduction of species," Esganikan said. "This is to deal with the obsession that groups have with *owning* the bank. It's not theirs to own."

"You've been following the row over patents on the crops, haven't you? That's why I asked Bari if he'd produce patent-free seeds and distribute them worldwide."

Shan was now back on her own turf, her last job before Eugenie Perault marooned her on Bezer'ej: EnHaz, environmental hazard enforcement. She knew all about licensing seeds. There hadn't been one legally available patent-free seed variety left for sale when she'd headed for Cavanagh's Star. But she'd brought the gene bank home, with all those non-GM varieties that anyone could grow, save the seed, and grow again, year on year. They could breed for drought resistance, salinity tolerance, anything in the heritage of these vintage crops, all the things that commercial production had taken away.

How could I have forgotten? Fuck you, agricorporations. Fuck you all. This is worth the journey. If Izzy and Jon died for anything, it was things like the right of people to feed themselves. I have to hang on to that. It wasn't in vain.

"The biotech boys will rush to court," Mo said. "You know what they're like."

"Commercial law won't count for anything now, and the staple crops aren't their product." It was a pity the mission hadn't had five years' lead time as planned; they could have arrived with a consignment of seeds and just dumped it on the market. *Never mind.* It would still get done. "The Eqbas don't use lawyers to settle out of court."

And there'd be more Eqbas ships in a few years. For all Shan knew, there might be even more after that. She was starting to see things as she used to, the little crusades and wrongs that needed putting right even if that meant a step outside the law, and that was something she'd lost sight of recently.

This was why I went to Cavanagh's Star in the first place; it's why I'm here now, Esganikan or not.

It was almost getting tempting to hang around and see what happened in the longer term. She resisted it.

"We're going to live through some interesting times,

then," Mo said. "You better get some more sandwiches down you."

It turned into an unexpectedly tolerable day, and Mo's grandchildren had the time of their lives on a brief flight in the Eqbas shuttle. Shan wondered how they'd look back on that later in life. It was a little miracle in its own right. Esganikan was definitely fascinated by children, possibly because they seemed almost a different species to adult humans. Wess'har kids were just scaled-down versions with limited databases that they filled up as time went on, exemplified by the terrifying astute Giyadas, arguing complex ethics with Shan as a six-year-old.

And now Giyadas was pulling rank on Shan as senior matriarch, and ordering her to whack Esganikan. My, how she'd grown. Nevyan must have been proud of her.

"This isn't Umeh, Esganikan," Shan reminded her, trying to resist the urge to record Mo's grandson giggling with delight that the "doggie"—Aitassi—could actually speak. "It'll be worth the extra time it'll take to clean up the place."

"Time," said Esganikan, "doesn't worry me."

I'll bet it doesn't, Shan thought. But Esganikan was still running out of it, and fast.

When they had landed at Rabi'ah, the sky was crammed with angry gunmetal clouds and the wind was whipping dust into their faces. Now a few fat spots of rain, rare precious rain, plopped onto the parched earth at their feet.

"You even brought us rain, Superintendent," said Mo, holding his hand out to catch the drops. "You're a regular miracle worker."

Shan saw just rain. If there were any miracles going down, they were all Eqbas technologies that would be coming to Rabi'ah sooner rather than later—desalinated water pipelines, biobarriers, temperature-energy converters.

"See you soon," said Deborah, waving as Shan got back in the shuttle.

She would. There were two funerals scheduled here in the next couple of days.

12

There is a fine line between exercising one's own responsibility and assuming too much of someone else's. Every individual has a duty to recognize their role in the fabric of life and events, and act accordingly; but when we believe that the whole cloth is somehow of our own making, even the threads woven by others, and therefore demands our attention and action, we risk crossing into the territory of seizing too much power, and then of thinking it our duty and right. As in everything, there is a balance to be sought. It should be the point of least harm to the greatest number.

TARGASSAT,
matriarch philosopher,
on the limits to intervention

En route to police headquarters, Kamberra.

"You said ten people at this meeting, tops. Why are we holding it at the police HQ?"

Shan sat in the back of the car with one eye on her borrowed handheld, watching the news headlines. She decided she would rather have faced a rioting mob than address a meeting of the key greens in the capital. But it had to be done sooner rather than later if the mission wanted more active allies out there in the human community, and she had the kind of credibility that spoke more to them than Esganikan's imperious approach.

And I kept saying I never wanted to be the Eco-Prophet, didn't I? But I play the card when I need to. I'm slipping.

Shukry was driving them into town. "Well, maybe a few more than ten. You know how hard it is to tell activists that they can't come. They all want to be represented."

It was her idea anyway. She couldn't complain. "How many?"

"Maybe forty." Shukry half turned in the driver's seat, looking as if he was waiting for her to explode. "The police HQ is the easiest place to secure when we let ordinary punters in. Creates a better impression than wheeling them into some ADF camp or worse, too. You didn't really want the greens crawling all over the reception center, did you?"

Shan thought of the Skavu. "Probably not."

"How about you, ma'am?" Shukry asked Laktiriu. Shan had persuaded Esganikan's deputy to come along for the meeting on the pretext that she needed to learn to work cooperatively with the greens. It sounded a whole lot better than telling her that she had to get up to speed before Shan blew her boss to Kingdom Come. "Are you okay with meeting a large group like this?"

"You're not the first aliens I've worked with," she said. "I have a method."

Shan wasn't sure if that was encouraging or ominous. Aras, withdrawn and silent, concentrated on the news feed as if he wanted to avoid being drawn into the conversation. The deaths of Qureshi and Becken had probably hit him harder than she thought, but she also knew him well enough to know that he felt alone among humans in a way he hadn't on Bezer'ej.

She tried to jolly him along. "Do you want to take a day or two away from the center to see some of the wildlife havens? We could make the time."

"I'm not in the mood," Aras said quietly. "And you have work to do."

He meant Laktiriu. She struck Shan as a thorough, dutiful *isan* with a less aggressive approach than Esganikan. Shan took nothing for granted with wess'har females, but she'd seen that they were capable of being cooperative with humans. Mestin, Nevyan's mother, and other matriarchs before her had managed to get along with human neighbors, so it was possible.

Laktiriu always had the human-specific pathogen to wave as her big stick if all else failed, but Shan didn't want to be

here if the Eqbas decided to use that. She'd seen what it did
to the handful of colonists who'd refused to leave Constantine. Maybe it was cowardice to shut her eyes and hope it
didn't happen on her watch, but she was getting used to the
idea that she had far less control of the situation than she
expected.

Things were happening faster than she could handle and
yet there was little conflict to see so far. No aerial bombard-
ment, no bioweapons dropped on cities, and none of the destruction seen on Umeh: everyone had been holding their
breath, expecting just that, but not all invasions started with
a bang and scaled down.

Apart from what Shan saw on the news feeds, the survivalists who'd taken to the mountains vowing to resist the invaders to the last man, she had no real grasp of how the
landings were seen by ordinary people outside Australia. It
struck her that she had now made the full transition to being
an alien among her own species.

"Sooner or later, there's going to have to be some contact
between the wider public and the Eqbas, isn't there?" Shukry
steered through a security arch picked out in warning chevrons over the access road. "The PR blokes have kept the
media off your backs so far, but you have to come out sooner
or later. Then there's the pressure on the PM from other governments. They want some contact too. Since his speech
yesterday, he's been taking calls for hours at a stretch."

"There's no *have to* with Eqbas," Shan said.

"What about you?"

"Not my decision," she said. "And I'm not going to be
staying. Anyway, all the time the Eqbas and their entourage
stay away from the public, they're not giving you a security
problem. Because that's what I'd be thinking of—how many
officers and how much money it was going to take to keep
public order indefinitely. How long do you think it'll be before humans have seen enough of aliens to enable them to
walk in the street on without causing a riot?"

"Maybe you better ask the police commissioner. You'll be
able to pop into his office on the way out."

It was tempting to slip back into old habits and offer the

local police the benefit of her experience, but it was also quicksand she planned to sidestep. If this had been the wess'har, she'd have known what to say, but the Eqbas were subtly different, a little more likely to behave like humans: they were interventionist. The Skavu—no, she didn't even want to think about it.

Humans bombed the first populated alien planet they ever landed on. Don't lose sight of that. This is what happens when you start a fight you can't finish.

The security arch loomed over them like a car wash, panels flickering with hundreds of moving sensor tiles. When the detectors were level with Shan, the vehicle stopped dead and the driver swore under his breath.

"Are you carrying something, ma'am?" he asked.

"Yes, and I'm not going anywhere without it." Shan leaned forward a little to draw the 9mm from her belt, and held it flat on her palm so the onboard safety recorder could see it. Shukry activated his head-up display and the security center sent a message to wait. "My permit was never revoked. Come to that, I might still have my authorization to decitizenize anyone I deem in need of a comeuppance."

"What's that? Shukry asked.

"In the good old days, we withdrew the civil rights of slags who habitually broke the law by reading them a legal warning. Then you could deal with them no holds barred, any way you bloody well liked."

"Jesus," Shukry said. "But that's Europe for you. Police state."

"Fine by me . . . do they still do decitting?"

"No idea."

Once again, Shan regretted Eddie's absence. He would have handled this so much better. He could have explained what a woolly liberal Shan was compared with an Eqbas commander, and carried out a magnificent hearts-and-minds campaign. But he wasn't, and she began to see all the small detail of what was needed here on Earth that hadn't seemed to matter on Umeh.

Liaison, getting opinion-formers on side, motivating people . . .

"Shit," she said under her breath, and walked into a room that held forty people, not ten. She sat down and looked at the expectant faces. Their expressions told her they hoped she might be the green messiah she was so determined never to be. And then they just stared at Aras and Laktiriu like kids. It was actually heartening to see pure wonder on adults' faces. She softened slightly.

"Where shall we start?" she said. "You'll have questions, so why don't we start there? This is Laktiriu Avo, one of the Eqbas commanders, and . . . my husband, Aras, who's restored ecologies too."

Don't mention that he had to, because he'd just killed every isenj in Mjat.

Silence.

"Hey, they speak excellent English," she said. "Feel free. Anyone?"

"Seeing as the Eqbas are vegan in every sense of the word, can we look forward to an end to livestock and dairy farming?" asked the man from the Compassion Alliance, identified by a T-shirt whose front was dominated by a video loop of slaughterhouse footage. It was hard to look away. Laktiriu's pupils were snapping away like crazy; it wasn't the best advert for humankind's baseline. "And what about cell-cultured meat?"

Managing expectation, Eddie liked to remind her, was the key to not losing support when things didn't turn out the way folks wanted. Shan finally averted her eyes from the repeating cycle of poultry carnage across the table.

"How far are you going to restore habitats?"

"What are you going to do about stopping deforestation in Europe?"

"How are you going to deal with the loonies who've taken to the hills swearing they'll resist the invasion to the last human?"

"Are you actually going to *cull* humans? It's about time. They could start with the survivalists."

Greens seemed a lot more *managerial* than she remembered. It used to be just fire-bombing unethical pharmaceutical and biotech corporations, measurable stuff that seemed

strategically logical to her, even when she still thought the
right thing to do was to prevent it.

"I think networks of like-minded people are going to be
very important in years to come . . ."

It was a long afternoon. Laktiriu seemed to be enjoying
herself.

She'd make a competent mission commander. She *had* to.

Nazel Island, Bezer'ej.

It was at times like this that Eddie could see the moral
heart of the wess'har, and understood the power of its appeal
to Shan. They could have taken a bezeri by force, but instead they asked if any of them would *volunteer* to be a research subject on Eqbas Vorhi.

It was all very civilized for a species that waged total war
and wiped out millions of isenj.

He trudged along the pebble shore behind Giyadas and
Lindsay the squid woman, trying hard not to stare at her. He
wondered if he was just giving into journalistic voyeurism
again, or if he really was trying to build bridges again with
an old buddy. Either way, he felt sorry for her.

"So what have the bezeri decided to do?" he asked. "Are
they going to play ball with us, or what?"

Shan might have written off Lindsay as an over-emotional
weakling who gave uniformed women a bad name, but she
was still sane as far as Eddie could tell, and keeping your
marbles together after what she'd been through took some
doing. Shan should have cut her some slack.

"None of them want to go to Eqbas Vorhi," Lindsay said,
indicating the huddle of bezeri watching from the cliff.
"They say it's too far and they'll be away too long."

Giyadas stood on the shore with her hands clasped behind
her back, human-style. It wasn't a comfortable position for
wess'har because of their shoulder articulation, and they
preferred to hold their hands clasped against their chest
when relaxed, looking as if they were in constant prayer.
With those elegant seahorse heads, the overall misleading

effect was one of angelic human piety. Eddie was sure that the example he'd set Giyadas over the years had been anything but pious.

She thought like a journalist. She even swore like him occasionally. Sometimes he felt that she was more his child than Barry.

"I can understand that it's daunting for them," Giyadas said. "That's a pity."

And that was where the illusion of similarity with Eddie's own species ended. Humans would never have taken *no* for an answer. Somehow, they'd have tricked or forced a bezeri into making the journey to the research center in Surang, because a bezeri was just an animal, however clever and articulate. It wasn't Us, it was Them, and their needs came a poor second. But wess'har—when they said they didn't exploit other creatures, they meant it. They wouldn't even ask the ussissi on Umeh to acquire isenj tissue samples; that would have compromised the odd neutrality that the creatures maintained. In the end, Eddie did it for them, and tied himself up in an ethical maze that he'd never quite escaped.

"I did try," Lindsay said. "But I stopped short of coercing them. I'm sorry. Bezeri are obsessed with place. Homebodies. Not exactly a colonial empire in the making even if their population expands like crazy. They only want Bezer'ej, and then only specific parts of it."

Giyadas tilted her head on one side to look at her, crosshair pupils flaring into four lobes. "I asked Shapakti about the possibility of biopsy samples, but he still needs a living bezeri to be certain that removal doesn't have other side effects in the host."

"Can't they model that?" Lindsay asked. "Even we could do that."

"The Eqbas can model perfectly well. Shapakti simply doesn't take even the remotest chance. If he's wrong . . . the bezeri really will be extinct this time."

There was an awkward silence. The human core of Lindsay, woken again by the hope of going home, was reminded of what she and Rayat had done all those years ago, and she seemed not to feel she'd atoned for that yet.

Come on, Lin. Shan said it. Rayat said it. It was tough on the bezeri, but if you'd known they wiped out a rival sentient race themselves—would you have felt so bad?

"Pili's tribe has expanded a great deal," Giyadas said. "We estimate about five hundred living aquatically now. Don't you want to reunite the clans?"

"How do you know that?" Lindsay asked. "You haven't done any oceanographic surveys."

"We upgraded the defense-grid satellites. We can detect their lights near the surface from time to time."

Giyadas swung her arms forward again and wandered up to the foot of the cliff. Sometimes she reminded Eddie of Shan, because she usually wore an Eqbas-like suit that was more like fatigues than the traditional white opalescent *dhren* of the matriarchs of F'nar. It gave her that uniformed no-nonsense look.

"You never told me."

"If they'd been making trouble for you, you'd have told us." Giyadas tilted her head back to look up at the bezeri. She was in earshot of them now. "Saib? Is Saib among you?"

The patriarch slid to the front and draped his limbs over the edge of the cliff, no doubt doing his leopard-in-tree impression to show how relaxed he was about talking to a wess'har. "I'm here."

"How do you feel about a few scientists coming here to test you?"

Saib considered the question without any display of lights. "How few?"

"No more than six."

"Six. . . ."

"We promised you that we'd keep the Eqbas out of here. These would be Eqbas personnel, but those are all we'd allow in."

"The tests might be dangerous."

"Yes. It might go wrong. Removal might kill you. I can't promise anything, not even how long it might take. Nobody can." Giyadas paused a beat. "Did you hear me tell Lindsay that Pili's tribe now numbers five hundred or so?"

"We hear now . . ." Saib rumbled.

"Well, will you allow the scientists to land?"

"They can land," Saib said. "And I'll volunteer."

"I'll let Shapakti know," said Giyadas, as if it was routine.

You can go home, Lin. Eddie felt the relief. *Leave the bezeri to it. You've done all you can.*

Giyadas walked back along the pebbles with Lindsay to the shuttle. There was no ussissi pilot. Giyadas was definitely a matriarch to break with tradition and habit.

"It'll be five years or so before the team arrives," she said. "You know the distances involved. But if you want, I can send you to Eqbas Vorhi now to be treated." *Treated* was an interesting word to use, not at all a reflection of how wess'har saw *c'naatat.* "In cryo terms, you'd feel you were back home in a few weeks."

Eddie expected Lindsay to jump at the offer. He'd started thinking of what he might do for her while she waited, how he could bring her up to speed with events on Earth in her absence and make it a little easier for her to settle back in to human society. A few days and she'd be out of here—tidy her limited affairs, steel herself to recovering David's remains, and then . . . home.

"You could see Eqbas Vorhi," Eddie said. "I haven't even been there. It looks amazing. Might as well go while you're in the neighborhood."

Lindsay seemed to be thinking it over. He couldn't judge her mood; apart from the voice, there wasn't a single human clue to her emotions, not a face he could read or gesture he could interpret.

She sighed, though. She actually sighed, a real crushed and weary sound that said it all.

"I can't leave until we've resolved the situation here," she said. "Thanks, but I've waited twenty-five years. I can wait another five."

Giyadas cocked her head, all curiosity, but didn't press her. "A responsible choice," she said, and climbed into the shuttle. Eddie, stunned at Lindsay's resolve, almost went back and grabbed her, but he didn't have the right.

It was bloody hard to accept it, though. He got into the shuttle and for a few seconds, he was sure she'd rap on the hull and say she'd changed her mind, and that she'd leave after all and put all this nightmare behind her. But she didn't. As she'd told him before, it was both her choice and her fault that she'd come to this point.

"Extraordinary," said Giyadas, lifting the shuttle clear of the beach.

"Yes, Lindsay's found a steel backbone somewhere along the line." She'd been quite pretty; blond and petite, quite the opposite of the Amazonian, dark-haired Shan. "Cometh the hour, cometh the woman and all that."

"Yes," said Giyadas. "Now you see why wess'har choose their males according to the genetic qualities they'll bring to the whole clan. A little element of Shan via *c'naatat* has transformed her."

Giyadas wasn't a cruel person—no wess'har was, not that he'd seen—but it was possibly the most accidentally spiteful comment she could have made about Lindsay. The woman had always been in Shan's shadow. Now not even her courage was regarded as her own.

One day, when it was safe to do so, he'd make sure history knew about Lindsay Neville, just an ordinary human who learned to be heroic.

Like he always said, everyone needed heroes. But the heroes who had to try hardest were sometimes the best of all.

Kamberra, en route for the Reception Center.

"Well, that was bloody awful," Shan said, leaning her head against the window of the car. "I'm sorry about that, Laktiriu. A baptism of fire, we call it."

They sped out of Kamberra on a deserted road. It might have been the heat, but Shan could see cordons at the intersections, and beyond those there seemed to be a lot of activity. The police were keeping people well away from the mission. The policing alone must have been costing them a fortune.

"It was most educational," said Laktiriu. She actually seemed pleased. Shan could hear a little *urrring* undertone in her breathing, not unlike Aras's when he was content. "To know that there are humans who think as we do is very encouraging. This is something we can build on. Their connections between nations . . . this is useful. This is what we can use. But those are not what Esganikan refers to as *your terrorists,* are they?"

Shukry glanced over his shoulder as he drove, but didn't join in the conversation.

"No," said Shan. "They're just people who take the environment and those sorts of issues very seriously. You'll get on with them just fine."

Laktiriu went back to gazing at the passing landscape. Shan glanced at Aras, and he tilted his head slightly in mute approval. It only took one meeting of minds to kick off a chain reaction. Maybe this was the tipping point of the mission.

"Shan Chail." Laktiriu lowered her voice. "May I ask your advice about a dilemma?"

Oh shit. I hope it's on existentialism and not Eqbas sex.

"As long as you understand I don't have all the answers."

"I have been asked to conceal an important fact. I think it's best that the matter is discussed more openly."

"Depends on the fact."

"Biohazards," said Laktiriu, in eqbas'u.

Ah. She didn't want the *gethes* up front to know about it. They spoke English in front of their hosts, so this must have been a *big* dilemma indeed. Shan was discovering just how different the Eqbas were from their Wess'ej cousins, who would have blurted it out regardless.

Shan turned towards Shukry. "Personal stuff. Don't mind us girls." She faced Laktiriu and switched back to eqbas'u. "Go ahead. What's troubling you?"

"How difficult is it to live with *c'naatat*?"

Here we go. Please don't let her be infected. Please. I can't take out the whole bloody crew . . .

"It has its advantages," Shan said carefully. "But it can be terrifying. It takes away a lot of your choices."

Aras joined in. He was, after all, the expert. "I spent five hundred years in exile, without even the companionship of humans for most of that time. It is a very, very isolating thing."

"Ah," said Laktiriu. "Thank you for being frank."

"Why is it bothering you?" said Shan. She knew anyway, but she played along. "Worried about us?"

"I was asked not to tell you, but I'm unhappy concealing critical information from someone I must work with. Esganikan Gai also has *c'naatat,* and she indicated she would pass the organism to crew members who wanted to experiment with it."

Aras let out a very faint hiss like air escaping from a tire. He was angry, and the car filled with that distinctive scent. Laktiriu froze for a moment, taken aback. Shukry seemed oblivious. Wess'har scent signaling went largely unnoticed by humans.

"Aras has very unhappy memories of sharing his *c'naatat* with his comrades during the wars with the isenj to reclaim Bezer'ej," Shan said. "He'd tell you spreading it was a bad move."

"You have no *idea*." Aras lost it. He didn't lose his temper often, but when he did, it stopped Shan in her tracks. "You have absolutely no idea what Esganikan asks of you, *chail,* but I do, because I was there and *I caused it.* I was the first to be infected. If I could go back and choose again, I would *never* have done it. *Ever.* I have a happier life now and a family I love, but I lost my first family, and I lost all my comrades, and in the end they wanted to die. I lived through it. It *costs.* And you have *no idea* how much it costs, none of you." He was so agitated that even Shukry looked back over his shoulder. "Don't do it. Don't let it happen to you."

"Wow," said Shukry. All he'd heard was a stream of eqbas'u. "This isn't about the wedding, is it?" He seemed to interpret *personal* as being connected to Shan's ménage à trois which she had almost forgotten would still attract attention in most parts of Earth. "I got it fixed. I know it's not the best timing what with all the . . . okay, never mind."

The last thing she wanted Shukry to know was what was really going on.

And that was how strongly Aras felt, was it? Shan wasn't sure that it hadn't been necessary at the time, because wess'har were far more self-sacrificing for the community than most humans. But in terms of personal pain, it was as bad as it got.

But that's where I am right now. And Ade, and Aras. And it doesn't feel so bad. Maybe, after centuries, though, it looks different.

"I don't want to cause problems for Esganikan," said Laktiriu. "But I don't think it's something I want to risk."

"Very wise," said Shan. "And I won't say a word to her."

After Shukry dropped them off, past a growing maze of security barriers and roadblocks that seemed to stretch out further from the center each day, Shan and Aras retreated to their room. Ade wasn't around.

"This is madness," Aras said. "Giyadas was right."

"Did you think she wasn't, then?"

"I thought it was extreme to ask you to execute Esganikan, but if she plans to spread the parasite, then this is out of control, and I agree with her."

"I know how many bad memories this brings back."

"When are you going to do it, then?"

"When I think Laktiriu is ready to step in."

"Make it soon, then," he said. "I want to go home."

13

Fourth To Die Kiir, something unexpected has appeared in the maintenance upgrade log. It is written in the human language, but you must come to see it for yourself. It appears to be a message from a human called Mohan Rayat.

MAINTAINER ASHID,
duty technician,
via emergency messaging

Immigrant Reception Center grounds.

There was plenty of unusable land around the center, enough to accommodate barracks for the Skavu. Esganikan walked around the perimeter fence with Laktiriu, Aitassi and Shukry to get an idea of how it might blend in with the center itself.

"I think we should create the accommodation before we reshape the center itself," she said. "Then we can move our own crew there while we reshape the rest of the center."

"What do you need us to do, ma'am?" Shukry asked.

"Nothing. Nanites will reclaim the materials and rebuild the center to our design. It'll be much more comfortable and efficient."

"How long will that take?"

"A week or two. Don't worry. When we leave in due course, the building will deconstruct itself and leave nothing." Shukry looked puzzled. "I apologize. Would you prefer the building to remain?"

"It's not that," he said. "I don't understand what you mean."

Esganikan decided it was time to give Shukry a show of Eqbas construction techniques. She remembered how mesmerized Shan had been by the construction of Eqbas buildings, and also by their rapid dismantling when Nevyan Tan Mestin had asked them to leave Wess'ej. Her Targassati non-interventionist sensitivities were offended by Eqbas policies, just like her ancestors who had left Eqbas Vorhi to live their isolationist life on Wess'ej ten thousand years earlier.

She asked for our aid. Nevyan summoned us to keep the gethes *out of Wess'ej space forever, and yet she thinks we interfere. We'll do more than confine the humans—we'll help them along with the rest of the inhabitants of this planet. Where's the wrong in that?*

"Find me an engineer, Aitassi," she said. "Just a small demonstration, a wall perhaps."

Shukry had that excited look, eyes wide, that all humans adopted whenever Esganikan showed them something new. "Is it going to be worth vidding?"

"You want to record it? Yes, you can."

An engineer was found and persuaded to start work on an outbuilding at one end of the complex. She released the template nanites on the concrete, spraying them from a canister, and walked off again.

Shukry held his recorder steady. "I can't see a thing . . . oh . . . hang on."

Now he could see it. The process was slow, but judging by his noises of approval, Shukry was impressed by a process that could take material, break it down into its components, and remake it into something new. He edged in closer and eventually just let the little penlike cam drop to his side while he stared at the transformation. The flat, flaking blocks were taking on a more curved form; there was a bloom on them, an almost velvety appearance.

"This . . . is the most amazing thing I've ever seen," he said at last. "We use nanotech, but nothing like this."

"That," said Laktiriu, "underpins everything—the ships, the way we remediate contamination, everything."

Shukry was an instant convert. Perhaps winning human minds was simply a matter of showing them little things that seemed like magic to them. Esganikan savored the sense of optimism and walked the rest of the perimeter to stretch her legs.

Now that Bari had started the human world thinking seriously about what changes would have to be made, it was time for her to show the decision makers what the mission could do to make the transition as painless as possible, and how long it took was up to them. As long as there was no backsliding, and they stopped breeding to excess and consuming so much, then they could reduce their population over many years, without killing.

There would be starvation and disease, of course. There was no point repairing this world simply to let humans fill it again.

The storms of recent days were still circling beyond the defense shield, and Esganikan considered changing the settings to let all the rain through, just to experience the volume of water in this arid land. It was at times like this that she longed for Surang and its greenery.

Only a few years, and then perhaps I can surrender command to the incoming fleet, if enough progress is made.

There were Skavu out on the landing strip, and not all of them were officers. Some of the engineers had also shown up from the Saint George camp; they must have been getting anxious to move the troops here too. Esganikan could see Kiir talking to them in a very animated way, and then looking in her direction, as if they were arguing and Kiir was threatening them with the wrath of *Gai Chail* for some shortcoming or other.

He did seem very angry. Skavu tended towards passionate anger. No doubt he would let her know if the situation required her intervention.

Records and Registrar's Office, Kamberra: shortly after the funerals of Qureshi and Becken.

Shukry was a gem, he really was. Ade had never met a bloke in his kind of job who was happy to do the donkey work, like driving and running errands.

He'd met the Eqbas shuttle from Rabi'ah at the reception center, and driven the funeral party into Kamberra so the detachment could pretend to be normal people for a while. They didn't even have to change out of their dark suits. They looked smart enough for a wedding even if their mood didn't match the occasion.

Ade had never felt less like celebrating, and he was beginning to hate himself for spoiling the day for Shan by having Izzy's and Jon's funerals in the morning. She never complained. She never did. But she had never been the type to want a fancy ceremony. If anything, she looked embarrassed and uneasy in a severe black dress. It would have been office-formal on anyone else, but on a woman he'd only ever seen in uniform, it was as exotic as a full white-lace rig and veil. They all sat facing each other on plush upholstered seats in one of the prime minister's official cruisers, Barencoin, Chahal, and Webster on one side and Aras, Ade and Shan on the other. There was no point worrying about it being bad luck to see the bride before the wedding now. They'd had fucking terrible luck so far, and it was hard to think of it getting worse.

"You've got legs," Ade said, trying to shift gear from a grief that made it hard to even eat. "Two of them."

"You've seen them before."

"Not like that."

"Is this okay? Be honest."

"You look the business, Boss."

"Nice dinner afterwards, yes? Damn, it's good to be able to access your account with a century's interest. God bless the Australian Treasury." Shan tried to draw the others into the strained conversation. "So when are you joining up?"

"We're supposed to get our papers next week," said Webster.

"I'm not sure I want to." Barencoin stared at his hands. He always scrubbed up well, except for the five o'clock shadow that he could never quite defeat. "I've been thinking about a civvy job. Anything. Police, fire, paramedic, whatever. I'm going to grab the first woman I find and marry her, even if she's ugly, and we'll start banging out kids. Although I reckon the Eqbas are going to sterilize everyone or license shagging or something."

"Us ugly birds are grateful," said Shan. "Good call, Mart."

They tried to laugh, but Ade found it brought him to the brink of tears and he was scared he wouldn't be able to make it through the ceremony. It was one of the things that he'd planned in his mind. They said blokes never had day-dreams about weddings, but it wasn't true. He had, and more than once. Not the day itself, the stuff that women seemed to care about, but the simple fact that it would be nice to be married and know there was someone waiting for him who wasn't just called *girlfriend*. It was a rubber stamp that said they weren't just marking time until something better came along, even if they were.

Most marriages ended up that way, of course, but people still got married; always had, always would. It was something humans did. If they invented something more than marriage—well, he'd go for that too. He'd make the biggest gesture he could for Shan because he loved her, and now she was just about all he had left.

The registrar's office was a mock-Georgian setting in one of the administration centers sunk into the city, not quite as grim as he'd expected. It was a rush job, after all, and Shukry was pulling out all the stops, without questions.

"You could have had my old parade lovats," Barencoin said, studying Ade critically. He stood where Becken should have standing as best man. That was painful. "I told you so."

"I'd look a complete twat. You're six inches taller than me."

"Ring?"

"Got it."

The registrar checked the information twice.

"Are these dates of birth correct?" he asked, looking at them both with faint unease. He obviously didn't get many couples who clocked up a few centuries between them on paper. "Twenty-two-fifty—"

"Yes, I'm over eighteen," Shan said. "How far over eigh-teen is my problem."

The registrar gave her a nervous smile. "We're bound to get a query on that. Confirm your full names, please."

"Shan Frankland."

"Adrian John Bennett."

"And you both confirm that you're legally free to enter into marriage, and that you do so voluntarily and not for the sole purpose of gaining residency permits in this country."

Ade swallowed. His sinuses felt flooded from suppressed tears. "Confirmed."

"Yes," said Shan.

"Are there any additional legal agreements you wish to submit now as part of the marriage contract, such as disposal of property in the event of a divorce?"

"No," said Shan. "It's unconditional."

Ade nodded once. "Nothing from me."

The registrar touched a few icons on his desk, a reproduction baroque-style table. It felt more like being hauled in front of the CO for a bollocking than the sweetly emotional moment that Ade wanted imprinted in his mind to tell him he was now Officially Happy. The registrar frowned at the text that appeared in the surface of the desk, hit another icon, and then seemed satisfied that it had accepted the information. It was probably their dates of birth again. They were both in the wrong century; they looked like errors. They *were* errors They didn't belong here.

"Now, you may exchange rings, tokens, and any personal vows you wish to make," said the registrar.

Barencoin passed the ring, and Ade slid it on Shan's finger next to the one he'd already given her when he had nothing but his mother's ring to offer. *Okay, you wrote out your vows, you know it by heart now—*

He took a silent breath, ready to launch into words he'd spent a long time composing, measuring, erasing, and parted his lips to speak. But the tears were going to get there first, long before the happier words, and he dried up. Shan didn't seem to notice. He hadn't told her he'd had anything special to say. The moment passed.

"Congratulations." The registrar held out his code stylus, expecting them to proffer their hands for their chips to be updated. "You're now legally recognized as partners throughout the Pacific Rim States and in all states that are signatories to the Beijing Convention. I can now revise your records."

"We'll take the paper instead," Shan said. "We're not wired."

And that was that, their big day, a day that started by burying two people he'd loved and who'd been his family before he met Shan. It was early evening, and Shukry had used whatever magic words a PM's bagman used to get them a table in a restaurant with a private area where no other diners would sit and stare at Aras. Ade had insisted that he come too. It seemed unforgivable to marry a woman and leave a house-brother out of it.

It was a good meal, all vegan, culturally neutral territory. Shan raised a glass and said: "Absent friends." It was Thursday, so the toast should have been to a bloody war and a quick promotion, but that would have been more than Ade could take.

"Shall we go and find a bar now?" Chahal asked.

"You go on," Ade said. It wasn't because Aras was with them; four marines could handle security on their own, Ade was sure of that, but he wanted to find some private silence to make sense of the last week. "We'll call Shukry and head back to the center. We'll go out on the piss before you take the Aussie shilling."

In the back of the car, Shan took his hand and just held it, comforting and not at all bridelike.

"You're a bloody good bloke, Ade," she said quietly. "It's worth every shitty moment I've ever had just to be your wife."

"Same here, Boss," Ade said. "Same here."

Reception center.

Aras didn't know how to make the day better for Shan and Ade so he kept quiet, and tried not to rub raw emotions.

He didn't need any memories transferred through Shan via *oursan* to know exactly how Ade felt about dead comrades. The concept of special days that were sacrosanct and so had to be kept free from the intrusion of unpleasant reality defeated him, though, and he simply accepted it. He'd seen many weddings in the Constantine colony over nearly two centuries. They were all part of the god-ritual that he could follow but never fully experience.

At the reception center, the hand of Eqbas technology was becoming more apparent. Nanites were busy digesting and reforming an area to the west of the entrance, shaping the architecture into new shapes and building in new functions, and the altered temperature and humidity within the defense shield—more important as protection against the relentless heat than attacks—had triggered long-dormant seeds. Plants were already struggling back to life. Aras took some pleasure from that.

"That's what Deborah would call a sign," he said, catching Shan by the shoulder and pointing out the scattering of seedlings to her. He thought of the isenj, clustering in bewildered excitement around a single imported *dalf* tree planted in a bomb crater, the first tree and the first glimpse of bare soil on Umeh for centuries. "I'm very encouraged."

Shan squatted down to inspect it. She didn't look comfortable in a dress, and kept tugging the hem down. "Actually, that cheers me up a little, too. And reminds me that the next thing I need to do is get Laktiriu pally with Deborah and Mo Ammad. A few people who get things moving, more people stick to the snowball . . . beats the Umeh experience."

"Better raw material," Aras said.

"I could have liked the isenj if I'd spent more time there. Maybe more than the bezeri."

Aras hadn't yet found out what the state of play was on Bezer'ej. He'd never flown a deep-space mission before, and was now realizing how disoriented he was by the apparent time he'd lost. Bezer'ej was only last week, the week before, a blink of an eye in these chaotic and awful days on Earth. But in the quarter of a century that had actually elapsed, what had happened to Lindsay Neville? Had the bezeri population exploded, or were they waging wars, or had some other major change taken place?

"How long do you think we'll stay?" Aras asked. Ade walked ahead, wandering into the lobby, in a world of his own.

"I think it might be longer than we want," said Shan. "Maybe six months, maybe even a year. Enough to get Laktiriu on her feet."

"But a second-in-command should be able to step in at a moment's notice, or forfeit the role."

"Okay, I'm getting soft in my old age." She stood up and tugged at her hemline again. "Aren't you going to ask me how I feel about the dirty work I've still got to do?"

She means Esganikan.

"I know. I've done it. Parekh. Josh." *Poor Josh.* But he had a choice. "You'll feel guilt, because humans do."

"I'll feel hypocritical."

"Isan, you have never sought to spread c'naatat."

"I'm such a saint," she said. "Come on, let's keep an eye on Ade. I let him down. I lost two of our own. Don't tell me I didn't."

The lobby still had some trappings of what had once been a lavish resort, with an aging wall-width video screen that ran from one side of the entrance to the central staircase. Ade sat on the bank of seats that curved against the facing wall, watching the image. As always, it was set to a news channel, one of the many BBChan options. The Eqbas and the ussissi treated it like an intelligence feed, a view of human thinking that they could match against what they observed worldwide from orbital remotes. Eddie would have been proud. But maybe he enjoyed his life more back on Wess'ej.

"It's ironic, isn't it?" Ade said, not taking his eyes off the display. "Poor old Eddie never got over his editor calling him a liar about *c'naatat,* and yet it's running in the Prachy story and nobody seems to give a shit about it."

The item on screen wasn't connected to Eddie's exposure of Prachy but Ade was obviously thinking about something else while he watched.

The report was actually on a dispute over a water pipeline that crossed the Sinostates–FEU border. The Sinostates had revoked permission for the construction because it had changed its mind on cutting down hundreds of hectares of forest replanted in the last century. The Eqbas noted the shift in policy, Aras was certain. They were probably meant to.

"What do you mean?" Shan asked, with that edge in her voice that said she was on guard and current concerns were temporarily forgotten. "When did that happen to Eddie?"

"Before we left," said Ade. You crashed into his interview with Helen Marchant, remember? His editor thought you looked too healthy for a girl who'd been spaced." Ade chewed his thumbnail and examined it. "He decided to take the shit and not admit what *c'naatat* actually was. Really hurt Eddie, it did. Reputation and all that. Never mind. The editor's long gone, and Eddie ran the story in the end."

"Is that a rebuke?"

Ade frowned. "No, Boss. Just feeling sad about wasted lives. Look, I don't even know if Eddie even feels that staying was a waste. He probably doesn't—"

"Are you telling me he exiled himself like some fucking martyr because he made a noble gesture to save me? So it's all my fault?"

"Hey, I'm not accusing you of anything. I'm just saying he made a choice."

Shan checked herself visibly. They were both closer to the edge at the moment than they'd admit. Aras prepared to step in and stop an argument. But Shan relented immediately.

"Sorry. I'm a stroppy old cow lately." She leaned over and gave Ade an uncharacteristically noisy kiss. "Look what you married. A monster."

Ade managed a grin, but Aras could tell he was a little hurt. "Mrs. Bennett, the harpy from hell."

The three of them sat watching the news for a while. A furious round of activity had followed Bari's stark warning at the UN, with Canada announcing draconian population controls, and the African Assembly banning the last cattle farming left on the continent. If the Eqbas could keep up with the demands on them for support, Aras thought, they might simply end up supervising a peaceful surrender. The small bands of individuals grouping in all parts of the world to stage a resistance didn't seem to understand that a war wouldn't be fought the way they expected. Most humans seemed to, though. For once, their embedded cultural myths about alien visitors seemed to be having a beneficial effect: resistance really was useless in the end. Nobody had ever fought the Eqbas and won.

But Aras was already feeling frustrated by the isolation here. He missed being able to work out what was happening in his world simply by walking around, as he had for so many centuries on Bezer'ej. Since Earth had become a large part of his daily life back on Wess'ej, linked by the fragile umbilical cord of ITX, reality had been filtered increasingly through cams and remotes, and even through unreliable humans, and now he worried that he was doomed to sit watching a screen and touching nothing for the rest of his life.

The rest of my life. It suddenly seemed a sentence and he'd never felt that before.

Ade jerked his head around, eyes darting across the glass frontage. "What's that?" There was a lot of activity outside, noisy boots and bright lights from small transports. "Oh, it's the fucking iguana boys . . ."

Four Skavu troops in the soft biohaz suits the Eqbas used, their hoods thrown back, strode across the lobby to the staircase behind Kiir. They plodded upstairs. Ade, always uncomfortable around Skavu, watched them move out of sight and turned back to the news, brow puckered. A minute or two later Aras heard the distant sound of slamming doors, and then the Skavu came back downstairs as if they were searching for something. They vanished through the doors into the maintenance area.

"I don't trust those bastards," Ade said. He looked around as if to check for his nonexistent rifle, then he ran for the doors.

Even Shan was caught by surprise. She pulled her handgun from her belt and went after him. It was the first time Aras had realized she'd carried it even during the wedding. By the time they followed the clattering boots and shouting to its source—Skavu voices, Eqbas protests—it was all too clear what was happening.

Nobody in a military base stopped an armed soldier, and unlike Shan, the Eqbas didn't eat, drink and sleep with their hand weapons close at all times. A few ussisi and Eqbas were now appearing from nowhere to see what was going on, clearly confused.

"Abomination!" Kiir was shouting. The door to the storage rooms was open, scuffed by boots, and the place was in chaos, shelving tipped over. Esganikan was pinned against the wall by two Skavu, now hooded. Kiir had hold of her bare arm, brandishing a blade. "Let's see! Let's see what you *really* are!"

He brought the blade down across her skin and blood— very dark, not human at all—welled from a long, deep wound. Then it stopped. Then, as Aras expected, the wound began to close and heal in seconds.

Then all hell broke loose.

14

Okay, here's why I think that's a bad idea. Yes, we could just have come clean with the Australians and done a deal to share the biotech if they grabbed Frankland for us. We've exhausted the Parekh story and they aren't stupid enough to think this is a point of principle over a dead scientist. Why would they want to help us? If they have any inkling of what she's got, they'll keep it. They don't need our geneticists, and we'll have tipped them off that they hold the most valuable asset in history. The Kamberra regime isn't our best friend right now. Let's bide our time. It's a small world, Eqbas or no Eqbas.

Head of FEU Military Intelligence,
during discussion with cabinet ministers
about acquisition of *c'naatat* parasite

Reception Center storeroom.

Shan now ran on old instinct: *armed assailant, hostage, bystanders, confined space.* She held the 9mm two-handed, suddenly back in another life where this sort of thing happened a few times each year.

Another instinct said *c'naatat, forget the knife, the Skavu's the one who'll end up dead,* but then she noticed the small explosive devices she knew too well. A grenade was the great leveler for *c'naatat* hosts. The parasite wasn't magic or true immortality. It could handle pretty well anything, but not fragmentation of its host.

"Kiir, back off and leave this to me," she said.

He had Esganikan by the collar now. She was scared. She was just like any other creature in fear of its life.

"Let me go, Kiir," Esganikan said. "I *order* you."

Shan watched him waver for a moment, but this was

practically a domestic, and she knew how they usually turned out.

"You're not doing anything useful by killing her," Shan said, putting on her let's-all-calm-down voice. "And you'll blow your head off. Nobody *wants* to die. Do they?"

Yes, a domestic dispute was a good parallel. Kiir was *emotional,* not impersonally vengeful. He glanced at Shan for a moment, "She betrayed us. She's *worse* than you. Her army invaded our world, but we finally saw the sense of Eqbas ways, even though they had *killed* us. We were *loyal* to her. *To her.* We changed our entire world, our whole culture, out of a new belief in the natural cycle of life."

"Okay, I know you revere her." Shan was trying to work out how the grenade operated. She'd seen too many different devices lately—human, Skavu, wess'har, isenj—and she didn't have Ade's training. "But just put the fucking grenade down and let me deal with her."

Aras stood to one side of her, seeming totally detached. If the bloody thing detonated it might even take them all. Shan played for time and calm. But that was for humans.

"I'm angry with her too, Kiir," said Shan. "She'll be dealt with."

"Stay out of this, *gethes.*"

All Shan could think of then was extracting Esganikan in one piece because it wasn't the right time to put Laktiriu in her place. The other Skavu who'd pinned the commander stepped out of the storeroom and paused for a moment, caught between Aras and Ade. He was on the threshold of the door as she backed out, eyes clearly on the grenade in Kiir's fist, and she knew him well enough to see what he was thinking. And he had his fighting knife in one hand. It wouldn't do a lot of good, but the Skavu didn't seem to be drawing weapons. Then she was aware of the Eqbas troops in position along the corridor with rifles trained.

I thought the Skavu were suicide troops. Nobody seems to want to die. Or maybe they think all the Eqbas are infected now.

"Back off, Ade," she said. "Kiir, let me tell you the usual shit. I can blow your head off before you detonate that thing."

She doubted it, but she knew she *looked* like she could, "I'll step away, and you follow me. No games. I won't kill you if you don't kill her." Kiir looked from Shan to Ade to Esganikan. There was the sound of running. *More tourists to frag. Great.* "Aras, somebody stop them coming in here. *Now.*"

She was so focused on Kiir's face with its hard-to-spot eyes that Aras and Ade were a smear in her peripheral vision. She took another step backwards. Kiir didn't move for a few seconds, but then he edged closer to the door, still with a fierce grip on Esganikan.

"There," Shan said. "We'll all be nice and calm again in a few minutes, and we can talk this out. Come on . . . few more steps . . . that's it . . ."

Ade must have seen something she didn't. He lunged forward but Aras knocked him to the floor, and Kiir threw Esganikan back into the open storeroom. The next thing Shan was aware of was a high-pitched tone filling her head and something that felt like grit raining down on her face. She struggled to sit up and saw Ade and Aras in a fog of dust, yelling soundlessly at each other, Ade trying to pull away from Aras's grip on his arm.

"Shit," she said. Her hearing started returning to normal. Some Eqbas tried to help her to her feet but she pushed them away. *In a fucking dress. I'm still in my fucking wedding dress.* She leaned inside the doorway of the storeroom and it was every bit as bad as she expected. Esganikan wasn't a problem any longer. She was spread around the room. "Fuck. Oh fuck it, it wasn't supposed to be like that." She grabbed an Eqbas. "Someone cordon off this room. Treat it as contaminated. Where's Kiir?"

Ade pulled free of Aras. As he passed one of the Skavu, he grabbed the saber from the man's back and ran down the corridor towards the lobby.

Kiir. He'd promised him he'd kill him. He'd been upset at the way the Skavu slaughtered unarmed isenj. The isenj were going to die anyway, just like Esganikan had been, but Ade had rules of engagement ingrained in him and there were just some things you didn't do.

"Jesus, Aras, fat lot of use you bloody are," she said, not

waiting for his answer. "Why didn't you stop him?" By the
time she crashed through assorted Eqbas, the debris and
the last doors onto the lobby, she had a freeze-frame view
she wouldn't forget in a hurry. Ade got to Kiir just a few
meters in front of an astonished Laktiriu and raised the saber two-handed.

Shan had a clear shot. She took it, double tap. Kiir went
down.

Even with her vastly altered physiology, she still had that
human tendency of disjointed memory. A few seconds later,
she couldn't recall the exact sequence. All she knew was
that Ade was standing over Kiir's body, taking big sobbing
breaths, and the Eqbas crew in the lobby were still frozen in
alarm reactions.

Ade looked around at her, then walked out through the
front entrance still carrying the saber. Laktiriu literally
stepped over the dead Skavu, totally in control, and looked
into Shan's face with her head tilted in that doglike curiosity.

"You thought Kiir would kill me?" she said.

Shan wasn't sure she would have done the same thing
again. Ade needed closure for the botched handover of
Prachy. She'd robbed him in a way. But she didn't want Ade
to cut Kiir apart and have to live with the memory.

"I'm trained to drop any threat," Shan said. "I wasn't taking chances after he killed Esganikan. Now, I'm going to
call the perimeter security and tell them not to worry about
all the bangs they've heard, or we'll just start another list of
problems."

Outcomes, only outcomes. Motive—maybe even the person responsible—didn't matter. Esganikan was gone, as Giyadas had ordered.

Laktiriu was in command now, ready or not.

Surang, Eqbas Vorhi: Place of Discovery of Life

Shapakti's equipment was surprisingly compact. Rayat
recalled how hard it was to get his equipment down to the

weight limit for the *Thetis* mission, and felt a pang of envy at how neatly it all packed away.

"Are you sure you want to come to Bezer'ej?" Shapakti asked.

"I'm sure. I haven't seen Lin for a long time."

Shapakti's family were going with him on the mission. The kids were all adults now, so his *isan* and all the house-brothers were looking forward to an adventure, a minimum ten-year round trip to Bezer'ej. Shapakti no longer did deep-space missions, and the days of his family being put in cryo to match time zones with him were over.

"I think we should leave your *c'naatat* in situ, then," he said. "Or else you have to wear a biohazard suit all the time."

"Good point." Rayat hoped he wouldn't have the urge to join the aquatic bezeri again. It had been fascinating and he now had insights into biology that no other scientist could imagine, but the novelty had worn thin. *I'm a man. I'd rather stay that way and sacrifice a few years than live for-ever like that. Lin's made of much sterner stuff than I thought.* "I have a request. Ask the matriarchs of F'nar if I can return there? Please?"

"Why?"

"Leave me on Wess'ej when this is over, and remove the *c'naatat* then. I can't go back home again, but I'd like to live out my days among humans. There are still people in F'nar."

Shapakti smelled upset. "I liked F'nar."

There *was* something wrong with him today. Wess'har never bothered to hide what they felt because they broadcast their emotions by scent, but Shapakti had been around humans a long time now. He'd learned to pull his punches a little with Rayat over the years, but not well enough to make him a poker player.

"Spit it out," said Rayat. "You've got a problem."

It was like a dam bursting. "You did it, didn't you? You finally got a message to Kiir."

"Oh. That." It had worked, then. Someone had found the note in the update. "Someone had to warn the mission."

"Kiir killed Esganikan. He attacked her. She's *dead*."

Rayat's success rate was better than he'd hoped. It was terrible that it had upset Shapakti so much, but that was one problem solved.

"I'm sorry," Rayat said. "I had to do it. You know better than anyone what the stakes are."

"Mohan, you had no need. I'd already got word to Shan, through Giyadas."

Oh, that was evolution in action. Shapakti had learned real deceit, a new trait for wess'har. "Well, thanks a lot."

"I warned you. Shan was better able to manage the matter. Now . . . now there is uncertainty, because Laktiriu has had to take command, and there is doubt that she can sustain discipline among the Skavu."

When a mission went awry back home, Rayat always had the option of calling for backup to manage the fallout. But the nearest help for Laktiriu was five years away.

"Well, what's Shan going to do now?"

"I didn't ask. I have other issues to worry about. Esganikan appeared to have plans for sharing *c'naatat* with the crew."

"Well, that alone should convince the matriarchs here that it's a bad idea."

"On the contrary," said Shapakti, crestfallen. "Varguti Sho says that the wess'har managed it safely under similar conditions, and so may we."

"That's insane. This is how the thing gets out of hand."

"I disapprove, yes."

"This isn't how wess'har do things. You have to stop this."

"I think you say the *thin end of the wedge*. I feel I have a duty . . ."

"You've lost me now."

"I don't think we should have this organism at all. I'm going to erase my research from the system, and take all the samples back to Giyadas. F'nar could handle the temptation to exploit *c'naatat*. They knew when to stop, when the threat had passed. We, like you, seem not to know when we start sliding. We begin with such good intentions. This is what you call the road to Hell, I think."

Rayat almost thought he'd misheard.

"Shap, do you know what you're saying?"

Shapakti shivered, a strange little gesture that Rayat thought might be bristling defiance. "I think removing research material it's a more acceptable form of asset denial than destroying an island."

Shapakti's scent of agitation filled the laboratory. He went on packing his equipment, head down, maybe from shame or maybe because he was thinking. Rayat racked his brains for another solution, but the more he thought about it, the more he came full circle to the same conclusion.

Shapakti went on packing in silence. Rayat wasn't sure the Eqbas could go through with this subterfuge, and had already started thinking of how he might sabotage the research and do the job himself—a terrible thing to do to an old friend—when Shapakti stopped work and knelt down for a breather.

"Help me?"

"Of course. This is exactly what I'm trained for. This is my job. But what'll happen to you when the matriarchs find out?"

"My immediate family will be in Wess'ej by then."

"You're running? You're going to ask for asylum?"

"I am."

Rayat was stunned. This was so out of character for any wess'har—communal, cooperative, embarrassingly unguarded—that he defaulted to type and began to wonder if this was a ruse, and someone was setting him up.

No, that was even crazier. If wess'har like Aras's ancestors had decided they disagreed with the fundamental tenets of their society and moved to another planet simply to follow a different ideology, then they were clearly capable of sudden dissidence. It sat oddly with their consensus politics and communal nature, but Wess'ej was living proof that they could—and did—kick over the traces.

He felt a lot better now. This was something he was familiar with. He helped Shapakti clear his laboratory.

"It's just like old times, Shap," he said, transferring data onto his *virin*. "I was a very competent spook. I was good at helping people vanish when they needed to."

"*Shan Chail* said you were a *slimy bastard* . . ."

"And slimy bastards have their uses. We do the dirty work nobody else will."

Shapakti didn't comment on whether he thought this was dirty work or not. "I'll carry on looking for a removal solution for bezeri and wess'har, but today we clear out all information and samples, and let Nevyan and Giyadas know that it's theirs to guard. We leave tonight."

Stripping the database was simple. Eqbas security measures were geared towards accidental loss, not theft. There was nothing to stop Shapakti taking all his research, most of which he'd ended up doing on his own over the years, or removing all the stored tissue samples, because Eqbas didn't steal; and Shapakti was going on a field trip. Nobody would notice. Rayat wondered if they would even care.

Did I teach Shap to be devious? Well, I'm bloody glad if I did.

Rayat felt oddly clean now, despite Esganikan's death. Whatever happened, and however he was judged if the truth ever emerged, he felt he'd taken the only safe and rational choice. His orders had been to secure the parasite, although that was when nobody had a clear idea of what it was, and asset denial was part of that. But it was his job to evaluate risks to national security, often on the hoof and without recourse to his masters—whoever they might be at any given time—and so he judged *c'naatat* to be more a hazard than an asset. It was his call. Nobody minded a *slimy bastard* saving them from disaster, it seemed.

"What about the rest of your family?" Rayat asked. He helped Shapakti load the small freight carriage. "Won't they be targeted when the matriarchs realize you've absconded with the project? Don't you need to get them out too?"

"You should know us better by now, Mohan." The biologist shut down his systems. "Why would my actions reflect on them?"

"They would on Earth. Your family would suffer."

"This isn't Earth, and we're not humans. If any of my family come with me, it will be because we want to stay together, not because we fear retribution for my actions."

It would turn into a circular argument, he knew it. Wess'har had a blind spot when it came to threats. It sat oddly with their all-out military strategies, part of that on-off switch they seemed to have.

"So are they coming with you?"

"Wait and see," said Shapakti.

When they got to the landing strip that night and transferred the cargo, Shapakti's brothers and *isan* were sitting quietly in the small ship as if they were waiting impatiently to go on a sightseeing trip. They greeted Rayat casually.

He nodded back. "Have you *told* them what you're doing, Shap?"

"Yes. Of course."

"Bloody hell, your whole family suddenly becomes revolutionaries? Just like that?"

"I don't understand why this troubles you."

"Never mind."

The bulkhead hatch closed silently like a wound healing. Rayat would never fully understand wess'har. It was as if bits of their legendary consensus broke off and spawned little deviant offspring, each of them harmonious in themselves but forever at odds with its parent.

"I still think you should have trusted me to handle the Esganikan situation," Shapakti said. "And told me what you planned."

"Sorry," said Rayat. "Old habit."

Shapakti lifted the ship into a vertical climb and Rayat found himself thinking, as he often did, what *c'naatat* might have been harnessed for if only mankind could have used it *sparingly*.

But it was a slippery slope. He was certain that it was best never to step on it at all.

Reception center, near Kamberra.

"Hi, Eddie." Ade leaned back against the headboard and wedged the *virin* between his bent knees to look at the tiny image transmitted from trillions of miles away. "Wait until I tell you what a shit day I had."

"Hi, mate. You took your time calling."

"Been a bit busy."

"I've been keeping up with the news."

"Then . . . well, you know about the Prachy job. Izzy and Jon didn't make it."

Eddie must have heard plenty of bad news in his time and had learned to keep going when the cam was running. But his face crumpled. Even in that small image, Ade could see he lost it for a moment. He'd really liked Qureshi. Ade had to remind himself that they were all faces from the past for Eddie, people he hadn't seen for twenty-five years, and perhaps that softened the blow a little.

"No," Eddie said hoarsely. "Oh no. Please. Oh God, I'm so sorry."

"I'm not done yet. Can I unload on you?"

"Anything you want, mate. It's . . . oh, sod it."

Ade was glad that Eddie didn't say it was tragic that they'd survived a deep-space mission and gone home to die in a pissy-arsed stunt that wasn't worth the effort. He didn't need reminding. The thought hung there just the same.

"We had the funerals today and then Shan and I got married. Then Kiir went nuts and killed Esganikan because she'd taken a dose of Rayat's *c'naatat*. I was going to kill Kiir myself but Shan slotted him before I got a chance. Did I leave anything out? No, I don't think I did. Like I said, a shit day."

Eddie was quiet for a long time. Ade could see his lips trying to form a response.

"You can do a journo answer if it's easier," said Ade.

"It's not, mate. And you're not okay, and don't tell me you've had worse."

No, Ade probably hadn't. "I just wanted to let you know."

"How's Shan? Aras?"

"About the same, I think. Can't even drink ourselves into oblivion, can we?"

"Well, it's looking better than Umeh did when the Eqbas started."

Ade didn't know what to say next. "I don't think Shan's even told to Giyadas yet. But let her know. She wanted Shan to finish Esganikan off, but Kiir beat her to it."

"Ah." Eddie looked as if he hadn't been privy to that. "I'll pass it on anyway."

"Better go now."

"I'd say take care, but it seems a bit sick. But for Chrissakes get out of there. Come home."

Ade closed the link and slid the *virin* back in his new black pants. Shan was in the shower; Aras was washing his tunic in the small basin. Ade found himself back in an earlier life again, restless and edgy in the aftermath of a fight, wanting to get out and visit a few bars just to blot out his thoughts with noise, beer and chatter.

"Why did you stop me taking Kiir down, Aras?" he asked.

Aras looked up. "I felt Kiir was right."

"But he fucked it all up. Shan wanted Laktiriu to have a bit of lead time before she took over."

"Shan," said Aras, "was tasked to execute Esganikan herself, so this is a very academic argument." He smelled angry. "There's also the chance that you might have got it wrong, too. *You* might have died."

Ade started thinking of objections to it all and then fell into the maze that was *c'naatat*: who should live, who should not, and who was a risk. He'd done what Esganikan did, in a way, and so had Aras. Only Shan had resisted the urge to infect another person. And even she applied double standards about who was allowed to live.

It was a mess. When people started playing judge and jury like that, without some rules of engagement, it scared him.

"I'm going out," he said. "The lads are at a bar Shukry found for them. I'll blag a ride into town from one of the cops on the perimeter. Tell Shan I won't be late."

She wouldn't mind. She'd understand, like she always did, and this was never going to be a normal wedding night anyway.

It took a while to find a police officer, but she was very obliging about running him into the city and making sure he found the right bar. It was a bigger shock in some ways than a truly alien world; some things had changed enormously in a century and some hadn't. He'd also grown used to the quiet and emptiness of Wess'ej. The flashing lights in the bar dazzled him as he walked down the steps into noise that felt like a brick wall against his chest.

"Jesus, Mart," he said, "I'm getting old. This is too loud."

"You can't even get drunk, can you?" Barencoin pushed a beer at him, one of a forest of bottles lined up on the table. Chahal was getting more at the bar. "Chaz, get Ade a few bags of nuts, will you?"

"It's all going pear-shaped," Ade said. "Kiir just fragged Esganikan. Shan shot him."

"Christ, Ade . . ." Barencoin shook his head. "How much worse is this going to get?"

"She had a dose of . . . well, what I've got, from Rayat." There was no point being careless with information in public when you never knew who might recognize you. "Deliberate."

Webster took a pull from her bottle. "Bloody mercy killing then. Who'd want that arsehole stuck in their head for the rest of their life?"

"How did Kiir find out?"

Ade shrugged. He never knew who was in touch with what when it came to Eqbas. And now he was past caring. He wanted to immerse himself in noise and the safe company of people who had been through exactly what he had.

The beer was blissful, even if it didn't touch him.

"You still want to go back, now that they can turn you back into mild-mannered normal Ade, or are you too attached to your neon dick?" Barencoin asked.

"Yeah, I want to go. I can always come back later when they've tidied this place up, can't I?"

They didn't actually manage a laugh. They talked a lot about Qureshi and Becken, and it helped. Late in the evening—later than they'd planned—they walked around the underground mall and found a curry house, the crowning event of a run ashore, and he felt guilty that it delighted him. Reality crashed back in when they had to summon

Shukry to get them transport back to the reception center, because no civilian traffic was allowed within five klicks of the site now.

"You better creep in quietly," said Webster as they made their way upstairs. There was no sign of the day's earlier events in the lobby, although the corridor to the stores was sealed off. "Women change when you marry them. Shan's going to be standing there demanding what time you call this."

As it turned out, she wasn't: Aras was asleep on top of the bed covers, and Shan was sitting on the balcony with her arms folded on the rail, chin resting on them as she looked out towards the sea.

"Sorry, Boss," he said. "Had to get out."

"Understood. Decent curry? I can smell it."

"Nice. Could have been hotter."

"So, do you want the perfect end to a perfect day?"

"Now what?"

"I needn't have worried about Laktiriu, sweetheart. She's all sorted." Shan sat back and put her feet up on the rail. "She says we have to leave. She wants all sources of *c'naatat* off Earth, just in case. And there I was thinking I was leaving her in the lurch. When I asked her how Kiir found out about Esganikan, she said that Rayat got a message to him through their engineering update system. Just like old times, eh?"

It could have been worse. The Eqbas could have solved the problem the explosive way. Laktiriu was taking the middle path and just sending them back, which was going soft for wess'har.

But Rayat—even light-years away, he was still a shithouse, and still a source of trouble.

It was good to have another motive to get back to the Cavanagh system.

15

Make your news (*456,761 uploaded features*)
How come Australia can find room right away for a couple of thousand Christians, but closed its ports of entry to Muslim flood refugees from Indonesia? Here's one family who didn't get a warm welcome.

A. TELLIO, MADRID. Viewer vote: True 65%, Bogus 35%

Why are we arguing about climate and immigration when our planet's been invaded? Take a look at Eqbas atrocities on planets like Umeh. Why is no government mentioning this or doing anything about it? I've been talking to people who've signed up to protect Earth.

J. MAURE, QUEBEC. Viewer vote: True 55%, Bogus 45%

Got a view? Got news? Send us your vid and legal waiver. Vote for the stories you believe!

BBChan open source news portal

Rabi'ah: one week after the change of Eqbas command.

The opinion-formers of environmental reconstruction toured Rabi'ah, making notes as an Eqbas hydrology team installed the new water supply. They looked baffled.

"Is that it?" A representative from the African Assembly stood next to the Eqbas engineers as they sunk boreholes the wess'har way. Like Bari, he'd expected to see big machinery and pipework. The Eqbas just had things that looked like old-fashioned drain rods, and were easing them gently into the ground. "Don't you drill?"

"The device inserts itself."

"How do you lay the pipes?"

"They build themselves once the template material is activated. It may take some weeks for the routing to reach the coast, but it *will* find its way there and attach to the de-salination system."

"Does it displace material underground? How does it move spoil?"

Bari was a lawyer by training, and expected the technology to go right over his head, but it seemed to be giving the experts a hard time too—even one from the FEU.

For all Mike Zammett's posturing, there were no official hostilities, and Bari saw the presentation value in holding open house. The FEU wasn't a stable monolith, and member states could be easily wooed by the promise of quick fixes on water supplies.

But what do we have to worry about anyway? As long as *the Eqbas are here, we have our big brother standing next to us in the playground. Go ahead, Zammett. Rattle that saber.*

Over the last twenty-four hours, the *as long as* bit had assumed a new significance. The Eqbas commander who showed up with Shan Frankland and another new kind of alien in tow wasn't Esganikan Gai. All Bari knew was that Esganikan was dead. He was finding it hard to get used to the Eqbas tendency to blurt out bald statements that would give his own PR team heart attacks.

Shukry appeared and discreetly beckoned him out of the knot of fascinated spectators watching aliens stick bits of wire in the ground, assured that fresh water would eventually come out at the dry end. The two men wandered away from the entertainment to a quiet spot at the edge of the protective canopy.

"It's true, sir, she's dead," Shukry whispered. "I've been trying to persuade Laktiriu that it's not something we want to talk about. Trouble is, if someone asks them a question, they tend to answer."

It was just as well that the Eqbas hadn't spoken in public yet. It was only a week or two since they'd arrived, and nobody was going to notice that the main player had vanished. Nobody really knew what Eqbas protocol meant anyway.

The change wouldn't invite questions, at least not for a long time—and it was relatively easy to keep the media away from the mission team.

"Shukry, key personnel from advanced civilizations shouldn't just drop dead after they've arrived," Bari said. "You know what I'd wonder? Freaky alien disease. And that either starts people thinking space-plague nonsense, or it makes the Eqbas look less than omnipotent, and frankly all that's keeping us from Arma-bloody-geddon is that we've seen what they did to Umeh."

"I don't think *killed by a disgruntled member of your own army* is any more reassuring, PM . . ."

"Oh God. Is that par for the course, or is it mutiny?"

"It gets worse."

"I'm praying that this is just teething problems shaking out early."

"Like I said, sir, ask and they answer. Frankland seems to be trying to teach the new girl to shut up. She's learning fast."

"So how bad is it?"

"The wrinkly-looking aliens form the bulk of the troops, the Skavu—remember the briefing notes? They're fanatical about ecology. Seems that Esganikan was carrying some bioagent—"

"Oh, that's a word we *don't* want to say, and *don't* mention it to the Chief of Staff."

"No, I don't think it's biowarfare. It's some condition that was supposed to make her invulnerable or something, and the Skavu hate messing with nature, so an officer assassinated her."

"Oh, that'd be the biotech the FEU was after when all this started. Good to keep up to speed via BBChan, isn't it? Well, it obviously didn't make Esganikan invulnerable. Scratch one rumor."

"PR's advising that we just ignore the personnel change unless asked, in which case the change of command is due to an accident."

"It's still bad. They're about to change the whole planet, and they have fatal accidents?"

"We just have to brazen it out and rely on the sheer welter of novelty drowning the who and why. A handy smoke screen."

That struck a chord with Bari. He could barely cope with the information coming in, and found himself taking refuge in whatever floated to the top, the big concepts. He still had time on his side. Everyone was still reeling. Twenty-five years' advance notice meant nothing, absolutely nothing, because there had been no communication while the Eqbas were in transit and humans were lousy at continuity over that time scale. Just the volume of data sharing on climate, ecology and communications specs since the Eqbas had arrived was swamping the scientists and technicians here.

"Smoke screen it is, then," said Bari.

It was time to cement the new relationship. Bari headed over to Laktiriu, seeing the Skavu soldier with her in a new light and noting the sword, which he assumed was ceremonial. Shan Frankland was probably now his best bet for keeping a handle on this. She was the only human on the Eqbas team, and the former FEU marine who went around with her was just a bagman as far as he could tell.

"Commander," said Bari, extending his hand to Laktiriu, "I'm very sorry about your colleague. We won't discuss it out of respect, and knowing how badly our media can distort things I'd advise you to avoid even referring to it." He could say *keep your mouth shut* a hundred different ways, a lawyer's gift. "I think fact-finding sessions like these are worth a lot more than statements, anyway. You could keep most countries' attention on the topic of water alone."

"Perhaps we should delay any announcements on reducing solar warming for a few months, then," said Laktiriu. "I realize we have more technology to transfer than your industrial capacity can handle in the short term."

"I'm happy to open to this up to some of the countries who are supporting our approach."

"That's commendable. Climate can only be managed globally. It's a pity we have no isenj with us—they engineered entire climate systems."

Isenj was rapidly becoming one of those words laden with darker meaning. Bari took comfort in the fact that the BBChan material showed Umeh as so devoid of natural life that he couldn't begin to imagine what a day was like there. They'd asked for it. But then one state had invited the Eqbas to help them out, and that parallel hadn't escaped him.

"I imagine this place will get a lot of media moving in afterwards, searching for scraps of information, now that they've worked out there are colonists here too," Bari said, targeting Shan as his best chance. "We'll do what we can to stop the buggers being a problem."

"They'll follow vessel and vehicle movements by satcam and descend anywhere the Eqbas stop," she said. "I don't think there's anything you can do to stop that. The police are zapping smartdust surveillance over the reception center area pretty well daily."

"Can't put genies back in bottles."

"We all get hoist by own petard sooner or later, speaking as someone who made a lot of use of aerial surveillance. I spent some time with Eddie Michallat, too, so I suppose you could say I'm more understanding towards the media than I used to be."

"So what's it—"

They were interrupted by a loud *shwoosh* and a burst of surprised laughter as water fountained from the borehole. It was just a demonstration of a self-creating pipe that had zeroed in on the water-recycling reservoir a few meters away, but it captured imaginations. The tame media—one heavily vetted and scrupulously searched agency man—had good shots.

"I was going to ask what it's like to be home, Superintendent," Bari continued.

"Horrible," Shan said. There was no expression on her face. "I'm going back to Wess'ej very soon."

As bombshells went, it was a small one, but Bari felt like a chair had been snatched away from under him. He'd have to find some other fast track into the Eqbas administration.

It was early days, though. He set aside his need to get everything instantly nailed down, defined and filed, and tried to think laterally.

There were always the ex-colony people, who knew

wess'har better than they knew their new human neighbors on this planet. And then there were the unfortunate former Royal Marines, abandoned by the FEU and now without even a corps to return to.

Maybe one of them wanted a job.

Eqbas reconnaissance patrol, on station over southern Africa.

"You know humans well, Aras. Why do they burn embassies?"

Joluti had activated so much of the bulkhead area as video monitors that Aras felt as if he was back in the church of St. Francis deep under the surface of Bezer'ej, bathed in rainbow light from the stained glass window. Images from dozens of broadcast and observation sources made up a quilt of frantic activity across the planet. Aras had asked to spend his remaining Earth time on patrols, so he could at least have a chance of seeing more of the world that filled his borrowed memories, more than the isolated, security-ringed compound of the reception center and the narrow corridor into equally cloistered pockets of Kamberra. The repeated images of violence at various embassies intrigued Joluti.

"Impotent rage," said Aras.

"They could channel their energy into locating the source of their grievance and resolving it."

"Us?" The patrol vessel—another craft metamorphosed from the main ship for this role, whose components might be a fighter tomorrow—spoke of the futility of stones and fire aimed at an Australian embassy in an African city. "I think that might demotivate most."

"Which is why I ask why they do it. We've made it clear in the past that we won't leave until we resolve what problems we can. I don't understand people who do things even though they know they have no effect."

"Humans react to symbolism more than reality." Animal toys were always the ones that bothered Aras. Humans adored fabric models of animals, but cared nothing for the welfare of the real thing. "They can never believe what they say, hear or see, either."

Human uncertainty—c'naatat *didn't select all the best traits for me. If I were still pure wess'har, would things look clearer to me? I don't even remember the way I used to think.*

"I'll avoid going in any lower, then," Joluti said. "I see no point making life worse for some wholly uninvolved person if our appearance causes rioting."

"Have we time to land in Canada?"

"Yes."

"The bird sanctuary. I'd like to see the macaws we restored from the gene bank."

Aras wanted to see a great many things, but now he'd run out of time even before he'd got around to listing the sights he wanted to see. The bird sanctuary specialized in recreating destroyed habitats; Shapakti would have found that fascinating, having created a patch of rain forest himself. Negotiating a point to set down caused some concern with Canadian air-traffic control, but eventually a compromise was reached and the patrol vessel hung two hundred meters above the sanctuary grounds, giving the visitors and local community an unexpected novelty.

Aras felt as much a specimen as the birds in the center. He was at ease with humans and found it disorienting when they reacted nervously, because he had almost come to see himself as looking just like them; but he had claws, he was two meters tall, and he didn't have a human face. However much *c'naatat* had modified him, it stopped short of making him appear fully human. The parasite behaved differently in every carrier, somehow responding to its hosts anxieties. By whatever process it used to rearrange and tinker with his genome, it seemed to have decided that he wanted badly to fit in with the humans among whom he was exiled, but didn't want to wholly surrender his wess'har nature.

If it had reshaped him totally into a male like Ade—and it had done little externally to his house-brother, except for adding bioluminescence around tattooed areas of skin—then he might not have struggled with his identity for so long. But his mind created that struggle. He knew that he craved his wess'har identity too.

Shapakti's macaws recognized him immediately, and greeted him with squawks of *"Uk'alin'i che!"*—feed me. Shapakti had taught them phrases in eqbas'u. They'd also picked up English, some of it quite profane. Not knowing what they were missing in their natural habitat, they seemed happy with other macaws in a small forest biodome that reverberated with their calls.

"What else would you like to see?" asked the sanctuary ranger. "We have a hummingbird breeding program. If you've never seen hummers in real life, I guarantee you a treat."

The plan to stay for an hour fell by the wayside. The hummingbirds, tiny jewels of birds, temporarily made him forget everything else that was preying on his mind. For the time being, he felt that the journey had not been wasted for this short and tragic stay, and that these creatures were worth the effort. He was happy for a few hours. The staff and visitors plucked up courage to ask to have their pictures taken with him, and he talked to the more confident ones about their feelings towards the Eqbas.

Most were clearly scared, but seemed reluctant to say so; some, though, were excited and saw the Eqbas as arriving in the nick of time. None were hostile. But maybe it was hard to tell an alien invader to go to hell when they were two meters tall and looming over you.

It was a wonderful diversion, one of the best times he could remember having, and wess'har had perfect recall. He felt suddenly robbed of the chance to explore this new world. Maybe, in centuries to come, he could return to Earth.

But the prospect of future hummingbirds in the wild was a slim incentive when so much of his past wouldn't leave him alone these days.

"I shall miss Esganikan," said Joluti, not rebuking Aras for keeping his vessel waiting several hours. "We'd served together for a long time. But Laktiriu may well work better with human society. She favors the gradual but sustainable path."

Aras had seen that path. It was the blind enthusiasm of humans who knew nothing much about Eqbas but were certain that aliens knew a better way to do things, and wanted to be good humans and help them. It was naive, and Eddie would have given them his benignly cynical smile, but it was the raw material that would determine if Earth went the way of Umeh or not.

Humans responded to inspiration rather than logic. And inspiration was talking to mesmerized kids about macaws that could speak an alien language, or getting humans to see that their species couldn't possibly be more special and deserving than an insect-sized bird that vanished in a blur of emerald light.

Yes, humans' imagination could be captured.

Reception Center.

The Australian Defense Force ground transport waited with its drive running outside the main doors. Ade cried, and didn't care. His detachment—what was left of it—had joined the Australian army.

"You're a big fucking girl, Ade," Barencoin sobbed. "See, you bloody started me off as well."

The two men hugged because this really was the last time they would see each other, except via an ITX link when Barencoin was in his fifties, and Ade still looked the way he did now. They absolutely knew it. There were no maybes or if-you're-passings to spare them the finality. It was a very tearful morning. The veneer of banter was showing cracks.

"If Ade gets snot on you, Mart, that means you're immortal," Chahal said. "No tongues, mind."

"I'll dribble on you now, then." Ade grabbed Chahal, and then the hugging and backslapping went on around the circle for some time. It was painful, not a terrible pain like bereavement, but a more bittersweet one knowing that these were his mates, his more-than-family, and every one of them was a fucking hero and a pro who he'd trusted with his life and always would. The pain was because they were the *best*, and he would lose years of knowing them.

"You better call the minute you land," Chahal said. "We'll have a lot of catching up to do."

"Well, Ade won't have much to tell us except how he threw up when he thawed out, so we can bore him with twenty-five years of derring-do," said Webster.

"We've got five minutes." Barencoin checked his watch. "Come on, Ade, show us your lights one last time."

Ade blushed and wiped his nose. "I'm sober. I can't do it sober."

"I've never seen them," said Webster. "I'm an engineer and I need to know how things work."

"Go on, Ade . . ."

"Light show! Light show!"

"Whip it out."

"I reckon it's batteries and he's been having us on."

It was a quiet corner and the Eqbas didn't care about human anatomy, so Ade unzipped and displayed his unique bioluminescence, certain he would die of embarrassment, until Webster howled with laughter and Chahal was almost coughing.

"You can tell he's not officer material," he said. "He'd never be able to whip that out in the officers' heads if he got a commission, would he?"

"It's a miracle," said Barencoin. "They can make lights so *small* these days."

Ade heard the transport honk its klaxon as a cue that it was leaving soon, and he zipped up again. "That's it, then," he said. "I'm going to sob like a girlie if I don't go now, and I've got to do this fast or I'll never be able to do it at all, and—shit, I love you bastards, all of you, and I don't care what cap badge you got now, you're all Royals and always will be."

He turned to go back to his room. For once, nobody had mentioned Becken or Qureshi.

"Send Shan down, will you?" Barencoin called. "She's not going to get away with not saying goodbye."

Ade had no idea how he managed to do it, but he simply

turned and ran up the stairs without a backward glance. The thought of eking out every last minute was like watching someone die. He had to go.

Shan was coming down the third flight of stairs as he went up. "Did I miss them?"

"Hurry up."

"Seen Aras?"

"No, Boss."

Shan disappeared beneath the turns of the stairwell. Ade went up to finish his packing. It took about five minutes, and that was because he'd already packed, and unpacking again ate up a minute or two. He'd embarked for Cavanagh's Star with what he could carry in his bergen and no more, and he'd lost a few items and expended rounds along the way. He was hanging on to the ESF670, though. The FEU owed him his bloody rifle. All his careful but unwritten lists of the stuff he would buy to take back to Wess'ej—food and other small comforts, mainly—had been abandoned. There was no time.

However pragmatically Laktiriu put it, there was no way of dressing this up. They were being kicked off the planet, *his own planet,* all three of them. *Fuck off, lepers.* It was better than being fragged so the Eqbas could save the cost of a shuttle, but it left Ade feeling bereft.

The video screen had been on in their room permanently since they arrived and had merged into the background noise now. But a familiar voice talking about macaws made him stop dead.

"Shit," he said. Aras was on the news, at the center of a small knot of people in what looked like a zoo, telling a kid about blue and gold macaws that had been born—not from eggs—on a world 150 trillion miles away. The angle of the shot suggested the recording was made by a visitor trying to get a better look through a crowd. They showed a lot of it, ten rambling unedited minutes, and Ade could almost hear Eddie ranting about crappy technical standards, but the media were short of material showing aliens wandering around Earth. The snatched footage of Aras must have been a godsend.

So he'd gone to see the bloody parrots, all the way to Canada. It was just as well the Eqbas worked on a scale that didn't need to worry about mileage. That was Aras all over, still capable of being stopped in his tracks by wondrous things even after centuries of seeing god knows what.

It was funny to see him on telly in an ordinary Earth setting among humans. He looked suddenly *alien,* really alien, not taken-for-granted family whose appearance you had to think hard about if someone asked for a description.

The item was over by the time Shan got back from saying goodbye to the detachment. She had her copper's face on, the one that said she'd switched off and was just processing data, not getting involved.

"Okay, Boss?"

"I don't mind admitting that was bloody hard," she said. "*Hated* doing that."

"Aras has been on the news."

"Tell me he's not complicated things."

"He's been at the bird sanctuary. Actually, he came across as a nice bloke who you wouldn't mind having invade your planet."

Shan took sudden and excessive interest in the contents of her wardrobe, which were about as meager as Ade's. "I'm glad she hasn't given me time to think," she said at last, obviously meaning Laktiriu. "It's always easier to just grab and run. I keep doing that. More to the point, I keep getting shunted around by politicians, and make no mistake, the new girl is one of those."

"You could have out-*jask*ed her, you know, if you wanted to hang on."

"Never occurred to me. What would be the point? How long is longer? Forever? She made a decision to keep *c'naatat* clear of Earth. Policy change. She's more cautious. That's a good thing."

You could wear a problem out by rubbing away at it, and Shan looked as if she had. She probably had the same things going around in her head as he had in his, all the why-didn't-I and I-should-have. This was a shock phase for everyone, from the planet to individuals. When the shock and novelty wore off, and the reality of a long-term Eqbas presence sank in, the problems would start. That, Ade thought, would be when people here started to feel it.

"I didn't even get to visit Uluru," Shan said. "Oh well. The good thing about *c'naatat* is that I'll always have time."

They watched the news in silence while waiting for Aras. They could have been out making the most of the last day, but it meant secure cars and cordons and having so many things left undone and unsaid that it felt better just to forget it and not even look outside the window.

"Here we go," said Shan, gesturing towards the screen at a new headline icon. "It's started."

The Sinostates border was now closed along its full length to road haulage from Europe in protest against the FEU's failure to meet the terms of a joint food surplus policy. It followed on their withdrawal of consent to continue an FEU water pipeline across the border because of deforestation.

"And the movies always show Earthlings uniting to fight off the aliens," she said. "But all we do is get competitive."

Aras returned with a small bag and tipped the contents out onto the bed. "Look what they gave me at the sanctuary."

It was a jumble of confectionery, snacks, promotional items, educational vids and other small novelties, the kind you got in any visitor attraction. Aras seemed to rate the gift pretty highly. He spent the evening examining every item with meticulous care. But he kept returning to one small packet so often that Ade had to find out what it was that kept drawing his attention.

When he looked over Aras's shoulder, he found that it was a small transparent pouch of tiny, iridescent green feathers.

16

I suggest you begin with a permanent ban on fishing. We haven't yet established our position on cell culture flesh, but there must be an end to the use of other animal species for food, entertainment, self-decoration and research. Those who insist on subsistence by hunting as part of their culture must accept that the only justification is a return to the conditions that made it the only nutritional option—which means a pre-Neolithic situation with extensive glaciations and a world human population of a few million. You already have excellent alternatives to eating your neighbors.

LAKTIRIU AVO, Adjustment Task Force Commander,
delivering an off-the-cuff comment to media inquiry
on what Eqbas thought of Earth food

F'nar, Wess'ej.

Eddie got the call from Laktiriu Avo a few days after the ITX had flashed up a message from Shan, saying that they were coming home. Shan's message—sent as a file, not live—had seemed an oddly abrupt way to announce she was going to vanish into chill-sleep for another twenty-five years after he'd just got used to seeing her face on the screen again, but the phrase "asked to leave" said it all.

No, actually, it didn't. It just begged questions that he wouldn't get answers to until 2426, when he might not even be around to ask them. He almost felt that she'd died, and Aras and Ade with her. It was a strange and distressing moment that left him unable to concentrate on much else.

And he never got the chance to tell her that Rayat and Shapakti had skipped Surang with the entire *c'naatat* resource. It gave Eddie a laugh at a time when there hadn't been much good happening, just unrelenting bad news that he could do nothing to assuage.

"Do you recall me, Eddie Michallat?" asked Laktiriu.

He must have seen her when the task force passed through Wess'ej, because she seemed to recall him, but she'd been just another Eqbas in a green uniform then. "It's been a long time," he said. "My apologies. What can I do for you?"

"I need your assistance."

Here we go again. "Go on."

"With Shan Frankland gone, I have no human to advise me."

"Well, you sent her home . . ."

"I felt the risks of having *c'naatat* carriers around outweighed the benefits. All I ask is to bring questions to you occasionally. Even if I employ a human to advise me, I can't evaluate the advice because I don't know if it's neutral. You might not know Eqbas Vorhi, but you do have long experience of Wess'ej, and so you understand us."

It was very flattering, and not sugar-coated. Eddie felt a surge of excitement at the prospect of being in the thick of things again. It was always a bad sign lately. "How frequent would this be?"

"I don't know. I have no way of telling when I won't understand something."

Eddie saw the specter of calls at all hours with pleas to sort things out. He'd given up being at the beck and call of News Desk a long time ago, and he was too old to start it again now. He hated firefighting, and that's what it would be; he'd get the call when the shit had already hit the fan.

"I'm too far away to do any good," he said. "But here's a suggestion. Let me see your plans in advance, and I'll go through them and tell you what looks like trouble to me." It was the kind of request that caused terminal paranoia in humans, but wess'har didn't like secrecy. "It'll be cultural and political stuff, just presentation and human-wrangling. I don't do science, but then you've got that covered."

Laktiriu did a little head-tilting this way and that, and the brown plumed mane that ran front to back across her skull shook a little. "Let me think about how that might be arranged."

Eddie closed the link, and realized that he'd probably just invited her to send him every single scrap of Eqbas business for the next five years. He'd probably get it. She had no way of knowing what was a minefield and what wasn't at the moment.

Well, that's going to brighten things up a bit.

Eddie knew what hell was. It was becoming a *viewer.*

He now had to watch news without having any input or redress, and it was a punishment worthy of Dante's imagination. Shan was in the limbo of space, twenty-five years away, and the aliens he'd had to himself for so long were now part of the fabric of Earth. Nobody needed him.

"You can't leave it alone, can you?"

He hadn't realized that Erica was standing in the doorway. "How can I tell her to sod off when she's gone in to make over our homeworld? Barry's going to want to go back some day, and I'd like to leave the place in good shape for him."

"You don't *think*, do you? What's Giyadas going to say about that?"

"How does it affect her?"

"You're getting slow. She ordered a hit on Esganikan and she's going to be left holding all the Eqbas *c'naatat* stuff. I say that makes them the *other side.*"

Eddie was surprised he hadn't seen that coming. On the other hand, if the Eqbas *were* the other side, having a friendly Eddie in the camp was pretty handy.

He just wanted to be useful again, after a working lifetime of mattering and dealing with decision makers, and—he was no longer in denial about it—he wanted to steer the Eqbas towards a lighter touch on Earth than on Umeh. As the years went by, and the more he visited Umeh, the footage he still had of the invasion troubled him more and more. It was hard to know the isenj as well as he did and not look back at that archive and see not spider aliens suffering and dying but the people he knew.

Ual. Damn, I don't think about him enough. The isenj
minister who started it all had been shot dead right next to
him, close enough for him to be splashed with the watery
yellow blood.

"You realize what we're doing here, don't you, Ric?" he
said. "We're the Targassat rift in miniature. I think I have
a duty to act if I can. You think keeping out of things that
don't directly concern you is best. There we have it, the
million-year history of the wess'har species, adapted for
audio and performed by the monkey boys."

"Okay, but don't expect me to approve, and you better
clear your yard arm with Giyadas."

Erica stuffed food, a flask of water, and surveying equipment into her rucksack before fleeing for the day on the
pretext of taking samples. She'd never made close wess'har
friends, and retired couples could get on each other's nerves
if they were cooped up with nothing to do. "Accept that it's
over, Eddie. You can't run the show any more. The aliens
are there, right now, and nobody's interested in what's going
on here, and you *can't change a damn thing* on Earth. You
don't even have a vote."

She stared into his face, more upset than angry—upset
for him, he knew—and then made an incoherent sound before shutting the door behind her with a thud. She hadn't
quite slammed it, but Eddie knew she wouldn't be back until
nightfall.

She was right about one thing, though. He needed to let
Giyadas know what was happening, if only out of courtesy.
It was a lovely breezy day up on the terraces, and a good
excuse for a brisk walk to her home.

He didn't have to knock. Wess'har didn't knock anyway,
but Eddie was family and could treat Giyadas and Nevyan's
homes as his own. Sometimes it was immensely comforting.

"Hey, doll," he said, "I got a new job. Spying for the Eqbas."

Giyadas was playing with her sons, Tanatan and Vaoris.
He didn't recall Nevyan spending as much time with her
sons, but Giyadas liked to do things differently, and Eddie

wondered again how much she'd been influenced—human-ized, in the literal sense—by spending so much time with him as a child.

"As spooks go, you have some way to go to catch up with Mohan Rayat," she said.

"Great cue," Eddie lifted Tanatan and whirled him around, playing grandfather. "The Eqbas aren't going to be thrilled when they find Shapakti's handing you their re-search, and let's not even think about the orders you gave Shan."

"So what have the Eqbas asked you to find out from me?"

"Nothing. Laktiriu's asked me to advise her on humanol-ogy and our cute ways, because she kicked Shan out. I sug-gested it would be easier if they kept me briefed on what they were planning for home sweet home, then I could tell them they were heading for trouble before they found it."

"Ahh. . . . Eddie the special political adviser!"

"You really should go to Earth sometime, doll. You'd have done a far better job than the Eqbas."

"I like irony."

"Aw, come on. You know Earth needed intervention."

"It still bothers me."

"Erica's furious that I said I'd do it."

"She thinks you're tormenting yourself," Giyadas said gently. "That's all."

"What, that I can't handle being nothing? That *nobody* hangs on my every word when I file a story from the end of the bloody galaxy?" All he could do was watch the car crash unfolding. It made him boil with *impotent . . . impotent what?* He didn't even have a word for it. He had phrases, though, like *those are my aliens, those are my friends, ask me because I could have told you that,* and *why don't they listen.* Eddie had all the outbursts of a man who had been the expert and go-to guy on outer space for as long as most viewers could remember, but had now been forgotten. He'd ceased to matter the minute the Eqbas stepped onto the desert at St George. "Yeah, maybe she's got a point."

"And you, having a choice, must make it." It was one of

those classic lines from the philosopher Targassat. "I understand the shame of doing nothing when action might help. The trick is to know where to draw the line of responsibility and interference."

Giyadas was his best friend. Just that fact on its own would have been enough of a miracle for any human; his closest friend wasn't Olivier Champciaux or any of the other handful of humans still hanging on to an obsessive exile light-years from home, but a wess'har matriarch who ran a city that had enough firepower to take on a small planet. She had bioweapons, too, but he didn't want to think about that. She'd been such a cute, funny, clever kid. The adult Giyadas still had that charm and glittering intellectual insight, but her legacy had been the desperate peace with Umeh that had been forged by a mutual need to see the Eqbas leave the system for good. It had taken the joy out of her. She was all duty, and that wasn't very wess'har, because all of them knew when to live for the moment. Her gravitas was a human taint.

That's probably my fault, too.

"You know how to crush a man, doll. I started all this, you know."

"Your initial reporting didn't cause Rayat to be sent here, or anything that happened after it." Wess'har concepts of guilt and responsibility were radically different from those of humans. "Knowledge should change the way you feel."

"In about forty-odd years, *Thetis* is going to arrive home. What's going to waiting for the crew?"

Thetis was an older ship, with a top speed that was a third of *Actaeon*'s or any of the wess'har fleet. She was still inbound with the last of the colonists and *Actaeon* personnel who'd opted for the slow, seventy-five-year journey home. It was easy to forget them. He hadn't.

"I think they made the right choice, because much of the adjustment will be yielding results," said Giyadas.

"You're humoring me, aren't you doll?"

She patted his hand. "I've known you even longer than your wife has, Eddie. But I think she's distressed not to be able to cut all links with Earth. This simply reminds her that every option for your son is a sad one—to go to a world where humans have an uncertain future, or to stay here, where there's peace but no possibility of a normal human life."

It was perfectly true, and it should have hurt Eddie, but it didn't. One thing he'd become used to was wess'har frankness, and the odd comfort—eventually—of knowing that he could say what he thought without editing a single word.

Tanatan tugged at the leg of his pants, wanting attention. Wess'har kids were wonderful fun, and the two boys spoke English with adorable little double-tone chipmunk voices. "Do you think they're old enough to visit Jejeno?"

Giyadas gave Eddie that same affectionate brush across the top of the head that he'd given her when he was the taller of the two. She was a head taller than him now, a full-grown *isan*.

"It's never too soon to get to know your neighbors," she said. "Or too late."

"I'm maudlin at the moment. Take no notice. I'm gutted about the marines and I'll be dead by the time Shan, Ade and Aras get back."

"I won't let you die, and you can stay in touch with the marines who remained. You have to concentrate on what can be done."

"Well, at least I know I'll be here to welcome my old buddy boy Rayat and shake him warmly by the throat."

"For Rayat," said Giyadas, "you only have to wait five years."

"And what are you going to do with *c'naatat*?"

"I'll think about that," she said.

17

After a while, I began putting a disclaimer at the beginning of every report I filed. I described who and what I was, so the viewer could judge the inevitable filter I put on my reporting. I strove to be the most neutral voice I could, just a proxy observer for the audience, but eventually I had to ask if that was what I was supposed to be doing. I had more and more days when I felt that being neutral— reporting news—wasn't adding to the sum of human improvement, but abdicating responsibility. People usually choose news to reinforce their views, not to change them. So what was the noble cause? It wasn't observation. In the end, I decided that it was better to save the drowning man than to report objectively on drowning, because people didn't rush out to learn life-saving techniques when they saw those reports. They just observed a man drowning.

I'm Eddie Michallat, human being, and I have to be involved in life to live. Those having a choice must make it. It took an alien to teach me that, and ultimately how to be truly human.

EDDIE MICHALLAT, Constantine diaries

F'nar, Wess'ej: March 2406.

The transport that brought Rayat, Shapakti and his family into F'nar from the landing strip outside the city hadn't changed since Eddie had climbed warily on board more than thirty years ago.

It was still a hovercraft covered with a valance as far as he was concerned, but wess'har didn't care how daft things looked, only how well they worked. Wess'har would have been a very tough sell for marketing men.

"Don't hit him, Eddie," said Giyadas. "You're not as young as you were."

"I'm going to be charm itself, doll. He did manage to do one honest thing in his life, even if it *was* robbing the Eqbas."

Da Shapakti didn't seem to have changed much, but Eddie never could gauge age in wess'har very well. The biologist came trotting across the flagstones, *isan* and house-brothers following, and hugged Eddie fiercely.

"It's good to be back," he said. "I feel at home." He gave Giyadas a courteous nod. "*Giyadas Chail,* thank you for your hospitality and refuge."

Rayat looked grayer, but he'd been on hold with *c'naatat* so many times that he still looked fiftyish. Eddie really wanted to see him raddled and spotted like the evil twin painting he was sure to have stashed in some attic.

"Hi, Eddie."

"Hi, Mohan." Eddie couldn't even remember what he'd called him in the past. He'd always just been Rayat. "You cleared the place out, then."

"It had to be done," Rayat said. "Last chance, really."

"And what about you? Are you staying undead for awhile now that Shap's got a cure?"

"No, I want it out of me for good now. I want to know my body's my own when I wake up in the morning."

Eddie wanted to say, "It's a trap!" but Rayat had no sense of humor and there was only so much tormenting that he could do before he lost the will to make Rayat's life hell. "Okay," he said. "Come back to the house and we'll give you a decent cup of tea, dinner, and bring you up to speed on Earth."

"Good to know it's still there."

"It is, but I've been working for the Eqbas for five years so I talked them out of turning it into parking lots."

"I haven't had chance to check the ITX," said Rayat. "Just give me the headlines."

"I think you need to watch the screen. I might even be able to get you a chat with the Aussie prime minister. He's still in office. Nice enough bloke. Den Bari."

Wess'har were already ferrying containers into the city on small pallets and taking them down into the tunnels that ran underneath F'nar. There was a lot of storage down there, but also an arsenal and fighter hangars with nanite production templates. Pretty little pearly F'nar and its deliberately agrarian ways might have looked like a theme park, but it was a superpower in human terms.

"Is that it?" asked Eddie, pausing to look at the pale yellow drums. They looked like hatboxes. "I'd expected something bigger."

"That's just the *c'naatat* materials in suspension," said Shapakti. "The equipment I need for the Bezer'ej project remains in our transport for the trip to Nazel. But we'd like to spend some time here before we go. "

"It's a bus ride." Eddie pointed up at the sky, where Wess'ej's twin planet hung as a fat, cloud-streaked crescent moon. "You forgot how cozy things are down Ceret way."

"And the macaws?" he asked. "My pretty friends?"

Eddie had to think. "Oh yes. They're fine. They're at a bird sanctuary in Canada."

"So *beautiful*," said Shapakti's *isan*, Ajaditan, looking around the caldera and up the steep steps that linked the terraces. F'nar was at its tourist-poster pearly best right then. "And so much climbing . . ."

They spent the rest of the day settling Shapakti's clan into their new home, and Giyadas saved Eddie a difficult moment by offering Rayat his own private accommodation. Eddie didn't think Erica would want a permanent houseguest, and he still wasn't ready to have Rayat at close quarters for the next twenty years, however mellow he'd become.

"Dinner," he said, pointing Rayat in the direction of the house, right at the far end of the terrace on the broken edge of the caldera bowl. "It used to be Shan's home, but we've exorcised the place with beer and holy water, so you'll be fine."

"Wrong religion," said Rayat. He walked ahead of Eddie along the terrace with the energy of a younger man whose body was self-repairing, and for a moment Eddie envied that.

The moment passed. "How is Shan, then? I'm a bit time-addled at the moment."

"She's on her way back. Hang on twenty years, and you can give her a nice big kiss."

"We wanted the same outcome, you know."

"Yeah, I know you're a matched pair of psychotic ideological zealots."

"Well, we put an end to the risk, between us, I suppose."

"She'll love the joint credit."

Twenty years sounded like an eternity. It would certainly be close to it for Eddie. But the thought of Shan catching up with Rayat . . . well, that was motivating. Eddie wasn't going to die until he'd seen *that*.

Kamberra, Earth: April 2406.

Den Bari, in his second term of office as Australian PM, stood outside Old Government House in the early autumn sun and marveled at how *tolerable* it all was.

"It's working," he said. "What a great day for them to arrive."

The air temperatures were falling. There were times when he resented how many taxpayers' resources had gone towards the solar-reduction layer, given that some countries hadn't contributed much, but climate engineering didn't follow borders. Water systems and land remediation, though—those could be withheld from nations who hadn't toed the line on population reduction or any of the other Eqbas diktats. It had been a few brutal years for the Sinostates, and overseas aid was a thing of the past.

This was how the Earth got fewer humans. You did it voluntarily, and met your zero-growth targets, or you got them met for you. Sometimes he felt guilty for not asking if the epidemics in the Sinostates were naturally occurring, and sometimes he felt the question was best not asked.

"I have difficulty with this, I admit." Deborah Garrod walked out onto the gravel expanse and shielded her eyes against the sun. "I know you're not a religious man, Den, but

I try to account to God for my inaction most days. Letting people die isn't much different from killing them."

She was a remarkable woman, and she'd done a lot to bridge the gaps with the Eqbas, but her rules weren't his. They agreed to differ and square their consciences as best they could. Now they were waiting to catch sight of the first ships of the main Eqbas Vorhi fleet, five years behind the vanguard that was now a feature of life on Earth.

"It's not collaboration," he said. "It's saving as many of my own as I can, and there's not enough world to go around—better to save a few than lose everyone by spreading the misery evenly."

Deborah just nodded. He found it interesting that she'd never tried to save his soul. They waited half an hour in the open air, something they wouldn't have been able to do before the Eqbas arrived, and looked hard for the familiar bronze ships with their chevron belts of light. Then it started; a low-frequency pulsing that made him screw up his eyes and ram his fingers in his ears to stop the itching that traveled to the back of his tongue. He didn't recall the first Eqbas fleet having that much effect on his ears. Maybe this lot came in lower, or closer, or—

"Oh my God . . ." he said.

Maybe this lot were much, much *bigger*.

The first ship cast a spectacular shadow, cool as an eclipse, as it passed over Kamberra. Six ships, Laktiriu said, but with vessels that could break up and reform into any number of units, the figure meant nothing. The flagship was followed by an assortment of craft of all sizes, some showing a definite blue bloom as they changed shape.

"Forty thousand personnel, Laktiriu said." Bari looked back at the building to see staff standing around with cameras and taking in the spectacle. "And all the others go straight home, bar the handover team."

"I've done a deep-space flight just once, and I'm still coming to terms with the time displacement," said Deborah. "How do they ever cope with doing this time after time?"

"Maybe society changes when you've got a lot of people doing it." Bari occasionally got a strong urge to ask Laktiriu if he could just pop back and take a look at Surang for real, but the logistics of dropping out of life for sixty or more years were beyond him, and always would be. "I'll always feel I've missed something big and important now that I know just how much is out there."

Bari left her to watch and headed back to his office. His handheld was already ticking with the influx of messages and requests to speak to this ambassador or that foreign minister. The Eqbas fleet might have been a welcome sight for him, but for others it meant a bigger Eqbas presence on Earth and all the fears that went with that scale of expansion. Two thousand Eqbas, and their Skavu troops, had changed the planet. What would twenty times that number of Eqbas do?

Sell it as less than four times the number. Add in the Skavu. Hell, you don't have to sell anything. *You just make sure Australia—and New Zealand, and the rest of the Pacific Rim, and every state that's played ball so far—goes on keeping its nose clean.*

Bari passed the groundsman who was raking the gravel level, tidying up the place for the meeting and greeting of the new Eqbas command. "Historic day, Kennie," he said.

"Seen one alien," he said, not looking up, "seen 'em all."

It was a good sign. Really, it was.

F'nar, Wess'ej: Undercity.

"We used to call this *sofa government*, you know," said Eddie as he followed Giyadas and the ruling matriarchs of F'nar down the tunnel. "Very informal."

"Do you miss democracy, Eddie?" Her Spartan helmet of a mane bobbed slightly out of sequence with those of the other matriarchs, whose numbers expanded and shrank as the occasion demanded, but which now always included Nevyan, Giyadas's mother, and her mother, Mestin. Giyadas was the senior in the group, a pecking order that was as unspoken and subtle as the hierarchy among the males of a household. There was consensus; but they all knew who was boss if push came to shove. "Mestin says you were fascinated by the lack of any formal politics here."

"And," Mestin growled, not turning her head, "it has been *millennia* since any *isan* has been killed for failing in her duty and not ceding. I wish you hadn't reported that, Eddie. You made us sound like savages."

Eddie had forgotten that story; the political editor had loved it, though. Office was thrust upon the most capable and aggressively competent females here, not sought; and nobody voted, and consultation and representation . . . it was chatting in the Exchange of Surplus Things or being waylaid by a neighbor with a point to make. Somehow, in this anarchic, osmotic process, responsibilities were taken and decisions were made. Eddie loved human politics as a game, but when he saw wess'har community life, he was ready to burn the ballot boxes. It was the most alien thing of all about them, really. He'd thought it was their double voices, or the polyandry, or the four-pupilled eyes, or even the transfer of genes between male and female during sex, but in the end, what made them most unhuman was the way they handled the concepts of responsibility and guilt.

Suddenly, the assassination orders that Shan was given made sense. Esganikan was an *isan* who had let the side down, and so her genes were obviously dodgy. She had to be taken out of the gene pool, at least by Wess'ej rules.

I get it. I get it, after all these years.

"How did Esganikan fail?" he asked. It was a failure by Wess'ej standards, obviously, but not by Eqbas Vorhi's. The genetic divergence in just ten thousand years was astonishing, and very visible. "What did she do wrong?"

"She kept information from her community that they needed to know," said Nevyan. "And she took too many risks with the safety of a world's ecology."

They were green hardliners here, although the Skavu made them look like woolly liberals. Eddie had a second or two's fantasy about enforcing wess'har need-to-know rules on Earth.

The light level increased as they walked further into the complex. Rack-lined tunnels and recesses branched off everywhere, filled with machinery, some clearly military, and some that could have been anything. There was a device for every purpose down here, most of them dating back to the arrival of the wess'har in the system ten thousand years ago, but still bloody useful and capable of indefinite replication by nanites. Some of the older-generation Eqbas metamorphosing vessels were stored down here, broken out into dozens of small shiplets that could coalesce into one large warship. It had never dawned on Eddie that the liquid-to-solid tech also made them very easy to store.

"Are we there yet?" he asked.

"Nearly . . ." Giyadas hung back a few paces and put her arm around his shoulders. "We value your wisdom, Eddie."

"Can I have that on my headstone?"

"Not for a very, very long time."

They turned right into a branch tunnel and then into a biomaterials area, where the duplicate Earth gene bank was stored. The walls were marked with biohaz warning symbols, wess'har style—this was also where they created and stored their bioweapons—and the doors were already open. Inside, Shapakti was waiting by a bench with what looked for all the world like a small thermal oven.

This was why they wanted his wisdom.

"We've debated what to do about *c'naatat,* Eddie, and our view is that we shouldn't keep these samples." Giyadas sounded as if the decision had been made, but the matriarchs still liked to canvass opinion sometimes. "If we keep them, temptation may lead us to use it. And one day in the future, we may not be as powerful as we are now, and there's no way of knowing what might happen to it. The proposal is that we destroy all the samples. All of them."

They valued his wisdom, they said, so he did his best to scrape up some of it and earn his keep. "But there's shitloads of *c'naatat* on Ouzhari. They couldn't even kill it off by nuking it."

"Ouzhari is always going to be an issue, but Bezer'ej is already defended by bioagents, and we'll assess new threats to its quarantine as and when they arise. But these samples—think of the hosts they've passed through, and the characteristics they embody. Aras, Shan, Ade, Rayat, even Lindsay. They're ideal for creating persistent, intelligent troops. This makes the material especially desirable."

"If anyone knew about it."

"Eqbas Vorhi does, for one."

"Ah. I'm with you. I get it."

"It also denies the asset to us, of course, but on balance, we feel it should be destroyed."

Eddie knew wess'har wouldn't destroy any living organism if they didn't have to. Their have-to thresholds bore no resemblance to those of humans, as the extermination of the isenj on Bezer'ej had shown. This was a big deal for them strategically, and maybe morally too.

"What happens to *c'naatat* when you remove it, Shapakti?" Eddie asked. "How do you actually do it?"

"It was a matter of stopping the individual organisms communicating. They then leave the body and remain inactive, permanently dormant. Or at least I haven't found a way of making them active again."

"So they're not actually dead?"

"No. But they can't communicate with each other, and so they can't act."

"And you can take the organism out of the host, but you can't take the host out of the organism."

"So far, yes."

So far. There was no telling what some clever bastard might be able to do in the future, and possibly not a wess'har bastard at that.

The extracted *c'naatat*'s fate struck Eddie as a depressing one: he had no idea if the organisms were sentient, but sentience was a very subjective thing, and the idea that this. . . . this *community* that lived within its host like the population of a planet was suddenly rendered blind, deaf and mute seemed desperately sad. Bacteria lived and died within every living thing each second of the day, though; there was a limit to how much even wess'har could mourn.

But Eddie knew what it was to be lonely, cut off from everything he knew. He decided he would rather be dead than totally, endlessly isolated. He had a brief glimpse of what

Shan must have endured, drifting alone in space, unable to die, just like the hapless individual *c'naatat*.

He hated it when life drew such stark parallels.

"I'm uneasy about biological agents in general," he said after a long pause. "We won't ever agree on that, and I still feel bad that I tricked isenj DNA samples out of poor bloody Ual to help you make that anti-isenj pathogen. So . . . yes, I think you should get rid of *c'naatat*. Just be sure that you won't need to use it to survive in the future."

And just in case the poor bloody thing knows what's happening to it.

The pause was long and silent, and then, without any discussion, Giyadas gave Shapakti a nod.

"Do it," she said.

Eddie didn't see anything happen in the little oven, and wasn't even sure what the method of destruction might be. But Shapakti pressed the top, there was a slight sigh of air for a few moments, and then he took his hand away and nodded politely.

"It's sealed, *isan've*. Now all that remains is the countermeasure, in case we ever need it."

"Is that it?" Eddie asked. "You killed it? How? How could you do that if Rayat couldn't even nuke the bloody thing to death?"

"You misunderstand," said Shapakti. "This is a biohazard container. It'll be launched in a missile directed into the sun. Into Ceret. That's the most certain destruction we know."

Eddie had never lost his sense of journalistic drama. He thought it would have made a lovely shot, Cavanagh's Star swallowing this bizarre burden. Nobody was going to land and fish out the container, that was for sure. He tried to see the funny side, but failed.

"Let's go," said Giyadas.

And that was wess'har strategic planning. Just a few minutes; just a few what-do-you reckons and nods, and a superpower had thrown away one of its greatest trump cards.

Only wess'har could do that, he thought, although the reasoning wasn't pacifism.

"So will you carry on working on removing *c'naatat* from wess'har, Shap?" Eddie asked.

"In computer modeling only, alas," he said. "But I was close, and I think a full range of countermeasures would be wise."

We've been here before, thought Eddie. *It'd be a shame to put Aras through all that dilemma again.*

He wondered what Ade and Shan would decide to do in the end. The challenge never went away. As long as Aras had to stay as he was, neither of them would take advantage of the cure.

Eddie wondered if they would even want to, and followed the bobbing manes back down the soft-lit corridors and back up to the city, blindingly pearl-bright in the sun.

18

Regret is new to me. While wess'har don't spend pointless hours imagining the different course of events that we could create by turning back time, we can recognize what we must not repeat. I regret calling on Eqbas Vorhi for help. Everything stems from that. The Eqbas are strangers, I fear further contact, and I will always worry about the Skavu now that Esganikan's restraining hand is gone. Like Giyadas, I now wonder if we were wise to destroy c'naatat, *which gave us the military edge when we needed it.*

NEVYAN TAN MESTIN,
in discussion with the matriarchs of F'nar

F'nar, Wess'ej: 2426: twenty years later.

Fnar hadn't changed.

Aras brought the shuttle in low over the plain as if he wanted to take in every detail of the terrain and make sure every stone, every pebble was still there.

Shan just wanted to get her boots on the ground as fast as she could. When the ship set down just outside the caldera, she didn't even grab her grip; she just ran all the way into the pearl city, scattering bewildered wess'har, and raced up the rows of terraces until her lungs made her stop for a minute before she could run again.

Her legs burned with the effort.

It's still the same. It's all here, nothing's changed, even Eddie's here—

The city still functioned in the way it was intended. Progress for the sake of it was meaningless to wess'har here. Nothing *needed* to change.

She waited a few moments outside Nevyan's door and took in the view, getting her breath back before facing Eddie.

We'd say this is stagnation. So? Where does progress take us? Where would we go?

Progress was like *freedom* and *democracy*. You had to define it before deciding if you wanted it, or it was just a Pavlovian trigger to get you to serve someone else's agenda. If progress was an end to disease, fear, and death, and having enough to eat, she had it all. There was nowhere else to go.

Get on with it.

She rapped on the encrusted door. The layer of nacre wasn't completely even. The varying thickness gave it undulations and ripples that added to the organic lines of a city trying hard not to stand out from the landscape. She thought of Earth—last week, last month, not a short lifetime away—and her only regret was that she couldn't show off F'nar to more people who would be amazed by it.

This time, she recalled nothing of being in chill-sleep. She took that as a measure of her relief at heading home.

The door opened. "You never have to knock," said Nevyan. No, wess'har just barged straight in, even if you were using the toilet. "But I've waited for that sound for a long time."

Shan couldn't imagine what it was to wait twenty-five years to see someone again. Her separation felt like weeks, not enough to really feel that gut-punch of recognition. Nevyan seized her in a fierce hug that took her by surprise, and Shan returned the embrace with appropriate caution.

"Hey," she said. "Tell me you're just middle-aged now and that we've got lots of time left."

"I shall not die for many years, my friend." The warren of chambers was as full of noise and cooking smells as ever. Damn, wess'har food actually smelled *homely* to her now. "Where do I start on events you've missed?"

"Try Eddie," said Shan.

Nevyan led her past curious youngsters—grandchildren, by the look of it—and into another chamber that looked out into the caldera. "I'll wait outside. I know you dislike others seeing your emotional moments."

It was a nice room, the sort you'd pay a lot for in an Earth

rest home; the hazy gold light reflected from the pearl terraces outside filled it, and for a moment she could defocus
a little and see it as a vast halo. An Eddie she'd never seen
before sat near the window, and struggled to turn his head
far enough to look at her.

"You're late, doll."

His voice still hadn't changed that much. There was a little creaking, hoarse undertone, and his breathing was la-
bored, but he didn't sound like a man in his—

Nineties.

Knowing that in advance didn't reduce the impact of what
a rotten bastard time could be.

*Dear God, and this is just time separation. This isn't
even* c'naatat. *What's it like after five centuries when you've
seen people age past you over and over again?*

Shan looked around for something to sit on and pulled up
a storage box of laminated *efte.*

"How are you doing, Eddie?" He was a painfully old
man, not quite as frail as she'd expected, but it was a job to
spot the bloke she'd known until she concentrated on his
eyes. Eddie was still in there. "We've got a lot of catching up
to do."

"You got fired," he said. "But that's good, because I
couldn't have waited for you much longer."

"I didn't belong there. I don't think I ever did." She took
his hand carefully. "Now I'm going to kick your bloody arse
for trying to be a hero."

"What?"

"You know what. You could have told BBChan that you
had proof about me. *C'naatat.* Nothing would have happened in the end."

"Jesus, that was a long time ago."

"You didn't have to protect me. And you certainly didn't
have to impose this exile on yourself."

Maybe it wasn't the thing to say to a man who probably
missed Earth and now regretted a pointless gesture that time
had covered in the silt of events. "Don't kid yourself that I
fell on my sword to cover your arse, doll," he said. "It was
more than that, a lot more. Now . . . have you *ever* stood up

and said what you really did to protect Green Rage? Even now?"

It was the question he first asked her more than fifty years ago, when she was freshly marooned here and he worked out who she was and why Perault might have shanghaied her. "Oh yeah, a copper telling the world she went native and helped eco-terrorism when she should have been crushing it is *really* something I want to boast about."

"Maybe you had to be there." Eddie took a rasping breath. "Look, it was more than my being too humiliated to go home. Why should I give a fuck what a news editor thinks of me? Something in me just switched off that day. I wanted to tell a different kind of story."

Shan checked her mental calendar. *Twenty-five years.* "When did you last do a program for BBChan?"

"Oh . . . maybe twenty years ago. It's gone now. You know that, don't you? BBChan's gone." He squeezed her hand. "You know I helped the isenj set up a broadcast network on Umeh? It's linked to Wess'ej too. Really something. I'm the bloody Lord Reith of outer space."

Eddie began laughing with the caution of someone whose chest hurt. Shan had no idea where to take the conversation next, because the things she wanted to know most were the most awkward, and there was too much water under the bridge to know where to start on the harmless stuff. It was a bad time to discover tact.

"So . . . about you, Eddie. Give me the bullet points."

"Erica's been gone ten years. Barry—I sent him off to Eqbas Vorhi with Olivier's lad when he was twenty, so he could get back to Earth with the next ship. There was no future for him here, not as the last of the species. Bloody shame that so many people went back. A few more humans here, and maybe we could have had a viable colony that could learn to behave like civilized sentients and fit in with the wess'har. Maybe even do something responsible with that second gene bank."

It took Shan a few seconds to do the maths, but that meant he'd heard almost nothing from Barry since. She didn't want to think about the big picture then, not gene banks or the sanctity of creation or the shape Earth was in. "So they're still sending support to the Earth mission."

"I think," Eddie said slowly, "that it's by way of checking up what's left and deciding whether to keep the garrison there, or decide that the humans can run the shop on their own, and pull out."

"Nothing I can do there now, but plenty I can do here."

"Predictably, the adjustment hasn't been completely seamless."

"Unless it really matters to you to tell me, I don't want to know all the detail . . . yet."

"You haven't had any news or messages since you left Earth?"

"No, I thought that catching up with my friends was the priority. Plenty of time to watch the bloody news."

"I'll give you my records. I spent a good fifteen years advising the Eqbas on policy stuff, so you can read a complete record of what went on each year." Eddie looked into her face and studied it, gaze flickering, eyes glazed with age. A slow smile spread across his face. "So, are you happy you've completed your mission now?"

"I don't know if I feel it's *job done,* but the case is as closed as it'll ever be."

"Good. Time to move on."

"I hope we can see a bit more of each other now. It's not like either of us have pressing duties."

"You've got Ade and Aras."

"They'll want to see you too."

"You know," he said, "I always fancied Ismat Qureshi. Pretty, *pretty* girl. Did she realize, I wonder? I never told her. Bloody shame."

Shan had been at Qureshi's funeral a week ago, in terms of her own timescale; late twenties or early thirties, a bloody good marine, and dead far too young. She wished now that the full twenty-five years' separation from Earth was something she had lived through, so that time could have taken the edge off her grief. But interstellar travel didn't work that way. Shan was effectively freshly bereaved, and still raw.

"I think Izzy knew," Shan said at last.

Eddie nodded a few times, then squinted into the shafts of bright sun piercing the window. "I know everyone says it, but nobody really takes it seriously enough. Tell people the good stuff when you can. You can't always catch up later. The shit and the arguments can wait."

Shan had always had good human radar. Something tapped her on the shoulder and whispered that unalloyed happy reunions were only for the movies, because she'd come back from the dead and knew how brief the breathless, grateful joy could be. She could see the limit of her time left to be Eddie's friend.

"I'll see you later," she said, and stroked the thin wisps of hair on Eddie's scalp. It looked like an infant wess'har's, all papery fragility. "Got to unpack. Did you leave the place nice and tidy, or will I find bottles and frilly panties down the back of the sofa?"

"You know the wess'har. Someone will have made the place ready for you. They always do." He clasped her hand again. "Be patient with Ade, won't you? And when you come back, I want to hear what you did on Earth. Just the fun stuff."

"You heard the rest, then."

"Yeah. I'm sorry. But . . . I'd have done the same. Too many what-ifs, leaving anything *c'naatat* there. It was never meant to leave this system. I'll tell you now—Rayat and Shapakti cleared every sample and piece of data from the Eqbas labs, brought the stuff back here, and Giyadas had it destroyed. No more *c'naatat* going spare. Just the countermeasures. And what lives on Bezer'ej."

Shan resented the fact that Rayat's name still produced a reaction in her. He shouldn't have still been able to jerk her chain like that.

Eddie could read her pretty well. "You might as well know. Shap got asylum here, but he brought Rayat back with him."

"Still here?" Her gut flipped. "Bastard."

"Minus *c'naatat* now."

"I'm glad they removed it."

"Oh, he wanted it gone."

"Now you're going to tell me he found God." No, it wasn't the time to vent. It wasn't fair on Eddie. "It's good to be back again, mate. First thing we do is have dinner. I'm not putting it off, not one more day."

He chuckled. "I'll try to stay alive, but you better not make any fancy desserts. I might be dead by the main course."

Shan wanted to tell him that she loved him like the brother she never had. She knew she didn't have a lot of time to do that. Tomorrow was running out for him.

But she had plenty left. She'd concentrate on his for a while.

F'nar: upper terraces.

Home: the place was still home after so many years, and it smelled fresh and clean.

"Got to call Chaz," Ade said, bounding over to the ITX. Time had simply closed up for him. "I promised. I said, I'd call the lads."

He dropped his bergen in the corner and sat down at the console. Aras watched him as he made tea, the first thing Shan would ask for when she got in, and wondered how long Ade would have to wait to find his friends after twenty-five years.

There was also a message from Shapakti propped against a bowl on the table, a real letter on hemp paper scavenged from the colonists. Aras opened it: he expected to see something about Lindsay or the bezeri, but it wasn't.

My friends.

Ten years ago, I succeeded in removing c'naatat *from be-zeri and wess'har tissue, and so we need not fear it again. If contamination happens, we have choices. I think those choices should be very restrained, in case we're tempted to use this as a convenience instead of treating it with rever-ence and caution. I await your homecoming.*

Aras closed his eyes.

Shan now had a choice, whether he wanted it or not.

It wasn't the first time he'd had to consider it, and when it had seemed possible a few years ago, he'd taken stupid decisions that ended in Lindsay and Rayat's infection with *c'naatat*. But the bad memories didn't stop all his conflicting longings overwhelming him again; his need and love for Shan, for a house-brother like Ade, for children he couldn't have with them, for children he might now have with someone else, for the life he had never fully lived—and for the life that he thought he would have to live, and want to live, forever.

How do I even begin to discuss this with Shan and Ade?
How do I tell them I might want to leave them?

Who will I be when c'naatat *is removed? Will I even recall my time with them? Just because it worked that way for a human is no guarantee for me.*

He hadn't even had chance to prepare himself for it. He stood staring at the pot of tea for a long time until he became aware of Ade not talking, but making an occasional *ah* sound. Aras turned to look, and Ade had his hand to one side of his face, eyes closed, listening carefully.

"Oh . . . I'd like that," he said softly. "I'm sorry that I bothered you. It's not like you can post it. But thanks. I'll try that number too."

Ade closed the link and sat back, then took a breath and stared at a fixed point on the wall. "Chahal teaches at Army College." He stood up and sniffed loudly. "That was his missus I was talking to. I'll get the other numbers when I'm feeling a bit more up to it. Sue's retired and Mart's a bloody police inspector. Christ, Shan's going to laugh her arse off at that. Inspector Barencoin of the Yard. Fuck me."

Aras couldn't even think of mentioning his own news. It was too selfish and potentially cruel; Ade had comforting news to help him buffer the aftermath of the short disastrous time on Earth. It could wait. He finished making the tea, and waited for the sound of Shan's boots on the terrace outside.

It was no time to start making decisions.

First, they had to work out what kind of home they had come back to. Not even stable, studiously traditional Wess'ej was immune to change. And then—

Shan swung open the door and stood there for a moment, looking around. "God, you'd never think Eddie lived a whole married life in here, would you? And guess what. Rayat's back."

19

Reforested areas in what was central Germany will be able to support reintroduction of previously extinct fauna within two years, according to ecologists. A joint team of Eqbas and Canadian biologists say they're confident the ecosystem will reach a sustainable state by 2435. Meanwhile, Indian authorities say the nation is on target for a planned reduction in population of at least 100 million in the coming year, thereby guaranteeing its access to water supplies under Eqbas Protectorate agreements.

(*The World Today*—morning bulletin, Channel 5000.)

F'nar: upper terraces.

Shan didn't look half as surprised as Rayat expected when she opened the door.

"Dr. Rayat," she said, with just an edge of ice, "how are you?"

She actually stood back to let him in. Rayat felt the temperature drop even further as he walked into the central living area, chilled by a blank stare from Ade. Aras never looked welcoming anyway, but Rayat assumed that he was still persona non grata with all three of them. He reminded himself that they'd missed living out the years that might have dulled the animosity.

No, they still loathed and mistrusted him, and he had neither the years left to him to work on that nor the desire to justify himself.

Shan went back to the table, where she'd spread out a selection of Eddie's meticulous records of the Eqbas occupation, and appeared to be working through them.

"So, what can I do for you?" She didn't look up.

"I'm sorry about Qureshi and Becken. I really am."

"Yeah."

"I didn't see any point sliding around trying to avoid you. F'nar's a small place." Rayat saw Ade turn his back to switch on the ITX, audio set low. Aras simply sat watching Shan. "So, you know Shap and I cleaned out *c'naatat* from the Eqbas."

"I heard. I'm glad. Been back to Bezer'ej?"

"Once or twice. You heard that Shap worked out how to get the thing out of other species, too?"

Rayat knew Shapakti had left a note for them, but the barely noticeable wobble in Shan's eyeline, just the hint of a double blink, told him that it was either a very sore topic or she didn't know for some reason.

"That's a lot of immortal squid to round up and treat."

"Well, I just wanted to break the ice so I didn't have to cross the whole bloody caldera to avoid you," said Rayat. "And, to be honest, I wanted to know if you were planning to remove your own *c'naatat* and Lindsay's so that we can get back to baseline here in terms of potential risk. You're the last left."

"Oh, yeah. Nice job stoking Kiir into fragging Esganikan, by the way." Shan closed the screen on the folder she was reading. "That's got to be the record for long-distance spook manipulation."

"Well, are you?"

"I'm damned if I'm going to be answerable to you."

"I did it." Rayat selected his best verbal knife. "You see, Lindsay has this very vivid memory of you stepping out of the airlock, and telling her she'd always hate herself for lacking the courage of conviction that you had. I just wondered how you might now justify *not* removing the thing from all three of you."

Ade turned slowly and got up, hands on hips, with that expression that turned him from an engagingly self-effacing man into someone who rang all Rayat's alarm bells.

"It's okay, Ade," Shan said. "It's how he gets his stiffy, seeing how far he can go before I kick the shit out of him again." She cleared the table and stacked the files on top of a cupboard. "Rayat, I'm a bit too preoccupied with Eddie, and recent losses, and trying to make sense of what I missed in the last twenty-five years to give you any entertainment. Let's have fun catching up some other time, shall we?"

She wouldn't look at him, but as she turned to open the door she couldn't avoid it; and in her usual unblinking stare, there was the slight frown of someone who had been forced to think about something they didn't want to.

Rayat pondered his own reaction as he walked back down the terraces to his home. Yes, he'd wanted to knock that saintly certainty off her face by reminding her that the only possible reason why she and her two lovers were still walking around as *c'naatat* carriers was that she was too swayed by self-interest to be consistent in her stance on it.

I stopped short of reminding her about the abortion. Maybe I'm going soft.

She *was* inconsistent about it. She'd veered from spacing herself and aborting her child to turning a blind eye to Ade and Aras. She had limits to her ruthless principles.

Rayat thought about his own reasons for wanting to be returned to normal, and tried to separate his own weariness with an exceptionally solitary life from the belief—so easy to cling to in doing his job—that *c'naatat* was too disruptive, destabilizing and open to abuse to be allowed to exist.

He didn't know. He also didn't know if he would take this to its logical conclusion and finish off the remaining *c'naatat* carriers himself.

All he knew was that he'd surrendered it, and she hadn't, and motive didn't matter. After a few decades, the wess'har way of thinking began to make sense.

Nazel, Bezer'ej

The islands didn't look any different from the way they'd been the last time Shan had visited, still as wild and unspoiled as the day she had landed in one of *Thetis*'s shuttles. Shan kicked along the shingle with Nevyan, scattering pebbles. *Thetis* was still twenty-five years out from Earth. She thought about the humans on board at times like this.

They're going to get a shock when they get home

"It's not that I don't believe you, Nev." She remembered her way to the bezeri settlement, which she felt she'd visited so recently. "But I have to see."

"I didn't think this would be a priority on your return," said Nevyan.

"Closure. That's all."

"Have you spoken to Shapakti yet?"

"Haven't had the chance. Still working through my list and trying to walk around the terraces without old neighbors going, '*Shan G'san!*' all the time."

"Then there are things I have to show you."

Shan thought she'd managed to get lost after all, but when she walked into an overgrown clearing she could see that this was the right place. The wattle-and-daub tree houses had crumbled, leaving fragments like eggshells, but the stone structures still stood largely intact. The bezeri had gone. She wandered around, peering inside. There were no artifacts, just the ruins of homes. The illusion of having been here recently was shattered. She'd last seen the place fifty years ago.

"Is this it?" Shan asked. "Is this what you had to show me?"

"Partly." Nevyan waited while she inspected all the structures. "They returned to the sea."

All Shan could think of was that bezeri were harder to track and find underwater than they were on land. With *c'naatat*, it was academic for bezeri, though. They could go anywhere they liked. They could even glide and fly in air if they felt like it. In the early days, they'd tried it all, taking full advantage of *c'naatat*'s ability to reshape their anatomy.

Maybe I could fly, too. What's the point, though? What does any c'naatat *want to be?*

"Lin too?"

"No," said Nevyan. "She's usually around somewhere."

"She could go home now. She could have gone home years ago if she'd had the transport."

"She was given the choice, and she declined both." Nevyan looked as if she'd had enough of the abandoned vil-

lage and began walking back towards the shuttle, where her
ussissi aide Serrimissani waited, and was probably getting
impatient. Age hadn't tempered Serrimissani's stroppiness.
"Lindsay persuaded the bezeri to be treated, but she thinks
not all of them. So we keep an eye on the situation in case
the Eqbas return at some time in the future, or even the
Skavu. It concerns me."

Shan felt an answering kick in her gut at the mention of
the Skavu. She had her doubts about the Eqbas now that
she'd seen that they weren't as wary of *c'naatat* as their
cousins, but she was even more conscious of the Skavu and
their extreme views. Anyone who looked like zealots compared to wess'har was a concern. Esganikan had given her
word that the Skavu would never return to this system and
take action against *c'naatat.* But Esganikan was dead, and
Shan had no idea what that meant in terms of Eqbas Vorhi's influence on their homeworld, Garan, which was a
little too close for Shan's paranoia. If nuking Ouzhari
hadn't eradicated *c'naatat*, she had no idea what Skavu
might resort to.

And . . . Kiir. Okay, he was either monstrous or simply
beyond human rules of engagement, but she'd shot him,
killed him, and he was not unlike her—a creature from another culture seduced into the ideology of wess'har environ-
mentalism, and used to enforce it. When Giyadas had given
her the order to kill Esganikan, she didn't question it. She
went right ahead with the plan, and would have gone through
with it if Kiir hadn't beaten her to it.

Shan shook herself out of that thinking, but mentally filed
it under the things that she had to remember to worry about.
"So what keeps Lindsay here?"

"She feels she has a duty to the bezeri, as Aras did."

Shan had never been able to empathize with Lindsay's
motives but she could follow them in a mechanistic kind of
way, tracking her from one martyred delusion to the next.

"What are their numbers like?"

"Hundreds now. They bred, or at least some of them
did."

"*C'naatat*-free."

"Those we can locate."

Shan almost said they were back to square one, but they weren't, and never would be. She'd almost expected Lindsay to be waiting for her. Shan walked away from the settlement, curious—how could the bezeri, the bloody squid supremacists, be talked into giving up their survival advantage?—and went back to the shuttle, Nevyan trailing her.

Paranoia tapped Shan on the shoulder again. It was hard to ignore. "You really think the Eqbas might come back and give you problems?"

"They were angry about Shapakti, but we made it clear that if they wanted the research back they would have to take it by force," said Nevyan. "It's academic. The tissue samples are gone."

"And you ordered me to assassinate one of their commanders. How do you think they'd react if they knew that? Act of war?"

"We wouldn't care if they found out, of course, but it never happened, and only outcomes matter."

If only human politics had been that easy. Shan was slipping back into the moral framework of Wess'ej again, a worldview that she now knew was subtly but significantly different from the Eqbas variety. It felt comforting. She wasn't out of step here.

"Can we swing by Constantine?" she said. "For old time's sake?"

If Lin had gone to ground anywhere, it'd be there, and Shan could probably pinpoint the area to within a few meters. Serrimissani took the shuttle low over the sea and banked to starboard to give Shan a better view of the ocean. The deck was resolutely opaque; the wess'har here hadn't made use of the Eqbas technology that Esganikan had left, and Shan now found it oddly frustrating not to be able to see through the hull. But she could see from the viewplate what Serrimissani was trying to locate. Beneath them, there were the telltale lights of a shoal of bezeri near the surface, watching them much as they always had until the shuttle passed.

Constantine was a carpet of amber and blue-gray foliage. Orange cycadlike trees and patches of bog streaked with shifting mats of vegetation gave Shan a jolt of *home, familiar, been here*. She reached out and tapped a point on the chart that tracked the shuttle's movement on the console.

"Okay, set us down about here, please."

Serrimissani's eyes seemed permanently narrowed in disapproval. "If you're going looking for Lindsay Neville, she spends her time at the old colony site."

"Okay," Shan said. "I'm looking for her." She turned to Nevyan. "How long has it been like this? Do you stay in touch with her?"

"Ten years. And only occasionally."

"Do the bezeri still want her around?"

Nevyan had a nervous habit of plucking at the collar of her *dhren*. The garment shaped itself to the wearer's needs anyway, but Nevyan always seemed to be giving it a helping hand. "She was your friend, once. Are you going to pursue her again?"

Shan hadn't got off to the best start with Lindsay when the *Thetis* mission reached Bezer'ej. There was a brief truce in the middle but then it went back to being as bad as it began. "That's not enough of a reason. Aras executed Josh, and they were a damn sight closer than Lin and I ever were."

"She does no harm, Shan."

Wess'har justice was sometimes a confusing thing even for Shan, who felt she had the measure of it. The bezeri hadn't killed Lindsay—not that they would have been able to even if they'd tried—but they'd had their opportunity for balance, as wess'har called it, and now the matter seemed to be closed, leaving only the issue of whether Lindsay was a continuing risk. It was a kind of double jeopardy.

She wasn't going anywhere, and humans couldn't get access to Bezer'ej. The only risk was the Eqbas, and even if Lindsay wasn't a host, the organism still lay dormant in the soil on Ouzhari. Not even nuking the place had killed it. There was sod all Shan could do about it.

And nothing I should do about it.

Shan knew the terrain well enough to find the place where they'd buried David Neville. The stained glass headstone was still standing, the top broken off where Lindsay had removed pieces of the floral design as a keepsake. It was hard to tell if it was tended or not, because the ground cover of short barbed grass never grew higher. Shan stood over it for a few minutes, wondering what awareness a baby had of being born into an alien environment, then locked down every thought that would flow from that and turned to walk back towards the remains of the colony.

"Do you want to be alone?" Nevyan asked.

Shan stopped and looked back. "No. Why should I?"

"You seem to be ticking things off a list, as always. Locking up the premises." It was an odd phrase for a wess'har to use, seeing as they had no locks. "I feel the need to treat you cautiously at the moment."

"Jesus, do I look that unstable?"

"You bury yourself in activity when you're upset. I don't need to smell your scent to know it. You don't have to suppress your scent, you know. Not now."

"Habit," said Shan. "Just habit."

Shan beckoned Nevyan to follow. It was a pleasant afternoon, overcast but mild, little wind, and the air was fragrant with a wet green scent almost like crushed rue—which was embedded in her memory as Constantine. Only the coordinates on her swiss told her where she was because all visible traces of the underground colony had been scoured clean by nanites, leaving the place to the reclaim of the wilderness.

The ventilation shafts and skylights hadn't been filled in; they were hidden by vegetation. She discovered one the hard way. One moment she was on solid ground and the next she was falling, stomach lurching until she hit the ground elbow first, meters below in temporary pitch-blackness. She yelped on impact. *C'naatat* didn't stop it hurting like hell. She got her breath back, cradling her arm and managing not to scream. The pain in her elbow was blinding and enough to stop her moving for a while until *c'naatat* carried out instant repairs.

Who gives a shit? Who am I trying to look hard for here?

But she didn't scream. She allowed herself a few grunts and a little effing and blinding.

"Shan? *Shan!*" Nevyan's voice was overhead. Shan's eyes adjusted to the darkness—a lot easier for someone with wess'har low-light vision and the infrared inherited from the isenj—and she saw long tangled roots and the suggestion of light at the far end of a passage. "Shan, are you injured?"

"Of course I am, Nev. But I'm healing fine." She listened for the sounds of falling rock. Once the joists and braces that held up the tunnels had been broken down by the nanites, the excavations were unstable. A rockfall would have been a real problem even if it couldn't kill her. "Can you bring the shuttle close in, and get a line down to me? I don't know if the passages are clear enough for me to walk out. I'm not even sure I could find the route."

"Serrimissani is on her way."

Shan felt stupid now. The pain was ebbing and she could sit up. Every trace of human habitation had vanished except the outlines of chambers and shafts that were clearly manmade—wess'har made, in fact, because Aras had helped build this colony even before he'd started to change and look more human. He'd wanted to fit in. He hated being alone. She'd seen a picture in the colony archive of a normal wess'har, gold and seahorse-headed, from the first days of Constantine, before she'd finally understood what Aras was and how he survived.

Damn, the things that happened down here. Ade and Mart hunted me down. Bloody well shot me, too. And poor Vijissi. If he hadn't killed himself, there'd probably be a way of removing c'naatat from him too, now.

Something moved to her left. She flinched, bracing for a cave-in, but reached for her weapon out of habit.

"That's not going to work," said Lindsay Neville.

Her voice hadn't changed. When she moved into the center of the tunnel, she seemed more human than the last time Shan had seen her; less translucent, more clearly bipedal, and wearing some Eqbas working clothes that must have come from Shapakti.

"Don't tell me you're living down here," said Shan.

"Hi, Shan. I'm fine, thanks for asking. How are you?"

Okay, she was going to play it that way. Shan got to her feet. "I'm just terrific. So you got the bezeri to revert."

"Persuaded some . . . forced others. Some must still be out there. What brings you here?"

"I needed to see for myself. I've been away for a bit. Why didn't you leave?"

"I have a job to do. There's no wess'har garrison here and the bezeri need someone."

"I don't mean to be a wet blanket," Shan said, "but not even *c'naatat* makes you the invincible defender of the planet. Even Aras needed a bit of backup, remember."

"Maybe so." Lindsay was a shadow even when she got closer. There was nothing a *c'naatat* could do to another without explosives, and she didn't appear to be armed with more than a small crossbow. "But if anything comes this way that seriously threatens the bezeri, I've got the ultimate defense for them as long as I'm here, haven't I?"

It took Shan a few seconds to work out what Lindsay meant. "You'd reinfect them."

I haven't really thought this through. Maybe it's too soon after being thawed out to make decisions. But I didn't come here for a chat about old times.

"If it's that or see them nearly wiped out again," said Lindsay.

Shan slid one hand into the deep pocket inside her jacket, just to remind herself what kit she still had.

I can't leave you wandering around here. Can I?

"You can't detonate that," Lindsay said wearily, knowing Shan's usual precautions: a grenade, or so she seemed to assume. "It'll take you too, and you wouldn't do that now. Not with Ade and Aras still around. They are, aren't they?"

"They are," said Shan, and heard the shuttle settling above. The smell of hot metal filled the shaft above her and Lindsay looked up, just that second's loss of concentration that gave Shan the edge she needed. She brought her fist up square under Lindsay's jaw—nothing like a hard human jaw, not at all—and sent her reeling, then jumped on her to pin her down, struggling to get a pair of cuffs on her. Lindsay lashed out—she still wasn't a fighter, poor stupid kid, not even with the *c'naatat* cocktail of hard bastards she had inside her—and caught Shan in the face, digging her fingers deep into her cheek, but this was just *pain,* and wounds lasted seconds. Shan had to kneel on her to get one cuff on and then jerk her arm up her back so hard that she heard something crack before she could lock on the other.

"There," Shan said, getting to her feet and wiping her face. The blood was dry and the gouges were just a vague tingling sensation. It hadn't been so long ago that Lindsay had hunted her down here, with Ade, Barencoin and Rayat, and left her no option but to space herself. She paused for a moment to be sure that this wasn't just some kind of neatly iconic revenge. "No offense, girlie, but you're going home. You did okay, but it's over."

"Home to what?" Lindsay demanded. "You're still the same arrogant bitch you always were. You always—"

"*I* didn't nuke Ouzhari. Did I?" Shan hauled Lindsay to her feet. "Earth's no picnic yet, but they might even *need* you."

Shan looked up into the shaft and waited for the line to fall within reach. She could have done with a winch and harness, but she could improvise. She could still tie a bowline. Ade had been impressed that she could do that.

"Nev?" Shan called. "Nev, Lin's coming up. Mind she doesn't lash out."

It took a lot more effort than Shan thought to get Lindsay up to the surface. The line burned her hands but, as always, that didn't matter in the end. She stood in the cool air, a little breathless, with no trace left of the fight except dried blood on her shirt.

"Lin's going home," she said. But she wasn't a monster, whatever Lin thought. "After we exhume David. That's what you want, isn't it?"

Lin, a strange insubstantial mannequin of herself, shimmering with occasional violet lights, might have been dumbfounded, but it was hard to make out an expression on her altered face.

She nodded. "I'm not going without him."

Shan had stood over quite a few forensics officers while

they unearthed bodies. It was easy when you switched off. She could do that just fine, even with the remains of a child. She'd exhume him. "Let's go, then."

This island had been Mjat when Aras was a young soldier—a teeming isenj colony, coast to coast, and then he wiped it out as pitilessly as the Eqbas had erased most of Umeh and then large swathes of Earth. This erasure had been going on since before her ancestors were born. She no longer felt wholly responsible for everything that had gone wrong, just a recognition that she had been a part of the chain of events.

And this terrain had been her first introduction to the wess'har. Josh Garrod had pointed out the unspoiled wilderness beyond the shimmering biobarrier that enclosed the colony's fields. She'd gazed upon nothing, baffled, and she could still hear Josh's voice.

The wess'har wiped it off the face of the planet. Welcome to the frontline, Superintendent.

No, Earth wasn't special, or the first, or the last.

She steered Lindsay Neville towards the shuttle, took a spade from the tool locker in the hold, and went to do a job that was kinder to spare a bereaved mother.

F'nar: later that day.

Shan had that unhappily satisfied look that she reserved for times when people had lived up to her worst expectations and she'd caught them out. There was a grim triumph in it; *isan* liked to be right. She was still trying to be kind to Ade, treading carefully around him, but Aras could see that part of her had moved on to the next task. Ade had now made contact with Barencoin, Chahal and Webster, and was distracted for the while.

"How are you going to send Lindsay back?" Aras asked. "The Eqbas might not send another mission for years."

Shan was checking out the cupboards. She'd brought a few small things back from Earth: tea that she didn't need, some packets of spice, and clothing, all of it utilitarian work clothes except for that black dress. In the intervening years, the food plants scavenged from Umeh Station had been productive and there was fresh avocado oil and preserved banana in jars, jobs carried out anonymously out of wess'har communal responsibility to neighbors. A modest but adequate life beckoned, a far cry from the overwhelming variety of things Aras had glimpsed in Australia.

"We can spare a shuttle," Shan said. "A bit of Eqbas ship. She'll be back around the time *Thetis* gets home, and she doesn't even have to pilot it, does she? But we have to give her Shapakti's therapy first."

Ade sat at the table making little headway with his meal. "You exhumed her kid."

"More like an archaeological dig." Shan paused for a moment. "Just bones."

"Are you okay?"

"I've done a lot worse." She turned to Aras. "And when did you know about Shapakti removing *c'naatat* from wess'har tissue? Why didn't you say? You knew, didn't you?"

"I don't believe he tested it on a live subject," said Aras. "It's still speculative."

"That's not an answer, sweetheart."

"I thought it might distress you for no reason."

Shan just looked at him for a few moments and then went on rearranging the cupboards. "Okay. Fair enough."

"Has Lindsay Neville agreed to be treated?"

"I didn't give her a choice. She's getting it either way." Ade abandoned his meal. Shan sat down beside him and watched him for a while, frowning, stroking his hair. "I didn't tell her about Izzy and Jon. I'll do it if you want me to."

"I'll tell her," Ade said. "Who gives her the . . . well, cure?"

"It's a transfusion. Nevyan can find someone competent."

"I'll do it," said Aras. "I know how to do that."

He'd seen *c'naatat* take hold of his comrades and even Shan. He knew what it did, the changes and the high temperature and the ravenous appetite while it rebuilt cells to its own taste. But he had no idea what it would be like in reverse. But what would be left of Lindsay Neville? Would it change the way she thought and felt as well?

A realization crept up on him. He wanted to know for his own peace of mind, to understand fully what he might be turning down. He was almost certain that he would—most of the time.

But how can any of us justify remaining c'naatat *now?*

"Can't be that big a deal if Shapakti processed Rayat more than once," said Shan. "Sorry, I'm not being very precise in my language. I've got no idea how to describe it."

"I'll talk to Shapakti," said Aras.

Shan reached across the table and squeezed his arm. "Thanks. I'll do it if you want me to, though."

"No need," he said. "I think your time is best spent with Ade, who has had a more unpleasant time." It would only distress Shan and Ade if he spoke with Shapakti in front of them. "I'll visit Lindsay. I can see Eddie at the same time. We must make the most of our time with him."

Aras walked along the terraces to Nevyan's home, enjoying the sunset that lit up the polished caldera. It was full of the sounds and smells of family life—clattering glassware, bitter spices, the cacophony of trilling voices—that were little like his own past; Iussan, on the Baral Plain, was in the cold north, underground and echoing. He'd never taken Shan there. It was time he did. Ade would probably enjoy it too, being an arctic warfare specialist from a world that had had little ice.

F'nar was full of children, or so it seemed to Aras. There were noticeably more sets of twins playing in the alleys, a sure sign of a temporary decline in the population being balanced by a brief burst in the birth rate. Wess'har physiology controlled fertility very precisely.

Another reason why we can't really understand the gethes. *They might not be able to do this naturally like us, but they can do it artificially—and yet they still want to spread to fill the space available.*

Nevyan took the influx of waifs and strays in her stride. Her home, a typical warren of passages and chambers, merged with Giyadas's and the place was alive with voices.

Eddie sat in the main room by the range, enjoying the warmth and apparently untroubled by the noise of the *jurej've* of the house preparing food and arguing over some minor detail of recipes. They acknowledged Aras and went on with their debate as if he'd only been away for weeks.

Eddie gave him a deeply wrinkled smile. "For a bloke with *c'naatat,* you really haven't changed."

"I was worried you might be dead by the time we got back."

"I was a bit worried about that, too. Bit of a bugger, being dead."

"And Lindsay?"

"She's taken to her room, as they say. I think we came as a shock to each other." Eddie moved his chair, a device like a scaled down version of the local transports that Ade called *hovercraft,* so that Aras could sit. "Livaor made this for me. Good, isn't it?"

"You can't walk?"

"Not enough to cover a city like this. But I don't need my arse wiped for me yet. I'm planning on dying before I do." He switched on the link, making the gold stone of the wall shimmer with images. "Shapakti might not be around at the moment. He's very keen on hiking. His kids even visit him here. Funny, that. If humans had someone defect with our sensitive tech, we'd hassle their family the minute they crossed the border."

"What would you do if you were me, Eddie?"

"How, exactly?"

"All of us can have *c'naatat* removed now. We shouldn't have it anyway, but we do, and I struggle between wanting it gone and wanting to stay as I am, and I'm unclear about my reasons."

"Motives . . ."

"Sometimes, they *do* matter."

"Heretic."

"As an aid to self-understanding. If I knew what I sought, I would make the right choice."

"You're looking for advice from me?"

"I am. You have a wide perspective now."

"You're even older than I am." Eddie paused. "But now? I regret not living life more fully. More emotional stuff, fewer causes. Family. Kids. Erica and I weren't the best-suited couple ever, but I wish I'd held my relationships together better and had kids when I could have some kind of life with them. It broke my heart to have to send Barry back to Earth, and I asked myself why we had him, knowing it would be inevitable. Why? Because it's what all living creatures do. Mate. Have kids. Care and fret over them. Gaze indulgently on their achievement. Have them take something indefinable into the future for you."

It was a view, not advice on what he should do. Aras still heeded it, because it was passionate, and given from a position where Eddie could see all the facts.

There was no easy answer; either choice would cause pain for a while. But for the first time in ages, Aras had a clearer idea of what was eating away at him.

"I'll find Shapakti," he said. "He can show me how to administer the countermeasure to Lindsay."

"It's okay," said Eddie. "I think you'll be a lot happier."

Lindsay—awful, alien, lost—huddled in the sleeping alcove and watched Aras. Her expression was impossible to see in that gel face, but Eddie could still read the basic human body language in her that said she was scared and hostile. Aras stood waiting with a device that looked like one of those old gas-operated corkscrews that they had in the National Technology Museum, a neat oval with a needle on the end.

"I'll try to think of it as being dewormed," she said.

"Like Jon Becken's joke?" Aras asked. He was fascinated with tapeworms, possibly because he had no real idea what one was. The Royal Marine's joke about removing one with the lure of a chocolate bar preyed on his mind, but then maybe you had to have a different outlook on sharing your body space with parasites to appreciate the concern.

"Sort of," said Eddie. "Lin, you're going home. Home might be fucked in places, but not all of it, and you get to join the chosen few in Australia. Sort of like heaven with alcohol."

"What did Shan do with David's remains?"

Aras stood waiting as patient as a mountain, transfusion kit held in both hands. "She treated them reverently. They're in an *efte* box that you can take back with you."

They'd be tiny things, little doll's bones. Eddie found the thought disturbing and wondered how Shan had felt about them for all her veneer of police unshockability. He'd never had the chance before she left to get beyond the "I'm-okay-ness" of losing her child. *No, she didn't lose it, not like Lin did. She got rid of it, she got rid of it herself, and she did it the hardest way possible.* Lin would be going home with a box of remains to a world where she knew few people and those few might not even be alive when she got there.

"Who's left?" she asked, almost reading his mind.

"Right now? Deborah Garrod . . . Chaz . . . Sue . . . I'm sorry, Lin, I don't know if anyone told you that Izzy and Jon got killed, not long after landing. Mission went wrong."

Intellectually, Eddie knew that it was fresh bad news, but the years had made it hard for him to fully gauge the impact on her. She said nothing. Aras still waited. He looked as if he could wait forever: he could, of course.

"Do it," she said.

She held out her arm. It didn't matter where Aras injected the plasma, but that was what humans did. It took as long to inject her as it did to infect her.

"Do you want me to stay with you?" Aras said. "It might be some comfort. It could be hours, or even a few days."

Lindsay, rapidly reverting to the body language and movements of what she had once been, rubbed her arm. "I think it would be easier to have Eddie sit with me. Is that okay, Eddie?"

" 'Course it is, doll," he said. "It's not like I'm going anywhere, is it?"

Aras didn't take offense as far as Eddie could see, but then he never did. Lindsay curled up on the thin mattress in the alcove—how did wess'har ever find those comfortable?— and began shivering within minutes. Aras did stay and watch for an hour or so, expressionless and utterly still, but eventually he left without a word and Eddie was alone with Lindsay again.

"I was scared of this when I got it," she said, "and now I'm scared because it's going."

Eddie wasn't sure if it was safe to hold her hand but he maneuvered his chair closer so that she could see him. "Doll, you'll be back on Earth before you know it. You'll be young again but with all the experience and wisdom you've gained. No human ever managed that before. You can live your life in the light of that—don't we all say we wish we'd known then what we know now?"

She seemed to consider it for a while. "It's still a scary place where I'm going. But then everywhere is scary when you're on your own."

He was going to a scary place soon, too, and nobody could go there with him. He understood. He reached out his hand anyway, and she took it.

20

On the path to becoming a man,
There will be times of suffering,
There will be times when things are unsaid,
There will be times of discomfort,
There will be times of tears.

Japanese proverb

F'nar, Mestin's home: three days later.

"I thought I'd come and see how you were," said Shan.

Lindsay, hair straggly with sweat, answered the question pretty eloquently without opening her mouth. She rolled over onto her back and stared up at something Shan couldn't see.

"Okay, you're not feeling too good now," Shan said. "But if it's any comfort, you look . . . normal."

"I feel like hell," Lindsay said.

"So now you're going to rail at me for forcing this on you."

"No."

"I'm sorry I didn't give you a choice. But it was that or fragging you. I'm clearing up. Rayat got me thinking about it. I still hate that shit-house, by the way."

Lindsay struggled to sit up but Shan didn't offer her a helping hand. Eventually she maneuvered into a position to prop herself on one elbow.

"I won't say I don't trust you," she said, "but let's say I'm wary."

"Yeah, and I won't insult you with the cliché that you've served your debt to society. There just comes a point when I'm done, and any further retribution is pointless."

"Meaning you think I've suffered enough, and you're not sure how to add to it?"

"Not meaning anything, but if I thought that having you dead was the best option, I'd have used a grenade rather than hauled you back here to make you wholly human again."

Lindsay stared back at Shan for a while as if she was trying to focus. "How do I get home? What the hell do I do next?"

Shan found she trusted her subconscious a little more now. It probably wasn't hers, and might have been the sweetly moderate core of Ade in her, or even Aras's ability to walk away manifesting itself. "I think you know more about the reality of devastation and rebuilding than most. You can have an Eqbas ship and it'll just take you home."

"In time for *Thetis* making orbit?"

"That too." Shan had a moment of completely purged anger that felt like nothing she'd ever known before. She found herself reaching into her pocket, unplanned. "Here. If the banking system hasn't totally collapsed by then, here's a kick start."

She handed Lindsay one of the credited chips she'd loaded up back on Earth. *Just money, that's all. Only a means to an end, and I have my end.* Lindsay looked at it in her palm, lips moving slightly in silence.

"Is this guilt, Shan?"

"The fuck it is. It's to leave you free to do a job. You need a purpose, don't you? I understand that better than anyone. What about picking up where I left off, and keeping an eye on that gene bank?"

"Ah, you're as obsessed with heritage as anyone."

Shan knew Lindsay resented the shadow she cast. Shit, she'd made sure she'd told her she'd never have the balls that Shan did; the judgment of a woman about to die left a lasting scar, and she'd intended it to be so. But now . . . now she just wanted Lindsay to get out of her life and do something useful somewhere. The only place for that was Earth.

"We have a duplicate gene bank. It's a little bit more than vanity, sweetheart." Shan leaned over her. "Just start over. Make different choices."

"And *you're* granting this gift . . ."

"And I'm not in your head any longer, am I? So the choice you make is all yours."

Shan turned to leave her to think about it. *Do I want that choice? What would I do with it?* But if she gave up her *c'naatat*, she'd be back to being middle-aged and out of time, a feeling she recalled all too well, and with nothing to show for it except a long catalog of fascinating experiences unique in human existence and nobody to tell them to.

But that didn't mean it wasn't the right thing to do.

"Lin, now it's gone, what's different?" she asked.

Lindsay raked straggly blond hair back from her face, looking as if she'd had a bad night on the tiles rather than the temporary company of an alien organism. She looked slightly to one side of Shan.

"It's like losing one stereo channel," she said after a pause. "Or realizing you're totally alone."

Alone was an odd choice of words. Shan thought Lindsay would have been glad to get rid of any trace of her; maybe it was someone else's memories she'd got used to having around.

So she had a second chance, like Earth, and that was a better deal than Shan had, in a way: Lindsay had her youth back, and the opportunity to make better choices. It was a benevolent sentence. The only drawback was that Lindsay had to serve it on an Earth in the throes of Eqbas restoration.

F'nar, the Exchange of Surplus Things: ten days after return.

"I promised you this," said Shan.

She cut a wedge from the cake, lifted it carefully onto the board, and sliced a bite-sized chunk from it. Ade expected her to put it on the rainbow glass plate and hand it to him; but she held it to his mouth, anxious and half smiling. He hesitated, embarrassed, then accepted it.

Wess'har didn't do weddings, receptions or any kind of formal celebrations. The vaulted hall was packed with them but they watched, bemused, and there was odd silence where humans might have clapped or proposed toasts.

"Yeah, we got there in the end, Boss," Ade said. He could have made better cake himself, but it was nice of Nevyan to put all her husbands on the job. At least they'd stuck to ingredients that came close to the real thing. "And it's good we don't have to have the first dance or anything."

Aras helped himself to the cake while the wess'har milled around and sampled it. It was routine for them to leave their surplus food and other produce here and take anything else they needed, no money changing hands or anyone keeping an eye on how much they took, but they had to be told that they should stay and socialize now rather than collect what took their fancy and wander off. Eddie hadn't taught them to party. Ade decided he would make it his pet project.

I'm never leaving home again. I can't stand it. I can't stand the time gap coming back like bad news.

"Human brains aren't made for interstellar distances," Ade said, wishing he could feel soppy and in love right then, but no amount of understanding how time and distance worked, or how his own extended lifespan meant that time didn't matter, could take away the fact that most of the people he cared about were the ordinary dying sort and he was a long, long way from them. "I hope I'm not ruining this for everyone."

No, c'naatat *doesn't make time less relevant. It makes it the most important thing there is.*

Aras handed Ade the rest of the cake. The plates were an assortment of wildly colored glass that the residents of F'nar had brought in for the event, everything from plain violet to what Ade could only describe as stained glass windows without leading. He tried to see what a wonderful communal effort this had been by his neighbors to mark an event they knew was important to him but that they didn't understand.

"'Ras, I think you should have a proper wedding too," Ade said. "I feel like we left you out."

Aras had been subdued since they'd got back. He always said that losing people never got easier for a *c'naatat* so maybe he was as upset by losing Izzy and Jon as anyone.

The unhappy memories of his distant past had seeped into Ade's mind via *oursan*, but there was nothing specific like whether he missed individuals. Genetic memory wasn't a complete record; it was just headline events, impressions, attitudes, the most raw emotions. All Ade could tell was that Aras was unhappy.

"I'm wess'har," Aras said. "This makes me feel no more neglected than if you didn't leave surplus crops here. The point is whether *you* feel I'm not part of the family because I haven't performed this ritual, or if Shan thinks less of me because I haven't."

"Of course we don't."

"There's your answer."

But Aras hadn't given him all the answers. Wess'har didn't lie, but sometimes they didn't think to tell you all the things you might need to know unless you asked, and they were a culture of askers. Aras had spent more time around humans than his own kind. And he had a fair dose of human in him.

He'll tell me if he's got any problems. I know he would.

Aras ate without enthusiasm, looking around at the crowd. Shan, Nevyan and Giyadas were having a loud conversation in wess'u. Ade still hadn't learned the language well enough to follow every detail, but he got the feeling Shan was sliding into becoming a governing matriarch. She couldn't leave stuff alone even if she wanted to. It was a compulsion, like Eddie said. She felt it was her duty to run the whole bloody universe.

"What's bothering you, mate?" Ade's stomach churned. "That you could be—well, cured?"

Aras looked like he was considering the idea for the first time, although it must have occurred to him a hundred times. "I think it is."

Ade wasn't in the best state of mind to take on more problems. They'd been through all this crap before, the last time Shapakti had thought he could do it. "Oh, terrific. Go on. Everything else has gone to rat shit and the only thing we have that's in one piece is the three of us, so why not start dismantling that too?"

"Ade—"

"Last time this came up, we did something stupid because you were trying to be the saint and leave so that me and Shan could have normal lives again. *No.* You don't make anyone happier by leaving us. For Chrissakes, stop being a martyr."

Ade had rebuilt everything in his life time and time again, after every death or crumbled relationship or disappointment. All the shit from his past was erased—or at least numbed— by a daily effort to reinforce normal life; he played happy families. Anything that might destroy that was a threat. He dug in.

"Ade," said Aras, "did you ever think what *I* might really want?"

He felt it like a slap in the face. "I *always* think about what's best for you, mate, and I was ready to butt out, remember? You love Shan. She was your missus before I came on the scene."

"And you had feelings for each other before she became my *isan.* Neither fact is relevant."

"What, then?"

"Possibilities are always unsettling. I need to consider what mine might be."

Ade wanted to tell him he was a selfish bastard, but then he realized he was reacting to the unsaid; he was assuming Aras would choose to revert to his original genome. He'd always had the choice of killing himself, but he'd never taken it, although Ade had seen him come to the brink once—and that was when Shan was presumed dead, not because he'd had enough of *c'naatat.*

Aras liked staying alive. There was the chance that he'd like staying alive forever. Ade decided he'd overreacted and that . . . well, they could take *c'naatat* out of humans, and Ade was content with that as long as Shan was, and he wanted as long with her as he could get. Finding the love of your life in middle age was too late if the first half had been a wasteland.

"Sorry, mate." Ade reached up and tugged at Aras's braid. "I'm not at my best at the moment."

"You grieve. I understand."

What happened to Ankara? Are the graves still there? Did they let nanites loose there too?

Eddie trundled towards him in his mobile chair and held his glass out for a top-up. "Don't stint on the beer, Ade."

He could always change the subject at just the right time, Eddie. "You still making this stuff?"

"I can't manage the pressure caps," said Eddie, holding up a gnarled, arthritic hand. "Nevyan's next-door neighbor makes it for me. They even synthesize the sugar."

Ade reached for the jug and refilled his glass. Eddie couldn't hold it as steadily as he once did, and so Ade erred on the side of caution by half filling it, cupping his hand around Eddie's until he was sure he had a firm grip.

"So you've been stuck with Rayat for a neighbor for twenty years, eh? Never wanted to gut him?"

"Hard to hate forever." Eddie beckoned to Aras. "He did do one decent thing in his life, anyway. Look, Shan said I could come to dinner. Got room for me this evening? At my age, you never know if there's going to be a next day."

Aras began clearing the plates and crumbs, and took over the social arrangements. "Of course. Come every day if you like. It was your house as well."

The exchange emptied fairly fast. Tomorrow, it would fill up as wess'har brought surplus crops and left them for any-one who wanted them. Somehow, everything got used, no-body took more than their fair share, and everyone was satisfied. It was survival of the most cooperative here. At every level, wess'har looked like they might have a lot in common with humans, and then Ade found every reason why they were fundamentally different.

Shan sat down beside him and slid her arm through his.

"No brawls, then," she said. "Not a proper reception with-out a punch-up."

"Miss being a copper?"

"Sometimes."

"Fancy old Mart joining the police."

"He still has to call me ma'am. He's a poxy inspector."

"I'm going to see if I can pick up the Eqbas ITX link,"

Ade said. "Why don't you take Eddie back to our place? I said he could come round for dinner tonight."

Shan nodded with that look on her face that said she knew he was saying he wanted a bit of time to himself. "If he behaves himself, I won't cook."

Even after the exchange had emptied, it took Ade a few minutes to steel himself to activate the link and search for views of Earth from the Eqbas orbital sensors. He didn't even have to hack his way in. The channel was open to anyone who wanted to access it.

Eventually, he plucked up courage to search for the coordinates of the Ankara cemetery and took the magnification as far as he could.

It was still an arid place with dusty pink stone chippings for soil, but dull green plants grew in the cracks. The white gravestones stood untouched—neglected, yes, because everyone who used to tend them was probably either dead or struggling for survival, but they were still there, and that was all that mattered. He tracked around the ranks of headstones until he found what he was sure was Dave's grave.

Ade wasn't much interested in the rest of the planet. He'd seen almost nothing of it anyway. All he cared about was either here with him, or dead and at rest. But now he knew he could also pinpoint the town of Rabi'ah, and the graves of Qureshi and Becken, when he felt the need. He knew he would.

Right now, though, the living mattered more. He closed the link and walked home along the terraces, rehearsing a sense of belonging.

F'nar Plain.

Lindsay didn't seem nervous as she contemplated the small bronze vessel sitting dwarfed by the plain.

Aras had expected her to be afraid. Perhaps that was one thing she'd learned to take in her stride after so much distance, grief, and shock, and the prospect of a long journey relying on technology she didn't understand—a worrying thing for a commander used to knowing every part of her ship—was just one more hurdle, a small thing set against becoming an ever-evolving hybrid of an unknown number of species.

Where did c'naatat *originate?* Aras had never worked that out.

"Jesus," she said. Lindsay walked around the one-man vessel, a small blond woman in beige working clothes, and stared at the ramp that extruded from the hull. "It's so bloody tiny."

"So is any ship in space."

"I suppose you're right."

"All you need do is settle down in the bay here." Aras walked her into the ship and made sure the bulkheads were set to opacity. He indicated the hammocklike structure in the heart of the vessel. "Are you ready? It feels like anesthesia, Ade tells me, whatever that feels like to a human. Like your own cryo systems, except for a tingling in the arms."

"I can handle tingling." Lindsay sat on the edge of the cryo bay and put a wary hand on the fabric. "At least it's nice and comfortable, not that I'll be in any state to appreciate it." She stood up and looked around the interior, apparently searching, and her gaze settled on the small *efte* box that held the remains of her son. Aras had wrapped the bones carefully; they were so very, very fragile. "Okay."

"Are you ready to leave?"

"Give me a minute."

Lindsay squeezed past Aras to stand outside and look around the plain. He thought she was taking a final longing look at the view, a blend of gold-bronze desert, purple and green vegetation, and the spectacular pearl caldera of F'nar that was visible only from a few narrow angles. But she seemed to be waiting.

"She's not going to come, is she?"

"Shan?"

"Yes." Lindsay seemed disappointed. Aras thought he saw her eyes glaze with unshed tears. "Ah well."

"I can call her. She would come. I didn't tell her you might leave right now."

"No, it's better this way. She'd only—no, she really did give me a second chance. I know she doesn't do second chances, so I'll quit while I'm winning, in case she decides I'm a waste of space anyway and finishes the job."

"She judges herself more harshly than she judges you."

"Shan always thinks she has to be the grown-up in a universe of children. It's not the best trait to face if you're someone who didn't get on with their mother."

My mother. Why do I always forget my mother? Iussan Palior Jivin. Aras stood on a shore about to be engulfed by a tidal wave of long-buried memory. "Are you glad to be going home?"

"I think so," said Lindsay. "And I'm glad to be normal again, I suppose. No offense. I just know more or less what happens to mortal humans, and nobody really knows how *c'naatat* end their days. I need a little certainty right now."

"Will you have another child?"

It was a question Ade would have told him was *tactless*. But he had to know, and he felt that Lindsay would take it for the question it was: a burning need to know if people could recover after grief and parting, and live fully again. He never had. Getting Shan back didn't count. She really was alive. He had no true bereavement to deal with.

"Yes," Lindsay said. "I will. And I'll be grateful that I can." She looked around again and paused. "Say goodbye to her for me, will you?"

"Yes."

"And Eddie too. I said goodbye a few times. It's hard to keep doing it. Just reminds him that he's hanging on by the minute, and I'm not."

"I will."

Lindsay squinted against the sun. "It really is beautiful here."

"Earth will be beautiful again, too."

Lindsay went back into the ship and lay down in the bay without a word. As the gel closed over her, Aras thought he saw a brief flash of panic in her eyes, and he raised his hand in a gesture partway between a wave and a plea to be calm, but in seconds she was unconscious and the bay was chilling her down to a state just a fraction short of death.

He watched for a few moments longer than he had to, checked the controls and navigation that would take her straight into Earth orbit, revive her and link her to the Eqbas fleet to land and disembark, and then left. The hatch closed behind him. As he stood back, the ship lifted with its belt of red and blue chevrons flashing, and soon it was a small dark speck in the sky.

Lindsay was going home. Aras thought there was no better time for him to return to Baral—his home city—and see how he felt about it after so many years.

21

Earth, August 1, 2426
Approximate population: 3.82 billion
Average daytime temperatures: 10.4 percent below datum
average for 2376.
Percentage of gene bank species restored or reintroduced:
37 percent.

Extract from Eqbas Earth adjustment mission record

Baral Plain, northern Wess'ej landmass.

Aras emerged from the underground transit tunnel onto a plain of short brown grasses studded with tufts of brilliant violet flowers. It was summer on the plain, the brief respite from the winter snows, and he could see people working in patchwork fields of yellow-leaf to squeeze as much food from the land as they could before the season ended.

Like Constantine, the city of Baral was largely underground. It was his model for the colony. But Baral had no imposing church with stained glass windows and a spire that almost thrust through the soil above like a tree—just a central Exchange of Surplus Things like F'nar's.

He hadn't been here for . . . how long? It must have been centuries. But these had been his people, and still were.

As he approached, they stopped work to stare at him, and then one called out: "Aras Sar Iussan, is that you?"

It was a sparsely populated planet and cities talked to each other. Everyone knew there was still a *c'naatat* soldier left alive from the isenj wars, the very last of his kind, the last of those who had driven back the isenj. He was, Ade told him, a war hero. It was a long way from being the Beast of Mjat.

"It's me," he said.

It was a strange homecoming. He knew his way to the city without even thinking: he knew the route down into the heart of the tunnels and galleries, sunlit as the surface, scented with familiar cooking. People stopped in their tracks.

"You've come home," said an *isan*. "Why now?"

"I need to remember who I was." He thought of Lindsay, who hadn't had time to forget who she was, but seemed to have nonetheless. "*C'naatat* can be removed. I need to know what I was before it took hold of me."

"Your clan will want to see you, too."

By the time Aras made his way through the vaulted passages to his old clan home, the entire city seemed to know he was back. Ussissi appeared out of the tunnels and watched. It felt like entering Umèh for the first time, random memories crystallizing from vague scraps of his past, and an absence of celebration.

The carving on the walls of the passages had been worn smooth over the years by the steady brushing of passing bodies, packages and children playing. But it was undeniably home; it smelled so familiar that he was suddenly here only yesterday, wondering which *isan* he would be taken in by to start his adult life as a *jurej*—husband, father, male. There was only one word for a male wess'har, and only one for a female, because the roles were universal and inevitable; there were no single wess'har. Males sickened and died without the constant repair of their DNA by *oursan*.

Aras had no role in this society. He felt like an alien. Shan and Ade—they came from a culture where the solitary and childless were routine and even the majority in some societies, but he didn't, and he felt a gulf opening between them and him as he faced his past at close range.

A group of children emerged from a doorway, four males and a female, the males following the *isanket* much as they would follow their *isan* in adult life. This was the natural order; even the Eqbas—juggling with their nature, adjusting the gender balance—still had a society based on dominant females with harems of males.

"You used to be one of us," said the *isanket*. For a moment Aras thought she meant wess'har, but then he realized these were his distant kin. He could see it; he could smell it. "Have you come home?"

Yes, I used to be truly wess'har. I used to be like this.

"I was curious," said Aras. "I wanted to see."

The little female beckoned him in. Somewhere in these passages, he'd grown up. He'd had brothers, sisters and cousins, and his father had taught him how to make glass. In the heart of the complex was a rooflight. He remembered it now: a dome, a glass dome.

Aras veered left, unerring. The *isanket* made an irritated hiss, but Aras knew where he was going—if the clan hadn't remodeled the layout in the intervening years—and he felt a strange excitement building in his chest. He slipped through a doorway, pushed aside the fabric hanging that serve for a door, and—

Home.

The room, a round chamber, was a well of rainbow colors. He looked up at the domed rooflight before he took note of the wess'har working there, staring into the colored glass and drinking it in until his eyes stung. He was a small *jurej'ket* again, a little male, helping his father Sar select and cut pieces of glass to form the design of the dome.

It was a landscape of tundra flowers framed in abstract shapes. The colors almost made him sob. Mjat and the white fire and the agony of both isenj and wess'har, both victim and aggressor at the same time, and all the unexperienced memories that *c'naatat* had given him now vanished.

These were the happiest times of my life.

Aras felt like a traitor, in every sense of the word. How could he be happier than with his *isan,* with *Shan Chail*, and his house-brother Ade? How could he feel like this when they'd been his rescue from unending loneliness?

And how could he turn his back on being . . . wess'har?

He brought himself back to the here and now. A family— *his* family, however separated by time and circumstance— stared at him in surprise, cooking suspended.

"I helped build this dome," Aras said. "Tell your names."

"I am Chuyyis," said the oldest male. "And this is your home."

Yes. It *was*.

F'nar: upper terraces.

"So did he say when he'd be back?" Shan asked.

Ade enjoyed cooking dinner, and having guests was a bonus. Here was a happy family home that he'd never had before; his dad wasn't going to show up drunk. The novelty still hadn't worn off and he hoped it never would. It almost took his mind off Qureshi and Becken, but he hardly dared be happy at the moment because as soon as it overtook him, he remembered them, and it slapped him down to the deck as hard as a punch.

"He said he was going to Baral." Ade concentrated on the bread. He didn't have Aras's skilled wrist action but the stuff passed muster as a pancake. That was easier for Eddie to eat, anyway. *Don't think about Izzy or Jon. You'll just look at Eddie and know he's next.* "He packed Lindsay off to Earth and just called to say he was going."

Shan sat with her boots up on the stool opposite her chair, doing a none too convincing job of looking unconcerned. Nevyan sat at the table, hands clasped. She was hanging around Shan whenever she could, seeming desperate to make up for lost time. "I didn't realize Lin was just going to bugger off that fast."

"You told her to go."

"I know. I just feel I should have said something."

"Like goodbye."

"Yes."

Ade wondered what had softened Shan's attitude. Maybe she'd run out of anger. Digging up the kid's body must have put a dent in her. "You did the right thing."

"No point de-*c'naatating* someone just to slot them."

"And what about us?"

"What?"

"I know what you're like." It was just a casual comment,

nothing more. "I know you feel guilty keeping it now that we can remove the bloody thing."

Shan gave him one of her long, slow looks, unblinking, possibly because it was a subject she didn't want to discuss even in front of her closest friends. "We had a way of getting rid of it before. It was just a bit more emphatic."

"Okay, so now it's easier, and I bet that makes you think you ought to take the option."

"Do *you*? Do you want to go back to the way you were?"

Ade thought of all the things he knew and could now do that he hadn't been able to do before; it wasn't just invulnerability. In fact, apart from a fall he'd had while rock-climbing that otherwise would have killed him, he hadn't had the parasite long enough to feel that he was pretty well immortal. It hadn't sunk in. What *had* sunk in was that he knew, absolutely *knew,* what Shan felt for him from right inside her head, and that was the most precious thing he could imagine: it was a certainty that no other man had ever had, except Aras. Ade valued it more than he could have imagined.

"No," he said. "I don't. I really don't. It's given me more time and I *want* that time. But that isn't the only issue, is it?"

"No, it's not. I hate that bastard Rayat being right, but he asked why we weren't going for the removal option, and I admit that it's been eating at me."

Ade went on slapping the bread on the hot plate to cook, wondering if he was selfish to hang on to this privileged life when too many of his mates were dead. Eventually there was a rapping at the door, and Eddie used his powered seat like a battering ram to push it open, followed by Giyadas.

"No Aras?" he asked.

"I think he's in Baral." Shan moved seats to make room for him at the table. "He'll probably get back while we're eating."

"Ah, your dinner is in the dog . . ."

"Lin's gone."

"I guessed as much." Eddie, a painful frail reminder of the mortality that Ade had dodged, gave him a sympathetic look. "I think we said our goodbyes anyway. You have to stop sobbing on each other's shoulders sooner or later."

"Took me several attempts to take my leave of the lads," Ade said quietly. "I understand."

They ate with Eddie most nights now. It seemed rude to want time to themselves when they had an infinite amount of it and he didn't. He ate slowly and with difficulty, helped by Giyadas tonight. Ade and Aras both tried to make meals that could be eaten easily with a fork rather than watch him struggle with arthritic and increasingly shaky hands. Ade sliced the flat breads into chunks to make it easier to mop up the stew.

"It's okay, Ade," Eddie said, not looking up from his plate. "I know I'm a senile old bastard. It's fine to acknowledge it."

Shan filled his beer glass. "You could just as easily say that you did bloody well to make ninety, and your liver deserves a medal for endurance."

Eddie chuckled. "Yes, I thought the thing wouldn't see seventy."

"So when are they going to do a Michallat lifetime achievement show, then?"

"I think I'm past that. I'm into obituary country."

At least he could joke about it, and that was something. Eddie had never been the self-pitying kind. Ade did what he always did, and tried to keep everyone's morale high, and that meant jokes, lurid stories and recollections delivered in that tone of fixed cheerfulness that didn't give anyone a chance to slip into reflection. Giyadas and Nevyan just listened.

Eddie was playing the game too. He never let on what he was feeling, not deliberately anyway. They finished the meal, still with no sign of Aras and no call from him, and went to sit on the terrace at the back of the house, the one that overlooked the desert. The other overlooked the city. Aras had chosen a bloody good spot when he excavated the home all those years ago; maybe he hadn't picked it for the view—it was right on the jagged, left-hand edge of the broken caldera—but it was nice anyway. On a balmy late summer

evening like this it was wonderful. It was actually autumn by
the F'nar calendar, but it was August by the Earth one, and it
was warm, so summer it was in Ade's imagination.

At least Eddie could still enjoy his beer. That was something. Shan sat on the broad wall that edged the terrace,
arms around her knees, looking out in the direction of the
network of supply tunnels that shunted small underground
cars from city to city carrying surplus crops and occasionally passengers. She was getting worried about Aras. Ade
could tell.

"It's so good to have you back," Eddie said, his chair
close up against Ade's. "I bloody well missed you."

Ade rested his arm on Eddie's. He wanted to hug him,
half out of comradeship and half out of regret and pity, but
it seemed like an admission to Eddie that Ade thought he
didn't have long to go. "You kept me and Aras sane when
we thought Shan was dead. You've always been a good
friend."

"I'm glad you think if me that way."

"I always will."

"Big word, always. Especially from someone with
c'naatat."

Shan joined in the storytelling, regaling Eddie with tales
of recovering elephants wandering loose on the motorway,
and arresting a man who was a serial stealer of women's
earrings while they were wearing them, and only the left
ones. It took all sorts. Eddie countered with a roundup of all
the awkward places he'd caught politicians trying to avoid
his persistent questioning, from hiding in a janitor's cupboard to getting their kids to tell Eddie that Daddy wasn't
home.

"I really hated pressuring small kids," said Eddie. "But I
did. A job's a job. Can't let the bastards use human shields,
can we?"

"I gave in to that once," said Shan, looking out over the
plain, keeping watch for Aras. "And I never will again."

"You mustn't agonize over *c'naatat,* Shan." Nevyan, in that
typical wess'har way, changed topics instantly and showed

what had really been on her mind while she was apparently listening to the stories. "Rayat made his choice. We didn't force Lindsay to make the same one, and as urgency is not an issue, you mustn't feel pressured."

"But I do." Shan was in gut-spilling mood tonight, which wasn't like her at all. "Targassat, remember? Those with choices must make them."

"That applies equally to us," said Giyadas. "And we have choices in this, too, and haven't taken them."

We could frag you, but we haven't. Ade understood that clearly enough. But Shan was scaring him now. She was so bloody *moral*; it was part of the reason why he loved her, the fact that she never did the expedient thing, but sometimes it got her into an endless loop of conflicting choices. Ade didn't want to lose this second bite at life. He was greedy for time with Shan. Would a few *c'naatat* who weren't going anywhere be that much of a risk? He was tied to whatever Shan did. He refused to imagine life without her. It wouldn't have been a life at all. She was his wife.

"You're quiet, Ade," Shan said.

"I'll do what you do, Boss. I don't want to go on a day longer than you."

That pretty well killed what little lightheartedness was left in the evening. They could all think it through. Even Eddie didn't have anything to say, and Giyadas and Nevyan took him home shortly afterwards.

Ade heard Aras come in a few hours later. He waited for the sound of running water that meant he was taking a shower—a basic stream of water from an overhead cistern, nothing fancy—and then timed him. He was taking a long time to come to bed. Shan was asleep, curled up in a ball with her back to him. Ade slid out of bed and went to find Aras.

He was sitting at the table, looking through what Ade thought was a book, until he remembered that wess'har didn't store data that way. It was a sheet of glass, or so he thought.

"Where you been, mate?" It was a daft thing to worry

about a *c'naatat*'s safety, but he said it anyway. "We were getting worried about you."

He looked over Aras's shoulder and saw that the glass sheet was something like a *virin*, a clear material with embedded displays and controls. It seemed to be full of moving images.

"I met my whole clan for the first time since the isenj wars," he said. "My *family*. Five centuries on."

"How did that feel?" Ade could see and smell how hard that had hit him. "I don't know what I'd do if I found I still had family on Earth. We weren't exactly close, not in the end."

"I felt both happy and unhappy," Aras said, not looking up. His gaze was fixed on images of an event that Ade didn't understand, but it seemed to be some kind of communal building session with the kids joining in, almost like raising a barn in the old days. "Happy that I could recall my childhood, and that it felt good, and unhappy that I didn't know if I wanted to be there or not."

Lindsay's restoration to plain basic human must have set Aras thinking again. It was inevitable. Sooner or later, Ade would pick up Aras's headline emotions via Shan, and he'd find out just how upset he was.

"Did they make you welcome?"

"Yes."

"It's okay, 'Ras. I understand. You can't pretend you're not wess'har." Ade sat closer and treated it like looking through a family album. "Are these your folks?"

"Most of them, to some degree or other."

Aras didn't seem to want to talk. He was engrossed in the images, either genuinely preoccupied or trying to make Ade go away, so Ade took the hint.

"Come to bed, mate." Ade worried that he took too much of Shan's attention and that Aras missed out. It wasn't that he kept a tally of who had sex with her most often, but he was pretty sure that Aras wasn't getting as much as he used to. "Shan's beginning to think you don't fancy her any more."

"Reassure her," Aras said. "But I have centuries of catching up to do, not just twenty-five years. I don't know why I avoided Baral for so long. The problem was all mine."

Ade went back to bed and wrapped himself around Shan, burying his face in her hair and trying not to wake her. She was sound asleep, breathing slowly.

"So what's up with him?" she said suddenly, and made him jump.

"I thought you were asleep, Boss. Did I wake you?"

"No. I heard Aras come in."

"He's got some kind of picture album. He met his family. The clan."

Shan paused for a few moments. "But is he okay?"

"A bit rattled, I think."

"I ought to help him through this." She let out a long breath. "He's had a lot of hard memories to face in a short period, and I don't think handling Lindsay's kid's bones helped much."

"What about you? It got to you, too, didn't it? Because of the abortion."

"No, it's because I wouldn't help Lin's kid survive by giving him a dose of *c'naatat*—but I'm happy to stay alive myself, so what happened to my fucking principles? When did I decide I should keep it? And why do I feel so bad about the loss of life on Earth when I spent most of my career thinking that humans needed culling? Where's my line? What *won't* I do? I've sat in judgment on so many people, and now I don't even trust my own sense of right and wrong."

See? I knew it was eating at her. All of it.

She didn't say anything else. He worried that she might do something stupid again, as stupid as stepping out the airlock to do the decent thing like some fucking mindlessly heroic general of the Victorian era, but it might have been a reaction to what happened on Earth—too much shit in too short a time, coupled with the realization of the time lost with people who mattered.

He'd still keep an eye on her.

"Do you suppose you might be staying *c'naatat* for me and Aras, knowing what shit we went through when we thought you were gone?" Ade whispered. But Shan was asleep, really dead to the world this time, and didn't hear him.

Aras didn't come to bed that night. Ade decided he'd need to keep an eye on him too.

22

*We must do what we can in life to tread lightly on worlds,
but we must also remember that just as other people have a
right to live, from the smallest tem fly to the living system of
a planet, so have we. Our lives might not be worth more
than others', but they are worth no less. Be considerate to
yourselves. There is no purpose in self-denial for its own
sake; only outcomes matter. When your actions do no
harm, enjoy them.*

TARGASSAT, on living each day

Jejeno, Umeh: August 19, 2426.

The city itself didn't look all that different to Shan's recent memory, but Jejeno *had* changed.

It was the noise that was different. The city once ran to a
permanent atmos track of rustling, clicking, chittering noise,
the sounds of millions of isenj, but now it seemed quiet. As
Shan walked along the wide streets between canyonlike
brick-red buildings, she had a sense of being in a ghost
town. It was totally misleading; there were plenty of isenj
around, tottering about their business, but there weren't
solid carpets of them moving in streams that needed traffic
rules to avoid crushes.

They had their wide-open spaces. The remaining three
continents—Pareg, Tivskur and Sil—were those spaces,
scoured clean by bioweapons and nanites, and now the isenj
of the Northern Assembly were dispersing across them.

"I thought they liked being crowded together," Shan said.
"The termite inheritance."

Nevyan steered her towards the dome of Umeh Station. "I
could say the same of urban humans."

Umeh Station—now called Njirot—had been designed to

house human explorers in hostile extrasolar environments,
so it had weathered fifty years in Jejeno with ease. Even
from outside, Shan could see plants thriving within. It
looked for all the world like a botanical hothouse. When the
doors parted, she found herself breathing lush, muffled air,
and surrounded by isenj taking in the sights in a way that
reminded her of Edwardian gentry on a Sunday stroll.

"I suppose all these plants come from Tasir Var," she
said.

"All except a few food crops." Nevyan led her through
unsettlingly familiar paths between foliage and blooms that
made her feel as if she was back in a greenhouse. Isenj reacted to their visitors with little clicks and nods that Shan
took as acknowledgment when Nevyan nodded back. "We
were able to breed the plants back a little closer to their wild
forms."

Shan had no idea that wess'har set any store by symbolism. Maybe she was misinterpreting the effort they'd put
into reverting a few lonely plants to their wild state. She
reached out and rubbed a thin, spiky leaf between her fingers, crushing a faintly fragrant oil from it.

"Any chance of visiting the other places?" she asked.
"Like Pareg?"

"I think it would distress you."

She had a point. It was sometimes better not to remind
herself of things she couldn't change.

I can't do a frigging thing about Earth, either.

She'd accepted there were limits to her own responsibility
and powers. It might have been a symptom of being ready
to move on at last.

*But if I haven't got some imagined crusade, how do I
justify my existence—a c'naatat existence?*

She had no excuses left, and it was her personal wishes,
enjoying precious and potentially infinite time, versus what
was prudent and necessary.

Nevyan beckoned. "We can come back here later. Let's
pay our respects to the senior minister."

There was a groundcar waiting for them, but Shan preferred to walk so she could look in detail at Jejeno. The last

time she'd been here, Minister Rit—widow of Minister Par
Paral Ual—had just staged a coup and asked the Eqbas to
back it. There were bomb craters that gouged jagged black
gaps in the city. Palls of smoke rose from the horizon. She'd
watched it all, as detached as a vid viewer, from behind the
protection of an Eqbas shield.

*Did Ual bargain for this when he invited the wess'har to
help his planet?*

It was impossible to tell what he might have imagined.
Jejeno was spacious. The isenj had opened up spaces—
parks, with trees. This was a world that had been literally
a coast-to-coast city with nothing left of the natural world,
a totally managed environment where survival hung on
the extraordinary skill of isenj engineers. But now it had
parks.

Shan stood at the huge doors of the government offices
and walked through into a reception chamber of polished
aquamarine stone. "Nev, do you ever think how different
this might have been if it had been the Eqbas who restored
this place, and not you?"

"Of course I did," said Nevyan, taking it literally again,
like any wess'har. "That's why I demanded that they left the
system and took the Skavu with them right from the start."

"Well, if you and the isenj can be allies, then I have hope
for the whole universe."

Embarrassingly, Shan found she did. Hope wasn't one of
her traits; any optimism she appeared to have was actually a
bloody-minded inability to withdraw from a fight. It was a
day of sea changes for her.

Minister Faril appeared the same as any other isenj to her,
all gem-beaded quills and a piranha-spider face with no
distinct eyes to focus on, plus a remarkably human outlook
on life that reminded her what *alien* could mean. He seemed
genuinely pleased to see Nevyan.

"This is my old friend, *Shan Chail,*" she said, introducing
her to Faril. Around them, ussissi—ubiquitous assistants,
oddly neutral, still an enigma to Shan—skittered on the
marble tiles. "She's just returned from Earth. It's undergo-
ing its own restoration."

"Ah, but you had diverse species, your own gene bank," Faril said. He spoke English. He managed to suck in the air and expel it in a bubbling baritone voice, bypassing the need for ussissi interpreters. "Do you realize how fortunate you were, to be able to restore your world, that you actually *saved* this diversity? The gene bank was a very fine thing." He summoned tea, something the isenj had learned from Eddie, and it turned out to be a herbal infusion that was foul but couldn't kill her. Shan sipped politely. "You have a duplicate."

"We do," Shan said. "Because I don't trust my own kind not to destroy Earth all over again."

"But those who survive will think *differently*."

The old Shan tapped her on the shoulder and told her that was a load of bollocks, because humans never changed. The Shan who needed to get used to living in a world where good things were not only possible, but even part of the hard-wiring of more truly communally-minded species, told her to listen. "Did you? Are the isenj who survived the ones who can override their instincts?"

"We don't *need* to override them," said Faril. "Those who are left *want* this."

How? How could any species like the isenj resist the need to fill every gap again? How could humans?

"Is this an education process?" she asked.

"No, selection. The tendency among citizens in the Northern Assembly was to want restraint, which made us relatively weak against the more expansionist elsewhere. This is . . . a memory. Our genetic memories predispose us to it. Once we had removed the tainted thinking, the tainted memories, we could live differently. Do you understand our genetic memory?"

Shan suppressed a human shudder at the idea of eradicating deviant thought. *What are you turning into, some kind of wet liberal?* "I understand it, all right," she said. "I have it."

"Of course. Nevyan did explain." Faril seemed perfectly happy. Maybe he was too young to remember the purge firsthand; old isenj didn't have wrinkles and distinguished gray, so it was hard to tell. "We have plans for the other landmasses. There may be Earth species that would adapt to life here."

Shan tried to take that in. It was usually anathema to introduce non-native species into an ecosystem. It set all her old EnHaz instincts on edge. But there was no true native ecology here except for a few vegetables; everything else was imported. The thought crossed her mind, then wandered back again and didn't show signs of leaving.

"Maybe," she said.

Oh God, no. Don't set yourself a new cause. Don't build a problem to solve.

She'd see. She'd keep an eye on how things went on Earth, and—

And that was the first paving stone laid, marked *Good Intention*. The wess'har must have done much the same when they colonized Wess'ej, if the modest scattering of zero-growth cities that hid in the landscape could be called *colonization*. Shan put the thought of manageable possibilities out of her head.

Nevyan settled down on one of the stone slab seats in the office. Unlike the rest of the seating it was padded, as if the isenj were used to making an alien guest feel more comfortable. It was a far cry from the war that Aras had fought, and even from recent history. Shan sat down on a slab cross-legged, which was a novelty act for both wess'har and isenj, who couldn't sit that way. And Faril was chatty. It was odd to meet a thoroughly enthusiastic quilled egg on legs that looked as if he could take your head off in one bite. Shan thought she should have been uniquely used to the biological diversity of the universe by now.

She had a little isenj in her, after all.

"I would suggest that you don't worry about *geth-ezz* coming back," Faril said. He even used the wess'u word for humankind, but gargled the terminal *S*. "We have an alliance. Together, we will be able to keep this system free of invaders. This is how our societies *should* be, stable, cooperative and convivial."

She almost expected him to quote Targassat next. *Nev must have played a blinder of a PR job.* Shan glanced at her,

catching a faint whiff of that powdery contentment scent
that told her Nevyan was very okay with the world, and had
to chalk that learned skill up to Eddie Michallat. Whether
he knew it or not, his influence had led to a kind of peace in
the end. It wasn't a minor achievement for a journalist. Shan
was instantly proud of him. He deserved a statue.

"I don't think humans will be spacefaring again for a very
long time, Minister," she said. "Tell me how things are going in Pareg."

It was quite a civilized afternoon, taking tea—of sorts—
with an isenj minister without the powder keg of war threatening to ignite at any time. It was almost enjoyable, right up
to the time that a ussissi came tap-tapping across the splen-
didly inlaid floor to give them bad news.

"You'll want to return to F'nar," said the ussissi. "Eddie is
unwell. These may be his final days."

Ussissi, like wess'har, had never been big on tact. Shan
faced up to the first pain of being *c'naatat,* seeing one of her
contemporaries overtaking her on the road to the grave-
yard.

F'nar, Nevyan Tan Mestin's home: August 23, 2426.

He'd hung on long enough, longer than he ever imagined
he could from sheer will, and now Eddie Michallat was the
last surviving ordinary human in the Cavanagh system.

Dying . . . dying wasn't what Eddie expected at all. He
was ninety-three, and each time in the recent past that he'd
thought death might be a possibility, it had lost some of its
formless dread and taken on another aspect. When he lay
awake in bed at night, struggling for breath, he'd always
wondered: *Is this the last one?* Was this the final illness,
the one from which he would never recover? Each time he
got better and returned to his daily routine—a little slower,
a little more careful of the steep steps cut into the terraced
city clinging to the sides of the caldera—his life was a
strange blend of relief at seeing another day and a regularly surfacing thought that this was *not* the end. The final

illness still had to be faced, and it might not be like the last one at all.

When he'd recovered from a particularly bad chest infection at eighty-six, it was the first time that he'd ever felt a sense of anticlimax.

Did I want to die then?

Was he fed up waiting for the ax to fall, or had he reached a new understanding of it, or did he just dread an end that would be even worse than that?

Now he knew. He'd done all he had to here. There was one last thing left for him to explore.

In the filtered gold light that filled the room, he'd reached the stage where he wasn't entirely sure if he was awake or dozing, and he had to press against the cushion under his hand to be sure he could feel it at all. For a moment he thought he'd slipped away and not noticed the point of death: he panicked to think he might have missed the last thing he had to observe and report upon.

But he was still alive. His breathing settled down again almost independently of him. His body would do as it pleased, which was a fair deal given that he hadn't let it give up while he was waiting for friends to come home all those years.

I had to see them back safely. It's not that I had so much to say, either.

"Eddie?" Shan blocked out the sunlight for a few seconds and then squatted down in front of him. "How are you feeling? Ade wondered if you'd like to go outside. It's a nice warm day."

"Just outside, on the terrace," he said. "I don't want to go too far."

"Come on, then." She stood up again. "Ade, give me a hand with the chair."

Eddie didn't know what the wess'her called the mobile chair. He'd picked up an awful lot of wess'u over the last fifty-odd years, but he couldn't speak it, not that double-toned khoomei singer's voice with its choral complexity. *I was doing pretty well to be able to make the sounds at all. Here I am, a bloody Tibetan monk almost.* He really would have loved to have spoken wess'u fluently. The chair moved smoothly down the passage, Ade steering, and into the daylight to settle on the terraced walkway itself.

Eddie remembered his first sight of City of Pearl, of F'nar, and how it took his breath away. It had looked just like *this*, right now. It had never palled.

He loved this city.

"Where's Aras?" he asked. "Is he okay? And Giyadas?"

"They'll be along soon." Shan sat down cross-legged at his feet and Ade knelt down on one knee next to her, so Eddie could have an uninterrupted view. "He's just getting some strawberries. The little wild ones. Specially for you."

Like Ade had always said, Shan really did have the most striking pale gray eyes, and on the rare occasions when emotion had broken down her barriers they had a genuine beauty, an unexpected and almost alien compassion. Maybe Ade saw that when the rest of the world never did, reserved solely for him and Aras, but now she finally seemed willing to drop her guard a little for Eddie.

You know I'm dying, don't you, doll?

"Do me a favor, Shazza." It was a nickname he once thought she hated, but she never told him as much. "Can you make sure I get a really good view?"

"What view, mate?"

"Bury me somewhere nice."

"Eddie, you're not going yet . . ."

"You never lied to me, Shan, so don't start now. Go on. Please."

The light switched off in her eyes for a moment, that instinctive jerk back to locked-down self-control. *Yes, you're upset. I can see from your reaction that I really am going now. But I know that. It feels different this time.* Eddie saw Ade slide his hand discreetly down Shan's back to steady her.

Look at that. He loves you, Shan. God, I miss Erica.

"Of course I will," she said at last. "I know a place with a great view. I promise. You can see the whole plain from there."

"Good." Eddie had a list. He reminded her every time he

saw her now, because he never knew which visit would be the last. "And you know where all my archives are."

"Check."

"My stuff to transmit to Barry when he comes out of cryo."

"Check."

Yes, Erica . . . if there's anything more beyond this, it'll be so good to see her again. If there's not . . . then the missing her will stop at last. Either way . . . there's an end in sight.

Shan reached up and laid her hand on his. She wasn't wearing gloves, and he couldn't tell if she had that gel coating on, but it didn't feel like it. She was instinctively careful about accidental contamination now. But it was much harder to infect a human with *c'naatat* than people thought. Open wounds were the likely vector. Rayat had told him.

Who'd have thought it? Rayat, self-sacrificing patriot. Lindsay, heroine. You never really know people until they're in the grinder.

"You're thinking something, Shan," Eddie said. It really was a lovely balmy day, high white cloud and a warm, almond-fragranced breeze—not flowers, but the scent of a red-and-white striped sluglike creature that lived in the crevices of the walls. *Aumul.* That was it. "Are you wondering what dying's going to be like for you?"

"Do you really want to talk about this, Eddie?"

"Not if it upsets you."

"This isn't about me. You can talk about anything you like, mate. I just didn't want to feel I was . . ."

"Okay."

"Yes, I think I'm a bit jealous. Is it okay to say that? I have no idea when I'm going to die. I know I can. Nothing's killed me yet. That's more unsettling than counting down the clock like I used to." Her face was still set. She'd switched off the emotion. "I used to have this constant low-level panic about running out of time. Not death so much as not getting things done."

This was what Eddie wanted. He didn't need platitudes, attempts to pretend he had years left in him, because he *didn't*. He wanted to see the innermost soul of another person again, to hear an absolute truth; he wanted one last good interview. What better than this? Who better than Shan?

She'd been a bloody hard interview the first time.

"How did it feel to stand in that cargo bay and see the airlock doors open, Shan?"

Ade looked down at the terrace floor and changed knees, uncomfortable either emotionally or physically, but *uncomfortable*. Shan inhaled slowly through her nose and seemed to be *making* herself look directly into Eddie's face.

He could see her weighing the morality, as she always did—tell him the truth and maybe distress him, or tell him what would comfort him because a lie now didn't matter.

Eddie knew what she'd do.

"I've never felt fear like it," she said at last. "And I split into two people, and the one who gives the orders told me to get on with it, because it had to be done. It was the worst pain I can imagine. I couldn't believe I was going through with it. And all I could think of was that I'd never told Aras that I loved him."

Her gray stare didn't waver, but she did blink, just a couple of times.

"Thanks for being honest, doll."

"And, yes, I broke the law over and over again to protect Helen Marchant's eco-terrorists."

"I know . . ."

"But I never admitted it when you interviewed me when we first landed on Bezer'ej. I never put my hands up to it before, not to anyone, but I'm doing it on the record now. For you."

She knew him better than he'd thought. "Thanks."

Eddie heard Giyadas coming. He knew her walk. She bent down over him and stroked his hair just as he used to stroke hers when she was just this funny, clever little alien kid who he adored.

"It's a lovely day," she said, suddenly very human. A wess'har would have told him he had run out of time and that he should make the most of the hours or minutes left. "Do you require anything?"

"I'm fine. Just sit where I can see you." He reached for her hand, but it was so much more effort than it used to be. Giyadas settled on the opposite side to Shan. "I'm glad you're all here."

"I don't know where Aras has got to, Eddie." Shan shifted position. "Ade, can you see him?"

F'nar was a natural amphitheater. Every part of the city was visible from the upper terraces, right the way down to the pearl-coated natural pillars that marked the entrance. Ade got to his feet and looked over the edge.

Eddie almost told him to be careful, because there was no barrier and a steep drop beneath.

But Ade couldn't die from a fall.

"Yeah, he's coming along the walkway by Taorit's house," he said. "A couple of minutes, maybe."

Shan's expression was unreadable. She squeezed Eddie's hand harder. "I can stop this, Eddie. I can stop it right now."

He didn't quite understand her at first. "Stop what?"

"Just say the word, Eddie. You don't have to go. I can make it all right, give you as much time as you want."

Giyadas didn't react. Ade turned slowly and looked as if he might intervene, but he said nothing. Eddie had always wondered how he might respond. Shan was offering to contaminate him with *c'naatat*. The prospect made his stomach tighten for a moment, but it was gone as fast as it came.

"No, you don't really want to do that, doll," he said. So this was how it felt to have choice of living forever: it didn't feel miraculous at all. "You were always my bloody hero, the woman who wouldn't give it away, not for anyone. Don't ruin my illusion. Don't give in to that impulse now."

He held her grip as tightly as he could. She looked at him for a few moments, and her carefully composed expression threatened to crumple.

Save me now, and I still have to go some time. Temporary reprieve, and I'll still be on my own.

"It's different for you," he said. "You've got a matching family."

Shan nodded. "Okay, mate."

She didn't mention it again. Aras arrived with a small

bowl and held it in front of Eddie at lap level for him to admire a few spoonfuls of brilliant scarlet fruits the size of
hazel nuts, studded with pinprick seeds. He could smell
them; when he managed to place one in his mouth, the flavor
was so intense at the back of his throat that it almost felt like
inhaling acetone. He tried to eat a few more, but the effort
was just that little too much for him then. He settled for
basking in the warmth.

"Ade," Shan said softly, thinking Eddie couldn't hear her,
"get Nevyan."

It might have been minutes; it could even have been an
hour, or more.

The sun was a lot brighter now.

"Eddie?"

He knew that wonderful double-toned voice. *Giyadas, my
little seahorse princess.*

"Worst thing you can have, doll. Regrets."

"Eddie, you have been a second father to me—"

"Eddie?" Was that—Nevyan? Shan?

"*Eddie!*"

The sun was really very bright indeed now, but it seemed
a long way off.

"It's been amazing being out here," he said. He should
have looked around to try to imprint those sweet faces for
his journey, but he didn't feel he had to now. "Absolutely
amazing."

"Eddie—"

The light was blue-white now, a narrow shaft. Ceret,
they said. Not the sun he'd left behind. And that was amazing too.

Yes, it really had been . . .

Amazing.

23

Yes, of course I'll do an interview about Eddie Michallat. I got to know him very well in the Cavanagh system. He's the reason I don't shoot journalists on sight, and I miss him. I miss him a lot.
Inspector MARTIN BARENCOIN, Australian Federal Police, responding to a media request for a tribute to veteran broadcaster Eddie Michallat

F'nar Plain; memorial cairn.

The soil on top of the butte was almost solid rock, and Ade knew how hard it was to excavate any kind of hole because he'd dug Shan's grave here.

Now she was digging Eddie's. It was the kind of heavy-handed irony that *c'naatat* always seemed to create. Ade felt uneasy about the memorial cairn that he'd built out of pearl-coated pebbles to give him somewhere to mourn Shan when he had no body to bury. It still stood intact, looking out from the top of the butte across the plain and the city, its nacre layer slightly thicker from fifty summers of *tem* fly swarms. Shan had never felt disturbed by it, she said. She could disconnect from her own mortality with surprising ease. But Ade no longer found it a comforting place to be.

But maybe it was easier to do that when you thought you'd already died.

"I could finish that for you," he said.

"I need to do it, sweetheart." Shan hacked away at the hard soil. Aras had buried one of his rats here, too, one of Rayat's lab animals until Aras had taken them from him, appalled at the things *gethes* did to other *people*. "I promised Eddie a good view. That's what he's going to get."

"Do you mind me asking something?"

"Have I ever?"

"Were you really going to infect him if he'd said yes?"

Shan straightened up and rubbed her nose. "No. I don't think so. But I'll never know now."

"I wouldn't have blamed you, but I think you did the right thing not to."

"Yeah." She rubbed the back of her hand across her nose, probably because she was sweating from the effort. She'd kept any tears to herself. "I know. But it was Eddie who said no. Where's Aras?"

"Wandering around."

"You want to tell me what's up with him?"

"He's had a lot on his plate lately."

"He hasn't touched me since he came back from Baral."

Ade knew that only too well. Aras had done so before when he thought Shan wasn't well enough, or when he was having a rough patch, but Ade didn't know if Shan was seeing what he suspected—that Aras was withdrawing from both of them. For the first time in his life, he really could go back to being a regular wess'har.

Maybe it *was* just a phase. It really had been a shitty few months: trauma, bereavement, reconciliation with an estranged family. Ade tried to imagine how he'd feel if his own family somehow showed up and brought all that past flooding back. It would definitely have killed any passion in him.

"He's doing that wrestling with his principles thing," Ade said at last. "Boss, you should understand that better than anybody."

She stood back and took a lot more time than necessary inspecting the grave. "Yeah, that's what worries me. Come on. Let's collect Eddie."

They walked back down to the city in silence, but Ade could hear all the unspoken stuff in her head if he thought about it: guilt, abandonment, and all the fears that Aras was going to do what he'd set out to a while back—to leave so that they could be two nice normal monogamous humans together. They'd fought about it last time. He was bloody sure they'd fight about it again.

Shan and Ade carried Eddie out of the city wrapped in a *dhren* shroud on a pallet, just as wess'har did. Wess'har left their dead out on the plain for the scavengers, and retrieved the shroud material; they were all about pragmatism. But Ade hadn't been prepared to leave Shan out in the open like that. He knew it made perfect sense, but it was bloody horrible, and he owed his dead loved ones a lot more than treating them like that. Eddie wanted a nice spot. He hadn't said he wanted to be lunch for some *srebil.* Aras could argue all he liked that it was the same as flies and bacteria doing the job, but it wasn't, it just *wasn't,* and never would be.

Eddie didn't weigh much, and Ade slung a couple of straps under the body so they could lower him into the grave. It was like any battlefield burial; Eddie had fought in his own way, and he was every bit a casualty as far as Ade was concerned.

"You're burying the *dhren* too?"

"It's Eddie," she said. "Can't bear the thought of soil in his face, I can always get another *dhren.* Never wore the thing anyway. Not my color."

So it *was* hers. She might not have said much—did she think he didn't know she felt things keenly?—but sometimes she'd do something deeply sentimental that would stop him in his tracks.

"That's a lovely thing to do, Boss." He held out the straps to her. She was a nonpracticing Pagan, and he wasn't sure which funeral rite she was carrying out. "Lower away, or do you want to say something first? I don't know how Pagans do stuff."

"Eddie wasn't Pagan. Orthodox Church of Hack, I reckon."

"Probably Christian. But we're fresh out of those."

"Which disposal did you put down on your form, Ade?"

"Christian."

"Well, then."

Ade knew how to do this, and he didn't feel self-conscious in front of Shan. He laid the straps down again and stood over Eddie's body at the graveside a small shape draped in opalescent white fabric, then took the bee cam from his pocket and laid it on the shroud so that it sat in a hollow. Ade had to shut his eyes hard to stop them welling. "You were a good mate to us all, Eddie. If there's a god, he'd better treat you to the five-star suite, and if there isn't, get some rest. You earned it. We haven't got a bugler for you, so just know that you were loved and respected."

When he opened his eyes, Shan was looking at him in that funny kind of way that said she didn't know he could do something so well. She swallowed and looked back at the body.

"Don't interview God, will you, you old bugger? He hates being misquoted." She bent down to pick up the straps on her side and laid her hand on the body, lips moving in silence for a couple of words. Ade couldn't work out what she'd said and didn't ask. "Goodbye, Eddie."

They lowered the entire pallet carefully into the grave and stepped back. There was nothing more to say. Shan took something from her pocket and threw it into the hole, then began shoveling soil; Ade didn't see what she'd dropped into the grave. It didn't take long to fill the shallow pit and build a cairn of stones on top.

Ade looked up at the sun. *Tem* flies loved shitting on smooth, sun-baked surfaces. "It'll be all nice and pearly in a few weeks."

"I'll plant some of those succulents up here, too," Shan said. They were like fat, shiny cacti without spines, just a coating of bubbles that mirrored the skylight domes that had once dotted the surface above Constantine. "Then maybe Aras can get his arse here to pay his respects, too. And Rayat."

She was pissed off that Aras hadn't showed. It probably wouldn't have seemed rude to a wess'har, though, and Ade hoped she'd cut him some slack. Ade was relieved Rayat had done the tactful absence thing. They walked in silence, and Shan made her way to the Exchange of Surplus Things, which was empty except for a couple of male wess'har tidying crates of fabrics. They looked up when she came in, nodded, and carried on.

"Tools," she said, holding out her hand to Ade.

He gave her his bag, unsure what she was going to do, but she was the Boss. She went over to the alcove where Ade and the rest of the Royal Marines used to play cards, took a sharp metal peg out of the bag, and began sizing up a flat slab of wall at eye height.

"Did Jon have a middle name?" she asked. "Or Izzy?"

"Michael," he said. "Izzy never used one. It was never on her paperwork."

"Okay."

It was another of those unexpected things that showed him how Shan's mind really worked. She began roughing out letters with the tip of the spike and stood back after a while to assess them, selecting a chisel and a hammer.

"Before I start hammering, did I get that right?" she asked. "And I need some dates."

MARINE ISMAT QURESHI, 37 CDO ROYAL MARINES

MARINE JONATHAN MICHAEL BECKEN, 37 CDO ROYAL MARINES

Beneath the scraped letters was a big space, presumably for the others in due course, and then:

COMRADES AND FRIENDS, GREATLY MISSED

"I know they were civvies when they died," Shan said, "but they were Booties while they were here. Anyway, it's not a war memorial." She looked as if she'd caught herself off guard, embarrassed by her own gesture. "Don't expect me to carve the emblem, though. I'll have enough trouble getting the letters right."

"Globe and laurel," Ade said, realizing again why he loved her so fiercely. "I can do that."

"I'll do a bit at a time," she said. "It'll take me a day or two."

She was a bloody good woman. *See, Izzy, I told you that you didn't have to worry about her.* Funerals always made Ade scared and clingy, forcing him look around his mates and dread that they'd be next. He thought he'd never have to worry about that with Shan. They had plenty of time. It made him feel relief each time he remembered it. It was the *only* thing, and now it didn't look so certain.

He took the peg from her hand, pausing to squeeze her

fingers, and then sketched the outline of the Corps' badge. It was pretty good, even if he did say so himself. Shan smiled.

"Clever," she said. "My old man's full of hidden talents."

Ade was happy to be her *old man*. Even in a painful time, it made him feel invulnerable in a way that even *c'naatat* couldn't.

He'd stick around as long as she would. The choice was up to her.

F'nar, Wess'ej: October 3, 2426.

I know this is right.

Aras watched two of Giyadas's grandsons playing on the rear terrace. He'd almost forgotten how different wess'har children were from humans; they were quiet and purposeful, observing and learning as much as they could. Shiporis and Citan were busy learning to pot up pepper seedlings under Ade's supervision. Ade was very good with youngsters, endlessly patient and quick to praise them.

Does he feel any yearning to have back the child he lost? Is this hard for him too?

"Okay, this is how you do it," Ade said. He held the seedling by one leaf and gently loosened the soil around its roots with a twin-tined fork. Citan watched intently with his head tilted to one side. "See? You have to leave the roots in one piece. Doesn't matter if you damage a leaf, it's the roots that matter. Then use your thumb to make a hole big enough . . . like that."

Ade held the seedling upright in the hole while Shiporis sifted soil around the roots. He showed them how to press on the surface just enough to compact the compost without crushing the fragile net beneath.

"Now we water it in. Go on, Citan. Just a steady dribble. Don't saturate it."

Ade had been a city boy; he'd learned cultivation from Aras. In a few short years, their worlds had come full circle.

It's not just what I have to do. It's what I want, too.

Citan and Shiporis seemed sufficiently confident now to pot up the rest of the seed tray on their own. Ade stepped back and left them to it, smiling to himself.

"Child labor," he said. "I'll get them making cheap rugs next. I'll be a millionaire by Christmas."

"They amuse you."

"Kids are great." Ade looked a little regretful, but there was no pain on his face. "So what are you going to do, mate? Not that I can't see."

It was the hardest thing Aras had ever tried to explain, but Ade knew, just as Shan did; it had been growing in him since the trip to Jejeno, the realization of what he had been and what he'd never had. The feelings were so persistent that they must have passed to Shan and Ade at some level. Visiting Baral had finally tipped the balance, and Eddie . . . Eddie could walk away from the offer of permanent, healthy life on his deathbed. If Eddie had ever reported a great truth, then it was this one: that there was a point at which life had to be lived to its conclusion and death faced. All wess'har knew and accepted that. Aras had forgotten how, until now.

"How can I do this to you, Ade?"

Ade shrugged. He couldn't suppress his scent like Shan could, and it was at odds with his expression. He was upset. "You have to do what you want, Aras. Don't live your life for anyone else. And nobody's responsible for making someone else happy."

Is he saying that to be brave? Or is he finally being human at last, and wanting Shan to himself?

"Shan opted to stay *c'naatat* so I wouldn't be alone," Aras said. "If I were to . . . have it removed, I know what choice she would feel she had to make too."

"Yeah. We've talked about that."

"You see my dilemma."

Ade wandered over to the low wall that formed the edge of the terrace and sat down beside him. "Tell me what you want to do. I know bloody well when you're unhappy, and you're not happy now. You haven't been really happy for ages." Ade snorted, that mock laughter that said something wasn't actually funny, but painful. "*Ages.* Listen to me. You know how long our relationship actually adds up to, all the days added together? The time we've actually been a family, the three of us? *Months* at most."

Ade stared at the flagstones, arms folded. Aras remembered building this house stone by stone, excavating the rooms, utterly alone and simply seeking to fill lonely time until he couldn't stand being surrounded by normal wess'har with families any longer. He thought he'd never forget Askiniyas, his first *isan;* but there came a time when he could barely picture her face even with his perfect wess'har memory, and the pain of her suicide had dulled to a vague sorrow after nearly five centuries.

Why did I carry on after she chose to die? Bezer'ej didn't need me, not with the garrison in place. I hung on because I didn't feel I'd tasted enough of life. I was greedy for existence, even one in exile.

If Shan felt the same way, how could Aras judge her after he'd burdened her with *c'naatat* in the first place? She never asked for it. He didn't even tell her he'd infected her. She found out the hard way, and she'd been distraught. She'd had a life of little else but duty too. Ade—Ade was just starting to live, it seemed. They had no debt to him or some wess'har principle.

Aras loved them both, *isan* and house-brother, and the pain of separation would be immense.

But Ade's always there for Shan. She adores him. And I must, absolutely must, *live out the life I never had. I have to try, at least.*

I must be a father.

"Eddie was wise enough to know when his life was lived, and that *c'naatat* wouldn't be a life for him at all," Aras said at last. "His decision made me think harder."

"Eddie didn't think about it. He just reacted right away and said no."

"And Jon and Izzy? I've seen the regret in your face. You sometimes wish you'd done what I did for Shan—saving their lives with your blood, without their asking. But you didn't."

"It was just that. A split second. Don't you think I hate

myself for that? I didn't even think of infecting them until it was too late. But they could have had it removed later, and that was a choice we didn't have when you saved Shan. Maybe I got to Jon too late, but Izzy would have lived. I don't know what that makes me—a stupid bastard who didn't think fast enough, or a callous one who let his mates die on a point of principle."

"Never callous, Ade. Never that. Don't think about it. You can't change the past."

"It's hard not to."

"Humans and wess'har have different views of *c'naatat*. That's the core of the problem. And I'm torn, because of my love on one hand, and my need for a child on the other, and I can no longer justify being *c'naatat*."

I started all this strife and killing. I was the first source of infection; I passed it to Shan. I even caused Ade to infect Lindsay Neville, and so the bezeri too, and Esganikan. Shan never really succumbed to the temptation. If Eddie had said yes . . . no, I think she knew in her heart that he'd refuse.

"You don't have to decide now, if you don't want to," said Ade. "The antidote thing will still be there."

"If I avoid confronting the choice, I'll live in limbo." Aras took Ade's arm. The contact didn't upset Ade now. There was a time when he would have reacted badly, the product of a childhood where any sudden touch was a violent one. "I have to do this."

Ade went quiet and just watched the two children, swallowing so hard that Aras could see the little lump moving at the front of his neck.

"When are you going to tell Shan?" he asked.

Aras had tried to imagine how she would take it, an alien thought process for most wess'har, because blurting out your views and intentions was simply how they did things. Shan would be upset. She wouldn't know why she was upset, whether at the prospect of losing a lover or because she feared he was making a sacrificial act again, but she would not smile and bless him on his way. He knew that.

"Soon," he said. "As soon as she returns."

"Just be sure why you're doing it, mate," Ade said quietly.
"That's all."

Aras was. For the first time in many years, he was clear
that he was making a selfish decision. Self-regard had probably kept him a *c'naatat* for far longer than he needed to be
one, because he was the last of his kind and had always had
an exit if he'd had the courage to take it, but now he faced
what a human might regard as shortcomings.

There was nothing wrong with being selfish. If you
couldn't act to make yourself happier when it harmed nobody, then you were what Deborah called a *martyr,* except
she regarded it as a fine thing. Humans seemed to value
their own pointless suffering, part of their constant attempt
to get their god's approval.

Motive didn't matter. That was the core of the wess'har
worldview.

"I'm sure," Aras said at last. "I'm wess'har."

F'nar; the Exchange of Surplus Things.

Shan kept chipping away at the *C* in the stone, refining
the name BECKEN and suddenly afraid to look away from it.
Carving the stone had taken much longer than she expected.
Now she was glad of the displacement activity.

The curve filled her field of vision. She wouldn't even
let herself register the peripheral stuff of the stone ashlars
and the crates around her. If she concentrated on that awkward curve, far beyond her carving skills, then her gut would
steady, the hot pounding pulse in her throat would ebb, and
the world would not fall apart. She was a child again, being
reminded that she was of no consequence.

Aras waited in patient silence. He was calm, exuding a
scent of male wess'har musk, a pleasant sandalwood aroma
that always caught the back of her throat and made her feel
good. It was one of the first things she'd noticed about him;
he smelled wonderful, and he was a strikingly beautiful
creature, so far outside her own human standards of aesthet-
ics as to be meaningless, but beautiful nonetheless.

He's leaving me.

Shan fought to steady her voice. "So you're going."

"Yes."

"It's not because of Ade, is it? It's not because you feel left out?"

"No." There was a rustle of fabric and rush of air as if he was going to put his hand on her arm, but she turned and took a step back. "I don't feel neglected. I never have. There was a time when I felt I made life difficult for Ade, because humans value monogamy, but I have never felt jealousy or pain. This isn't how wess'har think. You must know that by now."

"Okay."

"You're upset."

Shan was damned if she'd cry in front of him. "Well, when your old man walks out on you, you tend to feel a bit pissed off. It's a monkey thing. It's okay. I always pack a spare."

"Shan, please don't do this."

"What, end on a sour note?"

"Put on this act."

"I think," she said, in a moment of agonizing clarity, "that you're far braver than I'll ever be because you can face yourself. Your *real* self. Me, I'm still avoiding everything that makes me *me*. And maybe that's why I clung to this fucking parasite after all, because it made me someone else."

"No," said Aras patiently. "I think you did what you always do. You were stuck with it, so you made the best of a bad job."

"And now I don't have to. Rayat's right. I just won't deal with it."

She thought she was doing pretty well, all things considered. She hadn't shouted at him, or accused him, or even started crying or pleading. She'd never plead, even though he was precious to her and might well heed the appeal. She wanted him to be *happy*. She'd put her own needs aside all her life out of duty, out of what she suspected was a perverted instinct to be declared a clever, brave girl, and thus worthy of her parents' attention, but this was the first time she'd done anything without factoring in her own sense of self-worth.

Aras deserved to be happy.

"I would like to do this alone," Aras said. "This is hard for you and Ade. I know the process, and I'll go back to Baral."

"You should have someone with you. I'll—"

"It's not like dying, Shan. I can still see you both whenever I want, even if I'm different then."

But it *was* like dying. Once the parasite was neutralized, Aras was on borrowed time like every other wess'har—like every human.

"It might be frightening," she said. "Let us go with you."

"Lindsay could endure it, and I'm far more secure in my self than she ever was."

"You'd rather be alone?"

"I think so."

He was right. He wasn't playing games or being self-effacing because he was wess'har, however much human or isenj or whatever was in him. They didn't do that. But she still felt she was letting him give her an easy way out.

How can I forget him? He's in me. And he was the last thought I had when I was dying. That's where the truth is. That's when you know what your soul is made of, if any of us have one.

"Okay. Okay, we've made up our minds." She couldn't see well enough to carry on with the careful chipping away of stone to make Becken and Qureshi immortal in a more ecologically acceptable, less ethically fraught way. "Funny. We think we're bonded for eternity, and then we can walk away from each other in a matter of minutes."

"I haven't shocked you," Aras said quietly. "You could see this was coming."

"Yes." Could she blame him? If she'd been a less troubled soul and removing *c'naatat* could have given her a second chance of younger adulthood, she might not have been as torn as she was. Like she told Lindsay, this was that rarest of things, a second chance. All that removing *c'naatat* would do for her would be to restore her to a time when she'd made all her mistakes and lived with them grudgingly. "And I think you'll be a wonderful father. You *should* do it. I want you to do whatever makes you happy."

Aras turned and took a few steps, but then spun around, caught her by her shoulders and gave her an ordinary human kiss that broke her heart.

She thought of all the people she'd put a poor second to some goal that was far less important than being a normal creature of your own species. She had no right to sentence Aras to live his life as a freak to satisfy her own needs.

He'd do whatever I told him to. Wouldn't he?

That was no way to live.

"If I avoid you for a while," she said, "it'll be because I'm coming to terms with it. Be patient with me."

"You always were a bad liar, *Shan Chail*."

She was no longer *isan,* then. She turned back to the carving so she wouldn't have to watch him go, and worked on it even though she couldn't see the bloody shape any longer. Eventually she stopped rather than ruin the inscription, and thought that at least she wasn't so distraught that she couldn't think rationally. She never was. The lights in her hands rippled with shades of violet for a few seconds and then vanished again

"Sod it," she said.

When she got home, Ade was waiting, expression like a kid awaiting a thrashing, and started making the universal remedy of tea in total silence.

"Do we want to discuss this?" she said, flopping down on the sofa she'd built herself. It was still rock-solid. "He's gone."

Ade put her cup on the low table within reach and leaned over the back of the sofa to cup her face in his hands and look down at her.

"I bloody well love you, woman, and I always will," he said quietly. "And we'll cope. Shit, we'll even be happy again. I promise you."

That was Ade—dog-loyal, grateful for small kindnesses because he'd known so few, and able to snatch contentment and normality wherever he found it. He was totally admirable. He could also go after Kiir with a saber, intent on cutting him to ribbons.

"Ade, what happens to *us* if we revert back to normal?"

He pulled a face at her. It was hard to read expressions upside down. "I'd still want you, Boss. I fancied you something rotten when we were both ordinary, didn't I?"

"You did." She took a shine to him from day one, too. He was a choice rather than an accident made happy, whatever she'd once told herself. "I feel wrong carrying on with this thing when there's no justifiable *need*."

Ade walked around the sofa and sat down next to her. "*I* need us, though. Aras told me that doing a self-indulgent thing that wasn't harmful to anyone else was something everyone had to do. I've had a very short time of happiness in a life of shit. I want more. Is that good enough reason? I don't know. We could all have eaten a grenade and solved this once and for all, but none of us did."

"You always get to the balls of the argument, sweetheart." Shan ruffled his hair. Ade didn't make that contented *urrring* noise like a wess'har, but he lit up. "I'm going to do as my old man says for once."

They acted happy and acted eating a normal dinner with just the two of them. It was strained, but they would come through it, as they always had so far. If they could act it long enough, it would become habit, and then reality.

Ade had taught her that much. There were times when he showed her how intelligent she was but how very little she knew. She'd give it a few days to settle in her head, then go and tell Giyadas they'd reached their decision.

It was the right thing, but her guts were screaming that it just wasn't fair, not after she and Ade had both been through so much.

For the first time in her life, she wanted someone else to make the decisions for her.

Baral, northern Wess'ej.

Shan had told Aras that he shouldn't do this alone, but he wasn't. He was among family, and when he got to know everyone better, then he'd also be among friends.

"Will you require help?" asked Jesenkis. This male was

his kin, even more distant than Nevyan's uncle Sevaor, but definitely kin. When this parasite left Aras, he would value that. "Is it painful?"

"A fever," said Aras. Please, just check on me and give me water for a few days. I would rather go through this alone."

"Will you look normal afterwards?"

Aras had been so used to being regarded as exotically beautiful by Shan that he'd forgotten how utterly alien he appeared to his own kind.

My own kind.

"I will," he said.

Now he could think of his dead comrades with a greater degree of honor. His was a choice they'd never had, so would they have taken it? Of course they would. They chose to die rather than carry on as he did. Whether that made him stronger or more of a coward he didn't know. He lay down on the thin mattress, spread on the floor Baral-style, and stared up into the domed light above him. It was just a matter of inserting the needle into a muscle. He took a careless stab at his thigh and waited.

For the first few hours, Aras felt nothing. He wondered if *c'naatat* had yet again found a way to evade the countermeasure, a trick it had played before in wess'har tissue. But then he began to feel hot and feverish, and memories—truly forgotten memories, in detail he had never experienced before—began roiling in his mind: isenj cities, military barracks on Earth, scenes from high above the land and from beneath the sea, even the terrifying pain and cold of deep space—Shan's lonely space—and the dark cell where the smell of wet leaves meant his isenj captors were coming back to torture him again. Nobody was coming to rescue him.

It might have been hours. He wanted it to end. He wanted, and not for the first time in his life, to *die*.

Footsteps echoed outside in the passages and he even recalled Jesenkis bringing in water, staring down at him with a sharply tilted head and strong scent of agitation, then leaving again.

It was all Aras deserved. He was a killer of isenj civilians, betrayer of better wess'har who took the honorable way out, abandoner of his *isan*. He got what he had coming, as Eddie might have said. He *was* dying. Shapakti had got something wrong.

"Hang in there, mate," said a voice. Aras thought it was his disrupted mind, struggling to process the welter of recollections as he sweated out this fever, but a hand took his arm and someone wiped his face with a blissfully cold wet cloth. "Bloody daft. Who do you think you are, Captain Oates?"

It was Ade. Aras made sure he was real, grabbing his arm. "Is Shan here too?"

"No, I made her stay at home. It's better that way, mate."

Aras tried to sit up but Ade made him lie still. *My brother came for me. My brother came when I needed him.* Aras had lost any sense of the passage of time, but it was a long and painful fever made more bearable by the knowledge that Ade was always there, one soldier determined not to leave his comrade scared and alone to face his fate, and that was all Aras needed to get through this.

Am I really dying? Is Ade here because he knows that?

When *c'naatat* made changes to its host, there was always a fever. This was far worse. The parasite seemed determined not to let go. It was struggling to save its world just as he had struggled to save Bezer'ej.

I'm sorry, but I have to do this.

He was no longer sure who the apology was aimed at.

Now he was back on Ouzhari, an island that had once been a mass of black grass and white powder beaches, and then became a scene of destruction and black vitrified sand. He'd walked through snow there, watching the first *gethes'* bots, their mechanical vanguard sent to build a home for them, and made the decision to move them to an island where they wouldn't encounter *c'naatat*. The bots had carved a stone section of a building with words that had bewildered him, and even now he was no closer to fully understanding them: GOVERNMENT WORK IS GOD'S WORK.

The young navigator—long since food for the scavengers—

asked if he should fear the arrival of the *gethes*. Aras had
told him he would be long dead if the worst happened, and
he was.

But I'll live to see it. He would live to see it all.

And he had.

F'nar, upper terraces.

Ade hadn't mentioned Aras at all since he returned from
Baral and simply said: "It went okay."

After that, it was as if Aras never existed, although they
both knew damn well that they thought about him all the
time, and set one plate too many on the table, with that
catch in the throat that normally came with realizing someone was dead and never coming back for a meal again.
And it was a lonely bed, too. When Ade was in the mood
again, the memories swapped during sex would simply fill
in the awful gaps and nothing would need to be said or
discussed. Genetic memory might have been a sketchy record of detail, but it was meticulous about the intensity of
emotions.

He'd miss that layer of subtle communication. He'd missed
it when they had to use a condom. But he could get used to
being without it again. There were no more excuses. Aras
had shamed him.

"You coming to see Giyadas with me?" Shan said.

"Whatever we do, we do together." He tried to find respite
in harsh banter, just as he used to with the marine detachment. "I wouldn't have spent so much on that bloody ring if
I didn't want to be chained to you."

Walking to Giyadas's house felt just like the hours that
melted into minutes when he finally had to say goodbye to
his mates on Earth. The finality felt like an execution, even if
there were plenty of years ahead of them both, if Eddie's in-
nings were anything to go by. But somehow, it was like opening a wonderful gift as a kid only to have it snatched away
from you and a smaller, less amazing toy thrust in its place.

Grow up. Izzy and Jon didn't even get this far. You selfish bastard.

It was a full house. Giyadas's kids and grandkids, Nevyan, the usual domestic crowd. Ade squirmed. Taking the countermeasure would be like having to pee in front of the doctor, a loss of dignity at a vulnerable moment.

"Shapakti's here," Giyadas said. "You're sure you want to do this?"

"I'm sure I have to," said Shan.

Ade saw Nevyan's pupils snap open and shut. She probably felt bad about it. She adored Shan; they were best mates. She'd saved her life, found her drifting in that terrible mummified state when nobody else was looking for her because she *had* to be dead. Nothing could survive spacing.

But *c'naatat* did.

At least he wouldn't have to worry about a hull breach. If it ever happened, it'd all be over fast now. There were plenty of good things about *not* being *c'naatat*.

"I have to do this, too," he said. "Bring it on, doc."

Ade counted when things stopped happening. It was a habit. He couldn't remember when it started, or even if it had been quite this automatic before he got the parasite, but he counted the pauses in seconds. Nobody did anything or said a word for four seconds.

Nevyan just stared at Shan. Shan, usually a woman could make any bastard blink first, looked down at the floor. That wasn't like her at all.

"What's the problem?" she asked.

"I have a concern," said Nevyan. "The matriarchs all have, in fact. This is not something we want to force upon you, just as we never took your DNA for the weapons program against your will, but it concerns us. We no longer have a source of *c'naatat* should we ever be in dire circumstances again."

"There's Ouzhari," said Shan. "Plenty of it there."

Giyadas cut in. "We don't know if the organisms there have ever passed through a host, or what they might transmit to a wess'har host if they had. But we know what yours has acquired. It's a known quantity. It's been through our own troops before, and yourselves. And then we also gain whatever extra experience you acquire in living your life."

"And it's Rayat-free." Shan shifted to the other foot, looking like she was getting ready to move. She'd made up her mind. Ade knew how she hated last-minute changes. "So that's a bonus. But you could easily bottle my tissue samples, and Ade's. This is bullshit."

"Who are you trying to convince?"

"It's a point of principle. Not fashionable, but how can I go on when Aras did the decent thing, when I've got no real justification for staying *c'naatat?*"

Shan put her hands on her hips and looked down at the floor in silence again. Ade found himself counting.

"Aras wanted to have children, Shan. He was frank about that. His reasons were very different from yours." said Giyadas. "And what about Ade?"

"I do what the Boss does," he said. But he didn't want to, not at all; he wanted much more time with her. He felt resentful that he'd had a taste of a life he'd craved and now it was being taken away from him. For a moment he reminded himself that he never gave Qureshi the chance, so maybe this was his punishment for being a stupid selfish bastard, but that voice inside wouldn't be silenced. It was childish, selfish and needy.

"What do *you* want, Ade Bennett?"

He couldn't bring himself to say it. Shan turned and looked into his face, and she knew. She just *knew* he didn't want to go through with it. He could see it.

Ade did what he always had. He stayed loyal. "Like I said, what the Boss says, goes."

It was an awful moment. He'd put Shan in the position of taking something from him that he wanted. Nevyan tugged at the collar of her *dhren,* her little nervous gesture—rare for a wess'har—and stepped so close to Shan that Ade thought she was going to take hold of her.

"You'll never admit what you want," she said. "But I know what this choice is not Ade's, and he deserves better from you than to be dragged in the wake of your principled stands. So I'm going to do something you may never forgive me for."

Ade didn't notice it at first, but Shan did. She inhaled sharply. The scent of cut mango suddenly filled the room; *jask*. Nevyan and Giyadas had ganged up on Shan in pheromone terms, and asserted their dominance over Shan. That was how wess'har matriarchs enforced consensus in the group. Shan looked furious for a moment and then stepped back a pace or two. She'd been caught on the hop, and she was as susceptible to *jask* as any wess'har female.

"Well, that's a dirty trick," she said quietly. It didn't seem to make her give in like it was supposed to. Ade braced for a fight. "How could you try that stunt on me?"

"It's for your own good." Nevyan seemed taken aback. "When we took you in, we said you should be certain you would do your duty as a matriarch when needed. This is your duty; F'nar requires more than another twenty or thirty more years' service from you. Rationalize it as you will— living donor, whatever you wish—but I will not see someone I care about deny herself and her *jurej* some extended happiness over a principle. You represent no risk. Motive is irrelevant. Shapakti is forbidden from removing *c'naatat* from either of you until we have a very good reason to reverse that decision."

Shan straightened up. Ade caught Shapakti's eye and he said nothing.

"Are you angry with me, Nev? You think I'm ungrateful?"

"I didn't save you so you could indulge in pointless self-sacrifice. Follow Aras's example, and do something that you want but that harms nobody. A matriarch who has no regard for her own needs is, as you might say, not a selfless paragon but a *doormat*."

• Wess'har could be much, much more subtle than Ade had ever thought possible. The *jask* might not have worked as she'd planned, but Nevyan seemed to be playing an unusually crafty and very un-wess'har psychological game with Shan.

She wasn't telling her to indulge herself. She was telling her to stop being a martyr. That was bound to hit a nerve.

"Okay," said Shan. The quieter she got, the madder she usually was. "If Shapakti's following orders too, than we don't have much choice. The matter's closed until further notice."

"You're welcome," said Nevyan. "And however much I may have offended you, you're still my friend, and I won't stand idle if this proves to make you more unhappy."

Ade kept his mouth shut.

He should have felt relief or elation, but he just felt shaky. They left the house and walked a little way down the terraces in silence, not going anywhere specific, before Shan slowed to a halt and looked out over the city. The light was always changing, the view always fantastic, whatever the weather.

"Nev can really hit below the belt, can't she?"

"What, calling you on the martyr thing? Saving you from the decision?"

"Actually, no." Shan's eyes welled but she didn't crack. "Reminding me that Aras actually had *c'naatat* removed because he wanted to be a regular wess'har again."

Ade tried to think like a wess'har, drawing on the components of Aras that would always be within him. "They really do need the thing on standby, though."

"Yeah," said Shan. "Perhaps they do. But that's still an excuse."

"I'm bloody glad she forced you to keep it. I haven't had enough out of life yet. I want more. I really do."

Shan thrust her hands in her pockets and walked a few paces in front of him. "If you'd put it to me that strongly," she said, "I'd never have asked to have it removed."

He'd probably pissed her off, but it wouldn't last. He let the tension drain out of his shoulders and followed her. Now she seemed to be heading somewhere specific, and the direction became clear: she was going to Rayat's place, to see the only resident of F'nar who lived alone.

"No kicking or gouging, Boss."

She put her gloves on. "Don't want to spoil these."

When Rayat opened the door, he just stood back to let her in, but she stayed on the threshold.

"I just wanted to remind you that you can visit Eddie's grave," she said. "Aras and Lin have had *c'naatat* removed and gone home, if you didn't know already, but Ade and I are staying as we are." She held out her hand to shake but Rayat didn't take it. "Okay, now live out your life, and don't ever piss me about again."

"So you couldn't let it go."

"I can't be goaded, Rayat, and it's none of your business. So it's over, no more shit between us."

"I'd expected better of you. You're a hypocrite. You've cut this to fit your personal needs from day one. Who was the one tasked to keep this thing out of the wrong hands? Who did just that? Who had it removed, too? Who's been consistent about their duty? Well, it certainly isn't Superintendent Frankland, conscience to the world. *C'naatat*'s got to be kept out of everyone's reach, except yours and anyone you fancy fucking. Am I right?"

"Why don't you shut it before I shut it for you?" Ade said. He was itching to land one on Rayat, but Shan blocked him.

"Don't, Ade," she said. "He's just trying to forget that if I hadn't spaced myself, he'd have taken samples back to the FEU as he was ordered like a good little spook. And we all know where we'd be now."

She turned and walked away. Ade hung back for a second, and Rayat looked as if he was going to say something else but thought better of it. He was almost smiling, but not quite.

"You'd better do your bloody share of work on the Earth crops, too," Ade said, prodding him in the chest. "You're the only one who actually needs them to live on now."

Ade caught up with Shan. There was nothing more to say, and work to be done. A few days of digging trenches for spuds, pruning fruit trees, and getting used to being part of the fabric of Wess'ej; it was the best way of moving on.

Shan stopped and leaned on the parapet of the terrace. "Am I a hypocrite, Ade? He's right, isn't he?"

If she was, then so was he. They were in this together. "Who got the gene bank back to Earth? You completed your mission. You did it even though you were never supposed to. I think that more than balances the books."

Shan shrugged. "Let's go plant something, then."

"Job done, Boss," he said. "It really is."

In time, she'd come to see that. He knew she would.

Epilogue

Humans like clear definitions, like hero and villain, good and evil, black and white. There is always a personal line we draw between right and wrong, but they often forget that there is no unoccupied space between the extremes, just crowded shades of gray between which we must try to distinguish, and the color varies according to the light of the contextual day. Of all humanity's illusions, imagined clarity may be one of the most damaging in their understanding of their own reality.

Matriarch historian SIYYAS BUR

Michallat Butte, outside F'nar: January 30, 2429.

The snow had come again, thicker this time, and stayed longer. Shan had to admit she enjoyed it.

Coming from an Earth where snow was rare, she'd always treated it as exotic. Now that she could climb with some degree of confidence, she understood what Ade meant when he said there was nothing quite like scaling a rock face alone and looking out into a white wilderness that took no notice of you, and never would.

It really was a beautiful view from up here.

"There you go, Eddie," she said, coiling the rope around the length of her forearm and clipping it back on her belt. "Look what you made me do. Climbing a sodding mountain at my age, just to visit. They named the thing after you. You're on the map."

She would have given just about anything then to hear him tell her to fuck off and then laugh like a drain. She still missed him badly. She stood looking at the cairn of rocks, a miniature silver dragée mountain dusted with icing-sugar snow, and thought that if you had to have a grave, then this was the prettiest imaginable.

She had one just like it. A full grave and an empty one. Somehow it was usefully sobering to see her own cairn, if only to marvel at how devoted Ade had been when she hadn't deserved it. She worked every waking moment to live up to that adoration now, and for the first time she could remember, she felt content most of the time. Earth was a distant alien world whose fortunes she'd played a role in. She felt more divorced from it with every passing day.

The sun—Ceret, Nir, Cavanagh's Star, nobody minded what she called it now—was struggling to its high position. She sat down on her backpack and took in the near silence, remembering Eddie in as painless a way as she could.

Silly sod. The first batch of beer he made had lumps in it like . . . well, like someone had been sick in it. *God, that was funny. We needed the laughs, too.*

Shan lost herself thinking about the Christmas party with the marines playing pornographic movie charades while Eddie drank the most volatile eau de vie she'd ever sniffed. Even when worlds were falling apart, there were moments to savor.

A crunching sound of rocks giving way under snow jerked her out of her thoughts. When she looked around, a wess'har male stood looking at her, well wrapped against the cold.

He shifted a bundle in his arms. "I thought at first that I'd visit you as soon as I could, but then I found that it was easier to stay away, and then it became natural and painless. I never forgot you, though, Shan."

He looked like Nevyan; he looked like Sevaor. He looked wess'har, what he always had been at his core, because this was Aras.

Shan tasted that ozone tang of incipient tears in her sinuses, but steeled herself. He was still Aras, still the person she'd befriended and grown to love, and who filled her final thoughts when she reached the point of death.

She wondered if his memory would have gone with the

c'naatat, but Rayat had assured her that he recalled everything, including emotions, and so would Aras. "You didn't
forget me, then."

"Wess'har have perfect recall. Are you willing to talk
to me?"

How could she not? His voice was the same, still with
those infrasonics that made her throat itch deep inside.

"Of course I am. What have you got there?"

Aras held out the bundle. Now she could see what it was:
two tiny infants, little stick insect things. *Two.* He was gazing at them rapt, devoted: they were his. She couldn't bring
herself to spoil this moment for him by getting maudlin or
admitting that it hurt when a lover got on with a new life.
She'd got on with hers. They were even.

Wess'har infants weren't appealing, not even with her
dose of wess'har genes.

"Twins," he said. "They're both isan'ket've."

Twin females were a very rare event. If you were going to
catch up on a lost life as a wess'har father, then that was the
jackpot. Shan didn't ask who his isan was. That was one step
too far.

"They're wonderful." *I loved you. I still do, or at least I
love the Aras I have in my mind.* She looked into his face—
beautiful yellow sapphire eyes, black four-petalled flowers
of pupils, a sweet intelligent face that was still him, and yet
so alien she suddenly panicked about the time she'd spent in
his arms and what that made her. "Ade misses you. We both
do. Will you visit us some time?"

"I hope I can." The overtone in his voice was very noticeable now, very wess'har. "I have such happy memories of
you both. You saved me, Shan. You made this possible."

He smelled calm and content, and he was *urrring* with
pure paternal happiness. Seeing her for the first time in a
couple of years—whatever he remembered of their brief time
together—hadn't distressed him at all. That was a comfort.

And he'd die. In time, he'd *die.*

"No, you saved me, sweetheart," she said. "Over and over
again. Like Nevyan. Ade, too. I get saved a lot. You don't
owe me a damn thing."

Every fucker saved me. Every one.

Aras stood there in silence for a while. He seemed content just to stand and think.

"I came to pay my respects to Eddie, and to Black," he said. "Shapakti says he still has White's body in preservation, and that I can have it and bury it. I should have done that sooner."

White was another rat, Black's cage-mate. So Aras hadn't turned his back without a second thought after all, and the rats were still people to him. He stood at the cairn for a while in silence, and then they walked back down the long slope that led back down to the plain, trying to find things to say that bridged so wide a gap. Sometimes the gap was a wound, but it was healing.

It was too cold today for most wess'har to venture out; F'nar was usually mild, and only tough clans like those raised in Baral seemed to tolerate real winter. Shan made no small talk. There was both nothing to add and too many questions to ask. She was trying to be Superintendent Shan Frankland, who didn't give a fuck and never would. Today, she let herself fail. She was just Shan.

All Aras had ever wanted was to be a male wess'har, with an isan and children. *Job done.* She had no other claim on him that wasn't purely selfish, and whatever faults she had—killing, threatening, going beyond the law—she'd learned how to make a half-decent job of loving someone.

"I'm glad you don't regret it, Aras."

He cocked his seahorse head, considering the question. "Life is good. Is yours?"

"Yes." She tested that idea. Yes, she had Ade, and she was slowly learning to fit into a community rather than observe it from the outside. And apart from Eddie, her resolve hadn't been further tested yet by seeing those she loved age and die, leaving her alone. That time would inevitably come again, though. "I think it is."

"Do you keep up with events on Earth? Do you regret not being there to see your work vindicated?"

"No." She thought of Eddie's elegant apology to her when he'd wrongly accused her of carrying *c'naatat* as a mule for some pharmacorp. He quoted Rochefoucauld: *Perfect courage is to do without witnesses what one would be capable of with the world looking on.* "No, I don't need vindication. I did it because it needed doing, not for a medal." She wanted to change the topic. "What are their names?" she asked, indicating the twins. *I had a daughter, once, for such a short, short time.* "I bet you're proud as punch, fathering two matriarchs. Ade's going to be delighted."

"They are Haviklas and Sajikis," Aras said. "And I would like nothing more than for them to grow to be like you."

It almost upended her. But then she realized that she could feel that bittersweet pang, and instead of her long-practiced inurement against pain kicking in and snatching the messy emotion away from her to stop the damage, it lingered.

She could feel things safely again, good and bad. They were now at the point in the road where he would turn towards the transport tunnels, and she would head for F'nar, an iced wedding cake in a wilderness. They would return to their respective lives.

Maybe Aras would miss his longevity one day, but she looked at those odd little insectlike babies, so unlike the elegant adults they'd become, and doubted it. If he ever did—she had his genes and his genetic memories, and so did Ade. Everything Aras had been was preserved in their cells, locked into their genome. They'd still be there if he ever wanted them back to become what he once was again.

"Thanks," she said. "Just hope they grow up without the foul mouth and temper, eh?"

"Perhaps," he said, and carried on walking away. "Tell Ade I will visit. I haven't forgotten my brother."

Shan watched him go, letting herself feel that sorrow of knowing Aras was now as subject to time and disease as the rest of the world, and utterly unlike her and Ade because of it. But he could always change his mind, right up to the end.

She'd still be here for him, and so would Ade. They always would be.

Wings Bird Sanctuary, Canada: January 31, 2429

"I thought that would amuse you," said Den Bari, watching the two macaws prance up and down the branch, screeching. "They've never forgotten their first language."

The Eqbas task force commander who stood watching the birds—Jenesian Lau—was the fourth that Den Bari had worked with since 2401, and probably his last. He could have run for another term; but he was staring at seventy-five next birthday, and it was as good time as any to stand down. And this bird sanctuary was a good place to pose with Jenesian for the media. Photogenic wildlife saved from extinction summed up his life in office much more tastefully than the rows with the FEU and Sinostates about the cost in human life.

During his time as Prime Minister of Australia, billions of humans worldwide had died from disease, starvation, war and—although nobody had ever provided hard evidence—engineered pathogens. His own country and its allies had fared very much better. And so had Earth, overall.

"*Uk' alin'i che!*" one macaw said in a rasping voice. It was asking for food, in eqbas'u, as Shapakti had taught it, and then broke into English. "It's dinnertime! Dinnertime!"

Jenesian's crest of hair bobbed as she tilted her head this way and that in fascination. "These are the birds that Da Shapakti raised from the gene bank. How wonderful. They live a long time, don't they?"

Bari kept an eye on the cams darting around the two of them. He hated the idea of a farewell tour, but he was a world statesman and that kind of PR junket was expected.

"The macaws will outlive me, that's for sure," he said.

The gaggle of journalists broke into questions, too impatient to wait for the formal news conference. "Why aren't you planning to publish your memoirs, sir?" one of them asked. "Isn't that the first thing politicians do when they leave office?"

"I'll see what you pundits have to say about me first," he said. "Then I'll know if I'm the savior of the planet for letting the Eqbas help us out with our environmental problems, or the worst monster in history for not fighting them while billions of humans died."

There was a ripple of nervous laughter. Bari had long since learned to lance boils first in front of the media. He knew what was said about him; he still slept okay at night, and Deborah Garrod, now a member of parliament herself, had never once told him he should worry about his eternal soul. He shook hands with Jenesian for the cams before they left for the next engagement, and smiled. She was new in post. She'd spend the coming ten years on Earth managing the ongoing restoration. It struck him as a bloody long tour of duty.

On the flight back to Kamberra that evening—how extraordinary, he thought, to now find alien spaceships so routine—he gazed down through a transparent deck at the erased land on which European and Sinostates conurbations had once stood. If the ship diverted, he could look at the same reminder of the cost of restoration in parts of Africa and the South Americas. What looked like fresh new growth was built on death and destruction.

I helped that happen. I couldn't have stopped it happening anyway, but I made my choice, and I can live with it. I helped buy the world some time.

"Do you remember Esganikan Gai?" Jenesian asked.

"Yeah," said Bari. "Shame, really. I never got to know her as well as I would have liked." He wondered if he'd ever get around to those memoirs, and knew that if he did that he'd omit quite a lot of detail and crazy stories about immortals. "You'd have thought I'd have made better notes at the time. Politicians do that, you know. We always have an eye to our memoirs, right from day one."

He could always ask Shukry. He had a better memory, even now, and he kept notes. But there was plenty of time for that. Bari found himself thinking back to the first meetings he'd had with the Eqbas commander and her entourage, those disorienting first days, and tried to recall all the names around that meeting table when the FEU tried to get heavy with Esganikan.

There'd been a human copper, a woman the FEU wanted

badly. What was her name? Francis? Frankel? He'd have to look it up. She only stayed a couple of weeks, and then she was gone. There had been a lot of water under the bridge since then, oceans of it.

"What's troubling you?" Jenesian asked. "You're frowning."

"Bad memory," he said. "Trying to recall a name from way back. But it doesn't matter. Nobody important."

Franks?

Bari kept tossing the name around in his head, then gave up and started compiling a list on his handheld of the key people—human and alien—who had been pivotal in the restoration of Earth. He really should have started outlining these damn memoirs a long time ago. He'd need the material for a lecture tour, too.

Franklin?

He got on with his list. No, the name really didn't matter at all.